About the author

Barry Eisenberg is an associate professor of health care management in the School for Graduate Studies at the State University of New York Empire State College, a health care management consultant and a former hospital administrator. He and his wife, Amy, live in New Jersey. They have three grown children and one grandson. *Primal Calling* is his first novel.

PRIMAL CALLING

Barry Eisenberg

PRIMAL CALLING

Vanguard Press

A CIP catalogue record for this title is
available from the British Library.

ISBN 978 1 784657 30 7

Vanguard Press is an imprint of
Pegasus Elliot MacKenzie Publishers Ltd.
www.pegasuspublishers.com

First Published in 2020

Vanguard Press
Sheraton House Castle Park
Cambridge England

Printed & Bound in Great Britain

Dedication

In loving memory of two beautiful souls,
my sister, Roberta, and my brother, Larry.

Acknowledgements

A few years ago, as I turned on my car radio, I caught the tail-end of a human-interest story about a young man who had spent years looking for his father whose identity was a mystery. Although I missed the premise of the story, that tidbit of information piqued my interest and I began thinking about the anguish such a search can evoke. I decided to write a short fictional account.

I began reading about people searching for an unknown or lost family member and was transported into a universe filled with moving stories. The more accounts I read, the more I learned about the often-lonely road traveled by those undertaking such pursuits and the fierce determination exercised in doing so. I kept returning to the young man in the radio report, imagining that he must have been guided by the super-charged perseverance shared by those whose experiences I could not get out of my mind. The short story I set out to write blossomed into this full-length novel.

Working with Pegasus Elliot MacKenzie Publishers has been a joy and they have made the process seamless. The team have not only provided their expertise, but have been gracious, accommodating and generous all along the way.

I am fortunate to have many wonderful people in my life – family, friends, colleagues – without whose encouragement this project would have been daunting.

I have been bicycling with a group of close friends for almost thirty years. A couple of years ago, we decided to add a book discussion to the activities on our annual biking getaway. I was touched when my manuscript was chosen for the inaugural read and am very grateful to Lloyd, Danny, Jay, Howard, Bob, Mark and Peter for their valuable input.

My wife, Amy, asked her book club to read the manuscript as well. Avid readers, they came to the conversation brimming with questions and discerning observations, prompting me to revisit linkages between some plot elements. I am thankful to all: Eileen, Bobbie, Fay, Beverly, Rosalie, Toni, Anita, Jeanne, and Esther and her husband, Steve (who, sadly, passed away soon after that meeting).

My cousin, Shoshana, with whom I only recently and happily connected, edited a later version, making it more structurally and grammatically sound. Our friend, Maddy, offered initial sketches for cover design ideas. And Angel lent his artistic talents, providing a range of illustration options, including the one selected.

My dear friend, Tim, and I bonded many years ago when we were graduate students in Philadelphia. He sets a writing standard I could meet only in my dreams. I'm indebted to him for his insights and continuing support for this endeavor.

I am blessed to have the unending encouragement of my children, of whom I am so proud and always in awe, and their remarkable life partners – Kerry and Nathan; Jesse and Anna, and our grandson, who has brought an exhilarating sense of wonder into our lives; and Hallie and Jon.

Kerry's inventiveness and creativity, exemplified in her beautiful and distinctive writing and art, has always been a profound and treasured source of inspiration.

I cherish my conversations about writing, character development and motive – and just about everything else – with Jesse, an accomplished playwright, author and actor. Our discussions are master classes for me, and I learn more from him than he can ever know.

This book would never have seen the light of day without Hallie. Leading with thoughtfulness and her keen intellect, she dove into the task of editing the manuscript, honing plot points and adding flavor and texture to the dialogue. Moreover, she researched suitable publishers and managed the process of submitting the manuscript.

When I first mentioned to Amy that I was thinking of trying my hand at fiction, a departure from my usual focus on health care management, her enthusiasm erased any doubts. She has been by my side all the way, eagerly reading each iteration, helping to strengthen the flow and adding justification for character motives. Having Amy in my corner has helped bring this project to fruition. I am so grateful to her for a lifetime of love and devotion.

This book is dedicated to my sister, Roberta, and brother, Larry, who passed away within four months of one another some years ago. They were the best siblings one could hope for and I miss them every day. My father, George, who predeceased them, was a loving dad and ideal role model, instilling in me his sense of curiosity. My mother, Sylvia, lived for several years following their passing, soldiering on. If she ever felt despair or overwhelmed with sorrow, which she undoubtedly did, she did not let on. Her smile and adoring manner never wavered. In the most unassuming of ways, my mother was a model of courage, a benevolent spirit from whom I drew inspiration, especially when I thought about the inherent goodness of the people in my story.

We judge ourselves by our intentions and others by their behavior.

Stephen R. Covey
The Speed of Trust: The One Thing that Changes Everything
The Free Press

ONE

Failure never felt closer. It was at once punishing to Jack… tormenting, crushing. But, paradoxically, he sensed it could also be liberating. He was reminded of a film he saw last year, *The Incredible Shrinking Man*, in his film class when he was a high school senior. The protagonist had the misfortune of being exposed to an unforgiving chemical agent that caused him to get smaller and smaller. He struggled throughout the movie, frantic for a solution. None came, and by the end of the movie he was virtually microscopic. There was nothing left but to gaze into the universe, solemnly acquiescing to his destiny and its irreversibility. Along the way, his life was a nightmare. But now, with all hope gone, he lapsed into an unexpected peacefulness. Until that moment, there had been an intense search for a way out. But, strangely, coming to terms with destiny, even if bad, had the advantage of the struggle being over.

The movie had a way of filling Jack with self-pity because its theme of gloom and defeat felt familiar. But he was also beginning to relate to the big sigh that comes at the end of a long, lonely journey, even if it ends in failure, even if it proves pointless. Though he was getting close to this state of surrender, he knew he was not quite there. Futility was near, he understood, but he had yet to fully succumb to its apparent inevitability.

New Jersey Central College was a small liberal arts institution located about fifteen miles southeast of Cherry Hill, just across the Delaware River from Philadelphia. For many years it was known mainly for granting degrees in the field of teaching. But over the past few years, the college had invested heavily in a rapidly expanding computer science curriculum thanks to a gift from an alumna who created a very profitable software program for law offices.

Finals week was winding down. Summer break was all the more alluring because of the perfect weather.

It was noon and Jack Davies was finishing the first part of his

English class final. It was an essay on powerlessness. He knew firsthand how gradual but uninterrupted loss of hope can take a toll on your spirit. But you reach a point where it no longer matters. That's when you're free. In some respects, his tiny friend from the film had become a role model. Jack wasn't sure if he'd ever reach that point, because he hadn't quite reached despair yet.

The essay was becoming unwieldy. This stinks, he muttered to himself, but he'd let the chips fall where they may. He hadn't found a way to commit to this class, but the professor admired Jack's ability to create clever dialogue. Part two of the exam asked about the plight of the short story in American literature. Jack attributed the decline to the explosion of media options in which the short story has no place.

He tapped the desk, trying to think of something clever to say. But he was distracted by his own thoughts. And the open window next to Jack was a deadly concentration-breaker. He heard students cheering, celebrating the end of the term and letting loose. And he still had his computer research final to go. Jack remembered to include some lofty reference about barbarism creeping into the soul of American culture; the professor is a purist and will like this, he thought.

One o'clock. Test over. He plunked the blue book down with an anticlimactic thud atop the stack on the professor's desk. Jack and the professor exchanged perfunctory nods, a tacit affirmation of their failure to make a connection during the semester. Under other circumstances, Jack would have appreciated what this man would have to offer, but he had been too preoccupied to delve into the work this year.

The computer research final was scheduled to begin at one fifteen. Jack had just enough time to grab a sandwich from the cafeteria and get across campus to Spellman Hall. He anticipated being finished with the exam by four. This should be a cinch, he assumed with some justifiable confidence: he had become especially good at conducting research.

Jack walked across campus at a brisk pace. He almost always moved that way, slightly hurriedly, as though he were forever five minutes late. Jack was slender and angular, which exaggerated the rapid appearance of his movement. His mind was generally unaware of his speed, his attention to such a triviality rendered minuscule by thoughts of far more important matters these days. At great contrast to his physicality were his eyes. Deeply blue and set back, they suggested a more contemplative manner. His movement conveyed his need for getting there, his eyes for being there.

At about the same time, a gray Ford Taurus pulled out of an underground garage in a small office building on the outskirts of Arlington, Virginia. A man and a woman rode up front, while another man was seated in the back. The driver was in his early forties and a bit stocky; the tailor-made suit gave him a polished corporate appearance. The woman was in her mid-thirties and had a piercing gaze, an aura of equal parts intelligence and intimidation. The man in the back, slender and tall, seemed more haggard and impatient.

The car made its way up Interstate 95, and at about two thirty began a trek north on the New Jersey Turnpike. Conversation among the three was limited. They did not know one another well, having met only recently after being recruited to perform this mission.

New Jersey Central College had three entrance gates. The main gate opened onto a straight road lined with rhododendrons, azaleas and wildflowers, assembled into a grand mosaic of purples, reds and yellows that the school's small but very talented botany department maintained. Two other gates provided access to student, faculty and visitor parking lots.

At three forty-five, the Taurus entered the main gate of New Jersey Central College. The woman commented on how lovely the foliage was, and the back-seat passenger mumbled something about how much his wife loved to garden.

The car headed around the administration building and made its way toward the student parking lot. A few hundred cars were sprinkled throughout the lot, which was about one-fifth full. The Taurus slowly wove up and down the lanes, its pace steady and purposeful.

"There it is," the woman announced suddenly, pointing to a two-year-old red Honda Accord parked headfirst in a spot about twelve cars away. The Taurus pulled up behind the Accord. The driver glanced at a small sheet of paper that had been tucked in his breast pocket and verified the license number. He nodded to his companions, then steered the car to a nearby parking spot. He shut the engine and they waited.

At Spellman Hall, Jack was completing his computer research final exam. He felt right at home. For the past year he'd been working on a personal project that involved an inordinate amount of research. The final exam asked students to identify how to explore various Internet services for resources regarding the preservation of wild animals. Then they needed to create a spreadsheet with the results. Jack looked around the room. About thirty students were there, including several adults who had delayed going to college. Expanding the computer science curriculum had turned out to be a lucrative marketing strategy for the college, since many in the local workforce had needed to strengthen their computer skills over the past several years. Jack noticed a lot of grimaces and struggling looks. For him, this assignment was a breeze.

Jack finished his exam at three fifty-five. He printed out his test papers, brought them to the front of the room and handed them to the instructor. To his surprise, he found himself exchanging the same kind of detached nod as with the English professor. He exited the classroom and proceeded down a hall strewn with crude advertisements for tutoring, software programs and computer components, went down one flight of steps and was out into the open air.

Freshman year was history. Freedom was at hand!

Jack walked toward the student parking lot. It was late in the day for a final exam, and he didn't encounter any acquaintances on the five-minute walk to the parking lot. The driver of the Taurus spotted Jack entering the parking lot and turned on the ignition. Jack got into his car and backed out of the spot. His mother was expecting him home before dinner. He became preoccupied with thoughts of the important phone call he was scheduled to get the following morning.

The Taurus followed the Accord, the driver carefully staying sufficiently back to avoid arousing suspicion. After exiting the college, the Accord turned right onto Rockaway Avenue, a main thoroughfare that cut through several suburban towns. Rockaway Avenue had an eclectic mix of old shops and newer, trendy stores. A health foods store sat adjacent to a shop that sold antique toys. When Jack was a boy, he had loved to watch the Lionel train set displayed in the window. The sturdiness of the train cars and the authenticity of their appearance mesmerized him, as did the fantasy of hopping on board and being whisked beyond the confines of his community.

Jack turned onto Valley Mill Turnpike, a single-lane road that ran through a stretch of woodland. Jack was about seven miles from his home. About two miles onto Valley Mill Turnpike, Jack noticed that the Taurus behind him was getting much closer. That guy is in a big-time rush, Jack thought. The Taurus, gaining ground, was now about a car length behind. Jack gently tapped the brake to slow the car, hoping the Taurus would pass.

After a few seconds, the Taurus began to pass. Jack glanced into the Taurus as it pulled alongside. He noticed three people in the car, all of whom were staring directly back at him. It struck Jack as a look of scrutiny, as though to confirm their find. The female passenger, sitting in the front passenger seat, had a piercing, frightening gaze. She waved to Jack to stop.

Jack's mind was racing. His fear that this group would seek him out had materialized. But he knew he must try to avoid them, lest he expose Cathy to danger. He believed he had no choice but to dodge them and call her. He also knew he should not use his cell phone.

Jack hit the accelerator and his car lurched forward, pulling in front of the Taurus. The Taurus regained speed and, again, came up just behind the Accord. The driver was clearly skilled at this activity and, at once, was able to maneuver his car beside Jack's. Another wave by the woman to slow down. Jack needed to get away. As he fixed his gaze on the road in front, the driver of the Taurus, in anticipation of Jack's plan to try to race ahead, pulled his car in front.

Jack was now behind the Taurus. Both cars were moving at sixty miles per hour. Jack knew that a string of about ten stores, including a gas station, was just two miles up the road. Just then, the Taurus started to slow down. Suddenly, the deceleration became abrupt, and Jack couldn't help but get too close for comfort. He slammed on his brakes. Panic!

Jack tried to steer around the Taurus, but it shifted to the left, a deliberate attempt to prevent Jack from passing. The Taurus was slowing to a complete halt, and Jack was unable to steer past it. His only choice was to put the car in reverse and try to back out of the area. Jack took a deep breath and threw the car into reverse. The Taurus, now also in reverse, followed closely. Jack desperately wanted to turn the car around, and thought he had an opening. He spun the wheel and the car veered toward the shoulder. But Jack was no match for the driver of the Taurus. Before Jack could put the car in drive, the Taurus lunged back, tires screeching, until it was positioned directly in front of Jack.

Trapped!

Jack slammed the gear shift into park and bolted from the car, leaving it running, and darted directly into the wooded area behind him. The lanky man from the back seat and the woman scrambled from the car in pursuit. In the meantime, the driver of the Taurus repositioned both cars to the shoulder of the road.

Jack had no choice but to use his phone now. His hands trembled as he fidgeted for it, and the uneven terrain made it impossible to maneuver through his pockets. Then he realized his phone was on the passenger seat of his car.

The man shouted to Jack to stop. The woman, not far behind, screamed, "We're not going to hurt you." In the face of this madness, Jack found her tone oddly believable. Fearing no possibility for escape, Jack was left with no choice but to confront them.

He wheeled around, screaming, "What do you want from me? Who are you?"

They stood about twenty feet from Jack, separated by a small clearing in the thicket of trees. "We are not here to hurt you. We need you to come with us," the woman repeated.

Jack succumbed to a strange, paradoxical mix of panic and curiosity. He didn't know these people, though he had been aware they might seek him out. But he could not reveal this awareness to them. And he didn't know if he was in danger. "What if I don't? You can't do this to me." His wobbly voice managed a trace of defiance.

"Actually, we can," the man declared. His tone was powerful and convincing. That was it. With those three words, the man's authority — an unequivocal dominance over Jack — became deadly certain.

Jack stood there, frozen, while the pair walked toward him. He suspected he wouldn't be hurt, but he couldn't be positive. He was at once consumed with energy and sapped of it.

"Where are we going?" Jack asked, relinquishing himself to a fate over which he knew he had no control.

"Back to the car," the woman replied. "You need to come with us."

The woman led the way back to the highway. Jack followed, not wanting to provoke the man, whose presence loomed directly behind. Along the path lay rocks and tree branches. One of these might be used as a weapon, he thought. His mind raced; is there time to grab something? But other than a small tussle with a class bully in the third grade, Jack had not been especially schooled in the ways of physical confrontation. In fact, among the best of his social talents was conflict avoidance. No, he'd surely lose out in a physical struggle.

Jack pressed the pair for information. "Who are you? What do you want from me? Take my car. Take my money. Just please let me go." As Jack's pleas faded, so did any semblance of his resistance, and the pair offered nothing. No hint of purpose. No gesture of reassurance. The remainder of the short walk to the car occurred in silence.

As the group neared the car, the man told Jack to get into the back seat with him. The driver and the woman assumed their original positions in the front. She turned to Jack and instructed him, "You need to call your mother. Where's your phone?"

"It's in my car," he responded.

The woman retrieved Jack's phone from his car and handed it to him. Then she advised him on what to say: "Tell her that you were asked by Mr. Dwyer to help with a project at the department tonight." Holy shit, she knew his computer instructor's name. "If she asks what the project is, tell her the department is planning the installation of new hard drives on the school's computer system during the summer, and you've been asked to help with preparation." Jack felt a sense of terror — she knew about that too! "Tell her you'll be home close to midnight, but she shouldn't worry if you're running late."

"Is all that clear?" the man in the back asked with stinging bluntness. Jack nodded.

The man's stare was laser-like. "Be convincing," he said, which sounded to Jack like a warning.

Jack hit the call button and stared at the woman as the phone rang. The driver, who had not turned around during the entire time Jack had been in the car, kept his sights on the road ahead.

"I got her voicemail," Jack informed the group.

"Perfect," said the woman. "Just leave the message and tell her you'll be home late tonight."

Jack delivered the message as directed. The slight hesitancy in his voice was not enough to create concern for the group.

"Unfortunately, we're unable to answer any questions right now," she confirmed. "But I assure you our aim is not to hurt you." Then she exited the car, walked to Jack's car, and got into the driver's seat. Jack watched as his car made a U-turn. The Accord drove alongside the Taurus and stopped. The window rolled down, and the woman instructed the driver of the Taurus to follow her back to the college.

The trip back to the college was made in silence. Despite her cool assertiveness, the woman's presence eased Jack's fear. There was a cold, menacing steeliness without her, and Jack believed there could be harsh consequences if he showed any sign of resistance.

As they arrived at the college, Jack realized he had yet to hear the driver utter a single word. Jack watched as his Accord passed by the student parking lot and headed for the visitor lot. The majority of students at New Jersey Central College commuted to school, but about a fifth of the student body was from out of town. Parents and friends who visited were directed to park in the visitor lot. Jack knew that cars could be parked there for days without being ticketed by college security. Apparently, Jack's abductors knew this as well.

The woman parked the Accord and returned to the Taurus. Jack observed her placing his car keys into her purse, which had been on the front floor of the Taurus. The Taurus pulled out of the visitor lot, through one of the smaller gates of the college and then back onto Rockaway Avenue.

As the Taurus left the immediate area, Jack, impelled by trepidation, dared to question his captors again. His tone was pleading. "Who are you? Why are you doing this?"

"Everything will be made clear in due time," the woman replied, icily. "Now, please, no more questions for now."

Jack knew the car had been heading north, but he was unfamiliar with the route the driver was taking. After what felt to Jack like a distance of about seven or eight miles, the car pulled onto a small side road. It was desolate, eerily so under the circumstances. The lanes were narrow, not much wider than the car itself, and the quick succession of twists and bends in the road made it impossible to see beyond a few yards.

The car drove about five hundred feet up the road, then pulled off onto a dirt shoulder. The woman turned around and faced Jack. Jack's fear — this terror produced by a sense of imminent doom — caused his mind to scramble, scanning everything, anything for any possibility of escape. But there was no way out, and the fear manifested in jolts to his system. He could feel his heart beating in his chest. A strange numbness gripped his hands and descended toward his wrists. The tips of his fingers tingled and were overwhelmed by a paralyzing weightiness. A stinging electricity coursed through him.

"I can't tell you where we are going or why. And I'm not free to answer any questions right now. I need you to wear these for the remainder of the trip, though," the woman said, handing Jack what appeared to be a pair of sunglasses with shields that wrapped around the sides.

Jack slowly extended his hand to take the glasses from the woman and asked why he should wear them. "Just put them on, please. It's for your own protection." Jack sensed impatience in her voice, but with a hint of sensitivity. She was a model of efficiency. There was nothing wasted about her. Her words were delivered methodically without a syllable to spare. Her hair, shoulder-length with just a hint of a wave, had fallen back neatly into place despite a run in the woods. Jack felt his heart pulsing.

Jack discovered these were not ordinary sunglasses. They blackened out all traces of light. He had no idea where they were going.

Travel resumed. Jack felt the car make several turns in quick succession. He believed this was a deliberate strategy to confuse him. Until they had stopped, he knew they were headed north, but this jarring sequence of turns was disorienting. He knew only that there was no stretch of extended highway driving.

About twenty minutes later, the car slowed, pulling onto gravel. The front passenger door opened and the woman stepped out. The two men remained in the car. The woman opened the rear passenger door where Jack was seated. He made no move. The woman reached in and placed her hand under Jack's elbow. "Please come with me," she demanded, her tone firm but noticeably polite.

Jack slowly extended one foot out the door and felt a gravel incline beneath his feet. With the glasses still on, Jack was escorted by the woman for about twenty yards. He heard a door in front of him open and was told to go up one step and enter a house. The wooden floor felt like the floor in his kitchen at home. Its hard texture was offset by a suppleness that muffled the sound of shoes making contact with it.

Jack was advised by the woman that he was heading to a room in the back of the house. She led him straight for a few feet and then made a turn to the left. He surmised that a kitchen was to his right from the faint hum of what sounded like a refrigerator motor. He was also aware of the presence of other people in the house, not from voices, but from the dampened creaking of the floor. Another turn, this one to the right, then up five steps. The steps were carpeted, as was the hallway they entered on this elevated floor.

A door opened in front of Jack and he was asked to enter. The woman escorted Jack about five steps into the room, then guided him toward a folding wooden chair. Once seated, Jack heard the door to the room close.

"You can remove the glasses now," she said.

Jack squinted as his eyes adjusted to the light. The room was almost bare and small, about ten by twelve feet. In front of Jack was a small wooden table made from lacquered pine, flimsy in its construction. A plastic pitcher of water and two plain drinking glasses sat on the table. A small puddle of condensate had accumulated at the base of the pitcher. Jack was in one of four wooden-slatted folding chairs. The room had no windows and nothing on its bleak, beige walls. The light was dim, emanating from four recessed low-wattage lights in the ceiling.

"Would you like to use the restroom?" the woman asked, her tone softer than at any time earlier.

"No."

"Please help yourself to some water if you like," she offered.

"I'm not thirsty." Then, after a beat, "What am I doing here?"

The woman glanced quickly at the door. Her eyes were in a constant state of alert, radiating a confident vigilance. This woman has never known panic, Jack thought. She checked her watch, then fixed her gaze onto Jack. "We brought you here to meet your father."

TWO

Two theories compete for how Whistling Point, New Jersey got its name. A gully abuts the town to the west, just a few miles from the Delaware River. As the wind surfs through the gully it produces a shrill whistle. The sound has a supernatural piercing shriek on windy days in the fall and winter when the bare trees in the adjacent forest act more as a conduit for, than a barrier to, the rush of wind.

The alternative explanation has its roots in the development of the railroad in the area. In the mid-1800s, track was laid about fifteen miles to the east of the town. This was part of an ambitious effort to develop rail transportation along segments of the east coast, with Philadelphia as a hub. When it was discovered that the project's financing was mired in scandal, the project was abandoned, and the financiers jailed. But for a few years, railroad cars were moved along the half-built tracks for test purposes. Affixed to the front car, jutting skyward from the conductor's perch, was a behemoth whistle. A thick black cylinder, the whistle emitted a monstrous blast that could be heard for miles, especially in the district that was to become Whistling Point.

The corridor between New York City and Philadelphia was a province of economic stability for settlers throughout much of the nineteenth and twentieth centuries. Rich soil and a generally good climate made farming a safe venture. And of course, there was the access to two major centers of commerce.

Whistling Point was incorporated in 1922. At that time, small family-owned farms were being folded into large corporate enterprises, and the advent of new modes of transportation and communication paved the way for diverse businesses and occupations to flourish.

Mary and Kenneth Davies moved to Whistling Point from Kansas in the late 1950s. Kenneth took a job with a Cherry Hill-based accounting firm. This situation was perfect for the young couple. It seemed to Mary and Kenneth that many people who had been migrating to Whistling

Point shared their interest in an uncomplicated rural life, while craving some urban spiritedness. This then became the cultural foundation of Whistling Point: a seemingly contradictory mix of countryside quiet and city bustle. But it worked. Descendants of this socio-cultural stew emerged highly adaptable; they possessed a full arsenal of social versatility skills enabling them to assimilate easily into a broad spectrum of cultures.

As a result of growth in the area and Kenneth's business acumen, the accounting firm expanded. A few years later, Kenneth broke from the company in Cherry Hill and started his own firm. Shortly thereafter, Mary and Kenneth had their first child, Ken Jr. Eight years later, Linda was born.

Ken Jr. and Linda were part of the first large generation of children born in Whistling Point. As the community grew — and by virtue of its growth alone — it began to shed some of its rural orthodoxy. Ken Jr. went to college in Michigan and decided to settle there.

When Linda was twelve, she sprained her ankle in a softball game. The sprain was severe and required months of physical therapy. Helen James was a young and lively physical therapist who treated Linda in an exceedingly caring manner. Thereafter, Linda envisioned a career in some area of health care. When Linda became of college age, she wanted to stay close to home. She enrolled in a health care administration program at Temple University in Philadelphia.

In the summer following her junior year in college, Linda was ecstatic to be granted an internship in a small orthopedic hospital in central Philadelphia. Much of her job involved doing research for an assortment of behind-the-scenes projects, like evaluating pay scales for employees and gathering statistics on the side effects of certain medications. But it was contact with patients that had led to her interest in health care, and she desired more of that.

In the third week of the internship, Linda approached her supervisor to discuss potential opportunities that would allow for this, and she was offered the position of patient liaison, a relatively new role. Hospitals were in the throes of becoming competitive, a result of new restrictions on how much they could charge for their services. As a result, hospitals had an entirely new motive to keep patients satisfied: money. Many hospitals expanded the role of hospital ombudsman, an̄ could advocate for patients who experienced problems. As patient liaison team, Linda would meet with patients to gi̅ impressions of their care and respond to complaints.

Linda loved this new responsibility. In her second week on the j̅ Linda met a young man who had knee surgery as a result of a collision he sustained during a weekend pick-up soccer game. Stewart Jacobson had recently graduated from the New England Institute of Technology with a degree in engineering. He was in Philadelphia for three months as part of an orientation program for a new job with Meredith Oil, a colossal energy conglomerate. Stewart was a member of a newly organized team of highly educated engineers responsible for conducting feasibility studies for drilling sites. New computer and scanning technologies were being developed so quickly that they were becoming obsolete almost as soon as they were deployed. Meredith Oil invested heavily in assembling teams of young, fiercely bright go-getters who not only understood the emerging technologies but could also envision subsequent generations of them.

"So, how did that happen?" Linda asked, pointing to the cast which ran the length of Stewart's leg.

Stewart didn't look up. He had never been in a hospital before. He felt trapped and at the mercy of dozens of hospital workers, each of whom came in to poke and prod, make some entry on a chart, pivot in a military-like snap and move on to the next victim. He felt as if the knee was the patient and he barely existed. Stewart had always been physically active — not necessarily a gifted athlete — and now, suddenly, he was rendered helpless. To him, Linda was just one more hospital employee whose job it was to scribble a note and enter it into some godforsaken file.

"Busted it during a soccer game," he replied grudgingly. Then he looked up at Linda. He first noticed her eyes — not so much that they were pretty (which, it dawned on him later, they were), but that they were focusing on him. Eye contact. She's a human being. A rare breed around here, he thought.

"Are you with a league or something?" Her question struck him as naïve. It was probably the "or something" part. She was pretty; her

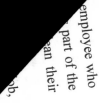

. Her tone was lively, but she had a tender
right now.

:ssing around on a Sunday afternoon."

u here?" Linda asked.

d. "Do you really want to know?" Stewart

added as if to authenticate her sincerity,
:inued, "By the way, I'm Linda. My job
...... are satisfied with their care. I looked at
your chart, Stewart, and from what I can tell the doctors and nurses think
your knee will be just fine in a couple of months."

Linda wanted to provide reassurance to this young man, away from
home and apparently alone. Her enthusiasm and generosity of spirit got
the better of her. But by offering something of a prognosis, however
accurate, Linda exceeded the boundaries of her role as patient liaison.
She unwittingly conveyed to Stewart that she possessed clinical expertise
and authority. Stewart inferred from her comment that he was invited
into a discussion about his medical condition.

"Well, for one thing, I've never been in a hospital before. I hate this
whole thing." The skin under the cast felt uncomfortably moist and
irritated, and Stewart was hit with a pang of exasperation. "Do you have
any idea when I'll be getting out of here?"

"That will be up to your doctor," Linda replied.

"Any idea how long I have to wear this cast for?"

"That will also be up to your doctor," she responded again.

Stewart wanted information, and he wasn't getting any. One more
try, "What about a smaller cast? Can I get something that'll cover only
my knee?"

"I'm afraid these are all questions only your doctor can answer.
What I can help with is—"

Stewart cut her off. "So, you're just another worker here who can't
give me answers. Great. Why don't you just go visit someone else?" He
was irritated and his tone defiant.

Linda gathered some courage. "Listen," she replied, a hint of
resentment in her voice, "I just wanted to see if there's anything you
might like us to do for you... to help you get through this. Your doctor

will be seeing you this afternoon. You can ask him all of those questions then." Linda waited a few seconds for a response. Stewart was swelling with anger at his predicament. Linda thought of herself as an innocent bystander, not recognizing she may have created for Stewart an unfulfilled expectation for a status report on his condition. She tried to give the visit closure. "All right, well, if you need anything, give me a call." She placed her business card on his bedside table, turned and walked out.

The next day when Linda arrived at the office, there was a message on her answering machine: "This is room two twenty-six, bed two. Hey, I'm really a nice guy. And I'm sorry about yesterday. I'm not always such a jerk. By the way, I spoke to my doctor and I'll be discharged in two days. And the cast comes off in six weeks."

Her day was off to a good start. As the day progressed, Linda could not help but think of Stewart in a new light. Stewart was an attractive guy, even with a scraggly three-day beard growth and matted hair. And his deep blue eyes conveyed sensitivity, despite his crabbiness. She found herself looking forward to seeing him again.

"How long will you be in Philadelphia for?" Linda asked while she had an apple and he ate his lunch.

"About ten more weeks," he replied.

Linda arranged for Stewart to have crutch training and physical therapy. A friendship between the two ensued, most of which occurred on the phone because of the tremendous amount of work required by Stewart's job. Linda and Stewart were fond of each other. But their lives were heading in very different directions, and each, especially Linda, sought to avoid the disappointment and even anguish that a broken attachment would produce.

Two weeks before he was due to leave Philadelphia, Stewart's cast was removed. Two days later he invited Linda to dinner to celebrate. They dined at a small French bistro one block off the Delaware River and got to know one another better over glasses of Bordeaux.

"Have you ever seen an oil refinery?" Stewart asked.

Linda blurted a laugh. "What a way to sweep a girl off her feet! Is that where our next dinner will be? How does Chez Cesspool sound?" Linda asked coyly.

27

Stewart laughed. "All right, all right. Some people see nothing more than smoke and stench coming from what looks like a gigantic erector set. I get that. But, you know, we would have a tough time getting around if it weren't for refineries. And you know we're working on technologies now where a good deal of pollution from the refineries is being eradicated. I've been to new refineries that are actually sanctuaries for birds and other wildlife."

"I don't know." Linda had a skeptical look, but was also secretly enjoying seeing how passionately he spoke about his work. "Listen, Stewart, New Jersey is great. Most of it is beautiful. But don't get me wrong. If you drive up the turnpike and pass the refineries near the airport, you're not going to convince me that it's a safe place for anything living. The smell alone can kill you."

"I know. I know," Stewart conceded. "But Meredith Oil hired a bunch of us to develop cleaner ways of getting oil out of the ground and processed. I mean, what choice do we have, make improvements in refining oil or stop driving?"

"What about all the alternatives to oil, like solar power or hydro-electric power?" asked Linda.

"Linda, I believe strongly, really strongly, that we need to develop those alternatives. But unfortunately, we're years, maybe even decades, away from those sources of energy having any real effect on our lives. It's just impossible to generate and store enough energy from those things to make a difference. But we'll keep trying."

"How did you get involved in this oil business?" Linda asked.

"I wish I had a more interesting story for you. When I was a kid, my dad and I rebuilt a car engine. It became something of a hobby for us. Later we rebuilt an airplane engine. That was probably the start of my interest in engineering. But I think that's just how my mind works. When someone tells me how beautiful the horizon looks, my mind begins to calculate how far away it is. Pathetic, huh?"

"No, not pathetic. Not exactly romantic, but not pathetic," Linda said, touched by his sincerity.

"Yeah. I know. I've been accused of that before," Stewart confessed sheepishly. "But what about you? How is it that you don't get discouraged listening to people's problems all day?"

"Sometimes it gets to me, I guess. But I can't think of a better place to be than a hospital. It's not just listening to patients' problems. It's making it better for them."

Stewart cut her off. "But don't you feel like you're swimming against the tide? I hated being in the hospital. All day there were people coming in and out of my room, and I couldn't get a firm answer about what was going on with my condition. If one more person said, 'You'll have to ask your doctor about that,' I was going to scream."

"Well, just like you want to take a necessary thing and make it better, so do I," responded Linda.

Stewart lifted his glass to toast. "Touché. Here's to making things better."

Stewart presented Linda with an itinerary of locations at which he would be stationed for work during the next few years. It was dizzying. Linda's affection for Stewart was growing, but he was clearly not one to settle down anytime soon, she conceded, and his passion for his career left little room for love and family. But these were matters for another day. The night was filled with laughter, warmth and affection. Linda and Stewart returned to his hotel to continue the celebration.

Linda and Stewart saw one another twice more during his final two weeks in Philadelphia. His job was immensely demanding, and it was not unusual for him to work twelve- to fifteen-hour days. He left Philadelphia and spent the next several months shuttling across the globe — first Boston, then the North Atlantic to a drilling rig, then to Louisiana, then Mexico, then San Diego, then Alaska, then Washington, D.C.

Stewart was becoming increasingly preoccupied with his job. Correspondence with Linda grew sparse. He cared for her, but after a short while the all-consuming nature of his job reduced his memory of their relationship to a brief fling. Linda felt Stewart's interest dwindling. Their contact eventually ceased. She never told him that she was pregnant.

THREE

"I hate school," an exasperated Jack shouted as he slammed shut the door to his mother's office. "Posner is an asshole."

"Jack, quit shouting. I have two patients in the treatment area," Linda responded, careful to muffle what would otherwise be a verbal blast directed at her son.

"Mom, there's so much noise in there they wouldn't hear a bomb drop. And, hey, why do you have patients in here so late?"

"This is why." Linda held up a report crammed with numbers, clutching and shaking the folder as if to strangle it. "Our insurance companies are dropping the rates they pay us. If I don't get more patients, I'm gonna start losing money. I need to stay open a little longer. But, hey, it's fine and it'll all work out. What's going on with Posner?"

Linda had graduated from Temple University eighteen years prior with a degree in health care administration just one month before Jack was born in July. Her first job after college was as a supervisor of quality assurance for a hospital in Cherry Hill. A year later she enrolled in a night and weekend physical therapy program. Her parents doted on Jack, and Mary was exhilarated at the prospect of caring for him while Linda worked and attended school. With financial support from her parents, Linda had acquired the physical therapy practice six years ago after working as a physical therapist and practice manager for five years before that. Linda had a few brief relationships with men over the years, but between raising a child and attending to the demands of her career, there was little time or energy left for romantic pursuits. Somehow, the opportunities for relationships just slipped away.

Jack was eighteen and in his senior year in high school. Twice a week he stayed after school to participate in the debate club. On these days he would walk from school to his mother's office — about a twenty-minute walk — and go home with her after work. The end of the workday was always busy for Linda. She paid bills, organized patient schedules, reviewed supply inventories and made sure the staff schedule was properly organized. Despite the hectic nature of the end of the day, she loved having Jack come by. He always had something or other on his mind related to school or friends, and its freshness made him quick to share it with her.

"Posner is a total asshole," Jack reconfirmed.

Linda pressed for more. "I got that part. What happened?"

Ronald Posner was a history teacher at the high school and its debate coach. He had been teaching at the school for twenty-seven years. The debate team never ranked above fourth place in regional finals and was generally dismissed in early rounds in competitions. Posner was bright but lacked interpersonal sensibilities. Students viewed him as inflexible and unapproachable. Sadly, he was never able to motivate his students to perform at the high-quality level for which some, perhaps many, had the capacity. Jack did not have a passionate feeling for debate, or for most school activities for that matter, but being on the debate team was an opportunity for mental exercise. And he could always count on the other kids being bright.

"I asked him if we could expand the topics the team can use for debate practice," Jack began.

"Since when do you care about adding topics to the practice list?" Linda asked, a little surprised at her son's enthusiasm.

"I read this article last week about the custody rights of divorced parents. I can't believe it. In some states, fathers have to petition the court to see their kids on special occasions, like birthdays, if it's not one of their regular visitation days. It's different for mothers."

Linda was a bit bewildered by Jack's sudden interest in parents' rights. When did this come about? And he wants to incorporate it into a debate topic at school? He never showed this kind of interest before, she thought.

"Yeah, I know things like that are not always equitable. What did Posner say?" Linda asked, projecting a contrived casualness.

"What do you think he said? 'We always use the same topics for practice, and I'm not about to change now.' Mom, if a kid on the team used that argument in a debate Posner would slaughter him. He's such a hypocrite!"

"Well, did you explain your interest in the topic to him?" Linda asked.

"What do you mean?" Jack asked.

Linda pressed a bit more. "Did you explain to him why you have a sudden interest in parental custody rights?"

"Yeah. I told him I saw this article and thought it would be interesting to do something different."

Jack sensed his mother's unease. He knew she wasn't on to him, but every now and then parents — all parents, it seemed to Jack — would say something or do something to indicate they knew things about their kids that the kids thought were top secret. Surely Jack's mother would not know what he had discovered in the attic three weeks ago. But, he thought, maybe it would be wise for him to subdue the animation with which he was presenting frustration with Posner and his newfound fascination with parental rights. "You know how I get, Mom. I see an article about something that's just totally unfair, I get crazy. Remember how I got over the dolphins that were getting killed in the tuna nets?" Please buy this, he wished.

Linda laughed. "Jack, just don't get too carried away with this. You know Posner can be a big, immovable rock. It might not be worth tormenting yourself over this."

Jack sensed relief. His secret was still safe.

When Jack was born, Linda had lived with Mary and Kenneth. Jack was five when Linda bought a small Cape Cod-style house on Oakmont Street. Lined with beautiful oak trees with rich plumages of leaves and sprawling branches, Oakmont was on the southern end of Whistling Point, in one of the town's older communities. Linda loved the charm of the neighborhood. Most of the houses on the block were built during the 1920s and 1930s when Oakmont was in what was then the center of town. Since then, much of Whistling Point had taken on the appearance of a sprawling suburban community, especially at its outskirts.

The houses on Oakmont were small, most no more than fifteen hundred square feet. Each was different, in contrast to the cookie-cutter model to home building that was prevalent in the 1960s and 1970s when Whistling Point experienced an expansion boom. Houses on Oakmont had character and history, and their quaintness was an asset, the essence of their charm.

Linda's house had a sloping roofline, which met white clapboard siding. The many windows were framed by the original shutters, basil green, slightly paled and distressed from age, with simple brass handles, Linda's favorite touch. The house had three levels. A small kitchen was on the first floor with a bedroom directly off it. This was the only flaw in the design of the house, according to Linda. For years she had thought about breaking the wall between the kitchen and bedroom to create one large kitchen. A small living room with a fireplace and a small bathroom rounded out the first floor. Linda and Jack occupied the two bedrooms on the second floor and shared the bathroom that separated them.

The third floor was divided into Linda's home office and a large storage attic. Jack had ventured into the storage area maybe two or three times in ten years, and the door to it was always closed.

A few weeks earlier, on a Tuesday, Jack had not awakened from the blare of his alarm. His mother, dressed and ready to leave for work, went into his room, tapped him on the shoulder to wake him, and realized he had a fever. "Oh, Jack, you're sick. You can't go to school with that fever. I'll call and say you're staying home today," Linda announced.

Jack, groggy and achy, lifted his head from the pillow. "I feel crappy, but it's probably just one of those twenty-four-hour things I get every now and then."

Linda brought Jack two Tylenols and a glass of juice. She also brought him a thermometer, which read his fever at a hundred point one. Linda decided it would be safe to leave him for a while and would check in an hour to see how he felt. At that time, they would decide if he needed to visit the doctor.

When Linda called an hour later, Jack was feeling much better. He even thought about going to school for afternoon classes, but Linda thought it best to relax for the day. "Watch TV. Read or something, just take it easy. It's okay to miss a day to take care of yourself," she suggested.

Jack rarely watched TV. At about ten thirty, he went to make himself a bowl of oatmeal. He felt bored and a little antsy, searching for something to do. Maybe he could look at some old pictures while he ate in bed, he thought. He'd get them first.

Jack trudged up the steps and opened the door to the attic. What a strange sensation! He realized that he could meander around any other part of the house blindfolded and still know where everything was, but the attic was foreign territory to him, completely unexplored terrain. Bored as he was, a modest adventure was in order. Perusing the contents of the attic seemed like just the right thing.

Linda had arranged the attic so that there were two piles of boxes with a center aisle down the middle of the floor. A few boxes were not identified, but most were labeled with neat Magic Marker lettering: 'baby pictures'... 'IRS/tax files'... 'old paperback books'... 'school yearbooks'... 'birth record'...

Birth record? Jack had never seen any documents related to his birth. Or anyone else's, for that matter. Jack lifted the box from the top of the stack and placed it down on the floor. Judging from the sealing tape's yellowed cloudiness, this box hadn't been opened in years. The tape on the box came off with barely a tug, its bonding potency diminished over time to Post-It note flimsiness.

The box was full of paraphernalia: old passports, original mortgage documents. Jack wondered how those got in there — Mom was so well organized. Beneath a stack of cards Linda had received congratulating her on Jack's birth was an envelope marked 'Jack - Birth Certificate'. No way, Jack thought. I can't believe I've never seen this.

The envelope was loosely sealed. Jack slid his forefinger under the end of the flap and ran it the length of the envelope. A single-page document was inside, folded in half. Jack's eyes were drawn first to a doll-sized footprint. Must be the logo from the hospital's labor and delivery department, he thought. He looked more carefully. It was his footprint. How weird — how could anybody's foot be that small? he mused.

Jack looked at the document more carefully. Then he turned ashen, his breathing became heavy and his head began buzzing with confusion. Jack's first recollection of a discussion with his mother about his father was when he was five years old. He had been lying in bed ready for sleep. His mother had just finished reading a story to him about twins who adopted two cats on a summer vacation. It was his favorite book at that time. But Jack had something else on his mind that night. It was

June, and his pre-school classmates were making Father's Day cards. Each year he made a Father's Day card for Grandpa Kenneth. A girl at his table turned to Jack and asked why he wasn't making a card for his father. Jack didn't know what to say, so he just averted his eyes and gazed downward at the collection of materials on the desk. It was the first time he was cognizant of a father being associated with him.

As his mother placed the book on the shelf behind the bed, Jack had asked, "Mommy, do I have a daddy?"

Jack remembered that his mother had leaned down and held him tightly in her arms. He had the sensation that her reaction was more intense than his curiosity warranted. Then she leaned up and began to stroke his face gently. Jack saw she had tears in her eyes that she struggled to contain.

"Jack, you are a very special little boy," Linda said. "Mommy wanted a baby just like you very much. And your daddy is a special man. I don't know who he is, but the people who helped Mommy get pregnant told me that he was smart and handsome and very nice."

Over the years, Linda employed this story with meticulous consistency whenever the discussion turned to the identity of Jack's father. As Jack got older, Linda embellished the story, sharing with Jack that she was artificially inseminated by an anonymous donor. She was eager to have a baby, she contended, and through research had identified superior clinics for artificial insemination. Linda reassured Jack that although it was not possible to meet the donor — not even his name could be disclosed to her — she was assured that his father was a very special man. It never occurred to him to question why she would pick that time in her life — she was entering her senior year of college, after all — to get pregnant. But now as this one question may have been answered, Jack's entire life was thrown into a tailspin. On this birth certificate, above the line where it said 'Father,' was a man's name: Stewart Jacobson.

Jack sank to the floor. He stared at the name on the birth certificate. A thick haze of nightmarish existentialism engulfed Jack, his very being sheared from itself. Weakened, pulverized, he felt as though he had abruptly transformed into a stranger. He had no mental category in which to place his discovery; the wrenching emotionalism sparked by his find had no corresponding rationale to temper it, to make it bearable. Here, in this speck of time that it took to see a name on a piece of paper, in this second, this one volcanic juncture — the snap of a finger, the blink of an eye — Jack saw his life as organically altered. But from what to what?

Nothing made sense now to Jack; he intuited only that the pillars of his life's history had, in a heartbeat, crumbled. His mother's partner in his creation was not anonymous, no longer someone about whom any fantasy could be constructed without challenge or judgment. Instead, in a flash, this person became a real human being. To Jack, his father had been amorphous, a concept without contour. In a perverse twist of fate, Jack had been the creator of his father; he could mold him into anything. His father's characteristics and qualities were pure invention, Jack's architecture. For years he had been Jack's silent companion and mentor, malleable to fit whatever role suited the need of the moment. His father could be brave and confident and supportive when Jack lacked assurance or conviction. But strangely, Jack thought, he rarely got angry at his father. Actually, never. Little could be pinned on this man since he bore no responsibility for creating a specific person with a specific person. His anonymity made him impervious to fault, let alone blame. But none of that was true any longer. This lifelong mental construct was shattered in this one instant. Now, fate had taken yet another perverse twist: Jack was no longer the creator, but the created.

Jack folded the birth certificate neatly back in half, handling the document ever so delicately, as if it were a sacred scroll. He placed it back in the envelope and carefully returned it to its place in the box. He draped the yellowed tape over the box, then returned the box to its place in the stack.

Jack went back to his bedroom, fell onto his bed, and lay there staring at the ceiling. Coherence escaped him. He bolted upright from his bed, ran into his mother's room across the hall and called her office. He was furious with her and was convinced he would be unable to contain his rage as he demanded to know why she concealed his father's identity from him.

"Davies Physical Therapy. Ann speaking."

"Hi, Ann. It's Jack. Is my mother there?"

"Oh, Jack. Your mom said you were sick. How are you feeling?"

"Better. Thanks. Hey, is she around?"

"No, Jack. She had an emergency with a patient and had to run over to the hospital. I'm expecting her back any minute. Do you need anything?"

"No, I'm fine. I was just checking in. I'll call her later."

Jack returned to his room and lay back on his bed. He looked around, taking in the room's contents as if he were seeing them for the first time. Above the head of the bed was a poster of three basketball players from the Portland Trailblazers, the team he had employed to fill in the blank when, as a youngster, he was asked which his favorite was. Hanging the poster and taking it down were of equal irrelevance, so it stayed. It occurred to him that he probably couldn't remember which players were on the poster even though he had slept directly under it for nine years.

While Jack felt physically immobilized from the shock to his system, his mind was drenched with adrenaline rushes. He had an analytical bent, and often felt confused as to where this trait properly fit in the matrix of interests and qualities that define people. Over the years, kids would talk about the things they had, this game or that, displaying an enthusiasm for their possessions that baffled and eluded Jack. It wasn't that he didn't get pleasure from being given a toy or a game, but he could never quite comprehend the unrestrained enthusiasm experienced by other kids about material things. Over time he became skilled at faking this thrill, this contrivance little more than a useful social entrance fee.

Jack continued to survey the room. There was a certain fascination to seeing things for what felt like the first time, despite the fact that they had been in his presence for years. Displayed on the wall to his left were three awards he had received. The largest was a plaque for a fourth-place finish in last year's regional debate tournament. Next to it was a framed letter of appreciation from the local emergency rescue squad. As a volunteer two years ago, Jack had manned a phone bank during a severe flood and provided invaluable support to a heavily depleted dispatch staff. Rounding out the display trio was an award for scholastic excellence in middle school, a period in his life that seemed at this moment like it was from another era.

Just below the awards was Jack's desk. A framed picture of Jack and his mother at a Halloween party from three years ago towered over the neat pile of school textbooks. The photo had been taken at a fundraising Halloween party for his school. Jack and his mother had gone dressed as a spoon and a fork. That picture had been in his visual field every day for three years, but it had disappeared into the background, becoming almost invisible. Resurfacing now in his awareness, the photo reminded Jack how much time his mother had spent making those costumes. A shiver cut through him as it occurred to him that there was a missing utensil.

Jack's head hit the pillow, and again he stared at the ceiling. He became overwhelmed by an explosive collision of truth and love, two forces he thought ought to go hand in hand. Jack adored his mother. And her devotion to him was complete and unconditional. He felt that love every moment; their bond was the rock-solid core of his self-esteem and his place in the world. Jack was at once powerfully grateful for that bond while he simultaneously took it for granted, compellingly diverse instincts that somehow fused into a single emotion.

But now, what had been their bond had been pierced. Why had she lied to him? No, this was not a lie, he decided. This was worse, a lifetime of deception. Even worse, it was deception about who he was. How could this be? Explanations scampered through his mind, Jack hoping to embrace one as decidedly — no, he'd settle for barely — credible. Maybe there was no Stewart Jacobson; maybe it was just a fabricated name, part of standard operating procedures at hospitals or fertility clinics. Maybe Stewart Jacobson was abominable, and his mother's sanity required that she erase his existence. Maybe Stewart Jacobson hurt his mother, and she wanted to prevent him from ever being involved in her life. Maybe his mother was waiting for the right moment to introduce the truth to Jack about his father. Maybe Stewart Jacobson made it clear he didn't want to have anything to do with a child and forbade his mother to disclose his existence to the child. Maybe…

For years, this unknown father, this anonymous man, had been a hero. Now that he was a real person, each explanation devised by Jack assigned him the role of villain. Jack so loved his mother that he began to accept that whatever motive may have been behind her anonymous donor story, it could not have been intended to hurt Jack. But he also believed she may not be ready to share the truth with him. Nor did he want to force her into it. He recognized her for what she was — a single parent, hugely devoted, working hard to build a life for herself and her son. Although Linda was successful professionally, and a person of strong character, Jack was instinctively protective toward her; after all, she was parenting without a net. It did not feel right to put her on the spot. There would be other ways to look into this.

The phone rang. The caller ID flashed 'Davies Phys Ther'. "Hi Mom," he answered, straining for an air of nonchalance.

"Jack, how are you feeling?"

"I'm fine. Fever's gone," he replied.

"So, what have you been doing?"

"Nothing, just catching up on some things."

"Okay, Jack, but call me if you start to feel sick again. I'll try to get home a little early."

"It's okay, Mom, take your time. I have lots of stuff to do for the rest of the day."

FOUR

"Hi, I'm trying to get some information about someone's birth records." Jack contacted the obstetrics department of Philadelphia Memorial Hospital where he was born. The receptionist informed Jack that duplicate birth records could be obtained by sending a request in writing to a state government agency.

"No, actually I have the birth certificate," he explained. "I just wanted to see if I could get some more information about one of the parents."

"Oh, I see. Well, I'm not the one who can help with that. You'll probably have to put your request in writing. Try the medical records department. I'll transfer you. Just hold on a minute."

Jack heard a transfer signal, and the secretary of medical records answered. Jack explained, "Hi, I'm trying to get some information about someone who had a baby at your hospital several years ago."

"When was the birth?"

"1990."

The secretary occasionally received calls like this, and most involved custody disputes. She provided standard policy details: medical records are the property of the hospital and ordinarily are not made available. Jack should forward a request in writing to the hospital.

In writing. In writing. The hospital must indoctrinate every person who starts working there with that phrase, Jack thought.

This was not going to be easy. Since his mother was well connected in the health care community, Jack was not comfortable revealing his name to anyone in the hospital. Surely if he wrote a letter to the hospital, someone there would contact his mother. And then there was the possibility that people in the hospital — people his mother knew, friends, professional acquaintances — would discover something about her that she did not want known. Not only would she learn that Jack had discovered the identity of his father but, he feared, the whole world could find out. Jack understood that he needed to exercise great care in his research; he would not want to undermine his mother's interests.

Over the next few days, Jack spent hours at the computer. He did random searches in the event that a Stewart Jacobson — *the* Stewart Jacobson — would materialize. He plugged the name into the white pages of various Internet search services across dozens of cities. A list of over three hundred Stewart Jacobsons was compiled. Jack printed out the list and stored it in a CD storage box he was confident his mother would never look in.

About a week later, Jack got the courage to call one of the Stewart Jacobsons on the list. He would experiment, he thought, a good way to break the ice with this project. He would have to make his call during the day to avoid being discovered by his mother. Jack rehearsed his plan in the event a man answered: please excuse the bizarre nature of this call, but it had come to his attention that Mr. Jacobson may have a child from a former relationship, and could he be the one?

Jack arrived home from school at three thirty p.m. He removed the list from its sanctum, unfolded it and looked it over. He decided to select an individual who lived within a hundred-mile radius based on the likelihood, he reasoned, that the person remained in the vicinity. He placed his finger on the top of the list and slowly ran it down, looking for an acceptable city. His eyes fixed on a target. Stewart Jacobson. Neptune Street. Vineland, New Jersey.

He picked up the phone and dialed the number. He elected to use the home landline instead of his cell phone since his mother had arranged to have the caller ID blocked from the home phone line. His heart was racing. The phone rang four times, the silence between the rings an eternity. Finally, a connection. The robot-like computer-generated voice intoned, "You have reached area code six zero nine…" He hung up. He sighed. A reprieve. But, oh, how anticlimactic.

Jack picked up the list and resumed his scan. There was another. Stewart Jacobson. Fourth Avenue. Cinnaminson, New Jersey. A woman answered, "Hello." Jack froze. Again, "Hello." And again, "Hello. Hello." Then she hung up. Jack felt drained, his energy sapped.

A few minutes later, Jack regained a measure of determination. One more try for today, he thought. Then he could resume this exercise tomorrow. Here's another good one, he believed, as he reviewed the list. Stewart Jacobson. Maple Way. Yardley, Pennsylvania. He dialed. After two rings the phone was answered. Jack turned pale. He quickly hung up, shaken by a voice he hadn't anticipated; it hadn't entered his realm of consciousness. He had been almost uncontrollably mentally immersed in this matter of his father since that day in the attic storage room two weeks ago. And yet, despite all the permutations of thoughts about the subject, despite all the juxtapositions of factors involving his mother and father that careened through his mind — their relationship, his whereabouts, the direction his life might have taken — the person who answered the phone introduced a frighteningly unforeseen possibility. It was a child. What if his father had a family?

Jack was caught in the turbulent whirlpool of radically conflicting emotional currents. His desire to locate his father, to know who he was, had become ever so quickly a vital force in his life, a passion teeming with vigorous curiosity. Jack's need was not to have his father occupy an ongoing place in his life; his thinking hadn't even gone that far. And besides, his mother was parent enough. But for the first time in his life he felt a void. He was within reach of discovering the co-supplier of his DNA and maybe the basis for his mother's need to prevent Jack from even knowing he existed.

On the other hand, Jack was tormented by the notion of opening a Pandora's box. If he pursued this endeavor, the hurt might extend beyond his mother. His father's children, if there were any, might be devastated to learn about Jack.

Making calls like this would have to cease. In addition to the harm to innocent bystanders, Jack recognized the strategy was plagued with other risks. For one thing, he could only make the calls during the day, when his mother wasn't home — but this was a terribly unlikely time to reach his father. For another, what would he say if by some miracle he got the right person? Suddenly, it occurred to him that he was not prepared for this eventuality. And then there would be the phone bill. His mother might see all the calls if she checked the bill. Thank goodness he thought of this now, hoping today's three calls would not catch her attention on the next bill. No more phone calls, he resolved.

Jack didn't have an alternate research plan. But he was becoming more and more dedicated to the prospect of finding his father, his zeal for the mission intensifying with each passing day. For now, though, it was a mission without a strategy.

He didn't want to use social media because it all felt so public. But there were countless websites, Jack discovered, for locating missing people... a universe of possibilities, the sheer volume bewildering. He surveyed several sites but didn't formally register on any of them. He would leave no record to trace, nothing that could come back to haunt him. At least not yet, he thought.

Jack was fascinated by this new world he poked his way into. The phenomenon of missing relatives touched the lives of an extraordinary number of people. And he learned there were thousands of people who worked in the field. Indeed, it was a field staggering in size. Jack was reminded of the time his mother took him to a flea market when he was ten years old. They had encountered a vendor who sold miniature doll house furniture. His mother bought a blue velvet Art Deco chair and couch set, thinking they would sit nicely on top of the small cabinet in the living room. The vendor asked Linda to include her name on a mailing list. Over the next few weeks, reams of catalogs appeared in the mail, seemingly daily, from miniature doll house furniture companies. Jack had thought the vendor was the only person on earth who sold the stuff. The arrival of the catalogs was eye-opening. They included endless displays of furniture from what seemed like every period in history, tiny frames for hanging on walls, kitchen implements of all types. Jack began to appreciate that there was an entire industry organized around these things, with some people devoted to designing the furniture, some to manufacturing it and still others to selling it. There were even competitions, classes, conventions and miniature doll house furniture shows. Some of the older and rarer furniture pieces sold for hundreds of dollars. The scope of this universe was mind-boggling to Jack.

Now another new world was becoming unveiled to Jack, its breadth similarly shocking to him. Exploring websites related to missing relatives was, among other things, highly enlightening. He became exposed to a wide range of related issues that seemed light years from his experience: abductions, custody battles, paternity suits, adoptions, inheritance disputes. Jack read about the psychological fractures experienced by children caught between warring parents. Their plight could be horrifying. He discovered that children in these situations often endured wrenching emotional pain — yet tragically, many concealed their misery for fear of being ostracized or misunderstood. Jack knew some kids at school whose parents were divorced. He wondered if any harbored such silent torture.

One website was especially interesting. Hoytgreen.com was a site developed by a California law firm, Hoyt & Green, that specialized in custody claims. Each week they presented a series of articles on how divorced parents could get squeezed out of their rights to visit their children. (The final paragraph was always Hoyt & Green to the rescue.) In some states, Hoyt & Green claimed, fathers' rights were severely restricted. Jack read one article about a father who had visitation rights on weekends, and the parents would spend alternate birthdays with their daughter. One year, the birthday fell on a Sunday. But this was the year for the mother to spend the child's birthday with her. The father contested, and the ruling by an arbitrator acceded to the mother's position. The arbitrator cited a seldom-employed 1937 statute that favored the mother in the event of such a dispute. Wow, Jack thought. How unfair. This topic fascinated him. He decided to present it to his debate coach, Ronald Posner, for the team's practice sessions.

FIVE

I was looking for my birth mother for three years. I couldn't tell my mom. I love her but thought she wouldn't understand. I posted a message on personlocater.com. Three weeks later my birth mother responded. It turns out she wanted to learn about me, too. Now I see her all the time and we have a great relationship. My birth mother told me she was only seventeen when she had me. She gave me up for adoption because she felt she was too young to raise a baby. It took a while, but my mom handled it great. My mom and birth mother have become friends. I feel like my life is complete now. Thank you personlocater.com
   A.W., Grand Rapids, Michigan

Jack was entranced reading testimonials on various websites. He was a skeptic by nature, and he concluded that many testimonials were nothing more than the creative handiwork of disinterested copy writers. Such marketing tactics angered Jack because he saw how easy it could be to prey on the vulnerabilities of those seeking lost loved ones. At the same time, he was mesmerized by how many people engaged in such searches. The number was extraordinary. His cynicism aside, genuine success stories were well-documented. And even if contrived, Jack recognized that the testimonials surely exemplified real people in real situations.

A couple of months had passed since Jack began to look for his father. Linda had been forced to spend more time at her physical therapy practice. The managed care companies, which accounted for an increasing share of her patients, were restricting the amount she could charge for services, and the practice needed more patients just to keep pace with revenue levels of prior years. When she came home, she had to dedicate hours to paperwork, despite the assurances by managed care companies that administrative tedium would decrease once affiliations with them commenced. With all that occupied Linda, she hardly noticed that Jack was spending much more time on his computer than usual.

Even though he was devoting much time to locating his father, Jack recognized that his approach had been relatively passive. He scanned people finder websites looking for messages from a Stewart Jacobson. He went to the library to search the newspaper archives for any notices about his birth. He even went to City Hall and, under the guise of doing a research project for school, reviewed census data from the area, hoping his father's name would surface. He checked property records, voter registration records and even property rentals. Nothing turned up.

Then one day, Jack experienced a rush of excitement. He was reviewing the message board of a website called docufind.com. Like many of the sites, docufind.com encouraged people to post and review notices. The message board was available to anyone who entered the website. But responding to a message required an annual subscription fee of twenty-five dollars. Docufind.com was one of about ten websites that Jack visited almost daily. The message he saw was riveting:

I believe I have a child from a failed relationship in the northeast. I don't know if the child is a boy or girl but should be about 18 years old now. I have not contacted the mother over the years because our relationship ended due to terrible misunderstandings. I worry that she will not permit me to see my child. She is a professional woman and quite capable of raising a child on her own. I hesitate to give out additional details but will be happy to do so if any of this sounds familiar.
S. Jacobson, Palo Alto, California

Jack read the message again and again, poring over each word. Although skimpy, the essential facts of the message were on target. Almost instinctively, Jack clicked on the registration page of the website. It asked that he assign himself an identification name and a password. Jack chose 'sjson'. He was assured from their statement of privacy that subscribers would at no time and under no circumstances be identified. Now the only trick was to figure out how to pay. He decided to take a chance and issue an electronic payment from his savings account. After completing the payment information, Jack was instructed to review his email for registration confirmation. A moment later he received notification that his registration was approved.

Jack crafted a reply to S. Jacobson in Palo Alto. After several reviews of his draft, he clicked the Send button and his message was on its way to a stranger's email box across the country.

My name is Jack. My mother and I live in a small community in western New Jersey. I am an 18-year-old high school senior. I never met my father, and my mother and I have never discussed his identity. I came across a record of his name a few months ago and have been looking for him ever since. I really don't want my mother to know I am looking for him, and right now, that's more important to me than finding him almost. His name is Stewart Jacobson. Could it be you?
Jack

Jack kept his computer on the entire night awaiting a reply. None came. He slept restlessly, waking periodically to check his email. Morning came without a reply. He left for school, dejected. He was distracted all day, awash in anticipation.

As soon as he returned home, he scurried to his computer. He was quivering — a reply from sjacobs77 was in his mailbox. He opened the message. The passage of time, if only less than a day, rekindled Jack's hopes. In the twenty hours since he had read S. Jacobson's message, he had grown confident, indeed positive, that this S. Jacobson in Palo Alto was his father. There was no way he couldn't be. But as he read the message, deflation overwhelmed him.

Dear Jack,
I wish you well in your search. I had been searching for a child I never knew, and I can understand the agony and frustration of trying to find a loved one. I debated with myself for a long time whether I should even embark on a search, fearing it could result in more pain than it alleviates. But my story has a happy outcome, or at least so far. I posted my message only recently and received four replies. Last night I discovered that I have a daughter. She lives with her mother and aunt in Rhode Island. Her mother and I had a stormy ending to our relationship, but she did confirm that I was the father. I don't know where this will lead, but I will get to see my daughter. Her name is Emily. My life feels

47

*like it has been changed forever. I wish you similar good fortune. Trust
yourself and never stop trying.*

 Stephen Jacobson

 When Jack set off on his journey, he was astonished by the
staggering failure rate associated with searches for missing relatives.
False starts. False calls. False alarms. False hopes. Searches that took
years. Searches that cost thousands of dollars. Tens of thousands. Wrong
paths and detours. Numbing derailments. Agonizing delays. Each step an
eternity. Waiting. Waiting for responses that never came. Waiting for
someone who never showed up. Waiting for an invitation, a plane ticket,
a phone call. Blind alleys. Dead ends. Disappointment and failure. All-
consuming anguish. Then, out of the blue, someone hits the jackpot. And
the spark of vicarious triumph breeds renewal. Once again, however
meager, hope and dedication nudge through oppressive melancholy. A
new day. Try again. Push forward. Slowly, but at least forward.

 Until now, Jack had never seen himself as a member of this club.
His search had evolved into something of a sports event. Sure, he was
driven, but it was massive curiosity and his sense of challenge that had
come to occupy the core of his inspiration. His father, the particularity of
this mysterious Stewart Jacobson, had, over the few months, grown
oddly incidental. Jack's motivation had become to win, to finish the hunt
successfully; the discovery would be the trophy, the means prevailing
over the ends.

 But this brush with Stephen Jacobson had been sobering. For the
first time, he had encountered the possibility of actually finding his
father. Jack realized that he was more emotionally invested in Stewart
Jacobson than he had come to believe. Over time, over the brief period
of a few months, this man had been remolded from a fantasy into a father,
Jack largely oblivious to this transformation taking place within. Jack
began to appreciate the turmoil, angst and futility to which people were
willing to submit, the immense sacrifices they were willing to make, in
pursuit of loved ones. For Jack, like the multitudes whose fate he realized
he now shared, his search had become an all-consuming drive in which
likelihood of failure, despite its incalculable probability, would not be a
deterrent.

Jack lay awake in bed that night. He understood he must reach more aggressively into this community, this Internet expanse of websites, if he was to have any chance of finding his father. Jack drafted a message and posted it on the message boards of five websites established to help people find missing family members.

Hi. I am an eighteen-year-old male who lives with my mother in the northeast part of the country. Until recently, I didn't know the name of my father. But a few months ago, I came across a document with his name listed as my father. I really am hoping to meet him. His name is Stewart Jacobson. I don't have any other information about him. My mother doesn't know that I'm looking for him, and I'm not ready to tell her. Any help would be greatly appreciated.
   Sjson

***

Whistling Point luxuriated in spring. The cold air that swept off the Delaware River could produce harsh winters, and the warmer weather descended with great relief, like a grand reawakening. Sometimes spring crept in so slowly — an increase in the temperature by a degree or two a week, it seemed — that the change was barely noticeable. Other times it would crash land, a thud of warmth, an unexpected reprieve. The horticultural heritage of Whistling Point was evident everywhere, with weekends devoted to planting and tending to yards. Spring produced a collective feeling of refreshment, people out and about, shops filled with customers, parks filled with young parents and their children. People burst forth from months of repression with communal bustle and renewal.

Jack had already been accepted to New Jersey Central College. He knew he had the academic credentials for admission to a more competitive college, perhaps even an Ivy League school. His mother had encouraged him to apply to other, more academically rigorous colleges, but Jack didn't want his transition into adulthood to occur with too abrupt a break from her. Even though New Jersey Central College was a commuter school, several of its programs were well regarded, and Jack

49

considered it an ideal option for the start of his college education. He reasoned that he could always transfer to another college down the road.

Two months remained in high school. Wouldn't it have been something if high school had always been this relaxed, Jack fantasized. Last year, as a high school junior, he was cramming for finals. Now, scholastic motivation shifted to the other extreme. One of Jack's classmates was disciplined for cutting classes. The school counselor filled out the discipline form and next to the box marked 'Reason for Suspension' wrote 'Excessive senioritis'.

Jack was spending much of his free time on his search for his father. Each day he would check the websites for any replies. And he would check the message boards of several other websites for any postings from someone who could be his father, or from someone who might know him. Weeks passed with no replies, except for emails from the websites marketing the investigative service offered by companies with whom many affiliated.

Jack's assemblage of classes could not have been better for someone who desired free time. The more challenging academic courses had been completed in his first three years of high school. Now his course load consisted of Physical Education, Health and Hygiene, Careers, English Literature and History in Film. Interestingly, with the pressure lifted to perform well, Jack felt a freedom in these courses to actually learn, which had periodically eluded him in previous years. History in Film was his favorite. The class watched movies and discussed their influence on pop culture. He was moved by the sense of torment in *The Deer Hunter*, realizing that could have been his destiny had he been born a couple of generations earlier.

At the beginning of the semester Jack had hated Careers, an elective course. The class had been introduced into the high school curriculum two years prior when the Board of Education thought there would be value in acquainting students with vocational opportunities. A noble goal, Jack thought, but the course started off horribly. It was taught by a former Physical Education teacher, Mrs. Samantha Kaye. Jack liked her and felt a measure of compassion for her since she was new to the subject matter and had been assigned the class only two days before it began.

Careers met twice a week for two periods per day. On Tuesdays,

Mrs. Kaye would lead the class through a discussion of a particular occupational field. On Thursdays, students would discuss their interest in that career and how their strengths and interests might apply to it. Week one focused on teaching, week two on finance. It felt dry and boring.

In the fourth week, Mrs. Kaye entered the classroom and declared, "I have a confession. I hate this class as much as you." The class emitted a collective gasp. It was the most attention they had paid all semester. She continued, "Look, I spent twenty-two years teaching Phys Ed. I love it. And I would hope that many of you who took my classes got something out of them." She was right. Mrs. Kaye had been regarded as a good teacher and a strong motivator. Too bad she wasn't the debate coach, Jack thought. "But from the looks on your faces each week, I can tell that you're all bored and, frankly, not getting too much out of this." The students were fidgeting a bit from anxiety. Seldom, if ever, had they experienced a teacher denigrating a curriculum. Was she going to admonish them for failing to pay attention for the first four weeks or hold them responsible for making this course a disaster for her? "So, we need to change things here. I got into teaching to make a difference in your lives. And so far, that hasn't happened in this class."

Jack was impressed. He had always respected Mrs. Kaye's demeanor. Her voice was firm and authoritative, but not in a way that overpowered students or bullied them into subordination. Rather, her tone and manner conveyed a certain dignity and high regard for her position. She drew in each student when she addressed the class, making eye contact with every person, seeing each as an individual. Mrs. Kaye had a methodical way of walking slowly around the room as she spoke, making sure she connected with each student.

"I recommended to Principal Blake that we change the curriculum in Careers. Theoretically, this should be a great course. Most of you will begin thinking about professions for yourselves over the next few years. And if all I do is read from that syllabus that I was handed the day before we met for the first time, I feel like you'll get turned off to some of the careers we discuss. We need to make this subject real for you, make it fun and interesting. I figure, why not bring in representatives from various professions to speak to us? Let's hear about different careers directly from the people in them."

The students were delighted. Jack regarded Mrs. Kaye as a certifiable role model. She continued, "Let's use the remainder of today's class to make a list of fields you want to learn about, and then we can figure out how to invite speakers in. What do you guys think?" Over the next half hour, the students compiled a list of about twenty professions.

On Thursday of that week, Mrs. Kaye distributed a schedule of presentations by practitioners from several fields. An executive from a hotel chain was scheduled to speak to the class next week. A lawyer the week after that. And in three weeks, Harvey Reitman would visit the class. Mr. Reitman was director of operations at West Jersey General Hospital.

Mr. Reitman's presentation was enlightening. Students hadn't realized the scope of opportunities in health care was so great. Mr. Reitman described the various careers in the order patients encountered them, from prior to the patient's arrival at a hospital until weeks after discharge. Mr. Reitman conveyed a sentiment similar to Jack's mother's: despite the complexity of details, activities and busywork, his belief was that the individual patient's well-being must remain the hospital's focus.

At the end of the session, Jack approached Mr. Reitman with a few questions. Jack was proud to learn that Mr. Reitman was aware of his mother's physical therapy practice. "She runs a great program," he said to Jack. "We're always pleased to refer our patients over to her for rehab. She's been putting in a lot of extra hours. I hope she'll be able to take some time off over the summer."

Jack nodded. "Summers have been tough. My mother hates to turn people down on their vacation requests, so she usually fills in for them over the summer. With summer vacations coming up, how do you have enough staff for all the patients?" asked Jack.

Mr. Reitman replied, "Summer is always a difficult time for that reason. Vacations are usually granted on the basis of seniority. But we're luckier than many other hospitals. We have a large volunteer staff to fill in the gaps. And we have a summer intern program that provides young people with hands-on experience while helping out the hospital."

The search for his father was ever-present in Jack's consciousness. He didn't view himself as a particularly manipulative person, but he came to recognize that he sought to exploit every interaction that had the potential for producing a clue. This tendency had become controlled by impulse. He saw no moral dilemma here; his gain, he was convinced, would not cause harm or disfavor to the unwitting provider of information. Jack was becoming more skilled at employing communicative nuance to move discussions in the intended direction. Now Jack's wheels started to turn: Could an internship be a ticket to get into Philadelphia Memorial? "Do all hospitals have internship programs like yours?" he asked Mr. Reitman.

"Many do. Why?"

"I guess I just wanted to know if it was common, that's all. I might be interested in something like that someday," replied Jack. "By the way," he continued, taking advantage of Mr. Reitman's expertise, "the paperwork requirements for my mom's practice have gone through the roof. Is that true for hospitals, too?"

"Jack, we probably have about a hundred employees who do nothing but paperwork. Health care has incredible record-keeping requirements. Most of it is for good reason, though."

"Really? Hey, how long do you have to keep records for?"

"Well, Jack, it varies," Mr. Reitman responded. "For some things we need to keep records for decades."

"That's crazy. Thanks, Mr. Reitman. Your presentation was great."

Jack concocted a daydream and was lost in it for the rest of the day: He would obtain an internship at Philadelphia Memorial Hospital, discover a way to break into the files in the labor and delivery department, retrieve the records from his birth and uncover a wealth of information about his father. As the afternoon progressed, he became determined to act on this fantasy.

When he arrived home from school, he immediately proceeded through his ritual of checking the websites and his email for any messages related to his father. As usual, none appeared. Then he called the administrative office of Philadelphia Memorial Hospital regarding summer internships for students. Jack was sure to emphasize who his mother was, hoping that would give him an advantage in acquiring an internship.

Jack was proud to learn that his mother's reputation was strong even on the other side of the Delaware River. The hospital representative explained, "Ordinarily, internships are limited to college students who major in a health-related field. But I'd be happy to help you out since your mother has contributed so much to health care in the area. How about if we arrange a kind of abbreviated rotation for you, say, for a two-week period? You can be assigned to a few of our departments for a few days each to learn about what they do. Do you think you would enjoy that?"

Jack knew the probability of discovering something about his father would be minuscule. But he had grown accustomed to the idea that a search for a missing loved one required the exploitation of all leads and opportunities, however staggering the improbability.

That night, Jack recounted Mr. Reitman's presentation to his mother, and told her that he was invited to participate in a two-week internship at Philadelphia Memorial Hospital. Linda was almost more excited than he was. "Jack, that's wonderful! You do know you were born there, don't you?"

"Oh yeah, right," replied Jack, hoping she didn't notice him swallowing heavily. Then, quickly, Jack changed the subject. "So, they're going to let me go around to a bunch of departments and observe what they do. And in return, I get to stock shelves and get coffee for everyone. If I do a good job, maybe they'll let me clean the toilets." They laughed.

"You know, Jack, we can laugh about it, but the truth is every job is important. I know it's a cliché, but the fact is there are some people who work at the hospital whose job it is to clean toilets."

"Yeah, I get that. I mean, I've never seen you act like you're more important than anyone at your practice. But in a big place like a hospital, I feel like it must be tough to be a janitor next to a doctor or nurse. Wouldn't you start feeling bad about yourself?" Jack asked.

"I think it depends. I don't know if I ever told you this story, but I learned my greatest lesson about managing from one ten-minute experience about fifteen years ago. I got a call from a rehab hospital that wanted to recruit me to manage their outpatient services. It was very flattering — the president took me out to lunch, and I was tempted to say yes. But you were so young, and I was afraid that the hours would be insane, so I didn't take the job. Anyway, after the interview, the president – Keith Pollan – and I were walking back to his office, which was down the hall from an inpatient unit. As we were walking past a patient room, we heard a patient moaning, so we went into the room. The patient was old, a woman. I'm sure she was in her nineties, and she looked very frail. Keith went over to her bed and took her hand. He asked if she felt okay, but she said she was nauseous. He said he would call her nurse. All of a sudden, she bolted up and threw up all over his suit. Keith didn't jump. He took a towel that was sitting on a chair next to her bed, and rather than wipe off his jacket, he wiped off her mouth and the blanket that was covering her. Then he leaned closer to her to support her better. He turned to me and asked if I wouldn't mind going into the hall to get a nurse. I went out of the room and saw a nurse down the hall, and I motioned for her to come. When I went back into the room, Keith was still sitting with the patient, comforting her, vomit all over his suit. When the nurse came in, he continued to sit with the patient, his arm around her back, supporting her. He explained to the nurse what happened, and she said she would take over. As he stood up, he took off his jacket and folded it so that the vomit was not visible. Then he helped the nurse move the patient into a chair and he continued to help her clean the bed and change the linen."

Jack asked, "Is that unusual? I mean, isn't that his job?"

"Yes, but that's too easy an answer. It wasn't just that he helped a patient and one of his workers. It was his demeanor. There was no part of that entire episode that was beneath him. Not just having vomit all over him but making sure that the patient was well taken care of throughout the whole ordeal. Some executives don't put themselves in the position of being in those situations. They cloak themselves off from the workers, and never get their hands dirty. This guy walked down the unit and took care of a patient just like any other employee is expected to. He didn't pass a grimy situation off to somebody else. And you could see how all the employees genuinely respected him."

"Fine, and that's nice and all, but if he's busy taking care of patients, won't that interfere with all his other work? Isn't that why he has nurses working there?" Jack knew he was being a devil's advocate, but he also felt there was something legitimate about his question.

"Jack, that place was run better than most. And it managed to have a healthy bottom line, even though it was in an amazingly competitive area. Every manager faces choices about what role they want to play. Keith explained to me that he wanted every employee to know that no one is above doing anything. And you know what… his employees worked harder and stayed there longer than most places. Like I said, I learned more from those ten minutes than I learned from anywhere else."

Linda and Jack hadn't really discussed his career aspirations, and the prospect of Jack pursuing an interest in health care provided Linda with some confirmation that her son was proud of her. It didn't matter if he went into health care; his interest in this opportunity did the trick.

The internship began three days after school ended. Linda arranged for Jack to commute into Philadelphia with a neighbor. On his first day, Jack participated in a new employee orientation. In addition to acquainting him with the hospital's mission and its rules and regulations, Jack was asked to review and sign a confidentiality statement. The document indicated that in the course of their work employees may be exposed to confidential information regarding patients and hospital business. By signing the form, employees agreed not to disclose the information. Jack wasn't sure how this policy would affect access to birth record information or what he could do with the information if he did get it.

Following the orientation session, Jack met with an administrator to organize his department rotation. Jack mentioned an interest in obstetrics, medical records, surgery, and admissions.

"Medical records? No one's ever expressed an interest in that department," the administrator noted, a bit puzzled.

Jack wasn't prepared for this reaction but was quick on his feet. "Yeah, well, I do a lot of work in database management at school, and I figured the medical records department would be a good place to see how all the information at the hospital is stored."

"But that would be mostly clinical information," the manager indicated. "Maybe IT would be better because you will see financial information, HR stuff, and reimbursement."

"But I was told that the medical information, which is what I'm more interested in, is kept in this department."

"No problem. Medical records it is, then," the administrator replied. "I'll arrange for obstetrics first."

The obstetrics department was managed by Gail Harmon, a no-nonsense nurse manager who had worked at the hospital for over twenty years. She had a manner that was at once uncompromising and sympathetic, an interpersonal balancing act that Jack marveled at. On his second day, it dawned on him why he found her manner so impressive: Mrs. Harmon reminded him of his mother.

Jack spent about two hours a day trailing Mrs. Harmon, learning how she organized the department. For the remainder of the day he performed assorted tasks, like replenishing supply inventories, moving wheelchairs about and filing patient charts.

At the end of his second day, Jack initiated a discussion with Mrs. Harmon about rules for maintaining records. "I can't believe the amount of paperwork you have on each patient. Was it always like this?"

Mrs. Harmon replied, "The amount of information we're required to keep never ceases to amaze me. Can you imagine how much more tedious this was before we had computers?"

"Yeah, nuts. I also saw that there are data sheets for the parents of each newborn. Did the hospital always have that?" Jack asked.

"For as long as I can remember," she replied.

"But is there room in the hospital for all that information? You'd need a storage cabinet the size of the Grand Canyon!" Jack exclaimed.

Mrs. Harmon laughed. "Jack, you're absolutely right. There's a federal commission and a state agency that require us to keep hard copies for a few years. The records from before we had our computer system are now stored on microfiche."

Jack had an inquisitive look which Mrs. Harmon interpreted as lack of familiarity with microfiche. She continued, "You know, they take a picture of a document, then reduce it in size to a tiny fraction of the original, then store it on film." Jack knew what microfiche was, but he didn't want her to stop talking about records, so he kept quiet.

"So where are the films stored? I mean, you probably can't keep that all in the hospital, right?" asked Jack.

"To tell you the truth, I really don't know where all the records are stored. The hospital has a contract with a records management company, and after a certain number of years, the records are transferred there. The medical records department handles most of that." Jack's hopefulness dulled. For sure, he believed, any records related to his birth would have already transferred over to this records warehouse.

In four days, Jack transferred to medical records. It was tucked away in the basement of the hospital, at the end of a large corridor, off of which were the hospital pharmacy and a cavernous storeroom where all the hospital supplies were kept. The medical records department appeared to Jack like a small, self-contained corporate office. Four rows of six workstations occupied the front portion of the department. In the rear was a large area, perhaps twelve hundred square feet of storage area. Was it possible, Jack wondered, that somewhere in that mass of data lay information about his father?

Jack was given an overview of the department's operations by the manager. She seemed very nice, but the demands on her impressed Jack as extraordinary. It was near impossible for her to spend any time with him. Her department was at the mercy of everyone in the hospital: doctors, nurses, administrators, lawyers, regulatory agencies — all needed her attention, and now never seemed soon enough for them.

As Jack was organizing some patient files to be returned to the file system, he recognized one of the younger-looking clerks. Barbara Lipton had graduated from Jack's high school two years before. She didn't remember him, but he recalled that she was on the yearbook committee. They struck up a conversation, mostly about which teachers they liked and disliked and whether the cafeteria food had improved since she graduated. (It hadn't.) Then Barbara explained that she had begun working as a temporary clerical employee at Philadelphia Memorial four months ago. In two months, she told Jack, she was scheduled to transfer to the admitting department.

Jack told Barbara about how he obtained his quasi-internship. He recounted his experience in obstetrics and described his amazement at the amount of information the hospital was required to keep. "How long do you need to keep records for?" he asked.

"Jack, it's incredible," she replied. "Some information we need to keep thirty years, some for twenty years, some for seven. I'm still learning."

"What's the oldest information you have?" asked Jack, experiencing a renewed optimism.

"I'm not really supposed to talk about this, but I've been working with records now from a birth from 1962. There's this guy who's claiming he's the father of a woman who was born here. She got killed in a horrible accident a couple of years ago. A drunk driver hit her while she was getting into her car. Her mother died a few years before she did. Now the guy comes along and says he's her father and is entitled to half of her money. The estate of the mother is claiming he's not entitled to anything because he's not the father. Now the lawyers are looking into the birth records that we have at the hospital."

"Jeez, that's crazy," Jack said. "You know, I was born at this hospital. I wonder if my birth records are here."

"If they're still here they'd be on microfiche. Otherwise the file would have been transferred to the warehouse that stores records for us," said Barbara.

"Yeah, someone told me that every few years patient records are transferred to microfiche," said Jack.

"It might be fun for you to take a look. I'll be done with this project in about an hour, but then I can show you the microfiche room if you want," said Barbara.

Jack's head was spinning. A strange fear — more like a powerful apprehension — was rumbling through him. Discovery of tangible information about his father had never been within reach, certainly not like this. Having become conditioned to expect disappointment, he feared succumbing to a profound sense of hope. He feared learning something about his father that he didn't want to know. A stasis had manifested within, a certain comfort with the situation in its present state. He feared that any movement forward carried the risk of gloom for his mother. He feared he would encounter leads that would lead to nowhere. He feared what he might find and feared what he might not. Most of all, he feared exhausting the only lead he had.

"C'mon Jack. I'm ready." Barbara's voice caught Jack off guard. He was filing patient charts in a back office, and her words shook him out of a stupor. "Hey, listen, I'm sorry, Jack, but I'm swamped. I won't be able to stay with you while you look through the microfiche records. But I'll show you how to use it, and you'll be fine on your own."

Was this too good to be true? Jack had been thinking about how to explain to Barbara that he would be happy to look through the records on his own so as not to disrupt her work. And now she was doing the job for him.

Behind a small file room, adjacent to the huge file area, was another storage room with "Microfiche" marked on the door. As Barbara escorted Jack into the room, he noticed a large table to the right with three large viewing machines and a computer monitor and keyboard on it. To their left were rows of metal cabinets, and much like a library, the end cabinet of each row had reference numbers indicating the range of contents in each row.

Barbara explained how to use the computer to identify the location of the desired microfiche file. "Okay, here you go, you enter the patient's name in this field. If there's more than one patient by that name, you'll be asked to complete additional fields, like date of admission. For births, the information is generally included under the mother's name." Then Barbara asked, "Have you ever used a microfiche viewer before?"

"No. But I think I can figure it out," Jack replied as he looked at the viewer. "It looks like you just thread the film through this spool here. The light switch is here. Then I just look through and move the film with these dials?"

"Don't tell anyone here you figured it out so easily. You'll get a promotion and all these people who've worked here for years will be gunning for you." Jack laughed. Barbara smiled at him. "Hey, I've got to run," she announced. "Good luck." If she only knew, he thought.

Jack moved over to the computer. He typed in Davies, Linda. One entry appeared on the screen, with a code next to it. "Oh my god," Jack gasped. The records were there.

Jack felt his breathing quicken. He moved from his chair and found the row of cabinets in which the microfiche film he sought was located. He opened the drawer and found the film organized into small boxes, each with a code. He saw the box with the magic code on it, then gingerly touched it with the tips of his trembling fingers. He was pulled by forces that tore at him: *Forget this*, it's useless, it will lead only to anguish. And then, *go forward*, you may never come closer.

He lifted the box, his movements, he sensed, controlled by forces outside himself; he was on automatic pilot. He approached the viewer, removed the film from the box and threaded it, then turned on the viewer's light. He peered in. The film was set to a table of contents page: Births July 1987 — June 1993.

It took about two minutes for Jack to find his records. There were about thirty pages of information photographically reproduced and included in his birth file. The first several pages looked like the medical record, detailing Linda's progress through labor. There were a few pages regarding insurance. All were signed by Linda. Jack scrolled through about twenty-five pages and saw no reference to a father's name. All signatures in areas for patients and insurance subscribers belonged to Linda or Grandpa Kenneth, who had agreed to pay for incidentals not covered by insurance, like phone and TV.

Jack's spirit was drifting toward malaise. Maybe it was true that Stewart Jacobson was an invented name. Jack had invested enormous emotional energy into the fantasy that this man existed and would be found, and now despair was beginning to poke holes in his spirit. Jack had only a few more pages to review. His hope exhausted, his energy sapped, he began to wish he had never found his birth certificate. This has been a torturous process, he thought with an air of surrender.

The next page was entitled Parent Data Sheet: Mother. It included Linda's name, address, next of kin (Kenneth and Mary Davies), occupation (student), marital information ('single' was checked), insurance information and education. No surprises here.

Then Jack turned the spool to highlight the final page in his birth record: Parent Data Sheet: Father. Jack looked at the page and was seized by an emotional reversal. He recognized the handwriting as his mother's. There was not much there. Only two spaces were filled in. But he knew now for certain that he had a father, that there was a real person with a known name who gave him life. Next to the space marked 'name' it said *Jacobson, Stewart*. And next to 'education,' the box marked 'college' was checked. And next to it was written *New England Institute of Technology*.

SIX

"Now make two wishes," Linda said, beaming at her son, who was turning nineteen on the last day of his hospital internship. Jack and Linda had a particularly joyous tradition for celebrating their birthdays. Ever since he could remember, on the actual day of their birthdays, Linda would prepare a special chocolate fondue, and she and Jack would cut up fruits and cakes for dipping. A single candle was planted in a small section of pound cake and the birthday celebrant would make two wishes, one for each of them.

When Jack was young, Linda generally had a small party for him and his friends. But it was this birthday ritual with Linda that was most special for him. He worried that today's two wishes were mutually exclusive. For himself: Please let me find my father. And for his mother: Whatever happens, please let it be okay for her. The wish for Linda did not completely soften his feeling of betrayal, but it took the edge off.

That evening, Linda's welfare weighed heavily on Jack. Weeks had elapsed, he realized, during which he had failed to devote much consideration to the impact his search might have on her. He was simply too absorbed with the search and its meaningfulness to him. It had overtaken him, shielding from his consciousness almost everything unrelated to it; during these periods all else was extraneous. And then, periodically, his concern for his mother flooded his mind in a deluge of worry. How could he do this to her, he lamented; there was no one on earth as sacred to him. He agonized over telling her about the search, how he came upon the birth certificate initiating the quest that was ever-present in his mind, that he pursued the hospital internship only for the remote possibility of discovering a piece of information about his father.

But, Jack reasoned, telling her introduced risks. She could be shattered, and hurting her was not worth it. On the other hand, if he found Stewart or discovered his whereabouts, his mother would certainly become aware of what he had been doing. Then she would be brought into the process at a later stage, one with a far greater potential for hurt. Moreover, who better than Linda could answer the questions about Stewart: *Who is he? Where is he? What happened?* Conceivably, she could solve in an instant what Jack had been straining to discover for months. But, on still another hand, Linda — for reasons she might not share with Jack — could implore him to cease his efforts to find his father. Then he would feel compelled to obey. Case closed!

Jack reconciled that he would tell his mother when the time seemed right. But now was not that time, and he was convinced Linda suspected nothing; Jack had become adept at concealing his activity from her.

Jack had been calculating his next step: He would contact the New England Institute of Technology. But he wanted to be certain not to squander the opportunity. If it hadn't been clear to him before, he certainly had come to understand that big organizations are not in the business of freely giving out information about their employees, patients, students, customers or whatever group they're in the business of serving.

He called the university's general number. "Um, hi there, I'm trying to get some information about a former student." The operator told him to try the Alumni Association or the Department of Student Affairs.

Jack did a search on the Alumni Association website, but no Stewart Jacobson appeared. A more detailed search could be initiated, but this would require registering on the site, which was limited to alumni. Hope was running out as Jack turned to his remaining option.

"Student Affairs, Cathy speaking." The voice sounded unexpectedly young to Jack. It must belong to a student with a summer job in the office, he thought.

"Hi. I hope you can help me. I'm trying to get some information about a former student," Jack began, feigning confidence.

"Is the student applying to another university or something?" *Or something.* Jack was relieved. He had been anxious for days about making this call. He had convinced himself that some bureaucratic ogre would answer, would see through his charade, then notify his mother, the FBI and the entire United States military. The young woman's tone immediately put him at ease. And then there was the "or something." Cathy was human.

"No, actually, it's an unusual situation," Jack replied. Then he launched into the speech he'd been rehearsing for days: "You see, I'm planning a surprise party for my mother. She has an old friend she knew from college days. I want to invite him, but I have no idea how to get hold of him. The only thing I know is that he went to your school. So, I thought if you have an email address or a phone number, I'd be able to invite him. My mother would be thrilled."

"That's so cool," replied the young woman. "By the way, what's your name?"

"Jack. Jack Davies. I'm calling from New Jersey."

"All right, let me see what I can do. What's your mother's friend's name?"

"Stewart Jacobson," he said. Jack realized it was the first time he had said the name out loud.

"And when did he graduate?"

"I'm not exactly sure, but can I give you a range?" Jack asked.

"Sure."

"Probably sometime between 1985 and, oh, I guess, 1993."

"Oh, that's quite a range. Would you mind holding on for a minute? I'm going to do a quick check in our database."

About two minutes passed. "Hi, Jack? Sorry, but nothing came up for those years. How do you spell Jacobson, with a 'c' or a 'k?'"

"I'm pretty sure it's with a 'c'," Jack replied.

"Yeah, that's what I checked for," Cathy said. "What about Stewart. Is it 'e-w' or 'u-a'?"

"'e-w'," Jack responded. His optimism, which had been soaring, was now in steep decline.

"Can you hold on again? I'll be right back," Cathy asked.

A minute passed. Then Cathy returned. "All right, so I see what the problem is. We have a number of different databases here for our students. Depending on the year of graduation and the major, the person could be in one database or another. I have to check a couple of things, then I'll call you back. Actually, I really don't know if I'm allowed to give out information like this about former students. Please don't take it personally if I end up not being able to. You're doing such a nice thing for your mom, so I'll try to help if I can. I have to check which database your mother's friend is in. A friend of mine — Peter — who works with me knows how to access all the databases much better than I do. I'll ask him when he returns next week. Is that too late for you?"

Jack was deflated but didn't want his voice to reveal it. "No, that's fine. And I really appreciate that you're trying to help me. I know if we can find this guy it would make my mom really happy."

"I'll do my best," Cathy said. "What's the best way to get back in touch with you?"

"Well, it's a surprise, so I don't want my mom to find out. I guess emailing me would be best."

"Sure. What's your email address?" Cathy asked.

Jack gave his email address to Cathy, and said he looked forward to hearing from her the following week.

The summer had been hot and oppressive. For the past two years Jack had worked as a summer relief aide at the library. When the hospital internship ended, Jack returned to the library for three hours of work per day. He continued his daily ritual of checking emails and website postings immediately upon returning home. Still nothing from or about his father.

Cathy proved true to her word. A week after their call, an email appeared from her:

Hi Jack. I had a chance to do some further checking about Stewart Jacobson. Please call me. Cathy

"Hey, Cathy. It's Jack."

"Oh, Jack, I'm glad you called. I think I have some bad news. We have no record of a Stewart Jacobson at all. We checked graduates in all university majors between 1975 and 1995. I'm sorry."

Jack was in denial. "That can't be. I'm sure he went there. My mother mentioned it a lot."

"Is it possible he was registered under a different name?" Cathy asked.

"I don't think so. And I'm sure I gave you the right spelling," said Jack.

"I'm sorry, Jack, but we checked a pretty broad range of years."

Jack's one flicker of hope had extinguished. "Well, all right. Thanks for your help. And thank your friend."

"Sorry. I hope your mom has a great party, anyway. Bye."

Once again, a dead end. This was the final lead. Jack had run out of ideas and hope. He decided to step away from this search for a while. It had become overwhelming, distracting him from focusing on, let alone enjoying, anything else. College was starting in a week, and he needed to remove himself from the suffocating clutches of this obsession.

SEVEN

Jack's first day at New Jersey Central College produced a myriad of impressions. He parked in the student lot and walked to the center of campus to Franklin Hall for an English class. He experienced an odd notion of asymmetry, as those walking around campus were of a variety of ages. Until now, peer relations were defined almost exclusively by age group. In a flash, other traits, such as common academic pursuits, could also constitute the basis for social engagement.

The lack of familiarity with his surroundings didn't ruffle Jack. Rather, it heightened his alertness. It occurred to him that all he noticed today — small landmarks like the surfacing roots of a huge oak tree at a grassy triangle adjacent to the parking lot, the aroma of brewed coffee wafting from a faculty commissary — would soon cease to beckon for attention; familiarity would push it all into the background. For chunks of the duration of his search for his father, his attention to his mother had languished. He had hardly visited her at the physical therapy practice. And between his hours at the computer and her heavier than usual workload, their time together diminished. Jack resolved to devote more time and attention to her.

That night, Jack and Linda went out to dinner. The Red Barn Diner was about two miles from their house. Linda had been taking Jack there for years. The food was good, plentiful and inexpensive. An ample supply of warm cheese bread and cinnamon bread with the most tantalizing aroma was provided at every meal. The Red Barn was big and almost always crowded, but the tables and booths were spread out and it was easy to feel a sense of privacy.

"So, how was your first day? And don't leave out a detail," Linda asked, filled with awe at having a child in college.

"Well, the classes seem pretty good. My English professor has a book published, a collection of short stories."

"Oh nice, what are the stories about?" Linda asked.

"I don't know. I picked up the book at the end of the day. It's required reading for the class. He told us that the short story is a dying art form in America. Years and years ago, families told short stories as a form of entertainment and passed them down from one generation to the next. The professor is pretty cool, but he blames television and radio, and now the Internet, for the demise of the short story." Then, with a sarcastic bent, "Welcome to the twenty-first century. Anyway, I hope his book is good."

"What about Spanish?" asked Linda.

"The class was canceled for today. Seems the Spanish teacher was returning from visiting relatives in Spain, and she was delayed in an airport for ten hours."

"Watch out for her mood tomorrow. Maybe you should cut class," teased Linda.

"Mom, I suck at Spanish. I don't know, maybe it doesn't interest me that much," he contemplated out loud. "But if I miss a day, I'll probably wind up failing the final. Hey, my computer class is terrific. The teacher is only about thirty, and he develops software programs for small companies. Half the class is much older than I am. They're taking the class because they're not as computer-savvy as they need to be for work. There's one guy in the class who's got to be sixty."

"You know, Jack, I'm halfway between where you are and where that guy is. I hope when I'm his age I'll still be interested in learning and taking courses somewhere."

"Yeah, you know what's great? He doesn't look the least bit uncomfortable. The younger students look like they're scared to say the wrong thing. But this guy just speaks so naturally, like being wrong or right or accepted doesn't matter at all."

Linda smiled. "Yeah, I suppose there are a few benefits to getting older. Tell me, what's the course going to cover?"

"Mostly how to use online resources for research. Like how to compare and use different search services for different projects. How to judge the quality of information. We're going to divide into groups for a project that's going to last the whole semester."

"Word to the wise," Linda intoned in a distinctly motherly way, "try to get in the older guy's group."

"Ha, right," Jack replied.

"Overall, what do you think? Is the workload going to be manageable? Harder than you thought? Easier?" asked Linda.

Jack thought for a moment. He hadn't intended to broach the issue of his parentage. In fact, the subject hadn't crossed his mind all day. But there was something about her question that triggered The Subject.

"I can't tell, yet. But I already see it being much more intensive than high school. I mean, it'll really take up a lot of time. You know, it had me thinking that I can't believe you were pregnant and taking classes and things." A morsel of bait was tossed.

"Yeah. Seems hard to believe after all these years. Gosh, you were so adorable."

Linda didn't take the bait. She didn't even seem to sense that Jack was fishing. Jack gave it another try. "I mean, how did you manage it, you know, being pregnant and being in college at the same time? Why'd you decide to have a baby then?"

Linda sat back in her chair. She sighed, then said, "Looking back, it seems like a crazy decision, doesn't it? But sometimes you go through with something because it feels so right, even though it doesn't make sense to a lot of other people. Not that it's the same thing, but I had these two friends back then, a couple. They were dating. And they took a cross-country trip when they were both twenty-one or so. When they got to California, they decided to buy a dog. They had no money and had to use their remaining traveler's checks to get him. At first, I thought they were nuts. This dog would force them into a relationship, and we all thought they were too young. It seemed so irresponsible at the time. But it ended up working out well. To this day, they're the happiest couple I know."

"Yeah, but, Mom," Jack shot back, "a dog isn't exactly a baby."

"True," Linda said. "But what I mean is that sometimes an instinct just needs to be followed. I knew I was ready for a baby. I knew I could take care of him and love him properly. And at the time I thought a man would only complicate things for me, mainly because I really wanted to get a jump on work. I may have been shortsighted about that, but certainly not about having you."

She wasn't biting, but Jack pressed a bit. "But why then? Why not wait till you finished college to get pregnant?"

"I wish I could tell you. But I don't have an answer. I had been in college for three years. I knew the routine and knew I could handle it. Grandma would be available to help watch you, so I could pursue my career and raise you without feeling stressed. I think it worked out well. Don't you?" she asked.

"Oh yeah, of course," Jack replied, a noticeable hesitancy in his voice that Linda mistook for questioning her judgment.

"Jack," she said, responding to her incorrect assumption, "Sometimes you have to follow your heart when you know it's the right thing. Having you was the most right thing, I ever did in my life."

Time to back off, thought Jack. She was not prepared to share the truth with Jack. Certainly not tonight. And he was resigned that he was no more prepared to force the issue than at any time before. His mother had her story. Jack knew it was deeply personal to her. To demand that she yield to his interest seemed grossly unfair, a course of misdirected self-indulgence on his part.

But there was more to Jack's relinquishment. The episode with the New England Institute of Technology had depleted the remaining traces of his optimism for his quest. He had grown accustomed to the likelihood of never finding Stewart Jacobson. And more, this very abdication had become a source of relief. He would still check the websites. But now even this had become simply a ritual, a habit without purpose beyond faithfulness to execution. The search was over. It was done. He could live again.

Weeks passed. Cooler weather was setting in. The area's rich soil produced an abundance of trees, which in turn yielded a bounty of leaves that made autumn a glorious visual delight. Reds and yellows, oranges and deep browns were scattered everywhere. New Jersey Central College was awash in leaves, and the crisp air had a vitalizing effect on the students.

Fall gave way to some early winter snows. Jack had adapted easily to college. The autonomy provided by a commuter school suited his frame of mind. He did make some new friends — acquaintances, really, who offered easy conversation during breaks. Jack had achieved a certain equilibrium. The frenzied emotionalism of the prolonged search for his father had produced a mental callous that made most things in his life seem less urgent.

On a Tuesday, late in November, he arrived home to find an email:

Hi Jack,

I hope you remember me. I work at NEIT and tried to help you out a few months ago when you were trying to locate your mother's old college friend. I have some updated information for you. Please give me a call.

Cathy

Once again Jack was thrust into an emotional maelstrom. His messages had been posted on several websites for months. No responses ever came his way. He had given his mother much opportunity (or so he thought) to tell him the truth about his father. He had taken a job in a hospital just to get some information. And what he had obtained was meager. What in the world could Cathy have unearthed months later?

"Hi Cathy, this is Jack."

"Oh, Jack, how are you?"

"Fine. I've been pretty busy. I started college this semester. How about you?"

"Great. Hey, how was your mother's surprise party?" Cathy asked.

Jack had almost forgotten. His recovery was quick: "Oh, it was great. My mom was surprised."

"Did you tell her that you were looking for Stewart Jacobson?"

"No, uh, as a matter of fact, I guess I just forgot to mention it to her. I managed to find a bunch of other old friends and got caught up in tracking them down. What an ordeal." Jack almost started to believe his own story. Then, slightly tremulous, he broached the subject, "So what's this news about Stewart Jacobson?"

"Well," Cathy began, "I only thought if your mother wanted to reach him, I had a little news."

"You mean," Jack asked, wincing with apprehension, "you know where he is?"

"No, sorry. But I came across the weirdest thing a few days ago. The school is selling off a few of its dormitories. So, they asked me to go through all these old files to see if any students still owed money for

71

housing. Not that the school would necessarily have them pay any money back, but the buyer wanted to make sure the properties had no outstanding debts or anything. Anyway, I'm looking through this list of hundreds, maybe thousands of students starting from like 1980 or so, and as I'm going down the list, I see the name Stewart Jacobson. Now I'm thinking, this is so bizarre. Here's this guy who apparently lived in the dorm, but we have no record of him in our academic files."

Stunned, Jack asked, "Has that ever happened? Can someone live in the dorm and not attend the college?"

"I guess it's possible, but I never came across a situation like that. So, I was getting curious. I checked with Peter, my colleague who works with the database management system, and he rechecked the databases, this time using Stewart's social security number. We got his number off the housing sheet because the school used to use social security numbers for IDs. Your college probably did the same thing. Anyway, we ran the ID through every possible database and came up empty. Pretty weird. Peter, who's now obsessing over this mystery, decides to go another route. We do credit checks through our office, you know, for housing and tuition. Peter enters the social security number like he's doing a routine credit check. Turns out that number doesn't belong to anyone. Like it was never assigned to anybody. Pretty strange, huh?"

"I don't know what to say. Are you sure he lived in the dorm?" asked Jack.

"Well, that's the other thing. I'm sure there was a Stewart Jacobson who lived in the dorm. We have housing application files for all the students. This place never throws anything out. So, I go to the archives and find Stewart's file. Inside is supposed to be all this stuff about a lease agreement, student loan information, method of payment forms for the dorm, you know, basic stuff. I looked through a few random files from other students from those years. All of their information was intact. But Stewart's was really weird. There's a file jacket with his name on it. And there was nothing inside. It was completely empty. But attached to the outside was a post-it note that says 'Deliver Contents to Security Office'."

"Did you learn anything else?" asked Jack.

"I called the security office, and they said they know nothing about it," said Cathy. "It's the craziest thing. Even the head of security said he didn't know anything about it. Of course, he wasn't even here when Stewart attended college."

"It's like he's a ghost," said Jack. "Do you think there's anything else we could do to find out about him?"

"I really don't know. I even went to the Alumni Association office to look him up in their collection of yearbooks. I went through every possible year he could have been here. No listing of him. No photo. Nothing. But we were wondering, since we're all confused, maybe you could just ask your mom about him? I'm sure she could solve this for us."

Jack hesitated. "Oh, sure," he stammered, "I'll ask her right away." Then he had a thought: "You know, it might help if I had his social security number. Maybe my mom will have an idea about a job he had, and the number can help us get his records or something."

"Yeah, all right. But don't ever tell anyone it came from me. The number is 182-46-0118. Hey, Jack," Cathy continued, "this has been driving Peter and me crazy. Not that it's any of our business, but if you find anything out, can you please let us know?"

"Yeah, sure. I'll let you know if I find anything," Jack assured her.

"Thanks. I hope we talk soon. And good luck finding this mystery man," said Cathy.

"Thanks for all your help," Jack said, his voice couched in muted bewilderment. Then, attempting to downplay the significance of his true interest in Stewart, "It was great of you to get back to me about this."

EIGHT

"Jack, listen, there's something going on that I need to speak to you about," Linda announced to Jack on a Saturday morning in December as he sat in the living room, reading a science fiction book. Linda sat on the chair opposite his.

Jack's heart skipped. She knew what he'd been doing for the past several months, he feared. He shot a glance at her, attempting not to appear worried.

She revealed her thoughts. "I'm thinking of selling the practice."

"What?" Jack shouted. "Why? What's going on?"

"Well, Jack, I've been thinking about it for a few months now," Linda replied. Hmmm, Jack thought, he wasn't the only one who'd been surreptitiously preoccupied around here. An unanticipated source of redemption, he mused to himself.

Linda continued. "It's just getting tougher and tougher to run an individual practice these days. I have no one to share my costs with, and we're not getting enough revenue from each patient to make ends meet. And we're not big enough to bump up our volume of patients to make this work."

"I know, Mom, but you've worked your whole life for the practice," said Jack.

"Yeah, well, that's the good news. Because it's been a well-run practice, it has some appeal to the chains. A few months ago, Southwest Therapies approached me about buying the practice. They're a big chain of physical therapy and rehab centers. They started in Phoenix and went west from there. Now they want to get into the northeast. My practice would be perfect for them. I've already turned them down a few times. But they kept coming back with better offers. I talked to Grandpa about it. He thinks we should consider it. I wanted to fill you in and get your ideas about it," Linda said.

Jack slumped back in his chair. A few months ago, Jack had helped

Linda reorganize a small storage room in at the physical therapy practice. The room was at the back of the facility, past the homey reception and waiting area; five treatment rooms; a common exercise area replete with stimulation devices, assorted weights and exercise equipment found in the most modern gyms; two consultation rooms; a main inventory area filled with canes, walkers and prosthetic devices; a smaller inventory room; three accessible bathrooms; a patient file area; and Linda's office. The small room housed equipment and supplies that were used infrequently. It was also where Linda kept old files on financial records, state inspection results, contracts with suppliers and general correspondence.

Linda had asked Jack to help relocate the storage and file cabinets to create additional space. He emptied a few of the drawers to lighten the cabinets. He saw records dating back at least ten years. Book after book and file after file were filled with Linda's handwriting; her imprint was omnipresent.

Linda's history and that of the practice had become interwoven. Four years earlier, Linda had remodeled the facility. The flat surfaces had a necessary hygienic sheen, but Linda managed to soften it with the relaxed feel of comfortably cushioned couches and chairs. The waiting area was sufficiently spacious, easily accommodating the wheelchairs and crutches and visitors that accompanied many patients, but it was arranged in clusters so that small groups could have private conversations. The walls were adorned with soothing landscapes.

This practice was indeed Linda's in all respects. Jack had come to recognize that Linda hired people who conformed to certain standards that had been near and dear to her for years. Staff had to be generous of spirit, not only with patients, but with one another. They had to be resourceful and decisive. And they had to exude a positive air. Over time, Linda had assembled a group of about fifteen people who fit the bill. There was a positive dynamic at the practice. Jack likened it to the nervous energy experienced by the debate team before an important event. The energy was purposeful, and Jack appreciated the synchrony of good energy and a noble mission.

"Great, so you've worked this hard just to make the place attractive to someone else." Jack was somber but resolved. "It just doesn't seem right."

Linda laughed half-heartedly. "Yeah, what a way to look at it. But I don't think the place can survive on its own. And the package Southwest is offering is very substantial."

"So, what do you want to do?" asked Jack.

"I've been thinking about this for months. I'm torn. I do know that things can't go on as they have. My practice will go out of business."

"Why does Grandpa think it's a good idea?" asked Jack.

"He says the value of the practice may be greatest right now. If I wait too long, the price I can get may go down. And in the meantime, I'll be losing money. He does have a good point."

"And what would you do?"

"I met with the executives of Southwest. We could work out an arrangement where I could still manage the practice. I would still work there, which would be good. And I'd be free from a lot of the paperwork hassles, which I imagine would also be good."

"That sounds like a plus. But would your heart be in it the same way?" asked Jack.

Linda drew a breath. "I just don't know."

The physical therapy practice was a constant in Jack's life. In a way it was like a member of the family, the attachment never more powerful than when facing its loss. The practice defined his mother's life. Not merely by the status in the community and the sense of achievement it provided, but mostly by the vast collection of small events that comprised the day's work: seeing patients inch toward recovery, consoling a patient who relapsed, reviewing a new treatment procedure, observing the receptionist's deftness in juggling appointment schedules.

"Are there any other options?" Jack asked.

"There is one other thing I'm considering. But I don't know if I can pull it off. There's a practice about ten miles from here, toward Cherry Hill. It's slightly smaller than mine. They take care of patients west of us, so between the two practices we handle about five communities. I've been toying with the idea of buying it."

Jack's eyes widened.

"If I do," Linda continued, "together we'd be in a strong position to withstand these chains overpowering us. Plus, I'd get the benefits of sharing expenses. I'm sure you've heard the expression 'economy of scale'."

Jack nodded. "That sounds great! So why not just do it?" he asked enthusiastically.

"Because it's not that easy. It's expensive. Don't forget, the value of that practice is also high. So right now, I'd have to pay a premium for it."

"What about Grandpa? He can lend you the money, can't he?" Jack asked.

"I've talked it over with him. He can lend some, but it probably won't be enough. I can get a second mortgage on the house, but that won't do it either. And since getting the new practice would not be an immediate income-producer, I really don't want to put the house up for collateral."

Linda thought this discussion would best be presented in increments, so she retreated a little: "Hey, listen, for now just think about it. I'm not going to be pressured into any decision. I want to make sure I make the right one. Maybe just give it some thought."

Now Jack had a new burden weighing on him. He understood the financial imperatives his mother had to consider. But he knew she would be miserable if she sold the practice and worked for a nameless, faceless management company with headquarters on the other side of the country. She loved the trust and rapport that had been built between her and her patients, and he worried that defending corporate practices and philosophies would smother his mother's spirit. He'd have to help her to understand that. But he quickly realized, she already did.

NINE

Winter was in full fury. Multiple snows hit Whistling Point in rapid succession. The landscape was blanketed with a grand white swath, its glow radiant, depriving night of its darkness. Trees were frosted with ice, its weight tugging at the branches, creating a vastness of luminescent archways.

Whistling Point, like most of the communities that dot the western part of New Jersey, was generally well prepared for harsh winters. Heavy snows would not ordinarily deter the town from carrying out its everyday routines. Linda's physical therapy practice had closed for a total of only five days in the past ten years, as the town's plowing schedule gave priority to health-related facilities.

New Jersey Central College was a majestic sight after a heavy snowfall. The college was established on the grounds of an estate of an eighteenth-century land developer. Many of his holdings were in the South and he incorporated much Southern flavor into the design of his estate. The library occupied what was the main house, a sprawling yellow pine expanse, three stories high. Just inside was a spacious foyer with an elegant sweeping staircase that spiraled up the center of the building. Cherry wainscoting adorned the wide hallways. A row of tall white columns emanated from the portico and ringed the building. Ivy crawled up the back of the building, adding an accent of New England charm. The snow concealed the flower beds, which, in summer, bestowed color upon the library and graced the various walkways that led to the building with a dazzling outline. But now the snow lent a scholarly character to the setting, evoking imagery of people immersed in their studies.

Jack enjoyed being at the college. He had a natural comfort with the coursework and was gratified by exposure to new subject matter. Some students had fixed ideas about careers. But Jack hadn't a clue. He felt no need to set his sights on a career path. It would come to him in due time, he reasoned. There was no shortage of pursuits to which his interests could be applied, and, in the meantime, he vowed to savor this indoctrination into the next stage of his life.

182-46-0118. His mind shifted focus to that number with extraordinary ease. He could be anywhere, doing anything. Despite the nature or extent of his mental preoccupation, a flip of the switch, usually triggered unconsciously, brought him magnetically to that number. It had been about five weeks since he first learned it. It was all he had about his father, other than the bizarre matter of Stewart's attendance at the New England Institute of Technology.

Jack was held prisoner by a harsh ambivalence. One paltry bit of information he accumulated about the identity of his father led to another insignificant bit, each successive one more mystifying. Moving forward with this search was taking its toll. When Jack was engaged in it, he was fully absorbed. He was at the mercy of the search, his mind wholly occupied. It sucked from him an ability to concentrate on anything else… school, friends, family. And despite the hours devoted to this activity, the portfolio of information about his father was only a scant more than he had when he discovered his birth certificate. The frustration of failing to make any progress would motivate him to turn him away from the project periodically. The messages on the websites produced nothing. It's hopeless, he would concede from time to time, and he would put the project on hold. Then, suddenly, he would be drawn to it again, driven by some uncontainable and inexplicable force.

Following midterm exams in February, Jack's computer research instructor assigned the class a new group project. Many websites offered information on exchange rates for international currency. The assignment: track, evaluate and compare sites for their clarity, accuracy and functional utility.

Jack's group met the following afternoon to plot a research strategy. Fred McNichol, the oldest class member, to whom Jack had been drawn, initiated the discussion by suggesting they compile a list of the categories of organizations likely to post exchange rate data.

"Banks," said one.

"Insurance companies."

"Stock exchanges."

"Credit card companies."

Like a rocket, Jack veered abruptly from the discussion and into his own thoughts. Banks, credit card companies. *Why didn't I think of that?* He was frustrated with himself, failing to think creatively like a resourceful investigator. Thus far he had limited himself to websites on the remote chance that his father was out there somewhere, and just as desperate — or at least eager — to reconnect with Jack. But this was pure fantasy and Jack knew it. If Stewart Jacobson wanted to see his son, it would be a cinch. Jack's mother hadn't moved out of the area. She hadn't even married and assumed a new name. Plus, she had a prominent business, one that contained her name in the title. No, if a rendezvous was in the cards, it would not result from the chance encounter of two people who mutually sought it. Jack came to the firm belief that meeting his father would result only from Jack's persistence and imagination.

Banks and credit card companies would be the place to start. And then, by chance, a third source was added. Across a website for the BankFirst Visa card was sprawled an advertiser's banner:

Do You Know What Lenders Are Saying About You?

Then the fine print:

Most people have never seen a personal credit report. But everything from mortgage companies to banks to car loan companies to landlords make decisions based on your credit every day. Credit Plus offers a thirty-day free trial. Waste no time. See what's in your credit report today.

This seemed too good to be true. Credit Plus would be added to Jack's list. And surely, reasoned Jack, Stewart had a bank account when he attended NEIT. Obtaining the names of banks that operated in the Boston area was simple, taking no more than five minutes. Most had websites which offered some history, in some cases indicating when they were founded. Jack was amazed at the high volume of mergers, acquisitions, name changes and even insolvencies, cutting deep into his assumption that a bank is a bank forever.

Three banks with branches within walking distance of NEIT's

dorms were still in operation: People's Bank of New England, Boston Trust Savings and Loan, and Eastern Mass Savings Bank. He crafted a letter, which he sent by email to the bank managers of the three banks.

To whom it may concern:

I have been searching for my father, whom I've never met, for the past several months. I learned recently that he attended the New England Institute of Technology near Boston, probably in the late 1980s and maybe into the early 1990s. The only information I have about him is his name and social security number: Stewart Jacobson, 182-46-0118.

I know this request is unusual and may seem a bit crazy to you, but it is my hope to exhaust all possible leads, and maybe my father was a customer of your bank during that time. If so, I was hoping you might have a forwarding address or any information about where he might be.

I would really appreciate any help you can provide. Also, if you could please keep this request confidential, I'd be grateful.

Thank you,

Jack Davies

The three banks had relatively similar procedures for responding to third-party requests for information about their customers. Each forwarded the letter to its customer relations department, and within a week Jack received three nearly identical replies. Each indicated that it would be a violation of company policy to disclose information about a customer without the customer's explicit consent.

Jack knew the bank route would be a long shot. Disappointed, but not surprised, and buoyed by a newfound eagerness, he went to the Credit Plus website. There was a lot of fine print, paragraph after paragraph, enough to cause Jack to second guess whether he should pursue this course. An entire section was devoted to fraud. 'It is unlawful,' Jack read, 'to use this service for purposes other than for obtaining one's own credit history; it is unlawful to misrepresent oneself or identify oneself as another individual; it is unlawful… it is unlawful…' The extent of legal verbiage was daunting. But Jack reasoned that if he was discovered, he would simply tell the truth, and he would depend on his innocent nature and righteous cause to bail him out, to mitigate any impression of him as sinister or criminal. So, he registered with Credit Plus under Stewart Jacobson's name and provided his social security number.

With financial institutions enlisted as a first line of defense in nationwide efforts to restrict the flow of funds to potentially dangerous organizations, Jack's letter was forwarded to each bank's security department. Each department reviewed archived customer lists and determined that Stewart Jacobson had never been a customer. Security personnel at Eastern Mass Savings Bank and at Boston Trust Savings and Loan placed Jack's letter in a file, and there it would remain with no further action taken on it.

But Jack's letter was handled differently at People's Bank of New England. Frank Carrera had been promoted to Regional Security Officer at the bank three months earlier. He was recruited into this newly created senior-level security position after the bank experienced a breach in which loans were approved to a local contractor who purchased materials of inadequate building grade. Because of the financial risk associated with this contractor, the bank was required to obtain more details about the purpose of the funds. Their review processes had been scrutinized by state and federal agencies that made the recommendation, among many others, that a more robust security program be instituted at the bank.

Frank had worked for a local consulting company for ten years, managing the implementation of security systems for regional banks. He was impeccably thorough and had the abrupt manner of someone who placed security light years ahead of customer relations. The president and board of the People's Bank of New England took pride in the customer-friendly tradition of the bank and had some misgivings about Frank's tendency to view all customers as potential security risks. But the era called for a more vigilant approach, bank management understood, and Frank's presence would certainly blunt any criticism that they were not doing their part to contribute to the security and safety of the public.

Frank read Jack's letter. He attached a memo to the letter indicating that Mr. Jacobson had never been a customer at the bank. But unlike his counterparts at the two other banks, who considered the matter closed, Frank placed the letter in a folder he kept in his locked drawer. The folder was labeled, 'FBI: Low Risk', and its contents were forwarded to the regional FBI office once a week.

Meanwhile, two days after Jack submitted his request for a credit report to Credit Plus, a reply was waiting for him in his email folder.

Dear Mr. Jacobson,

We are sorry to inform you that we were unable to complete a credit report for you for the following reason(s):

Error 210: Invalid social security number.

"Shit," Jack screamed at the computer, and he slammed his desk, scattering papers and pens to the floor. He was back to square one, the very place he had been when he was in contact with Cathy at NEIT. He grabbed a pad and started a list of other avenues to pursue: credit card companies, phone companies, utilities, cable companies (then he crossed off that entry, realizing cable hadn't existed in prehistoric times).

Credit Plus, like banks and other industries that exchange financial information, would report requests from the public that aroused suspicion to government agencies. The fine print, which Jack had actually read, pointed out that questionable requests may be reported to the Securities and Exchange Commission, local police departments or, in the case of nonexistent social security numbers, to the FBI.

Thus, in the third week of February, an FBI regional office in the northeast received two alerts involving Stewart Jacobson. One request apparently came from Stewart Jacobson for credit information about himself, and one was from a young man who wrote to the People's Bank of New England claiming that Mr. Jacobson was his father.

David Shearer, an information analyst, was in his second year in the FBI's Philadelphia office. He reviewed incoming communications, assigned case numbers to them and then performed the triage function of evaluating risk and routing them to the appropriate section in the office. As information was entered, the system searched case files for common elements.

On Tuesday, David received the letter from Frank Carrera of the People's Bank of New England. By initial appearance it seemed harmless enough and was assigned a low risk designation. A case folder was established, and relevant information was entered. Jack's email letter to the bank manager and Frank's accompanying note indicating that

Stewart Jacobson had not been a customer were scanned into the folder. The case was forwarded to Mariah Caldwell, an investigator who handled bank fraud and other similar white-collar illegalities.

On Thursday, another communication arrived on David's desk. It was a form letter from Credit Plus detailing the request from Stewart Jacobson for his credit history. David processed the report. Because of the potential for fraud, the report from Credit Plus automatically received a higher priority level than the letter from Jack to the bank. As the report was entered, the system was scanning all other cases for commonalities. A report to David was issued immediately. It referenced a case which was input only two days earlier, involving a letter to a bank manager from a young man searching for his father. Despite the hundreds of cases per day that David sometimes handled, he remembered the letter from Jack. A friend from college had spent considerable time and money looking for a birth parent, and David had come to understand the extraordinary efforts — at considerable cost of time, money and emotion — to which some people would go to locate a birth parent or child.

Mariah Caldwell's office had already conducted a cursory review of the case, confirming Jack's address and obtaining a personal profile from his Internet provider. The letter to the bank manager struck her as probably benign, if not somewhat naïve, and did not impress her as qualifying as an urgent matter.

Two days later another report made its way to her desk. It was certainly possible that coincidence could explain two matters involving a Stewart Jacobson within a two-day period. But more than likely the two were related.

Protocol ordinarily would involve behind-the-scenes gathering of relevant bank records, addresses and places of employment — for both Jack and Stewart. As required, before proceeding, Mariah filed her report with a regional supervisor for a higher-level security analysis of the data in her report. Here, the presence of more sensitive, secretive information in the report could be culled — for example, that which might have a potential bearing on national security.

On Friday morning, Acting Regional Director Anthony DiGregorio was in his office when Chris Spencer, a Senior Chief Information Analyst, burst in with a concerned look.

"Sir, I just received this report. You need to take a look at it right away," Chris said.

Anthony took the single sheet of paper and read it. His face reddened. "Damn it. Who knows about this?"

"To the best of my knowledge, no one, sir," Chris replied.

"Do we have any intelligence here at the bureau on Jacobson?" Anthony asked.

"No. All data about him is referred to DIA," Chris informed him, referring to the Defense Intelligence Agency, the Department of Defense agency that collects and provides information about military capabilities and aims of foreign countries to the United States' defense community.

"All right. Chris, get this over to Defense. Use the highly classified channels," ordered Anthony.

"I'll arrange for a courier, sir."

Jack's experience in attempting to locate his father had a bumpy cadence. A single lead, a bit of hope, produced a great swell of optimism. But each led to a dead end, and with it a crash of hopefulness. Nothing worked, it seemed, and every lead not only bore no fruit but also contributed a share of doubt about the very existence of Stewart Jacobson. February concluded with a reinvigorated eagerness on Jack's part to conduct an ambitious search. But the cold, formal responses from the banks dampened Jack's enthusiasm, and the Credit Plus confirmation that Stewart's social security number was invalid dealt a devastating blow to Jack's stamina to forge ahead. Jack was despondent as March began. Motivation to explore other avenues was diluted. Jack decided not to contact any credit card companies.

What Jack didn't realize was that his actions had triggered a secret investigation run out of an office in Arlington, Virginia. Jack was being watched.

TEN

The pile of fried chicken was about a foot high. "I guess I got a little carried away," Kenneth said. The aspect of Mary's and Kenneth's rural upbringing that had not vanished after they settled in Whistling Point was the love of preparing big outdoor meals. As each spring arrived, they cleaned out the barbecue pit and eagerly looked forward to arranging feasts for Linda and Jack.

"Your grandfather couldn't wait to use his new toy," Mary said to Jack. Kenneth was thrilled to try out his new outdoor frying vat. "We'll be eating that chicken for a week," she said.

April started out cool and misty. A surprise snowfall in the first week of April was a final fierce reminder of the past winter's fury. But now, three weeks later, the trees were saturated with buds, the grass was thickening and the forsythia were a vibrant yellow. Jack hadn't inherited his grandparents' love of gardening, and he couldn't distinguish one type of tree or plant from the next. But he loved the period in April when for a few weeks the forsythia glimmered a bright shimmering yellow. For Jack, it signaled the beginning of the season when school was winding down and summer was imminent.

"I hate this," Kenneth said as the phone rang just as he, Mary, Linda and Jack sat down to dinner. "I guarantee it's going to be one of those sales calls."

"Hello," Kenneth blared into the phone. Then, after hearing a sales pitch, he boomed, "No, I'm not interested, and please remove me from your list."

"Was that for re-siding the house? I got two calls like that this week," Mary said.

Kenneth started to laugh. "No. This was for a singles club," he said.

"Then why did you have your name removed from the list?" Mary teased.

"Yeah, Dad. Hey, you could probably do better than I could in a club like that," Linda said. "Oh, Jack, that reminds me," Linda turned to her son, "you started getting these kinds of calls. A sales rep from a bank in Boston, of all places, called to tell you about their retirement programs."

Jack froze. He feared that his letter to the bank manager had gotten him on some customer contact list. "That's weird. They probably get lists of students from college records," he said.

Kenneth jumped in. "Absolutely. Once you get into college you get on all kinds of lists. Banks and credit card companies want to get the jump on college students so that by the time they start on their careers, they'll have relationships with them."

"You're probably right. I didn't think of that," Linda said. "And I thought it sounded so strange that a bank in Boston would be calling Jack. So, I asked the guy how he got Jack's name and he told me Jack was already a customer."

Jack struggled to maintain his composure. "Can't imagine how I made that list."

Kenneth asked, "Jack, have you registered for insurance through the college, or did you request any information for a credit card or a loan for the car or anything like that?"

"No, Grandpa," Jack replied.

"And you don't have a secret bank account in Boston where you're hiding all your money?" Linda asked, feigning stern.

Jack took her seriously. "What do you mean by that?" he asked, his tone defensive.

Linda started to laugh, and she quickly caught herself. "Jack, I'm kidding," she said, "but why are you so jumpy?"

Relieved, Jack replied, "I don't know. We have a huge project for English, and I'm way behind. I'll catch up over the weekend."

Linda and Jack left for home about two hours later. Jack drove. He felt waves of tension, feeling the possibility — however slight — that Linda harbored some suspicion about the call from the Boston bank. He weighed the prospect of raising the issue again, just to test the possibility. "So, Mom, when did that guy from the Boston bank call?" Jack asked.

"Yesterday. Why do you seem so uptight about this call?" Linda asked.

Jack cut in, "I'm not! It's not the call. I just have a lot on my mind,"

Jack responded, getting comfortably certain that his mother did not suspect there might be more to the phone call from the bank.

"Anything you want to talk about?" Linda asked. She paused for a minute. "I mean, you're doing so well in school, I can't believe it would be stressing you out. I wouldn't complain if you had a little more of a social life. Is there a girl you're interested in?"

"No." Jack hesitated. "Well, there was one. She's in my English class. We spent an hour together talking the other day. But turns out she's married. Married! Thank god I didn't ask her out. What an idiot I would've been."

"Did she wear a ring?" asked Linda.

"Yeah, but it didn't look like a typical wedding ring. It wasn't gold. It was more of a red and blue mosaic. She told me she and her husband got matching rings on a Navajo reservation. They liked the fact that the designs have traditional meanings. Her ring means 'Enchanted One' and his means 'Sensitive Warrior'. Sensitive Bullshit if you ask me."

"Ha. Don't be bitter because she's already married."

"Yeah, to Mr. Sensitive Warrior," Jack said, oozing sarcasm.

"Have you thought about giving Blair a call?" Linda asked. Blair Foster and her family had lived five houses away from Jack and Linda for eight years. Last year the family moved to a northern suburb of Philadelphia. Blair's mother, Sue, and Linda had an acquaintanceship, and from the time the family had moved, Linda and Sue spoke on the phone every few months. The gaps between conversations increased as both women tacitly understood their primary commonality had been proximity.

"Mom, you've been trying to marry the two of us off since we were ten. I don't like her. I never did, and I never will." Jack realized the conversation had shifted from the Boston bank. Then, just to make sure this topic was even further behind them, "You know, in high school... never mind. I shouldn't be telling you this about her."

"Well, now you have to! What don't I know?" Linda asked.

"Ok, I guess." Jack continued, "She had a boyfriend when she was a junior. He didn't go the school. I never met him, but I think he was about twenty. Her parents had no clue she was seeing this guy. Turns out he was a dealer. Blair used to make drug deliveries for him at school.

When her parents found out, they decided to move."

"What? Blair? God, I know I can be naïve sometimes, but I never would have expected that from her. Sue told me they were moving because Adam's commute was becoming too much of a strain."

"Right. After eight years his commute was all of a sudden too much of a strain?"

"Okay, well, I guess we'll rule out Blair as a potential mate," Linda said as the car turned into their driveway.

"Yeah, but hey, maybe she'd make a good business partner," Jack laughed. "She has entrepreneurial experience."

Two weeks had passed since the sales representative from the Boston bank had called. Hoping the matter would simply disappear, Jack hadn't returned the call. He also had not resumed his search for his father by contacting credit card companies as he had planned. The bank route had proven futile. Of course, he should have realized, financial institutions would not disclose information about customers to third parties, especially without permission. And now Jack had doubts that he even had the correct social security number.

Final exams were only a couple of weeks away. Jack was well prepared except for his English exam. It consisted of two parts, an in-class section on the material covered during the course and a series of three short stories to be submitted two weeks prior to the end of class. These stories were due the next week and Jack hadn't even begun the first.

Jack was an able writer. He loved writing but typically felt blocked when faced with the constraints of a school assignment. Science fiction was his favorite subject. The professor assigned the class a series of themes on which to base their short stories: jealousy, revenge, love, despair, spirituality, fidelity, deceit, hope. Jack explained his interest in science fiction to the professor and requested his approval to develop at least one story based on this interest. The professor declined, noting that a "good writer begins by mastering the depiction of basic emotions."

Whatever, Jack thought.

On the first Sunday night in May, Jack sat at his computer staring at a blank screen. Yielding more to procrastination than creativity, Jack decided to check his email again, for the third time in an hour.

Surprisingly, a message had just come in:

Jack,

I'd like to speak to you. Call me in the office tomorrow. Use a public telephone.

Cathy
NEIT

Jack remembered that the email address used by Cathy in her previous email communications was cathy.admin@neit.edu. The email address from which this message was generated was clearly a personal account. He didn't know what to make of it, but if Cathy took what had been a business-related issue home, it could mean something, he thought.

An adrenaline surge thundered through Jack. He stayed awake until three a.m., and despite — or more likely, because of — the message from Cathy, he was able to write two stories for his English class. When he did sleep, it was uneasy, and he awoke with a start from the sound of his alarm.

Jack was filled with anxiety about calling Cathy. Their relationship — well, if it could be called that, he thought; more an acquaintanceship — was predicated on a lie. A shroud of mystery surrounded Stewart Jacobson, and could Cathy in some way be implicated because of some information she tripped across? Would he be forced to humble himself and reveal the true — or, at least, a less false — nature of his inquiry about Stewart? He finally decided he would call Cathy before lunch, during his break.

Adjacent to the cafeteria on the lower level of the Student Center was a lounge. Two rows of private cubicles were situated along the far wall. Students typically used this facility, which was equipped with phone lines and modems, for computer work. Jack believed he could best conduct a private conversation from one of these cubicles. And more importantly, if any anxiety-producing revelations were to surface, at least he would not be standing in public view.

"Hey, Cathy. It's Jack."

Cathy's tone was stern. "I'm going to call you from a public phone. Give me your number and stay where you are."

Two minutes later the phone rang. "Cathy," Jack blurted, as he grabbed the phone. His heart was pounding.

"Yeah hi," Cathy said. "Jack, there are things going on with Stewart Jacobson. Don't take this the wrong way, but I looked you up. I know you go to New Jersey Central College, but other than that I really don't know anything about you, and I suspect you weren't telling me the truth about wanting to invite him to some surprise party."

Jack cut her off. "Cathy, what's going on? You're freaking me out a little."

"Listen, I need to fill you in about some things, but not by phone, and definitely not by email. Shoot, I can't believe how stupid I was to email you last night."

"Cathy, what is going on?" Jack pleaded. "Can't you at least give me a hint?"

"No. Not now. But for whatever ridiculous reason, I feel like I can trust you. Or maybe I just want to, I don't know. But I can only talk to you in person. How far are you from Boston?"

"About five hours. But Cathy, I—"

Cathy cut him off. "I'll meet you somewhere in between. How about Albany?"

"Cathy, give me some idea about what's going on," Jack said, his voice quivering.

"When can you meet me?" Cathy asked.

"I don't have class on Wednesday until four," Jack replied.

"Fine. I'll arrange with Peter to get the day off. There's a Hyatt Hotel off the New York Turnpike three miles north of where it crosses Route Ninety. Can you be there by ten?" Cathy asked.

"Yeah. Fine. Ten's fine. But please can you tell me anything? I've never felt more nervous in my life."

"I get that, but I'm not saying anything over the phone. I'll see you on Wednesday."

"How will I know you?" Jack asked.

"Let's meet in the lobby by the reservation desk. I'll wear a light blue jacket," Cathy said.

Stunned, numbed, Jack could muster only, "I'll see you there."

Linda worked well into the evening on Monday, and by the time she arrived home, Jack, exhausted from a practically sleepless Sunday, was already asleep. On Tuesday, Jack was at school until eight p.m. When he arrived home, Linda was heavily engaged in paperwork. The temptation to disclose all to his mother had never been as intense. As he had for months, Jack wrestled with revealing that which had overwhelmingly consumed him for a year. He replayed the pros and cons of telling her over and over in his mind, and eventually determined, as he had innumerable times, that revealing his discovery could seriously dismay her or shut down the process. Once again, he decided, he would not tell her yet.

"Mom, will you be working late tonight?" Jack asked her as he entered the home office.

"Another couple of hours."

"One of our project groups is having an early morning meeting tomorrow. I have to leave early, by five, so we can get some of our final done before people get to work," Jack said.

"Five in the morning?" Linda exclaimed. "Who's scheduling the meeting?" she asked.

"Well, we have a couple of people with full-time jobs. So, we all agreed to have this one meeting before the workday begins. Let's hope this is the only time we need to do this," Jack said.

"All right. Go get some sleep," Linda said.

"Yeah, I think I will. Night," Jack said.

"Good night. And good luck with the project tomorrow," Linda said.

Jack experienced a surreal unease as he lay in bed. The strange combination of the Stewart Jacobson mystery and the deceit toward his mother would produce occasional moments, like now, of psychic nausea. Other than an occasional benign mistruth ("I didn't break the vase," at eight) and an occasional mistruth thought benign ("None of the guys were drinking," at seventeen), Jack simply didn't lie to his mother. Part of his motive now, he believed, was to protect her, although he wasn't sure from what. All sorts of possibilities swirled within. Protect her from the past. Protect her from having her lifelong lie to him exposed. Protect her from being hurt. Protect her from failing to protect him. But the other part of his motive was to prevent his mother from becoming a factor in derailing the search for his father.

After a predominantly sleepless night, Jack left for Albany at five fifteen the following morning. The drive to Albany was easy and fast, and Jack arrived at the Hyatt at about nine a.m. He got a cup of coffee from a kiosk in the lobby and settled into a thickly cushioned chair with a textbook. His eye continually wandered to the registration desk.

At nine forty-five, a young woman with a blue jacket positioned herself in front of the registration area. Barely a woman, she had the appearance of a young college student. Her dark wavy hair fell just below her shoulders. She was fair skinned and had an alert, intelligent appearance. She was also pretty, a quality that heightened the intimidation Jack already felt in anticipation of having to confess his lie to her.

Jack placed his book in his backpack, rose from his chair, and approached Cathy tentatively. "So, you're Jack," she said with a smile, drawing out his name. As with their first encounter on the phone, her manner put him at ease.

"Hi, Cathy. Nice to finally meet you," Jack said, unable to conceal his shyness as he extended his hand.

"Well, you are not what I pictured," Cathy said.

"Better or worse?" Jack asked.

"Well, not worse," Cathy teased. "Come on, let's find a private corner to talk," she said as she gestured toward a far end of the lobby.

As they walked over, Jack said, "You know, I haven't slept for two nights. Your call scared me to death."

"Sorry, I know I sounded really dramatic. But only because it felt super necessary to be cryptic like that until we could meet in person."

Jack and Cathy sat in a small, softly lit area in a remote corner of the hotel lobby. She began, "Okay, so for the past couple of days, I've been replaying all these events over and over in my mind. A few months ago, I got an unusual call from this young guy who told me he's looking to find out about an old college friend of his mother's." Cathy gazed out a nearby window, her hands stretched out, palms upward, not having fully reconciled her naïveté. She turned toward Jack. "You know, at the time I really loved that you were throwing your mom a party. But regardless. Okay. I have some information about things for you, but first I need you to tell me the truth. I know there wasn't a surprise party, but I do know that there's something else going on. I have some things that I want to share with you, but I need to feel like I can trust you first."

Jack's hands were clasped in a tight grip. His search for his father had become so private, so secret, that to share it with someone else seemed to constitute a violation of a sacred personal vow. And here he was with a veritable stranger. "Cathy," Jack began, "I can't believe I'm telling you this, but I think Stewart Jacobson is my father."

Cathy sat stunned, her eyes frozen wide, as Jack recounted how he found the birth certificate, learned of the college that Stewart attended and how his path led to her. "I never met him and didn't even know he existed until recently. And there were hundreds of times I almost told my mom about this. But each time, something stopped me. I don't know why she never told me about him — assuming he is my dad. I mean, if she had a bad relationship with him maybe she never wants to see him, let alone have him see me. So, if I don't tell her, well, at least I'm not going against her."

"Okay. That's a lot. But about your mom, you know if you do find him, he'll probably be reintroduced into her life, too. So, at some point she'll know you were going through all of this," Cathy said.

"I know, but I guess I don't want to lose the chance of finding out who this man is," confessed Jack.

"All right. Well, let me tell you what's been happening on my end," Cathy began. "Last Friday, the director of security called and asked me to come to his office. That's pretty common. From time to time our office is asked to gather some records about a student. I head over to his office, knock on his door, and when it opens, Mr. Jeffords, that's the head of security, says in this very formal voice, 'Cathy, please come in. I'd like to introduce you to a few people.' Sitting at his desk are three people, two men and a woman. We're introduced to one another and I'm asked to sit down."

"Who were they?" asked Jack.

"I'm getting to that. Or I should say I really don't know because there seemed to be a deliberate effort to be vague. Jeffords had this weird, almost grim look on his face, and he seemed so nervous. I remember their names, Mr. Gold, the other man's name was Cosgrove, and the woman was Miss Hovering. Or something like that. Mr. Jeffords told me they had some questions for me about an investigation of financial records related to the sale of the dorm. Remember I told you about that when we spoke a few months ago?"

"Yeah. Were they with a security company or the government or something?" Jack asked.

"Mr. Jeffords said that they were with a government banking agency. Which sounded like a bunch of crap to me. I don't know why, just how he said it. Then they said they were looking into the financial records of about fifty alumni. When I asked if they could give me details, they declined, and said they were not at liberty to disclose the nature of their inquiry. Mr. Jeffords said that I had to cooperate since it was a government agency. That made me feel really nervous, of course, so I asked if I should have a lawyer with me and they said that since I was not at all involved, I would not need representation. Then they showed me the list of alumni and asked if I had come across anything unusual about any of these names while reviewing financial records. I take the list and scan it up and down. The names were all arranged alphabetically. The only name on the list I recognized was Stewart Jacobson."

"What did you say?" asked Jack.

"I told them about the call I got from you about Stewart Jacobson. I mentioned that I was so impressed because it seemed like you were doing such a nice thing for your mom."

"Did they react to that?" Jack asked.

"These three were the coldest people I've come across in a long time. They didn't have reactions to anything. But they seemed interested in learning about all our conversations," Cathy replied.

"Did you tell them?" Jack asked.

"Of course I did! I didn't have a choice. But also, I had no reason to doubt your story. Look, I know we were completely confused because of his empty housing file, but I had no reason to think that Stewart Jacobson was some major mystery man."

"What about that empty file? Did you tell them about it?" Jack asked.

"They already knew about that file. In fact, they asked me how I found it and if I knew where its contents were."

"I remember you told me that there was a note on the file jacket that said the contents were to be delivered to the director of security," Jack said.

"Yeah, I know. But Jeffords said he was unaware of it. Apparently, he didn't know where any of it went," Cathy said. "Jeffords has only been the director of security for less than two years. The director before him had a massive heart attack and died the year before. I never met him. But anyway, this group was really concerned about the location of that file's contents."

"What happened then?" Jack asked.

"The conversation turned back to you," Cathy replied.

"What did they want to know?" Jack asked.

"They asked me how well I know you, what impressions do I have about you, did you tell me anything about your personal life, who your parents are, who your friends are, stuff like that."

"Well, what did you tell them?" Jack's voice was rising to a level of agitation.

"Don't freak out, it seemed clear to me these people have no interest in you except that you are on the trail of Stewart Jacobson. But I told them I was very uncomfortable discussing you. It felt like some kind of betrayal. Honestly. I almost can't believe I felt that way, either. I mean, I really didn't know you or anything about you. But the way they were asking me all of the questions about you started making me feel like it was an investigation of you. I reiterated that I was only trying to help you find him for your mom's party, nothing more. I think when they saw that I had some sympathy for you, they backed off. They said they understood that you were just a kid who by sheer coincidence was trying to find someone they needed more information about to help with the sale of the dorm. I can't say that I believe it all, but at least they reassured me that you were not involved. To them, you're an innocent bystander."

Exasperated, Jack shook his head. "I don't know, Cathy. This situation gets stranger by the day. Who the hell is this guy?"

"I asked them if they have any information about Stewart's social security number — why our records have a number for him that keeps coming up as nonexistent," Cathy said.

"And…?" Jack implored.

"This was the part of the conversation that upset me. The woman,

96

Hovering or Clovering or something like that — she did most of the talking. She said she didn't know anything about the social security number. Then, right after, when she thought I was looking at Jeffords, she shot a glance over to one of her colleagues. I read it to mean she thought I bought her explanation. Not that it matters much, because there's no way they would tell me about the social security number even if they did know."

"Then what?" asked Jack.

"They asked if I thought I would speak to you again. I said I didn't know, but I doubted it. Then I remembered you said you'd call if you found anything out about Jacobson. There was one other thing they asked that aroused my suspicion. They asked how committed you seemed to finding him. I said I really didn't know. The party for your mom was over, and I would guess that your interest in Jacobson was also over. They just looked at one another with this knowing look that seemed like code. Then they thanked me, and Jeffords asked them if I could leave. The woman said they had nothing further for me. But before I left, she said that it was very important that I don't tell anyone about this meeting. If I did, it would hurt their progress on the investigation and slow down the sale of the dorm. I assured them that I would speak to no one. Then we shook hands and I left."

"So, what made you decide to tell me about this?" Jack asked.

"Honestly? I know this sounds irresponsible, but there was something very sincere about your voice, even if the story you told me wasn't true. It was easy enough for me to verify that you were who you said you were. I contacted New Jersey Central College, and since I was contacting them as a representative of NEIT's administration, they confirmed your student status and address for me. Which, by the way, they're not supposed to do without your permission. You may want to pass that along to them some day. I debated whether to tell you about my meeting all weekend. Then I decided that if you were in any danger, I could never forgive myself if I contributed to it."

"I don't know what to say. I guess I should say thank you. But it seems so weak. For all of it... driving to meet me, trusting me. I hope you're not putting yourself at risk or anything. But really, I am so grateful," Jack said.

"Let's hope this investigation doesn't amount to anything," Cathy said with a reassuring tone.

"Do you have any idea what could be going on?" Jack asked.

"None. I spent the past few days agonizing over possibilities. Stewart Jacobson being your father was not one of them, I will say. I thought of all sorts of things. Most sound silly now. I kept coming back to the theory that Stewart Jacobson was some long-lost uncle who embezzled millions of dollars and you or your family were being kicked out of his will. I also thought he might be a business partner of your mom or dad, and he screwed them somehow and they were using you to try to help find him."

Jack laughed. "Your theories are less far-fetched than what's really going on."

"Yeah," replied Cathy. "Real life always seems to turn out to be more amazing than what imaginations come up with."

"What do you think I should do?" Jack asked.

"No question about it — tell your mother," Cathy replied.

"Can I tell her about our meeting?" Jack asked.

"I don't know. I assured these people I wouldn't tell anyone about what happened. Let me think about it," Cathy said.

"Do you think they've tapped into my email?" Jack asked.

"I thought about that right after I sent you the email. I don't know. Jack, I don't know anything about these people. But someone apparently has a great interest in your father, if he is your father. Sending three people to do an investigation is pretty intense. I wouldn't be shocked if phones and email accounts are being tapped."

"Maybe my mom is better off not knowing about this, then," Jack said. "I don't know what we stumbled across, but I don't want her to get into trouble."

"Of course, do whatever you think is best. But I really feel like you have to tell her. We don't have any idea what these people might want from you. Who knows what they're looking for? Maybe you're a threat to them. I don't know, to me it's insane to think you shouldn't tell her," Cathy implored.

"Fine. Fine." Jack's tone suggested capitulation. "But how can I tell her about the search for my father without telling her about what happened with you?"

"I know. Let me give it a few days to see if Jeffords has anything to say to me about what happened. If he doesn't approach me within a week or so, I'll follow up with him."

"What will you say?" Jack asked.

"I don't know exactly. I think I'll probably find some excuse to call him and ask him if there's anything else I should know about Jacobson or the meeting with the three people. Jeffords is tight-lipped. I doubt he'll tell me anything, and that's assuming that he actually knows anything. But I'd at least like to give him the opportunity. This case is completely out of his hands. He didn't control the meeting. In fact, he was in the same position I was in, just answering questions. And you could see that he was nervous too, sitting there with those people. I have a feeling that we haven't heard the last of them. That's another reason I'd like to give it a few days."

"Okay. But I'm going to hold off telling my mom until I hear from you. I don't want to tell her part of the story, then come back and hit her with something crazy like this," Jack said.

"All right. Now, let's make a plan for how we can be in touch with one another," Cathy said.

"How about if I call you in a week? Do you still have the number of that public phone at the school you called on Monday?"

"Yes," Cathy replied.

"My last final exam is next Thursday. It ends late in the afternoon, around four. How about if you call me at that number on Friday morning? I have to go into school that day anyway. I agreed to help with a computer upgrade."

"That's fine. Is ten okay?" Cathy asked.

"Perfect. Hey, Cathy, it's dawning on me. I don't know anything about you. Like what's your last name?"

"Morgan." She laughed.

"What's so funny?" Jack asked.

"I just changed my name. Morgan was my middle name. My last name was Cryzanski. Rolls off the tongue, huh? So, I started to use my middle name as my last name, and it just became legally changed three weeks ago."

"Well, congratulations on that. What about your job at the college? You work there full time?"

"No. Well, yes. I'm a student at NEIT. But I'm on a work-study program. I work twenty hours a week and my tuition is paid in full. But at the rate I'm going, it will take me six years to finish."

"How's the school? You like it?" Jack asked.

"For the most part. The program can be pretty tough. And the standards are high, and so is the workload. But I've always had an interest in studying alternative sources of energy, and one of the school's engineering programs has a special minor in that area. But I have to say, between my courses and work, I have little time left for anything else."

Jack had taken an immediate liking to Cathy. He felt comfortable talking to her, opening up to her. Maybe it was just the drama of the circumstances that swept them along. Neither had to strain to create conversation to counter an awkward silent pause. No, Jack sensed, it was more. Jack did not easily open up to others. But there was something about Cathy that made disclosing effortless.

"Really, Cathy, thank you so much for everything. I can't tell you how much it means to me."

"Hey, I'm glad I got to meet you, too. I'd better get going. I have to be back this afternoon."

"Me too. I'll talk to you next Friday," Jack said.

Cathy stood and faced Jack, coming to terms with the solemn nature of it all. "Jack. Good luck with finding your father. I hope when he turns up, he's a good guy."

"I just hope he turns up."

ELEVEN

"You brought me here to meet my father?" Jack's impulse was to shriek, but his voice was breathless from disbelief.

"Yes," his abductor replied, her look continuing to soften, though her methodical demeanor was unrelenting. "I'm sorry it had to be done this way. Your father will explain it to you."

Jack stared at her, frozen by the uncertainty of whether to be frightened to death or exceedingly appreciative. "Is he here? Will he be coming soon?" he asked.

"He will be with you momentarily. I have to leave you now. Please just wait here." As the woman reached for the doorknob, she turned back to Jack. "I recognize that this has been traumatic for you. I believe it will get easier from now on." Then, in her crisp manner, she turned toward the door and departed the room, the distinctive click of the door latch abruptly punctuating her departure.

Jack understood that he had tripped across something so sensitive that it defied his imagination. Is it possible, he wondered, that his mother was aware of something sinister about Stewart, something so callously inhuman that she was forced to expunge his existence from their lives? Instead of knowing nothing about him, perhaps she knew everything.

The juxtaposition of morbid dread and titanic anticipation was overpowering. This was a moment he had sought for a year; well, maybe not this way, but still sought, and sought with a fevered determination. But now that it was at hand, he was cringing with apprehension — maybe there are some things in the world best left unknown, he thought. Would he undo it all rather than discover a heritage blotted with depravity? There was no turning back, and he sensed he wouldn't even if that choice magically materialized.

A mounting frenzy gripped Jack, and he feared an inability to regain the sensibilities necessary to navigate his way through this moment. Then, with a shock, it occurred to him that he should consider where he should be positioned in the room when his father entered. He was grateful for this thought, for it obscured the larger, more tormenting aspects of the predicament.

Jack placed his fingers on the table. They felt stiff and cold. He lifted himself from the chair and delicately eased it in toward the table. He slowly walked to the opposite side of the table and leaned forward, his hands grasping the top of the chair. The droplets of water cascading down the opaque sides of the pitcher were the only disturbance to the conspicuous quietude of the room. If the door opened, should he stand there and wait for his father to approach him, or should he move to meet him?

He walked toward the door to test how he would feel in that location. His step exuded great caution. Should he stand near the entrance to the room? This way, he reasoned, he and his father could shake hands immediately and avoid a momentary awkwardness of calculating which greeting ritual would fit the bill. No, standing near the door had a clumsy feel. It would look planned, rehearsed, like he had been caught reading his medical chart left by a nurse before the doctor entered the examination room. And, by standing near the door, Jack felt he would be deprived of a crucial interval between seeing his father and having to react to him. Back over to his original chair. He pulled it away from the table and sat down.

Coherence eluding him, Jack's mind zig-zagged from one thought to another. How did he get to this place, to this moment? He struggled to fix his thoughts on some of his activities over the past year to get some perspective. Any perspective. But the events of the year were melding together into a feral murkiness. He tried to ascertain how he got onto the radar screen that led him to this place. He was unable to reconstruct the chronology of the past year, unable to isolate each of his undertakings to assess which could have contributed to his detection. Such a determination might produce some insight into why his father was so mysterious a figure, he thought. All those websites catering to people with lost loved ones. Not long ago, they were allies in his quest. Now Jack felt peculiarly detached from them, even angry at them. Did one betray him? Could one have been part of a sting operation, a lure to nail careless exploiters of others' despair over loss? Did one stand out now as suspicious? Jack couldn't focus — they all became jumbled in a confusing brew of dotcoms.

Maybe it was the letters to the banks, he thought. Couldn't be, he concluded — that all happened too recently. Did Cathy know more than she let on? Was she in on this grand conspiracy? No, that was absurd. Now Jack knew he was succumbing to baseless paranoia.

Jack remembered he was scheduled to speak to Cathy tomorrow. She was the only person who knew about his situation. Jack had never had a strong penchant for confiding in friends. Disclosing anything personal never felt comfortable. Or necessary. But now he was grateful for Cathy. He needed someone now. Desperately.

Jack's thoughts scurried toward his mother. Until now, having a parent had a stable meaning for him. Any unease or conflict in the relationship was simple — a difference of opinion or some natural adolescent rebelliousness when she tried to steer him toward her version of good. Her intent for him was unconditionally virtuous. Nothing blurred that motive, at least nothing that had the strength or endurance to replace or diminish it.

Jack's assumptions about family and parents and the bonds that link them suddenly felt fractured and tenuous. What explanation could Stewart possibly offer to restore even a semblance of honor to parentage? How can someone elect to stay away from a child? Yes, Jack encountered hundreds of accounts on websites of parents who willingly chose a life path away from their children. And as he listened to the parents' revelations of their needs, he became more accepting that some simply could not bear to embrace a life with their children. At first, that seemed alien to him and he couldn't help but view such a choice as morally wrong. However, as he became acquainted with the backgrounds of some of the parents, especially those whose lives were wracked with some variation of agony — whether psychological, life circumstance, financial — he felt disinclined to be judgmental. But at that very moment, the experience of his own upbringing led him to feel that leaving a child was a disavowal of some innate human drive, a turning away from a most fundamental part of nature's order. And to reclaim a connection by subjecting a child to the nightmare Jack just experienced — well, this was not merely unconscionable in a basic civic sense, but, Jack thought, a sign of a corrupt soul.

And how could Stewart justify abandoning his mother? Who would do that? Sure, she had her faults. But in Jack's eyes his mother was a woman of exceptional character, bordering at this very moment on saintliness. It seemed unimaginable to Jack that a man could arrive at a decision to leave her. Had they been married? (Oddly, this thought had yet to cross his mind until this moment.) Had they had contact over the years? How did they meet?

A rush of panic startled Jack. What if this was a trap? What if there was no father coming to see him? What if——

There was a knock on the door. Jack reeled toward the door, his body pulsing, the hair on his arms bristling with an electric tingle. His breathing was heavy and deep, almost labored, and felt both rushed and slowed from anxiety.

"Yes, hello," Jack tentatively said, his eyes widened and unflinching.

There was no response. The door opened, and a male figure stood in the doorway. For a second, a second that had shadings of an eternity, the two men remained frozen, shell-shocked by the extraordinary undeniability of their genetic link. There was immediate mutual recognition, albeit silent, that Jack was a younger, but almost identical, version of the older man.

"Hello, Jack. I'm Stewart," said the man, as he slowly entered the room and walked toward Jack. They continued to take one another in as Stewart neared Jack. Jack was overcome with the moment. Their eye color, a deep blue, was the same, and though Stewart's face and build were fuller, they possessed the same angular stature.

Stewart approached Jack and extended his hand. Jack reached out, and as they grasped hands, Stewart reached his left hand and placed it on Jack's shoulder. "I am so, so happy to meet you," Stewart said slowly.

"I don't know what to say," Jack said, his voice teeming with astonishment.

They released their clasp and stood staring at one another.

"Are you my father?" Jack asked, more by impulse than calculation, his voice an almost childlike murmur.

"I—" Stewart felt his voice quiver. He glanced away, as if to

104

summon the necessary composure, and continued, "I believe I am your father, Jack."

Stewart extended his arm, and again placed it on Jack's shoulder, a combination of affection and a verification that Jack indeed existed.

"I heard you've been looking for me," Stewart said. He was wearing a gray knit sweater and scrupulously ironed black pants. This man had a distinctly tailored appearance, including short-cropped light brown hair that reminded Jack of how his hair looked as a little boy in his photos from summer camp.

"Yeah. Yes. I have. For about a year now," Jack replied, mesmerized by the fact that he was standing in the presence of his father.

"Jack, I hope you will forgive me if I seem... overcome. I didn't know of your existence until three days ago," Stewart said.

"What? You mean you didn't know you had a child?" Jack asked, shocked, confused and skeptical. In the entire time of Jack's search, the thought never occurred to him that Stewart Jacobson was unaware that he existed. There was, for Jack, an almost supernatural quality to this fact: he had no mental or emotional folder into which this revelation could be filed.

"No. And when I did find out, I was overseas. I received an urgent message that you — that a child I had — was looking for me. Arrangements were immediately made for me to come see you."

"I, I don't get it. How could you not know you had a child?" Jack asked, his posture rigid and tense.

Stewart pulled out one of the bridge chairs and moved it next to Jack. Jack turned his chair so the two were facing one another. "I'm still trying to figure that out. How is your mother?" Stewart asked.

"She's great," Jack blurted out. Then, more slowly, he repeated, "Yeah, she's great."

"Is Jackson your real name?" Stewart asked.

"How did you know?"

Stewart let out a small laugh. "Linda, uh, your mother told me that she loved the mountains in Wyoming. She said that if you wake up in Jackson Hole you get the most extraordinary view of the mountains. She said it was a majestic sight, a landscape only God could create. She told me if she ever had a son, she would name him Jackson in honor of that awesome vista."

"She told me about that, too. We're planning to go there together, probably when I finish college," Jack said. Then he returned to the puzzle of the moment. "Nothing is making sense to me. How come you didn't know about me?"

"It's my understanding that your mom doesn't know that you've been searching for me. Is that right?"

"Yes. She told me that she got pregnant by an anonymous donor."

"Is that what you've thought all these years?" Stewart asked.

"Yes."

"Does she know you found out about me?"

"No. I think she still thinks I believe the donor story."

"How did you learn that wasn't the truth?" Stewart asked.

Jack explained his discovery of the birth certificate in a box in a storage area in the house. Then he raised the subject so central to the phenomenon of his father's enigma. "But honestly, aside from finding the birth certificate, everything about you has been a mystery. I—"

Stewart cut him off. "I know. I'm sorry that you've had to deal with such craziness. I'll get to that as best as I can. But can I ask why you didn't tell your mother that you discovered the truth?"

"I thought about telling her every single day for the past year," Jack sighed. "And I came close to saying something plenty of times. But I don't know, I was afraid that you might have walked out on us when I was a baby or something and my mom wouldn't want to have anything to do with you. That would be the end of looking for you, and I wasn't ready for that. And I wouldn't want her to be hurt, either."

Stewart was taking it all in. Every now and then he would simply stare at this young man, struck with the astounding sensation that this was his son. He watched how Jack formed words, a slight upturn of the mouth between phrases in a sentence. He noticed Jack's brow would furrow, not from confusion, but as if to fortify his ability to suck in and process information. He listened to Jack's speech and heard a measured cadence. He saw in Jack's eyes an intellectual curiosity. And as Stewart listened to Jack's story, he heard Jack's single-minded determination to accomplish a goal along with a compassion for a loved one. Stewart felt he was gazing into the mirror of his own youth.

Jack asked, "How is it that you never knew you had a child? I just don't get it."

"Well, Jack, do you know that your mother worked in a hospital before she entered her senior year in college?"

Jack nodded.

Then Stewart told him the story of how he and Linda met and very quickly established a connection. "But it didn't start off all that great. I thought your mother would never want to see me after I insulted her that first day. I should have known then that she had the right stuff to run her own company. She was so smart. She cared about the people she came in contact with. And she had the guts to do the right thing even when it was easier not to."

"Then why didn't you stay together?"

"Good question. We were both so focused on our own lives, and we were being pulled in different directions. I guess it was really my life that was the problem. I was going headstrong starting out on my career. I had recently taken a job with an oil company that required me to go all over the world. Your mom and I had contact after I left, for maybe two or three months. But you know how distance and preoccupation with other matters have a way of making it impossible to carry on a relationship. And I suppose your mother decided that having me in her life, and then with you, would complicate things. I moved along in my career and I never heard from her again." Stewart looked down, almost sullen. "And here you are now. A man. Only a few years younger than I was when your mother and I met. All these years you existed, and I had no idea."

Jack began to ask, "How did you—"

A knock at the door cut him off. Stewart rose from his chair, walked over to the door and opened it. Jack could see that a man was on the other side. Although Jack did not have a clear view of him, he did not recognize him as one of the men who brought him there. Jack heard the man tell Stewart they would have to leave in ten minutes. Then Jack heard Stewart say, "Okay, I'll do my best to be ready." Stewart closed the door and returned to his chair.

"Jack, I'm so sorry, I'll have to leave you soon. But before I go, I need to talk to you about my circumstances. I know that my life and my identity are, as you put it, a mystery," Stewart began.

Jack stared at Stewart, transfixed.

Stewart continued, "When I was told that I have a son, I was so overwhelmed. Stupefied. I still am. In my wildest imagination I could never have invented a moment like this, that I would ever be face-to-face with a child. My child. When I learned about you, and learned that we could meet each other, I also understood that there are aspects of my life that I wouldn't be able to share with you. I feel so sad about that, especially since you have been through such an ordeal with this for so long now."

Jack cut in, "Are you married? Do you have another family?"

"No," Stewart replied. "No, no, no. I was engaged to someone once. I'll tell you about her sometime."

That last phrase reverberated through Jack. It was a signal to him that Stewart intended for there to be a relationship between them, or at least further contact.

Stewart continued, "I'm sorry that my time is so limited today. But let me explain my story to you as best I can for the moment. After college, I—"

Jack interrupted, "Did you go the New England Institute of Technology?"

"Yes. I know you knew that already."

"It was the only bit of information I had about you from my birth record."

"I know. And shortly, we're going to need all the information you have gathered about me, and especially who you have been in touch with for information. But let me explain the story first. After college, I got a job with a big oil company, conducting research on new techniques for locating and drilling for oil. Like I said before, I did a lot of traveling and got to meet many people all over the world. At some point, our company increased the amount of work we were doing with the government. There were lots of good things we could do together. Like working on research programs on how to drill more deeply for oil and how to preserve the environment at the same time. For the past few years, I have been working on a very different kind of project that requires absolute and total secrecy. I was worried that by meeting me, you could be exposed to some risk. But my associates assured me that you would remain safe. But they also told me that any continuation of your search for me could very well put both of us at risk."

"Are you a spy?" Jack asked.

"No. No, I'm not a spy. But I'm not able to tell you anything now about my work. But there are a couple of things that are very important for me to tell you. First, in order for me to carry out my assignment, a new identity has been created for me. All of the records about Stewart Jacobson have been destroyed. I have a new name, social security number, address, the whole nine yards."

"What's your new name?" Jack asked, his voice filled with eagerness.

"Jack, I am so sorry I can't share that with you. Please understand that if I did it could put you in danger."

"I guess so," Jack replied, not fully understanding.

Sensing Jack's confusion, Stewart said, "I know it's cliché and probably pretty frustrating, but this is one of those times when what you don't know can't hurt you. And the second thing is that you must not tell anyone about me. Not that we met, not even that you know I exist. It needs to be as though your mother's story about the anonymous donor is true." Stewart looked directly into Jack's eyes to gauge his sensitivity to the importance of this point. "Jack, since your mom doesn't know that you were looking for me, I have to ask that you continue to keep this a secret from her. At least for now."

Again, Jack nodded.

"I'm sorry, I know that this is very difficult, but I need to understand that you will be absolutely faithful to this request. A lot is at stake, and our security can be seriously compromised if my prior identity becomes known. Or if people know you were looking for me. It's in both of our best interests, okay?"

"Yeah, I promise," Jack assured him.

"You know, Jack," Stewart said, a slight smile forming on his mouth, "I don't really know you very well, but I know your father, and he's a pretty trustworthy guy."

"I hope so," said Jack, a smile coming to his face as well. His mind raced back to the circumstances of getting there. "Why was I kidnapped to be brought here? I was scared to death."

"Yes, about that. I'm so sorry. I wasn't aware until you arrived here that there was some force used beyond what had been discussed. My colleagues said that they had tried to make contact with you on the road but that you resisted."

"Well, yeah. I didn't think I should just pull over for a random car somewhere."

Stewart smiled at this. "Understandable. Just like I hope that you will understand how sorry I am — how sorry we all are, for that matter — that you were brought here that way."

"Where do we go from here?" Jack asked. "Will I see you again?"

"I certainly hope so. But I'm not able to say exactly when or how. I'll be in touch with you somehow. If not directly, I'll arrange for a communication to be delivered to you."

There was a knock at the door. Again, Stewart went to the door and opened it. Whispers were exchanged between Stewart and the same man who appeared earlier. It was inaudible to Jack, except Stewart's final remark as the door was closing, "I'll be there in a minute." Then he returned to his chair.

"Jack, I have to leave now. I'll be going overseas for a while."

"When will I hear from you?"

"As soon as I'm able. I need to ask you one more thing. Donna Hoverdale is the woman who brought you here. I know you had a rough time with her, but I promise she's a good person, just sometimes over-committed to her work. She is going to need to know all of the steps that you took to try to find me. Obviously, we need to make sure there are no loose ends that could get either of us in trouble."

Jack nodded.

"I have to get going. There's a plane waiting."

"When did you get back in this country?" Jack asked.

"About two hours ago. I'm sorry I have to leave again," Stewart responded.

"You came here from another country for just a few hours just to meet me?" Jack asked in disbelief.

"Is that too much of an effort to make when you discover you have a son?" Stewart said, creating the first feeling in Jack's life of endearment for him from his father.

Stewart rose from his chair, and then Jack did the same. They shook hands, and as Jack's dropped to his side, Stewart leaned toward him, put his hands on his shoulders and drew him in for an embrace. Slowly, Jack put his arms around his father's back. It was awkward for both, but supremely fulfilling, almost magical.

Stewart walked toward the door and opened it. He turned back toward Jack and said, "I am so, so happy to know you." Jack saw that Stewart's eyes were moist.

"Yeah, me too," Jack managed to say, despite the lump in his throat. As Stewart turned to leave, Jack called to him, "Hey, I don't know what to call you."

Stewart turned to Jack and smiled, his eyes reddened, and said, "We'll work on that. Please take care of yourself. And your mother." And with that, he turned and left.

"Okay, thanks. Donna, I don't think I remember it all."

"Perhaps we can approach this a bit differently to save time," she responded. Then she reached into the briefcase and withdrew a folder. Inside was a stack of about twenty pages that she placed on the table in front of Jack. "This is a list of all the websites you have had contact with and other electronic correspondence that you've had. Let's review the list and then you can tell me the nature of your contact with each."

The sight of the list was bewildering. For the past year, Jack had thought he was operating in absolute secrecy — but his every move on the Internet had been documented over the past couple of weeks. He was aware that such surreptitious activity was conducted — wiretaps, phone taps, electronic surveillance — but he had never imagined there would be circumstances under which he would be subjected to it.

Jack skimmed the first several pages, which contained dozens of websites devoted to helping people find people. Listed beside the name of the website was some information about nature of Jack's communication with it. About eight or ten websites had accompanying information like 'Notes posted regarding search for father. No reply'. Next to docufind.com was a transcript of Jack's exchange with Stephen Jacobson.

Jack was awed by the comprehensiveness of the list. Nothing was private, nothing was sacred. He shuddered at the thought that he could never again feel confident that his life was shielded from furtive investigation. "I can't believe you have all this information about me. It's like a violation of my privacy."

"I know. I can understand that seeing all this is probably shocking," Donna said. "And yes, your privacy has been compromised. There's no question about that. But as I've said, you must understand that we have access to your activities only when a court deems it necessary for the security of our nation. A court must reach a conclusion that your right to privacy is superseded by the importance of protecting the public welfare. In your case, of course, you did nothing wrong."

"You mean you had to get court approval to get all this information on me?" Jack asked.

"Yes."

"But how in the world did you get all this information? You couldn't have known I was doing this from the very beginning?" Jack asked.

"You're absolutely right. But once we became aware of your activity, we recreated many of the steps we thought you might have taken. We obtained logs from several of the sites, some of which, by the way, are available to anyone. Most good investigating is done by retracing someone's steps, which takes an enormous amount of time and incredible attention to detail. A good deal of it tends to be quite boring work, actually. Now, can we go through the list?" Donna asked.

For the next two hours, Jack and Donna went through each item on the list. Of the twenty or so pages, the first twelve included the websites Jack had contacted. Jack could not recall visiting or having correspondence with any websites not on the list.

The last few pages included contacts with the three banks in the Boston area. Next to the entry for People's Bank of New England was a note indicating that the FBI was contacted by F. Carrera, Corporate Security Director. In turn, the FBI forwarded documentation to an entry that was blackened out. Jack surmised the concealed entity was the governmental agency his father and the others worked for.

There was a heading beginning on the sixteenth page called "Credit Analyses." Appearing on the list was the communication with Credit Plus and entries for the New England Institute of Technology.

As the discussion turned to the NEIT, Donna said, "We have compiled a record of your communications with this university in Boston. Your father briefed me on how you discovered that he attended the school. I must say I admire your investigative skills. We have advised the security department and Cathy Cryzanski in administration about the situation and informed them that all inquiries regarding Stewart Jacobson must cease immediately."

Cryzanski. Jack laughed to himself. So, he thought, this group is not as up to date as they think they are.

Donna continued, "I'm going to need you to cease all communication with people from that institution about this matter."
Then, "Jack, I know you received an email from Cathy two weeks ago. Have you had any additional contact with her?"

Jack was in a bind. "She just wanted to tell me that she had no further information about my father."

"But why would she contact you about something that had already been resolved?" Donna asked.

"I don't know. We had been in touch a few times. I originally told her I was trying to find an old college friend of my mother for a surprise party."

"Yes. I know. She told me. I'm concerned that she contacted you just a couple of days after we met with her. It would make no sense for her to call you except to tell you about our meeting," Donna said.

Jack agonized over whether to tell Donna the truth about his recent meeting with Cathy. But if he did, he feared he would get her into trouble. He took a chance and stuck with his lie. "From time to time she would call me to find out if I had solved the puzzle of who Stewart Jacobson is. That's all."

"Are you telling me the truth, Jack?" Donna asked.

"Yes."

Donna looked at Jack, assessing his credibility on this point. Maybe, Donna thought, Cathy's initial impulse was to inform Jack about the visit, but then she thought better about it after sending him the email.

"Okay, I'm trusting you here. And I hope I've made myself clear that this all has a direct link to the safety of your father. I must ask that you have no further communication with Cathy. She isn't aware that your father is doing important work for the government. And for all the obvious reasons, we must keep it that way. If she calls you again, simply tell her that you have no further information about Stewart Jacobson, that you no longer have a reason to pursue it," Donna insisted.

As the night progressed, Donna and Jack became increasingly impressed with one another, he for her meticulousness and dedication, she for his determination and unwillingness to be deterred, qualities that reminded her of his father.

"It's pretty incredible, Jack. You've been looking for your father for a year. For an entire year. And despite the fact you never had any real confirmation that he existed, you kept up your search. I have to say, I'm in awe that you never gave up. Do you mind if I ask why?"

Jack shrugged. "I don't know. If I knew in the beginning that after a year I still wouldn't even know if he existed, I probably would have quit. Or I might have told my mother. But now, looking back, it was like one day at a time. I guess I never thought about the search as a whole. It was more what I would do on each individual day."

"But surely you must have stepped back from time to time and realized that you weren't making much headway," Donna observed.

"It's tough to explain, and this may sound weird, but some days, part of me didn't even want to find him. There was one day that made me realize I probably didn't want to reach a final answer, whatever it might have been. I was on that Docufind site and saw a letter I thought could have been written by my father, you know the letter from Stephen Jacobson. In retrospect, it was absurd for me to think that my father would have to go through that trouble to find me. He knew who my mother was, where she lived, probably where she worked. Anyway, I guess I created this little fantasy that my father was interested in finding me. When I saw that other guy's notice, posted on Docufind, I started to panic. I wasn't ready to have my life or my mom's turned upside-down. If my father was found, there would never be any way to go back, to pretend he didn't come back into our lives. But on the other hand, I didn't think I could live with myself without finding out who he is. I guess as long as I was doing the search, I could convince myself that I might find him someday, but also if I didn't make too much progress, I guess I couldn't really get hurt. And neither could my mom."

"Well, that's very self-aware of you. And it sounds like a delicate proposition," Donna granted.

"I guess it was, but I didn't think about it that way at the time. And you know what? It never crossed my mind that my dad might not know about me. In a whole year, I never once considered that. Isn't that crazy? Before I found the birth certificate, I could make him anyone I wanted him to be, so I kind of always thought my father was some perfect human being. After I found it, I figured he was just some immature jerk who walked out on us. I didn't want to find out if that was true or not."

"That makes sense," Donna said.

"But what happens now? When will I see him again?" Jack asked.

"That's impossible for me to say. I know that's probably not the answer you wanted from me, but it's the only one I can give you right now."

"How will I know what's going on? If he's okay?"

"Your father is arranging for communications to be sent to you periodically. But I can't say when or how."

"Will you be involved in that?" Jack asked.

"Probably. But the details will need to be worked out, and we haven't been able to do that yet."

"Well, where do we go from here?" Jack asked.

"For the moment I don't know. But I need to talk to you about the situation we face. This is a very unusual set of circumstances for us. As Stewart, your father, informed you, an entirely new identity has been constructed for him. When we do this — and I don't want you to think that we have armies of people out there with phony identities — that individual undertakes an exhaustive review of every person he or she knew, and the likelihood of that person having future contact. The relationship between your father and mother was discussed, but it occurred so long ago that any future effort by your mother to reach out to your father was close to zero percent. We didn't think it was necessary to factor her into our concerns, and therefore we never examined her background. Obviously, if we had, we would have discovered you, and it would have been a whole new ballgame for us. To have a grown child emerge from the woodwork has introduced a serious challenge of confidentiality for us. We need to rely on you being absolutely faithful to the secrecy of what we've discussed and what you now know. I would appreciate if you can give me some assurance to that effect."

"I promise. I won't tell anyone anything. I don't want to hurt my father or anything you guys are doing. I guess I don't know what else to say about that. Will I continue to be watched?" Jack asked.

"Yes. But it is as much for your protection as for the people involved in our assignment. Obviously, there are groups in the world who are at odds with the United States. We believe it is highly unlikely that your activities have come to their attention. But we cannot rule out the possibility either. Therefore, we'll need to maintain the surveillance, to monitor whether other parties have been alerted to the possibility that your father is not who they believe he is."

Donna occasionally employed a vernacular Jack found chilling. He viewed phrases like 'other parties' and 'maintain surveillance' as code for 'enemies' and 'spying'. It was Donna's way, he thought, of

118

demonstrating that she meant business. Ironically, Donna's intent was for her euphemisms to buffer the sting a young man like Jack might feel from the sudden indoctrination into a world of harsh international political realities.

"I think it's time we took you back to your car," Donna said. Jack checked his watch. It was eleven p.m. "I hate to tell you this," she continued, "But we're going to need to take you back the same way we got you here — blindfolded."

Jack had a knowing expression. "Why am I not surprised?"

THIRTEEN

New Jersey Central College had a quirky feel of inactivity. Finals were over and a first summer session was not to begin for another two weeks. Groundskeepers were tidying up the lawns and flower beds. A handful of students rushed about in frantic quests to beat dreaded deadlines. A few graduate students milled about the library, working on research projects. Here and there, an instructor could be seen toting a box of books.

Jack arrived at the college at nine forty-five a.m. and headed straight to the lower level of the Student Center. Out of breath from rushing, he plopped himself into the chair in the designated cubicle and waited for Cathy's call.

Precisely four minutes past ten, the phone rang. Jack jumped on it. "Hello," he answered in a forced hush.

"Hi, Jack. I have no real news. I haven't heard a thing from Jeffords and those people from the banking commission haven't—"

Jack cut her off. In a restrained outburst he said, "You cannot believe what I've been through. Can you meet me again?"

"Sure, I guess. Hey Jack, can you give me an idea of what happened?"

"Not over the phone," Jack said.

"But we're both on public phones," Cathy said, seeking to reassure him.

"I know. But it's too serious for that and I'm afraid to be on the phone too long," Jack said, his voice sharp and convincing.

"Okay, okay. Tell me when and where."

"How about the same place we met last time? Is Tuesday morning all right with your schedule?" Jack asked.

"No, but I'll make it all right. Same time as before, ten. Good for you?"

"Yeah, yeah, it's fine. Don't breathe a word to anyone. Not anyone.

120

Not even Peter. Promise me," Jack implored.

"I promise."

"And don't email or call me. Not under any circumstances. Even if there's an emergency. If you run into trouble and can't meet me, call the front desk at the hotel and tell them. I'll check with them if I don't see you." Then, as an afterthought, Jack said, "And don't use our real names. If you leave a message with the desk, use the name... I don't know, I'm not good at this... call yourself Emma and use Paul for me. And if you do have to call them, make sure you use a public phone."

Alarmed by the urgency in his voice and the obviousness that this matter had well surpassed in intrigue what she imagined, Cathy blurted, "Oh my god, Jack, are you all right?"

"Yeah, yeah, I'm fine. I'll see you on Tuesday," Jack said quickly, then hung up.

For the next three days Jack made a concerted effort to avoid his mother. She had constructed an artificial lifelong reality for him. He was at once uneasy at having pried his way into her secret and angry at having been subjected to it. He believed it would be impossible to engage her in a casual way while these feelings were so fresh. Fortunately, he was scheduled to work at the college on Saturday and Sunday on the computer upgrade project. The college chose the weekend in order to minimize the disruptions to students and faculty caused by a shutdown of the computers. Linda worked through the weekend as well, finalizing a summer schedule and ordering a full inventory of supplies for the next few months. Attending to these tasks now could produce a little more free time during July and August.

Dinner together was unavoidable on Monday night. There was an unusual degree of quiet during the meal, and conversation seemed strained and filled with effort.

"When do you start work at the library?" Linda asked.

"I'm not sure what I'm going to do. The college offered me a job for the summer. The computer upgrade is going to take about ten weeks. The money is a little better, but the job is so boring."

"If the difference in money is not that great, do what will be more interesting for you," Linda advised. "Also, and I don't mean for this to complicate your decision making, but I did want to talk to you about

121

working at the practice with me over the summer."

There was no way Jack could do this. If he was with his mother, he would be restricted from easily receiving or initiating communications about his father. This was not a time to take such a risk.

Jack's feelings vacillated between anger toward his mother and guilt about his betrayal. Anger was behind his response to her now: "Why do you want me to work at the practice? You need to keep an eye on me?"

"What?" Linda exclaimed. "Why in the world would you say a thing like that?" Before Jack could respond, Linda continued, "You know, Jack, you have been incredibly irritable lately. I feel like I've been walking on eggshells around you. Do you want to tell me what's going on?"

Jack knew he had been appearing contentious. But he was unaware that it had registered so noticeably with his mother. "No, I don't want to tell you what's going on. Do you always tell me everything? Are you always honest with me?" He almost couldn't help himself. The words were coming out despite his understanding of the danger.

"What do you mean by that?" Linda challenged, her brow furrowed. "Are you accusing me of something?"

Jack had to climb out of the hole. "I guess I'm still upset that you were thinking of selling the practice and didn't talk to me about it right away."

"Really? I'm sorry, but I refuse to continue to pay a price for that," Linda said, her voice uncharacteristically stern toward her son. "I wasn't trying to hide anything from you, and you know it. It's unfair of you to call that deception. I just didn't want to concern you prematurely in my thinking. And you know it. Is protecting a child a crime?"

That was it. That phrase triggered Jack's anger just when he needed to contain it. "What else have you kept from me in the name of protection?" he demanded.

Linda drew back and stared at him. He knows, she feared. But, how could he? Jack and Linda continued to stare at one another, each considering how to inch toward The Topic without creating the appearance of doing so. Linda spoke first, repeating her question, but this time with a softer tone. "Are you accusing me of something?"

"I didn't say that," Jack responded. He knew it was time to

backpedal, but he worried that the damage might have already been done.

"Then what did you mean?" Linda asked.

"I mean I'm not five years old anymore, Mom. You can't decide not to tell me things because you're worried how I might handle it. Like if you sell the practice, how is not telling me going to make me feel better? One day I'll go there, and I'll find out it belongs to someone else. That's supposed to be better for me?"

"Oh, really, is that what you think I would do?"

"I'm not blaming you for anything. But now it seems you're accusing me," Jack responded.

"Jack, it's just hard for me to believe that you're still carrying a grudge because I didn't tell you that I was *thinking* about selling the practice immediately when I began thinking about it. In fact, it's hard for me to believe that you would be upset about that to begin with, but to *still* be furious?"

"I guess it's not so much about selling the practice. But if you kept that from me, I wonder whether you keep other things from me as well."

"Like what?"

"That's the point. How would I know?" Jack said, staring at her with a coldness that he could barely conceal.

Now Linda blinked. She always knew she would tell Jack about his father, but not now, not as a result of a fight, not without preparing an explanation about why she waited all these years. This episode had confirmed for Linda that the older Jack got, the more her control would slip regarding when and how to tell him, and how influential she could be in helping to manage his reaction.

"Let's just drop it, Jack. We're only going around in circles. If I kept things from you it's only because I thought it would be in your best interest. Not that it was always the right thing to do, but it's what I thought was right at the time. I love you. My intention is never to hurt you. Why don't we talk about your summer plans another day instead?"

"Yeah, okay. Hey, I'm sorry I blew up at you." The words were there, but the tone was unconvincing. In fact, he wasn't sorry. He was hurt and angry. And the feeling wasn't diminishing.

"So, what's on your agenda tomorrow?" Linda asked, her tone forced.

Jack was caught off guard. "Oh, uh, I'll be at the college all day. And I have to start real early again. There's a lot to do to plan for the conversion."

"What time do you have to be there?"

"I have to get there real early, like six-thirty or so."

"All right. Make sure you get enough sleep."

Jack fell asleep at nine-thirty that night. His sleep had been uneasy the prior two nights and it didn't take long for him to settle into a deep, uninterrupted sleep. At midnight, Linda quietly entered Jack's room and confirmed that he was asleep. Then she was off on a mission to test her fear that Jack had discovered the truth about his father. Linda understood that such a discovery could have occurred in a very limited number of ways. He could have been told by someone. But the only people who were aware that Stewart was Jack's father were her parents, two friends Linda had known since childhood, and two people who worked at the hospital when Jack was born. Linda was more than certain that Jack had not been told by any of these people. As improbable as it seemed to Linda, the only real possibility was that Jack had discovered his birth certificate.

Linda entered the storage area and headed straight for the box containing the birth records. The box was in the same place it had been for years. She removed the boxes that sat atop it and noted that the sealing tape felt as though it was simply draped across the line where the two flaps met. She lifted the tape; it was stiff and cracked, as though whatever bonding capability it possessed had long since perished. She held it up to the light hoping for some evidence that could confirm tampering. Nothing about the tape suggested it had been stripped from the box, and she attributed its loss of adhesion to age.

Linda opened the box and carefully began to search through the contents. Although she hadn't looked in the box for several years, she knew she had placed the envelope containing Jack's birth record deliberately at the bottom of the box. There it was, the envelope marked 'Jack — Birth Certificate,' just as she had left it years ago, purposefully sandwiched between two larger envelopes. As she lifted the envelope, she noticed it wasn't sealed. Was it simply a matter of the adhesive decaying from the passage of time? Or had Jack opened this envelope and, upon seeing the contents, done his best to restore the envelope to its proper place to cover his tracks? Now Linda, too, would wonder about Jack harboring a secret concerning this same envelope.

FOURTEEN

Jack arrived early at the Hyatt, about thirty minutes before Cathy was scheduled to join him. Before moving to the lounge area, Jack inquired at the desk if there was a message from an Emma for Paul. Told that there was not, he was relieved and excited that he would be seeing Cathy soon.

At nine-fifty, Cathy entered the lobby and Jack bolted from his chair, walking briskly toward her. After a friendly embrace, Cathy, barely able to contain her anticipation, asked, "All right, tell me! What is going on?"

"Let's go sit down. You are not going to believe this."

Both were energized by the drama they shared, and they moved quickly to the same dimly lit corner of the lobby as last time. As they practically sank into the plump cushions on the couch, Jack looked at her with a broad grin. "You'll never guess who I met last Thursday."

"The three people who came to our college?" Cathy asked.

"Yeah. And guess who else."

"Don't tell me you met your father?" Cathy asked, bursting with eagerness.

Jack grabbed her hands. "Yes! Yes, I met him. It was the most incredible experience of my life. I want to tell you everything, but if they ever found out that I told you it could be really bad for me and maybe even worse for my father."

"I promise I won't tell a soul." Cathy's voice was almost breathless from excitement.

"They even brought you up and told me that I wasn't allowed to have contact with you, like ever again."

"Really? They told you they saw me?" Cathy asked.

"Yes. They knew you and I spoke, but not that we met. Anyway, I'll get to that later."

Jack described for Cathy all that occurred on the day he met his father. Cathy sat spellbound, feeling like she was watching — no, participating in — a noir film from an earlier era, replete with espionage and shadow. "And you still don't know what type of work he does?" she asked.

"No. And they have absolutely no intention of telling me," Jack said, his enthusiasm seeming not to be shaken by this realization.

"What was it like to see him?"

"There was something so surreal about it all. I can't stop thinking about the fact that this man, this man sitting across a table from me, is equal to my mother, at least as far as being responsible for creating me. I mean, I really saw myself in him. Almost as much as I see of myself in my mom. In a strange way, even more, but that's probably because I was on high alert for it. But my mother is the closest person in the world to me. And this man, who has the same relationship to me as she does, is a complete stranger."

"Yeah, but he doesn't have the same relationship *with* you that you have with your mom. Don't you feel like that sort of discounts the fact that your mom raised you and you two have a whole shared life together?" Cathy said.

"Yes, yes, of course I understand that. I'm just saying that I'm the genetic product of these two people. And they had an equal involvement in creating a human being and I'm that person. I never had a clear image of a father — I mean a father of mine — having that role. The image was always fuzzy. It would float around in my mind. All those years when kids talked about their fathers, I just stood on the sidelines. I found myself moving away, waiting for the topic to change. Most of the time praying for the topic to change. There were times I felt jealous. I would have liked to have a father do things with me. But after a while I became, I don't know, numb to it, I guess. Don't get me wrong. I wasn't sad. I mean it wasn't like I had a father who I grew up with and then he died. Or left us. Amazingly, it's like the opposite. It's like he never existed all along and the next day he appears. Out of thin air. Oh! And guess what? He never knew about me either. I mean, he actually just found out that he had a child a few days before we met. I wonder how his life would have been different if he did. I know he's had some sort of very important and demanding career. But we'll never know how that would stack up against being a father. And I'll never know what having a father as a child would have been like. We're both deprived in that way. I mean, it's not like I'm blaming my mother. I'm sure her decision was based on what she thought was best for me. Well, maybe I am blaming my mother. Shit, I'm rambling, I'm sorry. But it's hard for me to accept that she would be able to justify herself. But as I was looking at this man, I kept wondering what it would have been like to have him in my life from the beginning. I watched how he did things, how he said certain words, how he smiled. It was all just like me. When he's thinking about what to say, he has this habit of glancing toward the floor for a second and squinting slightly as he looks up."

"You do the same thing," Cathy observed, smiling.

"Yeah! I never realized it till I watched him do it. And all I wanted to ask him the whole time we were together was would he have been there for me if he knew I existed."

"Well, why didn't you ask him?" Cathy asked, her tone suggesting this was the blatantly obvious thing to do.

"I guess I was afraid to. Here's this man who's got some incredibly important job having to do with national security and I'm supposed to ask him if he would have devoted himself to some child he just discovered he had. It would have made me feel like an infant. Or an idiot. Probably both."

"I don't know about that. But yeah, maybe it wasn't the right time to put him on the spot that way. After all, he just found out about you. But at some point, you should ask him."

"Maybe. We'll see. He's not in any position to think that one through anyway. He's got way too much stuff going on."

"Jack, you're upset with your mother because she never gave you the benefit of the doubt because she wanted to protect you. At some point you should give your father the same benefit of the doubt. When will you see him again?"

"I have no idea. The plan is that he'll arrange to contact me, probably through someone else."

"Hovering?"

Jack smiled. "It's Hoverdale, actually. Donna. Yeah. I hope so. She's a good person. Well, maybe not if you get on her bad side."

"Do you think your father is in danger?"

"I have no idea. But the government went to great lengths to create a whole new life for him. He must be at some kind of risk all the time. They were all careful not to tell me anything that would reveal even which agency of the government they work for. The only thing I know is that he spends a lot of time overseas. And unless he was lying, he got back here just a few hours before we met, and he was going back right away."

"And you have no idea what his new name is?" Cathy asked.

"No. He told me that what I don't know can't come back to hurt me."

"What about your mom? You're not going to tell her about this, are you?"

"No, definitely not. It was made very clear several times I'm not supposed to tell anyone," Jack replied.

"Then why did you tell me?" Cathy asked.

Jack blushed. The question was fired at him quickly and bluntly. He never had a doubt that he would tell Cathy, but he also hadn't anticipated that he'd be put on the spot with that question in so direct a manner.

"I don't know. I probably shouldn't have told you. But you took a big chance contacting me after you met Donna and those guys. And you came all this way to speak to me about it last time."

"And you needed to tell someone, didn't you?" Cathy asked.

Jack turned his head downward, then glanced up with a faint squint. "No, not really. I thought about that before you called me last Friday. I wanted to be sure I wasn't giving in to that type of temptation. After all, my father's life — hey, maybe even mine or my mom's — is at stake. I know I could keep this to myself. But you've been there for me since the beginning of this whole episode. I feel like I can trust you."

"I won't make you sorry you told me," Cathy said, reinforcing the message by placing her hand gently on Jack's forearm.

Cathy's phone rang. She looked at the caller ID. "It's Peter. He'll ask where I am."

She answered the phone. "Hi, Peter." She listened, then, after a moment, said, "Tell Mr. Jeffords I can't make it in an hour. I'm at least two, two and a half hours away... yeah, that's fine, I can see him later in the day... see you later."

Cathy turned to Jack. "Jeffords wants to see me about the Stewart

129

Jacobson housing file. Apparently, your friends are concerned that the contents of the file can't be located."

"This is getting crazy. Unless they told you the truth, what reason could they have for making such a big deal out of a file from twenty years ago? And a student housing file, no less," Jack observed.

"I don't know," Cathy said. "But based on your story, I'll bet Jeffords hasn't been told any more than I was. He probably thinks the sale of the dorm may not go through unless all the records are accounted for."

"Yeah, probably. But since they can't find the information in the security office, you'd think the last security director would've kept the records in his house, you know, because the situation was so sensitive," Jack suggested.

"That would make sense," Cathy said. "But he died... Hey, Jack, I wouldn't worry about it. I can't imagine those records are that important."

"You'll call me after you get some information about what's going on?" Jack asked.

"Of course," Cathy said. "Let's make a time to talk again."

"Can you call me again at the same number, say, next Wednesday morning?" Jack asked.

Cathy nodded. "Ten o'clock?"

"Perfect," said Jack. "By the way, what does Peter do?"

"He has a similar situation to mine, you know, in the work-study program. He's a technical consultant to the administrative staff. He writes computer programs for special reports."

"He's also a good friend of yours?" Jack asked.

"Yeah. Why the interest?" Cathy asked, feigning ignorance.

"I guess I just want to be sure he could never find out the truth about everything," Jack said.

"I can't believe you would have those doubts about me," Cathy said, knowing full well that Jack did indeed trust her, and amused by the awkwardness of his flirtatious tap dance.

"I know, I know. I'm sorry. I didn't mean that I can't trust you. I just mean if Peter is involved in any way for the search of the file, I would worry that he might become curious about why there's such a fuss being made about it."

"Jack, I can assure you that if Peter, or anyone else for that matter, learns anything, it won't be from me."

"And, just in case you're interested," Cathy continued, "Peter and I went out a couple of times. We're good friends, but as far as anything more than that, well, we pretty much discovered there's no chemistry there."

"I didn't ask," Jack said.

"Yes, you did," Cathy responded, a knowing smile on her face.

Jack laughed. "All right, I know you have to go. I'll speak to you next week."

Cathy leaned in and hugged Jack goodbye. "Hey Jack, you know your parents have a lot in common."

"What do you mean?"

"They're both trying to protect you by keeping your father's identity a secret. Your mother kept his first identity from you and your father's keeping his second."

Jack laughed. "Yeah. Just your normal average family."

Cathy didn't laugh. "You never know, it may just turn out to be."

FIFTEEN

Occupying a small office on the second floor of a two-story walk-up office building on Frederiche Strasse in Frankfurt was a German branch of A.W. Kassing, Incorporated, a United States-based consulting group whose clients developed software for manufacturers of technology used by the oil exploration industry. Established four years prior, the German branch employed three people, all highly experienced in the design of technologies for locating and evaluating underwater sources of oil. The company's files contained a list of select clients, the majority of which were firms with ties to the governments of the United States, England, Norway and Turkey. The German office was created to promote the company's access to business with Russia and other former Soviet states.

Two staff members, including Tom Gaines, the group's managing director, were American; the third, Hermann Busterich, was German. Tom arrived back from a brief trip to the United States and went directly from the airport to the office. Elaine Corrigan, whose business card identified her as Consulting Practice Manager, greeted Tom when he walked through the door. They sat in chairs in the small reception area located just inside the door to the office. The office was windowless, and consisted of the reception area, two small individual work rooms, and an even smaller conference area. Furnishings were sparse, and a few nondescript hotel-type paintings and decorative calendars dotted the walls. The majority of space was filled with desks, computer equipment and file cabinets.

"You must be exhausted," Elaine said.

"Not really. I slept on the plane."

Elaine laughed. "Wow. You never do that."

"There's a first time for everything. And this trip was filled with firsts. First time I didn't sleep for three straight days and—"

Elaine cut him off, as if to complete his sentence. "And the first time you met a child you never knew you had."

Tom laughed. "I wonder what other little surprises life will deal me."

"Come on, fill me in! What was it like to meet him? What's he like?" Elaine asked eagerly.

"I still haven't digested it all. He seems like a terrific kid. Kid?" he caught himself. "What am I saying? Elaine, he's practically an adult. He's in college. Oh my god, I can't believe it... I didn't even ask him what he's studying there."

"So much for your stellar reputation for being thorough."

Tom laughed. "Well, I guess that reputation is out the window." Then, after a pause, "But seriously, I have a son and I really don't know him at all. He's lived his entire life without me even knowing he existed. And he seemed so... centered... smart. He kept coming back to his mother too — wanting to make sure she was okay, wanting to protect her. That says a lot about him, wouldn't you agree?"

"Sure does. And wow, he spent a year tracking you down. Just amazing!"

"Amazing, for sure." Tom pondered. "Can you believe it? I don't know if I would have that kind of perseverance with so many dead ends."

"And it was confirmed that his mother is not aware that he was searching for you?"

"Yes. And as I remember Linda, she's strikingly perceptive. I can't believe he was able to conduct such a search and compile so much information without her catching on."

"Maybe you should recruit him to work for us," Elaine teased.

"Not a bad idea."

"It's so much to think about, huh? What do you think things would have been like had you known about Jack?" Elaine asked. "I know that's a loaded question, but—"

"You know, I haven't stopped thinking about that. I have no idea. Every time I have one fleeting thought about it, another very different one takes over. It's hard for me to imagine not wanting to be part of a — part of *my* — child's life as he was growing up. And one of the worst parts of all this is how to deal with Linda. Part of me feels like she did the right thing for her son, you know, keeping him protected from what she thought would be a life of frustration not getting to know his father. But I have to admit, a part of me is so... angry. I mean, I have a son and she decided not to tell me about it. There's something that feels so wrong about that! A person shouldn't have that right… keeping the existence of a child from the other parent. I don't know. Maybe she should have. Honestly, I feel like I'm not thinking this through rationally. At least not yet. Or logically. Maybe it's from exhaustion, but I just can't sort out all the thoughts that are racing through my mind about this yet. Including the pregnancy. I never even thought to ask Linda if she was using protection. I mean, I know I was naïve. But after all, she was bright, educated and a health care worker, no less." Tom sighed and closed his eyes.

Elaine and Tom had known one another for four years. Elaine was twenty-nine years old. An adventurer, she had injured herself during a freak mountain climbing accident while in college. Elaine had participated in a climbing expedition in the Rocky Mountains. Just as the expedition was leaving base camp for a twelve thousand-foot climb, Elaine slipped on loose gravel and fell about twenty feet. A broken pelvis and knee resulted in a permanent slight limp, but her adventurous spirit had not dampened.

Tom had personally recruited Elaine, and he had come to rely on her quite considerably for this project. She brought a perspective to decisions that was an uncanny mix of big-picture insight and extraordinary attention to detail. She could envision a complex assortment of consequences associated with various policy options and simultaneously organize any project into an efficient matrix of activities, an intricate To Do list.

Tom poured himself a cup of coffee. "Hey, where's Hermann?" he asked.

"He's still in Hong Kong. He'll be back tomorrow."

"Did he make contact with Christine?"

"I won't know until tonight. He couldn't get to a secure line," Elaine responded.

A.W. Kassing, Inc. was not the consulting group its appearance suggested.

Throughout the 1990s, there had been a progressive relaxation of restrictions on Russian business exchanges with the United States. Despite occasional detours to progress, there had been a steady easing of tensions between these countries throughout the decade. Differences over support for breakaway nations and Russian power-flexing renewed tensions periodically, but this all occurred in the context of significantly less hostility than during the Cold War. Naturally, each country had powerful interests in monitoring one another's activities.

Oil production had been a major industry for Russia. It was only in recent years, however, that its exports became profitable. Yet, in some ways, the country lagged in technologies for the exploration and refinement of petroleum products. It relied heavily on equipment and methods that were less than optimal with respect to controlling for spillage, loss and pollution. And although Russia had made strides in upgrading the industry's technologies, the national economy had been too challenged for many years to invest sufficiently in a state-of-the-art technological upgrade program.

The Russian oil industry was a subject of great interest to the United States. As one of the world's major producers of oil, Russia's oil production had an important impact on the world economy. Any loss of stability in Russia's oil industry could impair that country's economy. Or, if the Russians curtailed their oil production, for example, to jack up prices, the impact would be felt on the world oil markets and could hurt the economies of many countries. Ultimately, it could hurt Russia as well since other producers would become more attractive, so the Russians had to work at striking the right pricing balance. Too low would stress their economy and harm their reform progress; too high would send buyers elsewhere.

The United States had good reason to monitor oil producing activity in Russia as well as in other former Soviet states for reasons beyond the economic — peeking into the oil industry's technology and manufacturing practices could shed some light on the state of technology of Russia's military.

The Defense Intelligence Agency was extremely interested in monitoring Russia's military and had a long history of managing clandestine operations to carry out this mission. The German branch of A.W. Kassing was a bogus consulting company, created by the DIA to gather data about Russia's oil industry and make assessments about the pace of its advancement and, of greater pertinence, what it could reveal

135

about the state of development of its military apparatus.

The three A.W. Kassing operatives were recruited for their extensive experience in oil exploration and related technological development along with their interpersonal savvy and intellectual shrewdness. Prior to the launch of A.W. Kassing, each spent over a year undergoing an identity transformation. New names and new histories were created. Former employers, professional associates and even families were invented. Academic histories, right down to old transcripts and diplomas, were constructed. For a good part of that transformation period, each went through the exercise of living a new life, all the while studying everything about the Russian oil industry, including how and where its technologies were deployed, how decisions were made and who made them, where oil reserves were located, extraction methods, how oil was refined, how shipping occurred and the economic details corresponding to all these activities.

The German branch of A.W. Kassing had all the markings of an independent consulting firm. The plan was to integrate into the community of producers and suppliers in Europe and Norway and use these relationships to springboard into relationships with companies that produced oil under the auspices of Russia. The group's goal was to establish a clear and detailed analysis of the rate of technological development of Russia's oil industry.

But, as the result of a cancellation of one meeting, the destiny of A.W. Kassing shifted four years after it was established. Olaf Neelson was an assistant energy minister in the Norwegian government. Aware of Tom's real identity and purpose, Olaf had been attempting to introduce Tom to Vladimir Polanski, an official of Imstructov, a large oil refinery with large complexes near the Bering Sea. Meetings had been arranged twice in Oslo but were canceled both times because of bad weather.

"But, Tom, keep the date. There is someone else I'd like for you to meet," Olaf said. Tom always enjoyed listening to him speak. Olaf had spent several years in the United States, having attended an elite boarding school in Baltimore and then Johns Hopkins University, where he earned a master's degree in economics. He spoke with the characteristic Norwegian elongated singsong whoop, but his diction and command of English were flawless.

"Who is it?" Tom asked.

"His name is Abdullah Khalali. He is in the Saudi ministry and directs a part of their shipping and crude distribution program. As a result of his travel he spends much time in other countries and is highly knowledgeable about the scope of unrest in the Arab world. He has formed a quiet brotherhood — well, maybe that's not the right word, it tends to scare people — a fraternity, with people who have fundamentalist histories, but who have grown weary of violence. He would like to strengthen this coalition, but keep in mind he and his associates walk a fine line. You should meet him. It might be helpful for your government to know about his efforts."

"Well, thank you for considering an introduction. I'd be very interested, but I should first clear it with my government," Tom said.

"Of course," Olaf responded. "But, Tom, it would be easy for me to introduce you under the cover of your assignment. Abdullah is already aware of your work and believes that your company does consulting work and has no real political or government connection. Because of his position, he is always interested in meeting experts in the field of oil exploration. To introduce you to him would be easy. There would be no risk of suspicion."

"I understand. Okay, that seems reasonable. Please arrange the meeting," Tom said.

Nine days later, Tom arrived in Oslo. He was whisked by a cab to a government office near the center of the capital. The six-story building had few ornate trappings, its nondescript appearance conforming more to a basic office building than some of the citadel-like structures that housed many government departments.

Tom entered the building through a heavily guarded front door. He displayed entry authorization papers delivered to him by Olaf a few days earlier. Since he was not employed by the Norwegian government, Tom was escorted to Olaf's office on the third floor by an armed national security agent.

"Tom, so good to see you. Abdullah should be here in ten minutes."

Tom felt a special bond with Olaf. They shared a primary interest in technology, and both viewed politics as a necessary, but decidedly less desirable, aspect of their work. He remembered when they had first met,

Olaf saying, "Remove politics and religion, and somehow I think we'd all manage to get along quite well." They could talk for hours about emerging technologies that had the capacity to drill deeper and deeper under saltwater to extract oil. And Tom was always impressed with Olaf's ability to think two steps ahead of the talking-head economists by correctly predicting prices of oil on the spot market.

"How's your family doing?" Tom asked.

"Good, thank you. My daughter has her eighteenth birthday tomorrow. How quickly they grow. Tom, you should really think about having a family someday. We're not getting younger."

"As a matter of fact—"

Just then, Olaf's secretary entered. "Sheik Khalali is in the anteroom. May I show him in?"

"Abdullah, it's wonderful to see you," Olaf announced as the surprisingly diminutive figure entered the room. He had a gentle manner and an easy smile. Despite his small physical stature, he had an athletic appearance, tapered at the waist. His skin had more of an olive tone than Tom expected, and his eyes had slight circles below, the mark of someone who sleeps too little and broods too much.

"I asked Tom to join us because his firm has been very helpful in expanding our exploration strategies. I thought you might like to hear about his work," Olaf said.

Tom explained how his team had designed a computer model to aid in constructing connector rings for deep-water drilling apparatuses. Conventional sealing rings would lose some of their structural integrity in deep, frigid saltwater. Tom's team had developed a technique to combine certain alloys with carbon to make the seals stronger. "And now we are working on strengthening the alloys by pretreating the carbon," Tom advised.

Abdullah was impressed. "Tom, you live up to your advance billing. Tell me a little about your background."

"I wish I could claim the credit. I was just lucky to work with very capable people over the years. The short version of my story is a master's degree in engineering from Michigan State. Fifteen years at Texxon in exploration, and four years at my present firm."

"How do you like working in a small firm compared to a giant like

Texxon?" Abdullah asked.

"Our boardroom is smaller," Tom smiled. "I guess there are advantages and disadvantages to each. But, as I get older, I find I get less discouraged by the disadvantages. They tend to be more trivial now. But I do know it would have been impossible to do my job now without the Texxon experience. So, Sheik—"

"Please call me Abdullah."

"Thank you. Abdullah, if you don't mind, how would you characterize the state of your oil exploration capabilities?" Tom asked.

"What a broad question. Our economy is so dependent on oil. We have no choice but to constantly reinvest in newer technologies. Most of the time we discover that the reinvestment more than pays for itself by reducing loss. I'm sure that doesn't surprise someone with your experience."

"I absolutely agree. May I ask, what is the chief obstacle you confront?"

Abdullah looked at Olaf, who read the look accurately. "We have done considerable business with Tom. He is a good friend." Tom understood the term "friend" to mean "trustworthy."

"Tom, I wish I could tell you that our biggest problem has to do with equipment. Or with money. Our biggest problem is the potential for instability. Ever since oil became the most precious commodity in the world, our region has not seen one day of tranquility. We walk a tightrope. We must, on the one hand, have strong ties to the west. This is the lifeblood of our economy. But we also recognize, on the other hand, that there are many in our culture who see this link as a betrayal of our heritage. This is not an easy balancing act."

"Can that last indefinitely?" Tom asked.

"I suspect not without risk of eventual implosion. I, myself, am actively engaged in efforts to gain support for more peaceful, collaborative approaches to resolving this historical dilemma."

"Are you seeing success?" Tom asked.

"At the moment, the resistance enjoys considerable popularity. But there are many who believe in the principle that different people can live together peacefully. This principle is in dire need of momentum and leadership. Our group convenes to exchange views on this matter and to determine how this interest may be advanced. We are not necessarily a political force. Not even a political entity. We are more of what would be considered a 'discussion group'. But we have similar interests, one of which is to cultivate a point of view in which tradition and modernity are not seen as mutually exclusive. Unfortunately, I cannot go into any more detail than that, however."

"I understand," said Tom. "Thank you for sharing."

"Tom, I have an idea, though it's off our topic. There is a meeting held bimonthly among a small group of oil executives who are responsible for shipping. It is an informal group consisting of about thirty people. Occasionally we have a speaker. Perhaps you can join us and give an overview of trends related to oil exploration as you see them. We would be more than happy to express our gratitude with a handsome honorarium."

"Well, thank you for considering me. I'm flattered, truly. Let me give it some thought. I love talking about my work, but I'm not sure I consider myself a speaker."

Following handshakes, Tom departed Olaf's office as talk turned to the lease of a Norwegian tanker to Saudi Arabia.

Two weeks later, Tom received a call from Olaf. "Abdullah was impressed with you. He asked that I extend that invitation for you to give a brief address to his group on your ideas about the future of oil exploration. He suggested that you should, how did he put it, oh, yes, 'fantasize about the future,'" Olaf laughed.

"Olaf, you are going to get me into deep trouble," Tom responded with a laugh, knowing that Olaf could be trusted completely.

"This will be a harmless exercise. And I do think that Abdullah is refreshing and a good contact for you. I must confess, I am hoping that his group offers opportunities to your country. I've known him for many years, and at heart Abdullah is a man of peace. And reason. Who knows, someday his group's vision may see the light of day."

"All right, give me the details. Where? When? Who will be there? And, of course, before anything, I'll have to review the invitation with my government."

Tom flew into Riyadh, Saudi Arabia, three weeks later and was met by one of Abdullah's aides. Together they drove in a Mercedes Benz to the center of the city, where Tom saw a cluster of government buildings. Amidst the buildings was a relatively understated hotel that projected a business-meeting aura.

The meeting was held in a moderate-sized conference room on the second floor. Contingents of security were present outside the room in which the meeting was held. The meeting was in progress and Tom was asked to wait for about ten minutes until it was his turn on the agenda.

Shortly, a stately woman dressed in western clothes emerged from the room and asked the security guard at the door if Tom had arrived. Overhearing her question, Tom turned to her and announced, "I'm Tom Gaines."

"A pleasure to meet you. My name is Nawal. I'm an aide to Abdullah. Please come in. We are ready for you."

As Tom entered the room, he first took note of the seating arrangement. A large square comprised of adjoining tables was organized a few feet in from the room's perimeter. Each side was about twenty feet long, and only thirty occupants were seated around the table. Tom thought that it seemed an unusually spread-out configuration. Abdullah was seated at what appeared to be the head of the table, but only because it was in the front of the room. He motioned for Tom to join him.

"I am most pleased to introduce our guest, Mr. Tom Gaines. I had the pleasure of meeting Mr. Gaines in the office of our dear friend, Olaf Neelson. Mr. Gaines, as you know, is a principal in the firm of A.W. Kassing, and I invited him because he has a wonderful sense of how our industry's technology is likely to evolve. His company works with several exploration engineers and they are deeply knowledgeable about the state of alloy development and deep-water exploration. I asked Tom to spend a brief period with us to share his views about technological trends."

As Abdullah was presenting the introduction, Tom was looking at the conference attendees, sizing them up. Olaf had indicated that the group would consist of about twenty-five high-ranking oil industry officials from Mideast countries. From the information provided by Olaf he had learned their names, some key background elements and their relationships to Abdullah.

141

Tom spoke for about half an hour. The group was clearly impressed by his knowledge and creative forecasting and charmed by his unassuming manner. His talk was well received, and Abdullah invited him to join the group members for hors d'oeuvres and mingling following the meeting.

The atmosphere in the banquet hall was marked by a cordial diplomatic formality. Tom observed an eagerness among group members to coalesce into dyads and small groups, a tendency to depart from the political correctness demanded by the context in order to have frank and meaningful exchanges with important colleagues.

As Tom was ordering a club soda from the bar, he felt a tap on his shoulder. As he turned around, he saw a man with an olive complexion, intelligent eyes and a neatly cropped beard. "I was very impressed with your talk," he said. The voice was familiar to Tom, but he could not place it. "I'm not surprised you don't remember me. Maybe a little insulted," the man laughed, "but not surprised. When we last saw one another I had hair here," he said, pointing to his head, "and not here," he continued, pointing to his beard.

"Oh, my god," Tom reacted, visibly shaken. "Rafiq? How did—"

"Don't worry," the man cut him off. He leaned close and whispered, "Your secret is safe with me, Stewart."

SIXTEEN

The engineering programs at the New England Institute of Technology were a brainiac's delight. Many of the students, by virtue of their cerebral endowment and hormonally charged competitiveness, would have preferred to work more independently than the computer technology of the 1980s permitted. Only crude personal computers were available then, most jerry-rigged by the more inventive students, but most large-scale research projects required data analyses to be performed by the college's substantial mainframe systems. During midterms and finals, students would have to coordinate their schedules to be certain that they had sufficient opportunity to use the computer. Some students gathered into work groups, and members would occasionally alternate turns inputting their members' data.

In his junior year, Stewart had been invited to join a work group comprised of students whose academic concentration was chemical engineering. He was invited not because of a scholastic prowess, but because he possessed a host of attractive personal characteristics. He was a talented social facilitator and negotiator. And he had a charismatic charm and quick wit and was appealingly self-deprecating. His easy manner was a welcome antidote to the ever-present fierce competition of a college teeming with high achievers. He could carry his weight academically, but he was by no means a member of the top tier at NEIT, a college inhabited by students whose mental acumen was stratospheric.

Stewart enjoyed the affiliation with this intelligentsia. But he recognized his limitations, and he doubted that it would ever be his fate to advance the state of engineering theory or achieve notoriety for some breakthrough discovery. While he knew a Nobel Prize was not in his future, he also knew that he was smart enough to apply the principles of the field in a productive way. And besides, the purity of the subject matter wasn't as exciting to him as its application, whether entrepreneurial or in terms of technological deployment.

Stewart's work group consisted of six students. One was a bright young Lebanese transfer student named Rafiq Farid. For the first month the two had little opportunity for interaction beyond the study group activity. Then, an incident occurred that became the basis for a quick bond. Elias Hobst taught a class in metallurgy. Professor Hobst was among the most demanding professors at the university. He insisted students attend every class, and any absence, no matter how legitimate the circumstances, was inexcusable. His tests were impossibly difficult and his manner gruff and intimidating.

Metallurgy was taught in a large lecture hall. About two hundred students attended the Monday afternoon lectures, and then broke into smaller lab sections later in the week. One Monday at noon, about a month after the formation of Stewart's work group, Rafiq received an urgent call from his sister in Lebanon that their paternal grandmother had passed away. She had been sick, and her passing was expected. Rafiq's father, a currency trader, was visiting the United States on business, and on that day was in Chicago. Rafiq was to contact his father to inform him of her passing. He began by calling the hotel and, unable to reach him there, called a couple of his father's business associates in Chicago.

The first colleague informed Rafiq that he was not due to see his father that day. Rafiq got lucky with the second, who told him that Rafiq's father was on his way to his office for an appointment. He would have his father call him as soon as he arrived. Rafiq provided his dormitory's phone number to the colleague.

Class time was approaching, and Rafiq's father still had not called. Stewart was passing Rafiq's room and asked if he would like to join him for the walk over to Professor Hobst's class. Rafiq filled him in on his family's situation and that he had to wait for his father's call.

"Oh, man, I'm sorry about your grandmother. If you're skipping class, I get it. But you know Hobst. He's such an asshole, I feel like he wouldn't care about that," Stewart said, knowing quite well he was not telling Rafiq anything he didn't already know.

"I'm not leaving until I speak to my father. I'd feel terrible letting the day pass without him knowing that his mother has died," Rafiq insisted.

"I totally understand. You do know your grade will be lowered,"

Stewart reminded him.

"I know. But this is more important."

Stewart was impressed. Rafiq made a moral choice and was willing to live with the consequences. Stewart realized he hadn't often seen principled decisions made up close, when the willingness to absorb an adverse outcome was so secondary as to become irrelevant compared to doing the right thing. Maybe this wasn't the most earth-shattering situation, Stewart thought to himself, but it was the situation Rafiq faced right now.

The first ten minutes of each class consisted of Professor Hobst taking attendance. He had a long list with the names of the students on it. Professor Hobst would call each name and mark each student present as he heard "Here." As the names were being read, it occurred to Stewart that Professor Hobst rarely looked up during this exercise. Stewart studied Professor Hobst carefully as he proceeded through the attendance list. He doesn't acknowledge the student visually, Stewart noted; he just listens for "Here" and moves to the next name on the list.

Professor Hobst was an imposing man, dispassionate, burly. His manner was harsh and uncompromising. Reading glasses were perpetually perched on the end of his nose, and when he directed his visual attention to a student, he peered over the glasses with a scowled look, as though the student was incapable of uttering anything but the most outrageous inanity.

Rafiq's name was about to be called. Stewart gulped nervously.

"Rafiq Farid," said Professor Hobst.

The lecture hall was cavernous. Seating was arranged in tiered rows, about twenty-five from front to back. The ceiling was high. Surfaces — desks, floors, walls — were hard, slamming words back in the room with a turbo-charged punch. Each syllable blared and produced a tinge of reverberation. Sound had never resonated so conspicuously, so incapable of being concealed or subdued. Any delay in responding to Professor Hobst would derail the rhythm of the attendance ritual.

"Here," announced Stewart quickly, his heart palpitating.

Several students spun their heads in Stewart's direction, stunned and confused by a display of raw audacity.

Professor Hobst paused for a millisecond, as though something might be amiss, as though this was the wrong voice, or it emanated from an unexpected part of the room; perhaps Stewart's "Here" failed to fit the pattern of responses to which Professor Hobst had become unconsciously accustomed. Stewart felt a sense of panic. If discovered, he would experience a penalty far worse than Rafiq for failing to attend class.

Professor Hobst didn't look up. "Kevin Fenton," he continued. Crisis averted. And a moment later, "Stewart Jacobson."

"Here," announced Stewart.

Stewart headed straight to Rafiq's dorm room immediately after class. Rafiq was sitting on the edge of his bed.

"Did you hear from your dad?" Stewart asked, short of breath from the scamper over from class.

"There was a traffic jam. He got to his meeting an hour late. But he did call me as soon as he got there. My grandmother was so sick. She had two heart attacks and a stroke in the past year. She was in a coma-like state. We had to have people come into the house to massage her just so her body could continue to function. My father was due to return home tomorrow," Rafiq said.

"I'm so sorry. That's so horrible. Is he very upset?" Stewart asked, his voice filled with consolation.

"I think he was more relieved than anything. He and my aunt had a hard time watching her go from being a strong woman to becoming this, this helpless creature. They knew she wouldn't want to be like this for very long. She had too much pride. Her suffering was almost too much for them to bear."

"Well, Rafiq, if there's anything I can do..." Stewart offered.

"Maybe you can help me study for Hobst's final to make up for the lousy grade I'm going to get for being absent," Rafiq said, mustering a smile.

"Well, Hobst thinks you were in class today."

"What? You're kidding! How? What happened?" Rafiq asked incredulously.

"I don't know what came over me, but when he called your name, I just said 'Here.' Really, it was no big deal, nothing like what you guys are dealing with." But Stewart was feeling unashamedly prideful.

Rafiq laughed. "You're crazy, Stewart. You could have gotten into

146

big trouble."

"Yeah, I guess, but to tell you the truth, I didn't really think much about that at the time. Plus, it's Hobst's fault — he never looks up when he takes attendance."

"I like that strategy: blame the victim. I'll have to remember it." Rafiq laughed. "I really owe you one."

"Nah," Stewart said. "You know, I hate to admit it, but it was kind of fun."

"I didn't think of you as such a risk taker," Rafiq observed.

"Neither did I," Stewart said, smiling.

Senior year was a frenetic period for NEIT students. They constituted the pick of the crop for engineering firms, and the top fifty percent of the graduating class could virtually select the firms they wished to work for. Stewart evaluated a few excellent offers, eventually choosing Meredith Oil because of its new program set up to empower self-directed oil exploration teams. The company's cutting-edge technology and opportunity for travel provided additional lures.

"So, Rafiq, what will it be for you? Big bucks right away or graduate school?" Stewart asked.

Rafiq challenged him. "Guess!"

"I'd bet all my money, anything, that you'll be heading to graduate school next year," Stewart said with a confident swagger.

"And you'd be a richer man," Rafiq replied.

"Why not take a job for a little while and make some money before heading back to school?" Stewart asked.

"You know, I don't think I'm cut out to take a basic engineering job somewhere. Where I come from, there is a lot of suffering. What you will earn next year from Meredith can feed an entire town in Lebanon for, like, that entire year. I just don't want to contribute to the brain drain," Rafiq said.

"So how would a graduate degree help?" Stewart asked.

"Education is so different in Lebanon. The whole way of life. It's amazing… if you saw the poverty and injustice you would be appalled. I feel it's important to prepare myself to help."

Stewart and Rafiq had become friends, but their friendship tended to be based on common interests, like athletics (both enjoyed soccer and

147

rugby), computer science and, to their surprise, music. Rarely had they discussed one another's background, particularly Rafiq's. It occurred to Stewart that there was an entire part of the world that he was unaware of. His life had been so sheltered, and on top of that, he had never been asked to fit in to a culture that was foreign to him. Rafiq's support of a country that left him with conflicting feelings was inspiring in some way to Stewart, even if he could not entirely relate.

"I don't know. It would be easy for me to say that our whole region has been exploited, and it would be equally easy for me to say that we haven't done anything to move into the modern world," Rafiq replied. "Either way, I hope I can do something to make that part of the world a little better." It was the most inspirational sentence Stewart had ever heard.

SEVENTEEN

"I would have recognized your name. It wasn't on the list they gave me," Tom said.

"I received a last-minute invitation from the Saudi oil minister, so I'm not surprised I wasn't on the list," Rafiq responded.

The two men exchanged a warm handshake. "My god, it's been a long time. How many years?" Tom asked. Then, answering his own question, "Must be more than twenty."

"Yes, it would be about twenty-one years since we last saw one another, I believe. Time has treated you kindly. You look great," Rafiq said.

"And you as well. Please, fill me in — how are you?" Tom asked.

"Well, I handle legal affairs for the oil ministry, now. Funny that our paths should cross again in our professions."

At that moment, Abdullah interrupted the two. "Tom, your presentation was fascinating. Rafiq, it seems you and Tom know one another?"

"Yes, we do," Rafiq said, coolly calculating the situation. "Tom and I met last year at a conference on drilling technologies. I was just congratulating him on a wonderful talk tonight."

"You must have much in common," Abdullah said. "Tom, Rafiq is one of the few people I have ever met whose technical knowledge is matched with a gifted command of international law."

"Yes. We were just catching up," Tom responded. "I hadn't realized his background was so extensive."

"Well, let me leave you to continue catching up. I hope we will have the opportunity to continue to learn from you, Tom," Abdullah said, then walked away to chat with another colleague.

"Let's go sit in the corner." Rafiq motioned to a quiet section of the lounge. "Perhaps I should be calling you Tom."

Tom's shock from the surprise was fading. "Thanks. That would be a good idea," Tom said, smiling.

"I assume that you are unable to bring me up to date."

"I would love nothing more than to be able to tell you everything. But yes, unfortunately you assume correctly," Tom said.

"I read your biography. It came with the meeting agenda. Naturally, I had no idea that Tom Gaines would turn out to be an old friend," Rafiq said. "I assume you are with the government." Rafiq paused, the reality of his friend's circumstance crystallizing. "Don't respond. We'll leave it at that," Rafiq reassured him.

Tom winked. "You are a good friend, Rafiq. Now, I'd like to hear about you."

"My life has been a series of ups and downs. Some unfortunate, tormenting downs," Rafiq began. "But I can tell you about that in a bit. Let's see. Where did we leave off? I did go on to get my master's degree, as I had intended."

"If I remember correctly, your plan was to go to graduate school and then return to work in Lebanon, right?"

"Exactly. And after a few years it became clear that many of our problems were rooted in the black-market system, so that it was impossible for the average person to benefit from the region's oil wealth. During this period, my mother's family, who are Saudis, if you recall, suggested I could have more of an impact in their country, so I joined a project on accelerating the refining process. Well, one thing led to another, and I guess the oil minister took a liking to me and suggested I further my education — he felt it would help me and help the industry as well. So, I went to law school at Oxford and then at the university in Riyadh."

"No one will ever accuse you of not having enough degrees," Tom observed with a laugh.

"That's for certain." Rafiq laughed, too. "And here I am today, many years later, representing the legal affairs of the ministry."

"You know, I've never forgotten a conversation we had in college about you hoping to help your country one day. It was eye-opening for me as a nineteen-year-old. And it always stuck with me. It was such a mixture of childhood idealism and an understanding of the world that life hadn't forced me to have," Tom said. "Can I ask, and only because we're old friends, do you feel like you've lost that if you're representing the monarchy, which is so wealthy in the midst of poverty and struggle?"

"A fair question, Tom. It's quite the balancing act, I can tell you. Ensuring that we do not lose our culture to progress, while also working to keep up with modernization. There is a delicate balancing act we must perform. If our government tilts too far toward the west and modernization, we will surely fail. From the outside, our middle-of-the-road approach can seem hypocritical. But when you live it every day, it makes sense."

"Fair enough. I'm still inspired when you speak, Rafiq, I must say. After all these years I still learn from you. But please, I'm enjoying the update. Continue telling me about your past twenty-one years," Tom said with a smile.

Rafiq slumped in his chair. "Tom, do you have a family?" he asked.

"Funny you should ask. That's an interesting story for another day. Why?" Tom asked.

"Well. Two years ago, my wife and I celebrated our eighteenth wedding anniversary," Rafiq said with a solemn look.

"Congratulations," Tom offered, meekly, knowing the stage was set for a letdown.

"We had two children, a lovely daughter, Fayza, and our son, Abdel. Fayza was lost to us, Tom, in a tragic accident. It was two years ago. She was only fourteen. She was going on a school trip near the Kuwaiti border. The group was going to explore an archeological dig. Fayza loved history, and she was so eager to attend this trip." Rafiq's eyes moistened. He sighed and glanced away to compose himself. "A few of the students wandered a short distance from the dig site," Rafiq continued. "Maybe fifty yards, no more. There was an explosion. The teachers came running. Fayza had stepped on a mine. Another student was also killed. I'm just so grateful Fayza did not suffer. The blast took her life instantly. Her body could not even be recognized, Stew… Tom." A tear ran down his cheek, which he quickly wiped away with the back of his hand.

Tom sighed, mesmerized by the obvious pain his friend was feeling. "Rafiq, I am so sorry. I cannot begin to imagine the suffering of losing a child, especially that way," Tom said, reaching out his hand and placing

151

it on top of Rafiq's.

"It has been said to me that one never recovers from the loss of a child. The loss of a parent, well, that's the natural order of things, I suppose. But the loss of a child... this haunts the soul forever."

"Please, can you tell me about her?" Tom asked.

"She was just the most curious person I have ever known." A soft smile briefly brightened Rafiq's face. "She would ask question after question about everything. When she was two it was constantly why, why, why about everything. Why does the sun shine? Why does the car move? Why does sound go to our ears? When she was twelve, she volunteered for a peace committee to correspond with children in another part of the world. Fayza's group corresponded with children in Israel to learn about each other's lives. The principals in the schools were attempting to arrange a meeting of the pen pals, and maybe even an exchange program. Tom, she was beside herself with excitement. She helped the teachers organize this project and became absolutely immersed in it. Fayza was something of an idealist. I have no question that she would have made this world a better place. A more peaceful place."

"It sounds like she already accomplished some of that," Tom offered.

"Yes, perhaps she did. In my world, she did. Thank you, Tom."

"How have your wife and son handled this?" Tom asked.

"Jamila, my wife, has never recovered. I suppose I haven't either. She became overwhelmed with grief, consumed by it. As strong a person as she is, she just cannot seem to climb out of her despondency. But my son, he's another story. He's seventeen now. At first, we were startled by what seemed to be a lack of reaction. We couldn't understand it. Life went on for him. He went to school, got together with friends. Perhaps we were so preoccupied with our sadness that we weren't noticing changes in him. In fact, we were happy, even quite relieved, that he seemed quite able to resume his normal activity. And maybe that contributed to our failure to see the changes that were really quite subtle. But he was seething. Deep inside, a rage was building, Tom, a rage we could not reach. Over this past year, I know he has had contact with fundamentalists. I hear things creeping into his language. He blames our ties to the west for Fayza's death. If it were not for western interests, Fayza would still be alive. This is what he believes. To him, her death represents something very ominous, the larger death of our history, who we are. He is becoming increasingly resistant to other, more moderate points of view. I can see the hatred in his eyes and it frightens me."

"What can you do about it?" Tom asked.

"Jamila and I feel powerless. The more we talk to Abdel about our point of view, the more resistant he becomes. We talk about peace and he talks about hate. We talk about building bridges and he talks of exploding them. We have suggested that he attend a different school — anything to alter his sphere of influence — but he resists. He has become defiant. We don't want to push too much for fear this will intensify his defiance and make things worse. We talk about Fayza's dream of peace and friendship, but he counters with 'Look where it got her.'"

"What about moving your family to another country? Even the United States. Surely you have senior-level connections elsewhere," Tom probed.

"We explored that with Abdel. He was adamant — he said he would refuse to leave. And he is of the age when he could make such an independent choice. In some ways I feel like I still have my daughter with me, and at the same time I fear I'm losing my son."

EIGHTEEN

Jack jumped to answer the pay phone. It was Wednesday. He hadn't taken his eyes off the clock on his cell phone. 10.02 a.m. "Hello," he said, his voice bursting with eagerness and energy.

"Hi, it's me. I have some news. How's tomorrow?"

"I'll make it work. Same time?" Jack asked.

"See you there," Cathy said.

How quickly their communication had achieved high-level efficiency, like that of operating room team members. No waste, no imprecision. It was synchrony produced by urgency, repetition and common purpose.

Jack was growing very fond of Cathy. During his drive to meet her, he listened to Radiohead and thought of her. It was a crude mix, almost a struggle as the music and thoughts of Cathy vied for his attention. Somehow, he made the tug-of-war work.

Jack hadn't had much romantic experience. When his mother discussed 'dating' with him, it had an archaic ring to it. Despite his recognition that his mother was youthful and impeccably aware of — and, in fact, enjoyed — many popular culture trends of Jack's generation, her notion of dating sounded like a ritual long into retirement. In some ways it was hard to imagine his peers engaging in such activity the way Linda described it. She would always encourage Jack to 'ask a girl out'. This had a particular sequence: select a place to go, agree on a time, pick her up, and deposit her home later. But the bulk of what he had observed while in high school seemed different, less bound by such formality of structure and convention and gender role assignment. Cliques of boys and girls dominated the social scene, and relationships seemed more fluid and less rigidly contoured than the descriptions of dating presented by his mother. Relationships would materialize within the cliques. These would come about less as the culmination of the dating ceremony as his mother conceived of it, and more, it appeared, from a transitory mutual sexual interest. Then, just as suddenly as the relationship would form, it might evaporate, as though it never existed.

Jack had spent a good deal of his school years feeling socially isolated. His high school was crammed with kids who pretty much all looked the same — white suburban kids from middle-class families with middle-class incomes and a spoon-fed propensity for upward mobility. As a result, there were not many options for identifying with and blending into a sub-group; popularity was measured largely by interest in, knowledge of or, better yet, talent in sports. Sure, there were other activities sponsored by the school, but these were considered fringe and generally irrelevant. That's one of the reasons why the debate team was directed by a teacher who was not especially experienced or skilled in the area; debate, like other facets of the arts and humanities, was an 'extra' at the school. Running one of these activities was tossed off to someone with some free time, or who made the fatal mistake of not showing up for the faculty meeting when assignments were distributed.

Jack was friendly and amiable, and he had a natural ease with others, or at least an ease that he could make appear natural. But his group affiliation needs were not strong and could certainly never compete with his preference for privacy. So, participation in a tightknit group was out, although his friendly nature enabled him to avoid becoming the target of social derision. But this nebulous social world that dominated the school environment worked best for those most comfortable in groups, so Jack was at a distinct disadvantage when it came to reaching out to girls.

Then along came Cathy. Jack brooded over the basis for his affection: Did he like her just because she was smack at the center of the most major event in his life? Or was there something more genuine about his affection for her? He wished he was more inclined to act on impulse when it came to initiating communication with girls — then the chips would fall where they may and that would be okay, he thought. But he couldn't escape his nature, and he was fearful of miscalculating Cathy's interest in him because he didn't want to get rejected or, worse for Jack, embarrassed.

When Jack arrived at the hotel, Cathy was already there. Their hug was friendly and polite, much like a greeting between family members. Jack was caught in a conundrum of his own making — did he stiffen during the embrace and dull the opportunity for something more tender? Were he and Cathy destined to be just friends? Or, depressingly, it occurred to Jack, were they merely partners on a project brought together by some bizarre accident of fate?

They immediately, almost mechanically, ambled over to 'their corner' of the lobby. They tumbled into small perpendicular couches, swallowed by the bulky softness of the cushions.

"How was your drive?" Cathy asked, her eyes sparkling. Her normal state, Jack realized, was effervescence. Not bubbly mindlessness, but liveliness, an animation that didn't crowd out her intelligence or intellectual curiosity. It didn't take but a millisecond of being with her — he admitted to himself that he was smitten.

"Uneventful," Jack replied. "How about yours?"

"Fine. But I was thinking. Let's go somewhere more interesting. This place is making me feel like a spy. In a creepy way."

"Where to?" asked Jack.

"You'll see. Let's go," Cathy said, and grabbed Jack's hand for just a second as if to activate him.

As they walked out of the hotel lobby, Cathy said, "I'll drive," and led Jack to the parking lot and toward her late-model Nissan.

"Where are you taking me?" Jack asked as they got into the car.

"Not far from here."

"You know... last time I was in a car and wasn't told where I was going, I thought I was going to be killed," Jack said, grinning.

"I promise, there's no long-lost parent where we're going," Cathy said with mock reassurance.

For the next twenty minutes, Jack and Cathy talked about their families, friends, interests, and aspirations. They acknowledged how strange it seemed that they knew so little about one another when they had become so intimately bonded around the most momentous experience in Jack's life. "Probably a little like what it's like to be in a foxhole with someone," Jack said.

Cathy turned onto a narrow gravel road over which hung a sign that said, 'Whispering Woods Arboretum'. "I haven't been here in years, but it's a great place for a picnic," Cathy said. "I hope you didn't eat yet." She drove about a hundred yards through a magnificent landscape of trees in full bloom. To Jack, this seemed like pure nature, nothing but foliage. Off to the side was a small clearing. Cathy pulled in and parked.

Cathy retrieved a brown shopping bag from the trunk of the car. "I couldn't find an official basket, so this will have to do."

Jack was enchanted. Cathy had planned a picnic for them. He tried not to embrace the fantasy that she might like him for fear of having it shattered, but he was at least entertaining the possibility. They walked through the European collection with sprawling English oaks, spruce and birch, all leafy and richly green.

"Those are my favorites," Cathy said, pointing to a field of flowering trees. "Let's sit over there." Cathy led Jack to the base of an Elizabeth Magnolia with a radiant yellow bloom. "My parents used to take me to this place once a year on our way down to New York City. I found it kind of boring in the beginning. But I fell in love with this yellow tree. It was like a friend, here for us every time we came."

Jack's mind was searching for something interesting to say, to fit the moment, but all he could mutter was "Yeah." Idiot, he thought.

Cathy had prepared some tuna sandwiches on whole wheat bread and brought along some cut-up fruit. They found a bench near a deep green Cypress tree, and as they sat down to eat, Jack asked, "What's going on with the file?" He was conscious of his every gesture and syllable, and his fear of making a mistake drove him to the safe terrain of business.

"Well, I met with Jeffords last week, and he told me that Hoverdale had been calling him about your father's housing file. She kept asking if he found it, or if he can think of any other places to look. He even went to the last security director's house and checked with his wife. She knew that her husband kept some records in a safe in a small utility room in the basement, so Jeffords looked through the safe with her, but your father's file wasn't there. Jeffords kept pumping me about the file. Could I think of any other places it could be? I mean, how would I know?"

"Did the wife have any information about the last time someone looked in the safe?" Jack asked.

"That's everything I know," Cathy said.

"Do you think Jeffords has any idea that this is not about selling the building?" Jack asked.

"No. I'm pretty convinced that's what he thinks. He's worried because he thinks he'll be in trouble if he doesn't find the file. He knows he's not personally responsible, but if the deal is blown, the trustees of the university may blame the Security Department. You know how these things work. They always find someone to blame."

"This scares me a little. If Donna is so interested in finding some old housing file, there must be something to it. I feel like my dad is in some kind of danger or something."

"I know. That's why I wanted to tell you about it. Maybe you should try to find out from Donna what's going on with the file," Cathy said.

"She'll never tell me. Plus, she has no idea that you and I talk. She doesn't even have an idea that we ever met. She'd kill me — this time for real — if she knew I didn't keep my promise not to speak to you."

Cathy laughed. "Yeah, right. She might be your father's girlfriend for all we know."

Jack was pensive, but nervous. "I just hope my father's not in any danger over this file thing."

"That's why I think you should try to find out. Don't ask her about it directly. But at some point, you can ask if there's anything you did that might have exposed your father. See what she says."

Jack looked incredulous, and he was adamant in his response. "Cathy, she's not going to tell me anything. I'm not in on this situation. They're not my friends. Their job is to protect my father and whatever it is he's doing. They don't owe me anything. I'm a major nuisance to them. An obstacle. And you know the incredible thing? I have no way of even reaching Donna. I have to wait for her to contact me."

"Right. I forgot about that," Cathy said. "Hey, I have to start back soon. Let's take a walk."

As they stood, Jack looked upward. The sunlight shimmered against the leaves on the upper branches, producing a sweeping golden glow. He had never seen a tree with distinctively yellow leaves. "This really is a beautiful tree. How many years have you been coming here?"

"About fourteen."

"We have a tree in our backyard, a big oak. When I was about four, my grandfather built a swing on it. He made the seat from a solid piece of wood and tied it to a giant limb that was about twenty-five feet off the ground. He used thick pieces of rope. I remember it was hard for me to get my hand entirely around the rope. My mother was scared because it was attached so high. She thought I would swing way up and fall off." Jack laughed as he reminisced.

"Did you ever fall?" Cathy asked.

"Yeah. First time I was on by myself. Boom. I fell right back and hit my head on the ground. My mother came flying out of the house. She thought I had a concussion."

"Did you?" Cathy asked.

"I don't know. I guess not."

"Is the swing still there?" Cathy asked.

"Yeah. The rope is pretty frayed, though. It's funny you ask, because I don't think I even noticed it in the last ten years, other than when I have to clear leaves in the yard. And lately anything that comes up makes me think of how things would have been different if my father had been in my life. Like with the swing. I have these vivid memories of sitting on my mother's lap on that swing. She would read to me while we sat on it. I was no more than four or five, I guess, but I remember that like it was yesterday. It was one of my favorite things. It's crazy, but even with something as silly as that, I keep wondering what it would have been like if he was there."

Cathy took Jack's hand, then she leaned in and kissed him. It lasted only about three or four seconds because they were both nervous. They held hands as they walked in silence back to the car.

"Could we plan to talk next week?" Cathy asked as Jack was leaving her car.

"Can you call me at ten on Tuesday?" Jack asked.

"Yeah. Same number," Cathy said.

Jack was feeling numb and awkward. "Thanks. For everything. I'm not sure what to say."

"No need to say anything," Cathy said, her warm smile comforting and alluring at the same time.

Jack's drive back to New Jersey took about four hours. He was spellbound with thoughts of Cathy. As he approached his block, he was jolted from his stupor by the quick beep of a car horn behind him. He looked in his rearview mirror and saw that it was Donna. Jack slowed down and Donna pulled alongside his car. She motioned for Jack to follow her. They drove for about two minutes, and Donna slowed down and parked on a heavily trafficked street. Jack pulled into the spot behind her. He practically leaped from his car and entered the passenger side of her car.

Before he could speak, Donna shot him a fierce look. "Jack, you haven't been honest with me," she said, her voice cold and hard.

Caught completely off guard, Jack could only nervously mumble, "What do you mean?"

"Oh, Jack, come on. Cut the bullshit. Where were you today?" This was the Donna first encountered by Jack. Tough. Menacing.

Nothing but a complete confession would do. His voice was full of appeal. "I'm so sorry. I didn't think it would cause any harm. Please tell me my father's all right. Honestly, Donna, I would never have gotten together with Cathy if I had the slightest idea it would be a problem. I never—"

Donna cut him off. "You would have no way of knowing whether it would cause a problem, would you?" She was blunt and stern. And she was right. "How in the world could you know if it would add to an already dangerous situation, not just for your father, but for you, and maybe for your mother? This isn't a game, Jack. And I'm not just disappointed because I trusted you. I'm angry. You lied to me. Why did you lie to me?" She wasn't softening.

"I don't know. I've gotten to know Cathy better than I let on to you. I would have told you, but I was scared she might get into trouble. That I might get into trouble. Then I thought I just had to keep up the charade. It wasn't intentional. I was just scared. And she was the only person in the world I could talk to about my father. If I had the slightest fear, the slightest fear that telling her would get any of us into trouble I never would have done it. Maybe you won't believe that, but it's the truth."

"Jack, is there more going on between you and Cathy?"

"Maybe. I don't know," he responded with a hint of sheepishness.

"Jack. Are you two romantically involved?"

Jack was exceedingly uncomfortable at the thought of disclosing anything personal to just about anyone. And topping the list of topics that produced the most discomfort, bordering on making him petrified, were feelings about a young woman. But Donna gave him no way out.

"No," he stammered. Donna stared at him, knowing he wouldn't be able to hold back. "Okay, we kissed. Kind of. But it wasn't a big deal."

"No big deal! Tell me then, what would be a big deal?"

"Well, maybe it is a big deal. I don't know. Look, Donna, I don't know what to make of it. It's not like she's my girlfriend or anything. Just tell me what you want me to do, and I promise, I'll do it."

"I spoke to your father about an hour ago. I told him you were with Cathy today," Donna said.

"Is he okay? Hey, how did you know I was with her?"

"Jack, I hope you can appreciate my hesitancy to share information with you. If we are going to work together in any way, I need transparency and honesty from you." Donna's eyes were riveted like lasers on Jack.

"I know, I know. I'm sorry. I promise Cathy is the only thing I lied about. I haven't told my mom or anyone else. I don't want to hurt my dad. I promise."

"Jack, I want you to be aware that we're able to listen in on some of the other phones you've been using."

"Really? So, I have literally no privacy."

"You should assume you have no privacy for the time being. At some point it will come to an end," Donna said, the anger in her tone diluting.

"Is my father all right? Was he angry with me?"

Donna smiled. For Jack it was like a nightmare abruptly and shockingly coming to a peaceful end. She said, "He asked if Cathy was a nice girl. I said she's smart, she's pretty, but she doesn't have the savvy to protect Jack without it showing through like a Fourth of July fireworks display. He didn't ask if she was trustworthy. That means he trusts you. You must have made quite an impression on him. He said to let you go ahead seeing her. He said bringing the two of you together was the first thing he's done for you in your whole life."

Jack had a look of shock and exuberance. He wanted the day to end right now, right at this moment, so it could go down as one of the greatest days of his life.

"But," Donna continued. "We need to have a few ground rules. You need to stop using that same public phone. Find some other phones, and not just on campus. And she should use a different phone as well."

"No problem," Jack said. "What else?"

"Quit meeting at the hotel. I don't want anyone who works there to get suspicious about two kids who keep showing up. You can have your relationship — whatever it is — more out in the open. Figure out some reason to tell people how you met if need be."

"Yeah, well, I can't tell my mom about her at all. I could never come up with anything that she'd ever believe."

"That's true. You need to keep your relationship with Cathy a secret from your mother for now. In time, if your relationship continues, she can know about it," Donna said.

Jack's mind was scrambling. "What about Jeffords? He keeps pumping Cathy for information about the lost housing file."

Donna laughed. "Oh, Jeffords. We've had that housing file for years."

Jack cut in. "I don't get it. That's why Cathy wanted to get together with me today. She's been worried because Jeffords keeps asking her about the file. He told her that you call him all the time to see if he found it."

"I think Cathy had other reasons to get together with you today." Donna smiled. "But as for Jeffords, he's snoopy. I ask him to look for the file because it gives me an opportunity to keep tabs on him. I don't want him to start poking around without having an excuse to talk to him every few days. He needs to be on a short leash. And it gives me a chance to reinforce the story about the sale of the dorm."

Jack laughed, but it was a nervous laugh. He was grateful that Donna gave him some background, but felt uneasy knowing Jeffords was being manipulated. Donna read his look correctly and said, "Jack, we constantly have to make choices about what we need to do to protect people like your father. With someone like Jeffords, I just can't take a chance. When we first met him, I had a feeling he suspected this issue was beyond a building sale. I don't want him making calls to government agencies or even telling the administration of the university about this matter. By keeping him on a wild goose chase, I get to keep him busy and distracted, and I can keep an eye on him."

"I get it," Jack replied. The gravity of the matter was becoming

162

clearer for him. "What can I tell Cathy about Jeffords?"

"If you feel she can be trusted, tell her the truth," Donna replied.

Jack was mystified. Donna was giving him more freedom in managing his communication with Cathy than he ever thought possible. "Thank you for trusting me. I know I screwed up before with things. It won't happen again."

"If you give a little to me, I'll give back, Jack. I'm here to protect your father. And now you."

"When do you think I can see my dad again?" Jack asked.

"I have no idea. He may be coming back to the States in a few weeks. If possible, we will try to arrange for you to see him. He would like that very much," Donna said.

"He would?" Jack sounded giddy.

"He'd like nothing more," Donna responded. "How is your mother doing?"

"She's fine. She seems a little stressed lately. She told me she may have to sell her practice."

"Why? I thought she loves what she does."

"She does. Apparently, there have been tons of finance changes in health care, and they're hurting her business. She's weighing her options, but I know none of them are what she wanted when she got into her field. She might buy another practice to share costs, but I doubt she'd be able to get enough money to do that. I don't know. I know I haven't been helping her much…"

"You know we've obviously had to look into her background, mostly to see who else might know that your mother had a baby. You should know that she has an incredibly good reputation. You should be very proud of her," Donna said.

"I am. Every now and then someone comes along and tells me how great she is at what she does. The older I get the more impressed I am."

"Any reason why she never told you about your father?" Donna asked.

"No. None that I can think of. And now that I know my father, he seems like a great guy… but I guess I really don't know him at all."

"You would be equally proud of him," Donna said. "Now you better get going. I'll be in touch soon."

NINETEEN

"What do you think?" Linda asked. Linda, Mary and Kenneth were standing in the storage area of the attic. Kenneth was pointing a flashlight toward the envelope that contained Jack's birth certificate and Mary was studying the flap.

"Linda, I really can't tell. I think if the envelope was forcibly opened, it would show in this section, you know, it would be rough here," Mary said, rubbing her finger along the front edge of the envelope flap.

"I know, but it's smooth, except for this one small area," Linda said, pointing to the center ridge of the flap. "I looked at it with a magnifying glass and there's this tiny spot that looks like it's been pulled open. But really, I can't tell. Dad, what do you think?"

"Don't ask me. Even with a magnifying glass, my eyes can't make that out."

"Well, whether he already knows about Stewart — or doesn't know — I've decided to tell Jack the truth about his father." Linda presented her declaration to her parents as though she was simultaneously attempting to convince herself the time was right.

"You know, I assumed this day would come, but we haven't talked about this for so long, it almost didn't feel real to me anymore," said Mary. "Do you want to tell him because you think he knows? Or because you genuinely think the time is right? I think you should really think about your motivations before jumping into anything."

"I know you're right. I have a lot on my mind about what's driving me. Yeah, part of it is that I'm worried Jack knows. And if he does, he'd be incredibly angry with me, that's for sure. He's been acting so standoffish lately. Irritable. And you know that's not who he is. I really don't know what's going on with him, or if it even has to do with this. I doubt it does. But who knows, maybe it does." Linda was mulling over her thoughts. Everyone who knew Linda viewed her as confident and sure, not prone to ambivalence or waffling. "But lately there's this tension between us," she continued. "I told him I might have to sell the practice and he jumped all over me, accusing me of keeping things from him. On the face of it, it's ridiculous that he would react that way. Absolutely absurd! It's like he latched onto that issue so he could attack for me another one. And it's not going away. That's why I think he might know about Stewart."

"Is there any other way he could have found out?" Kenneth asked.

"I can't imagine. He'd never have access to the people who know. And besides, they'd tell me if he ever got wind of it and approached any of them. No. Definitely not."

"There's one other possibility," Mary said. "Do you think there's any way that Stewart might have initiated contact with Jack? It's been known to happen."

A chill ran down Linda's spine. "Okay, Mom, now you're scaring me. No, I don't even want to think about that. Don't you think either or both of them would come to me if Stewart was reaching out to Jack? And let's not forget the main issue — how in the world would Stewart know he had a child? No. That idea is way too out there."

"Have you thought through how you're going to tell him?" Kenneth asked.

"I've thought about little else since I looked at the birth certificate a couple of nights ago. I'm just going to tell him outright."

"How do you think he'll handle it?" Mary asked.

Linda sighed. "As well as I think I know my own son, I haven't got a clue on this one. I could see this going all different ways."

Kenneth jumped in. "Two things are for sure. He's going to need a really good explanation for why you kept this from him all of these years—"

Linda cut in. "That's all I've thought about. I think I just need to be honest with him about that. And he'll either be understanding or furious."

"Maybe both," Mary said.

"Dad, what's the other thing you were going to say?"

"Jack is going to want to find his father," Kenneth responded.

Linda stared at her father, her face becoming pale.

"Linda, you look surprised. Don't you think that would be a natural reaction for someone who discovers he has a parent?" Mary asked, noting

Linda's ashen expression.

"I've considered it," she began, her tone pensive. "And I guess I'll have no choice but to step aside and let it happen. Jack's an adult now. He won't need my permission to go out looking for Stewart. He won't even need my cooperation. And if he's angry with me, I worry that I could lose him." Linda's eyes began to well with tears. "And you know what else... what if Stewart is upset with me as well? I've been keeping a child from this man for twenty years. He could be completely furious. And I wouldn't blame him."

"But we really don't know exactly how Jack's going to react, and we know nothing about how Stewart is going to react, or even if he'll actually end up coming back into the picture," Mary countered.

"I think it's incredibly shortsighted to think that Jack is not going to pursue this like a bull in a china shop," Kenneth insisted.

"Maybe. Maybe not," Linda said. "After all, it's not like he had a father who was in his life, and then, poof, he vanished. Stewart was nothing to Jack. I hate to put it this way, but he was nothing more than a sperm cell. Why would Jack become adamant about finding him? I'm not convinced. Look, I've thought about this. Naturally Jack will ask me lots of questions about Stewart. And I'm sure he will ask me where he is now and maybe even if he can see him. But I haven't spoken to Stewart since before Jack was born. It wouldn't be easy for Jack to track him down, and I'm sure once he sees how impossible it would be, he'd probably give up. I can't even remember where his family was from."

"Linda, I think you're seriously underestimating Jack on this," Kenneth said.

"You need to trust me on this one, Dad. I think once Jack realizes that we have no way to track Stewart down, he'll give up. I know my son."

"But Linda," Mary said, "Let's say Jack does want to find Stewart. What happens if he finds him? I get that you're worried that Jack might shift his allegiance to Stewart out of anger towards you, and while I don't see that happening, I understand your fear. But there's something I am worried about. What if Stewart has no interest in him? What if Stewart has a family and doesn't want to jeopardize it — or complicate it — with some kid he's never met? Jack would be devastated. He may be

166

devastated by what he discovers from you. Then he could be completely destroyed if things don't go well with his father."

"I still need to tell him. I owe him the truth," Linda said.

"I have an idea," Kenneth said. "Why don't you try to find Stewart first? This way you can see his circumstances, and then decide how best to deal with Jack about it."

"I agree with your father," Mary said. "The most important thing is Jack's welfare. So maybe you can find out where he is and what his life is like first, without having to talk to him," Mary said. "Once you see what's going on with him, you can decide whether it makes sense to talk to him before you tell Jack about him."

"Right. Makes sense. But, wow, I wouldn't even know how to begin looking for him! I wonder if he still works for Meredith Oil. I can always start by calling them."

"Good idea," said Kenneth. "By the way, one of the guys I play golf with — Ben — did some consulting work with Meredith. If you run into any problems getting information on Stewart, maybe he can help."

The following day, Linda searched Meredith's website and got the phone number of their main location in Houston. After being routed to the Human Resources Department, Linda asked, "Hi, I'm trying to track down and surprise an old college friend, Stewart Jacobson. Is there any way to find out if he still works there?"

"You know, we're not allowed to give out information about employees, but let me take a quick look," the Meredith representative said. Then after a few seconds of searching the employee database, "No, I'm not showing a Stewart Jacobson."

"Well, I guess I'm not surprised," Linda said. "We haven't spoken in almost twenty years. Do you know how long ago he left?"

"I'm really not allowed to give out any information. I'm sure you understand. But just to tell you, this database has every employee who ever worked at Meredith, and there is no Stewart Jacobson on the list."

"Are you sure? I'm positive he worked there. J-A-C-O-B-S-O-N?"

"Yes. I'm taking another look. No Stewart Jacobson. Probably one of the other oil companies."

"No, I'm sure it was Meredith. Well, anyway, thank you for checking," Linda said, stunned by the results of this conversation.

She called her father and told him about her phone call. "Dad, I'm positive it was Meredith. Stewart and I talked about the company all the time. He must have left a long time ago — maybe that's why he's not in their records. Do me a favor — please call your golfing buddy. Maybe he can find out when Stewart left and where he went."

About an hour later, Kenneth called Linda back. "This is the strangest thing. Ben did some economic forecasting for Meredith last year, and he knows some of the people in the finance department pretty well. He had them check about Stewart. They did a query on him and came up empty. I told him you were sure Stewart worked for Meredith, so he called back and asked if maybe Stewart wasn't in the database because he hadn't worked there in a long time. But every employee who ever worked there, no matter when they left, is on the main employee database. They said they could check one more place and would call him back. A few minutes later they called back and said they confirmed there never was a Stewart Jacobson at Meredith."

"This is completely absurd. Bizarre. Dad, Stewart worked for Meredith. Period. This is like some weird alternate reality."

"Well, who knows, maybe he used a different name at the company? I know you don't want to reach out to his family — then you'll have no choice about speaking to him."

"And not only that, I can't even recall the city he's from. I'll never be able to find him that way," Linda said.

"What about his college? Maybe you can find him through the alumni association," Kenneth suggested.

"That's a thought. But you know, if I can't find him, Jack won't be able to either. Maybe I'll just tell Jack about his father, and I'll tell him that I tried to find him but couldn't. Maybe it'll put an end to this whole thing."

"At least you tried to find him," Kenneth said. "What more could you do?"

"I really don't know what else. I'm completely overwhelmed at work, so I'm going to hold off for a few days, but when the time is right, I guess I'll have to just bite the bullet and tell him everything. You know, Dad, I never really thought I'd be in this position."

***

In 1991, Meredith Oil had opened new corporate headquarters in Houston. A towering complex of glass and steel, it created a dazzling shimmer that symbolized its premier status in the energy industry. Joseph Donnelly had been a research economist at Meredith since joining the conglomerate in 2001. He farmed out projects to consultants and was responsible for synthesizing the information and reporting it to his boss, Fred Lassiter, a company economist and primary liaison to the chief financial officer at Meredith. Most of the projects had to do with tracking reserve utilization rates and correlating them with spot market prices. Ben Frazier, Kenneth Davies' friend, had worked on a few projects for Meredith over the years, but had retired to western New Jersey to spend time with his grandchildren and play golf. On behalf of Kenneth, Ben asked Joseph to check if Stewart Jacobson was still working at Meredith.

The following day, Joseph met with Fred for their weekly standing meeting. After completing their agenda, Joseph said, "Did you ever know a guy named Stewart Jacobson who worked here?"

"Stewart Jacobson? Stewart Jacobson. Hmmm. I'm blanking. Why?" Fred asked.

"I had a call from one of our former consultants who felt sure Jacobson worked here, but there's no record in our database. I thought maybe Jacobson could have been a contractor who wouldn't show up in our employee system."

"Stewart Jacobson. Jacobson. Nope. Never heard of him," Fred said.

An hour later, Fred had a meeting with the chief financial officer of Meredith, Harvey Foster. As an officer of the corporation and a member of the board, Harvey was privy to the most sensitive and privileged information in the organization. After the meeting, as Fred was on his way out of Harvey's office, he wheeled around. "Oh, Harvey, by any chance do you know someone named Stewart Jacobson who supposedly worked here?"

Harvey's eyes widened. "Why are you asking?" he asked.

Fred recounted the story for Harvey. "Yes. The guy worked here, but he left several years ago," Harvey said.

"So why is he not showing up in the databases?" Fred asked.

"A few employees were set up on a separate payroll because it was easier to pay them through one of the offshore spin-off companies. All his records were transferred," Harvey said.

"Got it. Should I let Joseph know he can call the consultant back and at least let him know that he was right about Jacobson working here?"

"You said the consultant — what was his name, Ben? — was calling for someone else. Do you know who?" Harvey asked.

"I think Joseph said it was Ben's golfing buddy."

"Do you know Ben? Did you ever meet him?" Harvey asked.

"I met him once or twice. I have no real impression of him," Fred replied.

"Do you know his friend's name, and why he might need information on Jacobson?" Harvey asked.

"No, the conversation didn't get that far. But you seem concerned about all this. Why?"

"Fred, let's be careful about this situation. I'm sure it's harmless, but see if we can find out who Ben's golfing buddy is, and why he wants to find out about Stewart Jacobson."

"Okay. Should I have Joseph call him back?" Fred asked.

"No. Why don't you do it yourself? Find some pretext. Tell him you just spoke to Joseph and you thought you would call him personally to ask if he'd be interested in future consulting assignments. But be casual, and don't tell him Jacobson worked here."

"Why the secrecy about this?" Fred asked.

"Fred, I'm going to ask you to just do this my way. Jacobson was working on a couple of sensitive projects for us and I don't want to have a security breach on our hands. Let me know what you find out. And please take care of this ASAP."

A short while later, Fred went into Harvey's office. "I got the information on Jacobson," Fred said. "Ben said he was calling on behalf of his friend, Kenneth Davies. Seems Davies' daughter knew Jacobson a long time ago and was trying to reach him."

"Did he say why the daughter was trying to get in touch with Jacobson?" Harvey asked.

"I asked him about that. He said—"

Harvey cut him off. "Was he getting suspicious about why you were asking all these questions?"

"I didn't get that impression. After I asked him about future work for us — which, by the way, he turned down — we had a few laughs about how much Joseph can eat for lunch. So, it was just a friendly chat. Anyway, he said he had no idea why Davies' daughter wanted to find Jacobson, only that they were old friends."

"Ben has no reason to believe that Jacobson might have worked here, does he?" Harvey asked, in need of one final dose of reassurance.

"No. In fact, I told him we took one more look to see if Jacobson worked here and came up empty again."

"Thanks, Fred. I'm sure there's nothing we need to worry about."

As soon as Fred walked out of Harvey's office, Harvey made a phone call. "Greg, we may have a problem. It's about Stewart Jacobson."

Greg Saunders was executive vice president of government relations at Meredith. Harvey was asked to document the incident and forward it to Greg as well as to Meredith's CEO and the board chairman. Following a brief conference among the three, Greg forwarded the documentation to the FBI, which in turn forwarded it to the Defense Department.

TWENTY

Linda was acutely aware of an air of unease at her physical therapy practice. The staff were well tuned into what appeared to be an unfixable financial predicament. The practice was caught in a no-win situation and the staff were all feeling it. Over the years, Linda had observed with melancholy as small shops run by families — the grocery, the office supply store, the hardware store — found it impossible to compete and survive in an era dominated by giant department stores and chains. The phenomenon was now extending to health care.

Linda's staff could get jobs wherever they wanted. Not only were they well trained, but there was a shortage of therapists, and pay rates for skilled therapists were escalating quickly. They all knew the quandary Linda was in, and she understood that her staff might feel pressure to find other jobs if they were aware of an imminent sale of the practice. On the other hand, she knew that waiting too long to tell them would not give them enough time to consider their options. She spent a good deal of the day alone in her office. To her staff she seemed moody and distant, a sign to them that the business outlook had become more unsettling. On this day, however, she was preoccupied with the mystery surrounding Stewart. Unless she made some headway figuring out what had happened, she could not tell Jack about him. And she could not wait much longer because Jack's disposition, other than some moments of inexplicable gleefulness over the past couple of days, was not improving.

Linda stared down at her desk, a gleaming mahogany her employees had given her as a gift on the tenth anniversary of the practice. It produced a deep shaded reflection that would periodically capture her attention. This was often a welcome relief, however fleeting, from an episode of frenzy. Here was Linda's moment of irony. It occurred to her that she was surrounded by tons of information — her life was overflowing with mounds of paperwork and documentation. She could get her hands on information about any of the thousands — maybe tens of thousands — of patients who passed through her doors. In not much more than a flash, she could also access every detail related to any of the thousands of regulations governing patient care. She had virtual dossiers on every employee who ever worked there: their names, addresses, work histories, schools and training centers attended. But about the one person on earth with whom she created a child, she had nothing. Nothing! Until now she had worked on this project quietly and behind the scenes. She dismissed her father's suggestion about contacting the administration of the New England Institute of Technology. For sure that would be a dead end, she thought. It was too long ago, and the university was unlikely to keep track of where Stewart was twenty years later. Linda's anxiety about talking to Jack about his father was peaking, and it was made all the more intense because of the utter madness of the situation involving Stewart and Meredith Oil.

Amanda Roberts had been working for Linda for about two years. She was a physical therapy assistant and, at Linda's urging, was working toward her degree in physical therapy. In fact, Linda had been paying part of Amanda's tuition in exchange for a promise by Amanda that she would work for Linda for at least three years following graduation. Linda called Amanda into the office.

"Amanda, I want to talk to you about something," Linda said, her eyes intently focused.

Amanda settled nervously into a chair opposite the desk. "Is the practice in trouble?" she practically blurted. "Everyone is worried about it, Linda."

Linda laughed, easing the tension of the moment. "Yes, the practice is in trouble. And I'm working on that. But I need to talk to you about something else."

"What is it?" Amanda asked.

"Amanda, I've known you a couple of years. Patients love you. They trust you. I trust you as well. But I must ask you to promise me that what we discuss today stays in this room. Promise?" Linda asked.

"Of course."

"Your brother is a police detective, isn't he?" Linda asked.

"He was actually promoted a few months ago to captain."

"That's great. Where does he work? Isn't it on the west coast?"

Linda asked.

"In San Francisco. Hey, Linda, are you in some kind of trouble?" Amanda asked.

"No. It's nothing like that. But I may need a little help looking into something," Linda replied.

"Do you want to tell me about it?" Amanda asked.

Linda's demeanor shifted from grave to pensive. "I really didn't want to discuss this with anyone. At least not yet. But I need some help. It has to do with Jack. When I got pregnant, I told everybody that I was artificially inseminated," Linda began.

"I know. You mean, it's not true?" Amanda asked, tentatively.

"No, it's not," Linda continued. This was the first time she was revealing the truth to anyone in twenty years. She felt an odd detachment from the words as she spoke them, as though she was speaking about a predicament that was not hers. "I was sort of seeing this guy. He was very nice. Actually, a real terrific guy. He had just gotten a job with one of the giant oil companies as an engineer. He was hired to travel all over the world, looking for new sources of oil. It was very clear his job was going to be the main priority in his life. To make a long story short, I got pregnant, and things ended."

"He ran out on you?" Amanda asked.

"No. It wasn't anything like that. He left this area right after I got pregnant. He went overseas. We wrote and called each other a few times, and that was it. I wasn't even aware that I was pregnant for the first couple of months. He never knew he had a baby."

Amanda paused. "You didn't tell him? Why?"

"In retrospect, I should have. But I didn't. Anyway, now I'm trying to get some information about him," Linda said.

"Oh, my god. What's going on now?"

"Well, I'm not sure, but it's possible that Jack discovered that his father is not some anonymous donor, but a real person who was in my life back then."

"How did he find out?" Amanda asked.

"I think he may have seen a birth certificate with his father's name on it," Linda replied.

"Has Jack tried to reach him? Are you sure this guy is unaware of

Jack?"

"I've asked myself all these questions over and over. And I just don't know," Linda said. "But I do know it's time to tell Jack about it. My parents are convinced that Jack will want to find him. I wasn't so sure at first, but that was just wishful thinking on my part. Of course he's going to want to find him. So, I thought I should try to find him first, mostly to protect Jack. I would hate so much for Jack to spend time looking for this man, only to get rebuffed if he doesn't want anything to do with him. I have no idea what his life is like now. He very well could have a new family, and just not want to make room for a twenty-year-old."

"That shouldn't be too hard. I'll bet it's really easy to find someone by doing an Internet search or contacting the oil company he worked for," Amanda said.

"That's what I thought too, but, wow, was I wrong. I'm having serious trouble locating him. And that brings me to why I wanted to talk to you, because I thought maybe your brother could help. Stewart — that's Jack's father's name — worked for Meredith Oil when we knew one another. I called Meredith to see if he still worked there. Not only did they tell me that he doesn't work there, but they say he never worked there at all."

"Are you sure you got the right company?" Amanda asked.

"I'm absolutely positive he worked for Meredith." Linda was adamant. "Stewart and I talked about his job and career all the time. I had his business card with the company name on it. When I would call him, the receptionist would answer, 'Meredith Oil'. I know I'm right about this. My father knows someone who did consulting work there. He checked it out, and they told him there's no record of a Stewart Jacobson ever working there, though. I know it sounds like I'm crazy, but I'm certain — a hundred percent certain — I have this right."

"What do you make of it?" Amanda asked.

"I don't know! Maybe he used a different name at Meredith, or maybe he changed his name. But that seems too weird, and I can't think of why he would have done that. Something just feels off to me. And I have to find out what it is before my son goes out looking for some mysterious man somewhere. So, I thought maybe your brother could help me out. What do you think?"

175

"Let's call him," Amanda said.

Doug Roberts was a captain in the San Francisco police force. He had just arrived at work when he was told he had a phone call from his sister in New Jersey. Amanda told him she was with her boss, and Linda explained her story.

"Okay, what would you like me to do?" Doug asked.

"Is there any way we can locate Stewart?" Linda asked.

"There are all different ways to go about this. As a first step, I can see if there's any arrest record on him, any fraud record, name changes, aliases, social security number changes. This is routine. Give me an hour and I'll call you back."

About forty-five minutes later, Doug called Linda. "Sorry. Nothing came up on a Stewart Jacobson who would be in his early forties now. A few Stewart Jacobsons popped up in the search, but none anywhere near the age of the guy you're looking for."

"Thanks so much for checking," Linda said. "Are there any other options?"

"There are lots of things that can be done. But most involve talking to others, so it would no longer be just a private search. If you knew where he grew up or who his family is, that would help. Or if you knew what college he went to — they typically keep up with former students. If you want, as a next step, I can put out an inquiry to police departments throughout the country to see if they have any information on him. That might be a safe route."

"What's involved in that?" Linda asked.

"It's not a big deal — we issue a request for information on a police network. It doesn't mean the person is in trouble. A good deal of the time it means we just want to talk to a person who might be helpful in an investigation we're conducting. I'll need a description of Stewart. That might be the best next step. The only thing I need to let you know is that if I come across confidential information, I won't be able to share it or even let you know I found it."

"Okay, I guess," said Linda, a little unsure because it was dawning on her that this search was becoming more real and more open.

"What can you tell me about him?" Doug asked.

"Wow. Well, it's been about twenty years since I've seen him,"

Linda said. She had an image of Stewart etched in her memory. It was their final night together. It was dusk, and they were strolling through Rittenhouse Square, a charming park occupying one square block in the center of Philadelphia. The park felt larger than it was, yet more intimate, at dusk. The final rays of sunlight quietly streamed through the branches. Linda knew it could be her last night with Stewart, and she tried to memorize each facet of the experience and how he looked.

Linda's years of experience as a physical therapist provided her with enormous ease and skill at describing a clinical condition. But she felt helpless and awkward at Doug's task. "Let's see. Stewart was about six feet tall, he had blue eyes, attractive features—"

Doug cut in, "Any outstanding features: protruding ears, scar, birth mark... what about hair color?"

"No, there was nothing especially distinguishable about him that I can think of," Linda said.

Doug asked a few more questions, and he entered information provided by Linda into his system. After a few minutes he said, "All right. Here's what I'll put out on the network. For now, we'll keep it simple. Jacobson, Stewart, possible paternity suit. Early forties. Engineer. Expertise in oil exploration. Last known employer — Meredith Oil, 1980s, 1990s. The New England Institute of Technology. Physical description is from complainant who last saw subject approx. twenty years ago: six feet, Caucasian, blue eyes, moderate build, light sandy hair, fair complexion, no outstanding features."

"So, what happens next?" Linda asked.

"If any of this rings a bell out there, I'll be contacted," Doug responded.

"Thank you for everything," Linda exclaimed, relieved that something — anything — was being done, but also not terribly hopeful.

"Let's keep our fingers crossed. Talk to you soon," Doug said.

TWENTY-ONE

About two hours after Doug put out the information bulletin, he got a phone call and was instructed to take the call on a secure line. Donna Hoverdale was on the other end, livid. After explaining that Stewart's identity was a confidential matter with the Defense Department, Donna demanded, "Tell me exactly what was discussed."

Following his recounting, and Doug's apology for letting his intention to help his sister's boss blind him to the possibility that the matter might not be routine, Donna asked, "Are you sure Linda said her son discovered his father's identity?"

"She said it was possible. I don't think she said probable," Doug replied.

"And you're certain that the son didn't prepare or advise his mother to do this?" Donna asked.

"I can only go by what she told me," Doug responded.

"Do you believe she is prepared to go other routes to get information about Stewart?" Donna asked.

"For the moment, I doubt it. I think she'll wait to see if I come up with anything," Doug asserted.

"Obviously, if she calls, tell her you've come up empty. We'll handle it from our end. I need to have a few conversations here first," Donna said.

"Let me know if I can help you with anything," Doug said.

Donna immediately convened a meeting with the Defense Intelligence Agency officials involved in the case. Julius Gold and Emmett Cosgrove were with a DIA detail responsible for domestic security management of overseas agents. Deirdre Rothstein was an attorney, and Carl Hodges was Donna's supervising agent. The group's job was to perform a risk assessment. There was some good news: local police departments rarely pay much attention to paternity suit matters unless violence is involved. Also, there were no photos, and the complainant offered a description that was twenty years old. Not only was it going to be perceived as outdated, but it could evoke a 'why bother' response from anyone who saw it. The bad news was that Stewart Jacobson's name and occupation were spread all over a national police network. There could be no guarantee that the report wouldn't metastasize to other information networks.

Multiple contingency strategies were in place for dismantling the A.W. Kassing consulting group and providing an exit cover for the team. The most desirable was the natural phasing out of the group, which was scheduled to occur in ten months. Of course, a blown cover would require a more urgent and immediate dissolution of the group. At the meeting, Donna suggested they wait a day or two before finalizing a decision to trigger an exit option.

"Where's Tom on this?" Carl asked.

"I couldn't get through. The software on our secure lines is being updated. I'll be able to reach him in about two hours," Donna responded.

"What about Linda Davies? What's your recommendation about her?" Carl asked.

"I'll speak to her. There's no way to avoid it. I just don't know if she started looking for Stewart because her son told her about this. I want to speak to him first," Donna said.

"But don't you think he would have told her to lay low on this?" Emmett asked, stating the obvious.

"Yes," Donna replied. "But who knows what she may have done on her own. She might have thought getting the police involved keeps it safe. I have no idea. Besides, she's his mother. Maybe she thinks if she goes through the police, her son would be protected from danger. But no matter what, if he told his mother, I'll be furious."

Carl was stern. "You should be furious, Donna. You trusted him. Against my better judgment."

Eight thousand miles away, another discussion was taking place. "Tom, can you spend the afternoon with me?"

"Rafiq, today?"

"My friend, yes, it is urgent. I have taken the liberty of making travel arrangements for you to meet with Olaf and me in his office. I'm en route now."

Two hours later, Tom was on a chartered plane headed from Germany to Norway. Two hours later, he was in Olaf's office. Rafiq looked grim. "Tom, early this morning one of my colleagues stopped by my office and asked if I attended The New England Institute of Technology. I mentioned that I did, and then he asked if I knew of a Stewart Jacobson. I said the name had a slight familiarity to it, but I couldn't place the individual. Why? I asked. Obviously, we monitor as much information as possible that has to do with the security of our oil industry. Stewart Jacobson's name came up on a police report in the States. He was identified as an oil exploration expert who attended the New England Institute of Technology and worked for years at Meredith Oil. Because of our long-standing ties to Meredith, the report was sent via email to a handful of our ministers. One of them knew Stewart Jacobson, and it seems he was a well-respected engineer at Meredith. Then, one day, he dropped off the face of the earth. Now, the police in the United States are looking for him. We become nervous when somebody just disappears. It has been our experience that the person resurfaces as a spy."

Tom looked shell-shocked. "I don't know a thing about this."

"This news is brand new, just from today," Rafiq said.

"I haven't been informed of this by my colleagues," Tom said.

Rafiq asked, "Tom, do you know anything about this? How such a story would come about?" Before Tom could answer, Rafiq advised, "You must find a way to quickly vacate your operation. Once there is suspicion, it is difficult to quell."

"I have to say, I'm shocked about this. But okay. I'll have to figure this out with my colleagues. I'm not in a position to decide what to do. Do you have a copy of the report?" Tom asked.

Rafiq nodded and handed the report to Tom. "A paternity suit?" Tom gasped. "How in the world—?"

Rafiq cut him off. "A planted story, I'm sure."

"Do you have any idea who would try to expose you?" Olaf asked.

Tom was quiet, his lips pursed. "There is someone I need to protect. I don't know if this is related to it, but there is someone who could wind up getting hurt. And I've got to make sure that doesn't happen."

"Look, Tom, I'm sure there is much you cannot tell us, but—" Olaf reacted with a hint of uncharacteristic impatience, but Tom cut him off.

"This one may be tough to believe, but the person I need to watch out for is my twenty-year-old son who I never knew I had until a few weeks ago," Tom revealed.

"What?" Rafiq reacted. "You didn't tell me you had a child."

Tom knew he needed to explain, and he was among friends. He smiled, and it had the effect of reducing the tension in the room. He took pleasure in telling the story to these men. He had known Olaf for several years and had a deep respect for his integrity and intellect. Rafiq re-entered his life at its oddest moment, and after more than twenty years of separation he still had an abiding affection for him. His comfort with and admiration for these men enabled him to talk freely, and it was an opportunity to convey pride — albeit tacitly — about being a parent. A peculiar sensation had settled in: while he didn't feel like a parent, as he told his story, he recognized a protective instinct was beginning to form. As Tom finished his story, he asked, "What's your assessment of the risk?"

Olaf began, "I'm surprised you haven't had contact with your colleagues yet."

"Our security communications system back to the States is being upgraded, and our backup isn't reliable. Hopefully, we'll get in touch over the next couple of hours," Tom responded.

"If a photo comes out, you know you and your project will be in serious jeopardy," Olaf said.

"Honestly, Tom, I would love to put your mind at ease, but I am in no position to fully foresee the consequences." Rafiq sounded resigned. "The story may have been planted because your situation with Jack has leaked."

There was a knock at the door. Olaf's assistant poked her head in and indicated there was an urgent call for Tom. A line secured from the United States embassy was transferred into an anteroom adjacent to Olaf's office.

Tom took the call in private. Elaine was on the other end. "Tom, it's safe to speak. Our lines have been backed up. Listen, Donna called. We have a major identity situation going on," Elaine began.

"Yeah, I've seen a report about a paternity suit. Rafiq showed it to me," Tom said.

"The story is making some rounds," Elaine said.

"Apparently. The Saudis monitor police bulletin information. From what I understand it's easy to get. The oil industry expertise reference raised a red flag. Do you have any details on this?" Tom asked.

"Some," Elaine responded. "Turns out that Linda, Jack's mother, is trying to find you. She was in contact with a San Francisco detective—"

Tom cut her off. "San Francisco? Why San Francisco?"

"This detective is the brother of one Linda's employees. The story from the detective is that Linda thinks Jack may have found out about you and she wants to find you before he does. The detective put out an announcement on a police network. Donna doesn't know much more now. And she didn't know anything about Jack's involvement. As of now she was figuring out how to get ahold of him as soon as possible. Why are you in Olaf's office?" Elaine asked.

"Rafiq thought this would be a safe place to talk about the story," Tom replied.

"Donna is concerned. The team met. They need to find a Stewart Jacobson and issue a police report that he has been found. That should do the trick, but it has to be done pronto," Elaine said.

"Let me get a read from Olaf and Rafiq. I'll call you back," Tom said.

Over the past couple of years, Tom had amassed a wealth of information about the state of Russian oil technology. He had spent considerable time and effort tracking and detailing the status of the equipment the Russians use to find and extricate oil from underwater sources. He could identify water depth and temperature thresholds below which Russian equipment could not work effectively. He could identify salt densities that impair Russian capability to find more oil. He had documentation on many existing and planned technology upgrade projects. He knew their strengths and weaknesses. But he was not at a stage he considered appropriate to conclude the project. He was in the midst of documenting some of their new refining techniques, and this would be a premature time to walk away from the program.

"Tom, the most absurd aspect of all of this is that much of the Russian technology is easy to monitor without such secret measures. You would lose some ability to determine the relationship to defense, but you can probably fill in some of those gaps," Olaf said. "Do yourself a favor. Go home. Do what you enjoy without the risk, without the danger. This espionage business is not for you. It never was."

"I made a commitment, Olaf. I'm not about to abandon it unless I'm forced," Tom said indignantly.

"But now you may be forced," Olaf observed.

"I don't know," Tom muttered pensively. "Twenty years ago, we used to lose about seven percent of the oil we extracted to waste. That's been reduced by seventy-five percent. You know why? Because of all the technologies that engineers and scientists developed. Not because they're bad people who don't care about pollution. Because most of them are terrific, bright people who believe they're doing good things. The Russians are behind in these technologies. It's almost frightening how far behind they are. You know as well as I do, that we can pull up hundreds of millions of cubic feet a day of gas from over a mile underwater. The Russians have a long way to go. Understanding the technology gap is so important for us."

"All I'm saying, Tom, is there are ways of doing that without exposing yourself and others to risk," Olaf said.

"But what is your estimate of the risk?" Tom demanded.

"It's time for you to leave," Olaf said.

"What do you think, Rafiq?" Tom urged.

Rafiq had been silent. He hadn't been in the United States for many years. And there was something about Tom's presentation that rekindled the peculiar way he felt like an outsider while he was there. He had an image of Tom from twenty years ago as a risk taker for a noble purpose. But the purpose seemed naïve now, unlike twenty years ago when it seemed to Rafiq that Tom's rescue was heroic in both action and intent. Now Rafiq was feeling that his impression of Tom's deed that day was inflated by youthful idealism. He admired Tom, but felt that Tom, at this moment, reflected what he regarded as a distinctly American impulse to reduce the world to a brand of raw adventurism, stark in its black and white simplicity, right and wrong so easily framed as unidimensional opposites. Rafiq viewed his own world as bubbling with subtleties and fine lines. Survival depended on sensitive radar for reading nuances, for fashioning implicit understandings which housed seemingly mutually exclusive positions. Allegiance to the state could interfere with allegiance to religion. Politics, government and tradition were held together by some complicated definition of compatibility, and it took enormous work to sustain it. On the other hand, Tom's motive to aid his country seemed uncontaminated. He was not forced or pressured to do the right thing, let alone feel and think the right thing. It was hard for Rafiq to understand Tom's persistence with his mission in another way. He held Tom in high esteem, but it was impossible for him at this very moment to separate him from the culture that shaped him.

Rafiq thought for a moment. "Once there is suspicion, it is hard to subdue," he said. "Do your colleagues have a plan for responding to this report?"

"A police report will be issued indicating Stewart Jacobson has been found," Tom responded.

"How soon?" Rafiq asked.

"As soon as possible," Tom responded.

"If two days go by, we might be in trouble," Rafiq insisted.

"Why would the urgency be so great? This is about a paternity suit," Tom said, a slight impatience in his voice.

"To you it's a paternity suit. To us, it's about an oil expert who disappeared. When that happens, as I said, the person usually materializes as a spy," Rafiq said.

"Can you go back and spread the word that Stewart Jacobson has been found? Tell them the story was some minor issue. Make something up," Tom said.

"You are asking me to take quite a chance. If there was a report, I'd be happy to circulate it. But without a report that Stewart Jacobson had been found, and if it was later determined that I knew this man quite well, well, I needn't tell you what the punishment would be," Rafiq said.

Tom turned to Olaf. "May I use that secure phone again?"

"Yes, Tom. Please ask my assistant to put the call through for you."

Tom was able to get through to Donna in Washington, D.C. "Donna, I spoke to Elaine. Is there anything new? Have you spoken to Jack or Linda yet?" he asked.

"Not yet, but I'm working on it," Donna replied. "Any news on your end?"

"I'm sure Elaine told you that the story is making its rounds in the Saudi ministry. When will a police update be issued that Jacobson has been found?" Tom asked.

"That's all taken care of. The information will be on the police network tomorrow," Donna said.

"Tomorrow? Any chance it could be handled today?" Tom asked.

"I don't know. I have to see if the same detective in San Francisco can arrange it. Isn't tomorrow soon enough?" Donna asked.

"I don't know. Rafiq doesn't want it to wait. He believes it takes very little to stir suspicions, and once out there they don't die quickly," Tom said.

"I'll see what I can do. Talk to you later," Donna said.

Tom returned to Olaf's office. "The update that Jacobson has been located will be in tomorrow's police report at the latest. But they will try to expedite."

"Good," Rafiq said. "Let's hope that will put an end to this matter."

Olaf volunteered his opinion: "Tom, no matter what happens with this story, I still believe that you should conclude your mission. You've done enough, and there is no point in continuing this effort. Especially if you have any desire to become a part of your son's life."

"That's a separate matter, and what happens with him won't be affected by my mission here," Tom said. "I can't just abandon what we've begun."

Rafiq wanted to be helpful. But an underlying frustration was beginning to surface. "You know, I cannot help but think back to my days in the States. There's something about the country that makes people believe they need to save the world. But you have an opportunity to make a new start for yourself, and to have a relationship with your son. You should take that chance with him. How much more do you hope to gain by continuing on?"

"Look, Rafiq. I appreciate what you're saying, but any relationship with Jack will happen whether or not I stay here and finish my job. Don't you believe in the work that you're doing for your country?"

"I do. Of course. But we are a tiny speck trying to survive." Rafiq stood up and walked over to the window. "Tom, you know how much I admire you. I never forgot what you did for me all those years ago, you know, when you rescued me from that situation with Hobst. It has been a source of inspiration for me. I spent several years in the United States. It was a fascinating experience, and I came to appreciate the people immensely. But there are such great differences between the cultures. I live in a place where traditions go back thousands of years. Relatively speaking, your country is brand new. It may be difficult for Americans to understand the importance of a national history that is so extensive."

"Our history is definitely not as lengthy, but its founding ideals are based on inclusion and bringing rights to everyone. It's definitely not perfect, far from it, and many people still don't reap its benefits. But in the country's heart, I do believe that the goal is for all of its people to experience opportunity. I hope that one day more people benefit from its principles. It would be enormously gratifying if I could promote those goals through my mission."

Rafiq smiled at his old friend. "Your youthful idealism is what connected us in the first place. I am proud you have not lost it. I sometimes worry I have lost mine. Tom, I first came to the United States to attend college. I was terribly nervous in my first few weeks. Not because I couldn't handle the work. But because I felt I would never be fully trusted. As a result, I felt I would never truly fit in. You were one of the few people I met who never placed a barrier between us because I was from another place. But even more, you took a risk to protect me all those years ago in Hobst's class. Why was I worth it? I thought about it all these years. Because you are able to see past differences to do the right thing. The moral thing." Rafiq hesitated, then continued, "Today I feel ashamed because I'm not prepared to take the same risk for you."

"By not saying Jacobson's been located? Don't be crazy. You have a family. Back then I had no family to worry about. And what was the worst that could've happened to me — suspension? No, I could never ask you to fabricate a story now. A suspension pales in comparison to the consequences you'd face," Tom said.

"Gentlemen, I must intervene," Olaf said. "Tom, we have to get you back to your office."

"Rafiq, before I go, how is your son?" Tom asked.

"Unfortunately, the situation is growing more dire. I fear I have lost him completely. His radicalism has become overwhelming. He spends much time away from us, and we are certain that he is affiliated with groups fomenting violence. My wife is filled with despair," Rafiq said.

"Is there anything you can do?" Tom asked.

Clearly sullen, Rafiq said, "There may have been an opportunity shortly after our daughter's death. We misread his appearance of normalcy for, I guess, normalcy. As a result, we grieved without bringing him into our grieving. We erred drastically. His sadness turned to anger. He needed someone or something to blame. He found it. He hates the world, and maybe he even hates us. I don't know. I don't want to give up on him, but I don't know what we can do."

"Perhaps you can send him elsewhere for a while," Tom suggested.

"We thought about that. Now he disappears for days. We are losing even our ability to communicate with him," Rafiq responded.

"Maybe someday this episode will be behind you. Perhaps one day our sons will meet," Tom said.

Almost as if to complete his sentence, Olaf said, "I pray it will be in a climate of peace."

TWENTY-TWO

Donna and her colleagues had been trying to reach Jack for two hours. Now she was driving through Delaware, halfway between Washington, D.C. and the library in New Jersey where Jack was to have been working. However, she learned from his supervisor that he had called in sick. His phone was not receiving calls. Time was of the essence, and she had to talk to him before she spoke to his mother. The detective was convinced that Linda would let the police report run its course before she took further action to find Stewart. In the passenger seat beside Donna were three mobile phones. One looked like a version of a walkie-talkie device, set to a frequency that was impervious to eavesdropping, enabling safe communication with colleagues. If one of her partners had gotten through to Jack, she would have been contacted.

Donna's mind was a perpetual to-do list. She had always been this way. Donna Alweather grew up in the San Fernando Valley of Los Angeles. Her father was a police officer with the Los Angeles Police Department. He worked in the homicide division. Her mother spent her life worrying that bad news would come any day. Growing up, Donna was fearless. Swimming and diving were popular activities for kids in the Valley, much like soccer was on the east coast. At seven, Donna was diving with twelve-year-old's, doing somersaults from a twenty-five-foot board, giving Donna's mother something else to worry about. Donna was popular and bright. Her lone fault, if it could be called that, was impatience. She was forever prodding her friends to do this or that — take a job, take a class, learn a craft, join a club — incessantly choosing motion over deliberation. Her patience was tested most when friends wanted to 'hang out'. It seemed to her a form of social aimlessness.

After high school, Donna entered the University of California, Los Angeles. She knew she was destined to enter law school or work within the criminal justice system. She was acquainted with several people who worked for the FBI through her father, and she was intrigued by the combination of action and problem-solving and the methodical nature of the work. Law was appealing but, she thought, there was too much talk. So, she went the criminal justice route.

Following college graduation, Donna did an internship at a regional FBI office. It was mostly note-taking, filing, and transcribing, but the experience was great. Donna was happy to learn from the bottom up because she was able to discover how things really got done. She earned a reputation for having a quick and agile mind. There, she also met Cyrus Hoverdale, an FBI agent assigned to narcotics trafficking. Eleven months later they were married in a small church overlooking the Pacific Palisades, just down the coast from Malibu. Four months later, Cy's sting operation went south, and Donna was a widow. His death added a tinge of hardness to Donna that, although it softened over the years, never completely dissipated.

The following year, Donna became an FBI agent. Assigned to desk work, she handled mostly white-collar corporate crimes. Periodically, she went overseas to examine foreign accounts as part of broader efforts to seize assets of corporate bigwigs who were hiding embezzled company funds from United States authorities. She became a familiar and well-respected presence in foreign embassies. The Defense Intelligence Agency recruited her to participate in the security management of agents working abroad. It was an exciting opportunity and Donna relished the idea of traveling, believing it might also yield some therapeutic benefit. As she rose in the ranks, she found herself traveling less frequently while directing the globetrotting activity of her subordinates.

Donna was not pleased when the Stewart Jacobson case came her way. To begin with, Stewart was completely inexperienced in the ways of gathering intelligence. He was an expert in a highly technological field, and when she was first briefed on the assignment, she feared he would lack discretion and finesse in managing relationships in a world of secrecy bubbling with complex and clandestine motives. Moreover, what fun would there be in gathering information about the Russian oil industry? Donna believed that the United States could get the same information simply by using other, less covert strategies. But Defense had the notion that surveilling Russia's oil extraction technology would be one more means of understanding the state of their military technology. A waste of money, Donna thought. Thus, when the assignment was handed to her, Donna felt she had a high-risk project leader in Jacobson and a low-payoff project potential. What a crummy deal.

To her surprise, Donna took an immediate liking to Stewart. They met for the first time in a diner in a suburb of Portland, Oregon. Stewart was there for a six-month orientation period following his recruitment, and Donna stopped there on her way back from Japan to meet him. Stewart was the antithesis of Donna's image of a techno-geek, and Donna turned out not to be the hard-charging, no-holds-barred commandant that Stewart envisioned. They spent about two hours in the diner, and Donna had to leave to catch a plane back to the east coast. Romantic relationships between people in superior–subordinate roles were prohibited, and relationships among colleagues were frowned upon, so Donna did not really consider Stewart a prospective love interest. And, as Donna learned at the end of their meeting, Stewart had been engaged to be married, but it had come to a bleak conclusion, robbing from Stewart, it seemed, an inclination to be in a committed relationship.

Throughout their time together, Donna had developed a special affection for Stewart. She respected his willingness to take a huge risk for his country. It wasn't simply that he would take an assignment as an undercover agent in which physical danger was possible. In fact, from Donna's perspective, the physical risk in this situation seemed minimal. After all, Stewart and his group would be consulting with various companies in Eastern Europe, Norway and Russia, and all the while attempting to glean information, some of which was virtually available to anyone with Internet access. The real risk, as she saw it, was to give up a life and career with no opportunity to return to either. For all intents and purposes, Stewart Jacobson would cease to exist. Tom Gaines would be created, a new person with a new identity, a new history, sporting his very own expiration date. Once Tom's work was completed, someone new would be invented. It wasn't the risk that Donna admired, it was the sacrifice.

Now, Donna thought, here she was driving to see Stewart's son. They were all faced with a situation no one could have dreamed up. Here were these innocent people in the middle of New Jersey, Donna thought, having stumbled into a set of circumstances with precarious international ramifications. Just like Alice when she fell down the rabbit hole, Donna mused.

Just then, one of Donna's phones rang. She could see Jack's phone number on the caller ID. "Jack, finally," she said, assuming her default tone of seriousness.

"Hey, is everything all right? I saw you called a lot of times, but the calls weren't getting through and I couldn't get a call out," Jack said.

"Where are you?" Donna asked.

"I'm on my way to see Cathy," Jack said. "What's going on? Is everything okay?"

"No. How quickly can you make it back to your area?" Donna asked.

Jack felt a rush of panic. "About an hour."

"Turn around and head back," Donna said, her voice resolute in that hard, controlling demeanor Jack knew was never more than a hair's breadth away. "Call Cathy and tell her you have to cancel. I'll meet you in the college parking lot." Donna's tone was tough and direct, too direct for Jack's comfort, but, Jack realized, it had lost some of its shock value on him.

"Can you give me a hint?" Jack asked.

"No. We'll talk when I see you," Donna said, and hung up.

Jack arrived back at the college fifteen minutes before Donna. His main fear was that something had happened to his father. Jack had no idea what his father did, although he understood it was somehow for the good of the country. But he had no clue about the details and knew quite well that he couldn't ask about it.

Donna's car pulled alongside Jack's. She didn't look happy. She motioned for Jack to get into her car. His anxiety was escalating.

He got into the car. As Donna handed him a piece of paper, she said, "This is a police report that is spread all over a national police network. Do you know anything about it?"

Jack quickly read it. "What? Oh my god! No! Of course not! I don't know anything about this. I swear. Where did this come from?" His heart was racing.

"Jack, I need you to tell me the truth about something," Donna

191

demanded.

Uh-oh. Jack had heard Donna utter these words to him before. And that time she had caught him in a lie.

"Jack, did you tell your mother that you know about your father?" Donna asked, her tone stern, controlled but with a fierce edge.

"No, Donna, I swear, absolutely not," Jack said, relieved that no matter what the problem, at least it wasn't because he told his mother anything about his father.

"All right. I didn't think so, but I had to check," Donna said, and as with the last time they had a conversation that began this way, the harshness in her tone began to ease.

"What's going on? Can you tell me?" Jack implored.

"It seems your mother is also looking for your father," Donna began.

Jack's eyes widened into a look of intense shock. "Really? Why?"

"Well, she thinks you're looking for him, actually. I'm sure you know Amanda, who works for her. Her brother is a police detective in San Francisco. Your mother contacted him to get some help finding your father," Donna said.

Jack was stunned. "How in the world could she know I was looking for him?"

"I don't know," Donna replied. "But I did need to hear directly from you if she learned any of this from you."

"Donna, I haven't been doing anything about this for weeks. Not online. Not on the phone. Nothing. Since the time I met him. And I never talked about him," Jack said.

"Well, something has given her the impression that you are looking for him," Donna said, encouraging him to consider possibilities.

"I have no idea. I've honestly been so quiet about this. I mean, well, I don't know... a few months ago when all the searching was getting to me, I may have said something about parental rights. But that was before I actually met him. Or met you. I've never said a word about him, though. I promise," Jack said.

"Well, we can speculate until forever. But we have to put an end to this. It's time to talk to her," Donna said.

"What do you mean?" Jack asked. "What are we going to do?"

"We're going to get her and talk to her," Donna replied. With that,

Donna shifted the car into gear and began driving.

Jack's throat tightened. He had envisioned multiple scenarios in which he and his mother discussed this subject. Ever since the day he was abducted and taken to meet his father, he had understood that the circumstances under which his mother would be informed could spiral out of his control. But he had never considered the possibility that it would occur around a crisis. And he had never considered that Donna would be involved in disclosing the story.

"How are we going to handle it?" Jack asked, his voice filled with nervousness.

"You'll go into her office. Tell her you need to see her for a few minutes outside. You need to be calm and convey nothing. We can't afford to have anyone's curiosity aroused, and we certainly can't afford to have your mother react in a visible way. Just tell her you want to show her something outside. I'll handle the rest when she gets into the car."

"But what if she's busy? What if she can't come out right away?" Jack asked.

"Find out how long it'll be. If it's a few minutes, tell her you'll meet her outside. Just don't stay in there with her," Donna affirmed.

"But what if she asks what it is?" Jack asked.

"Smile and tell her it's a surprise," Donna said, smiling slightly.

Linda's practice was about ten minutes from the college. Jack was surprised that Donna knew exactly how to get there, including one small shortcut off the main thoroughfare. During the ride, Jack probed about his father. Has any of this affected him? Is he okay? When would Jack see him again? As Jack expected, each answer came in the form of a polite but firm 'no comment'. Donna did acknowledge, however, that this police report could be troublesome, but said they were developing a plan to respond to it and were hopeful that they would be able to overcome this problem.

Davies Physical Therapy occupied a freestanding, two-story building off a main street just on the outskirts of Whistling Point. There were parking areas on both sides of the building. Each lot could accommodate fifteen cars. As Donna and Jack drove up, Jack noticed that the parking lots were only about half full, a good sign that his mother might not be occupied with patients. Donna parked in one of the lots, and as Jack got out of the car, Donna mentioned that she would wait for him there.

"How should I introduce you?" Jack asked.

"I'll take care of it," Donna replied.

Jack had been in this building what seemed like a million times. As a child, he would run up the wheelchair ramp that led to the front door from the parking lots and the street. As he walked up the steps now, it occurred to him that he hadn't been on that ramp in about ten years.

He whizzed by the receptionist with barely a hello and walked toward Linda's office down the main corridor. Her door was open. Linda was on the phone as she noticed Jack in her doorway, and she motioned for Jack to enter. Linda was talking to a supplier, complaining about a pending cost increase. Jack could see that his mother's plea was going nowhere. She's going to be in a crappy mood, he thought.

"Hey, what brings you here today?" Linda asked as she hung up, surprised to see her son.

"That didn't sound like such a promising call," Jack said, mortified about having to get to his point.

"You know, they're all starting to sound like broken records. 'Linda, I'm sorry, but I have no choice, if I don't raise my rates I'm out of business.' Yeah, and if your customers go out of business, then you're really out of business. Anyway, why the surprise visit? Aren't you supposed to be at the library?" Linda asked.

"Yeah. But hey, can you come outside with me? I actually do have a surprise for you," Jack said, unable to completely conceal his nervousness.

"Jack, are you all right? You seem a little uptight. Are you sure you're—"

Jack cut off Linda. "No, no, I'm fine. Just a busy day, a lot of running around. But can you spare a half hour or so?"

"Of course," Linda said. "Let me just let the front desk know I'm going."

As they left the building, Linda asked, "Which side is your car on?"

"Actually, we're going to a friend's car. Here, this way." Jack motioned to the right side of the building. He walked briskly, keeping ahead of his mother.

"Is everything all right, Jack? Your car okay? Who's your friend?"

"It's just over here," Jack said, pointing to Donna's car.

Before Linda could ask who Donna was, Jack jumped ahead and opened the front passenger door for his mother to enter. As she did, Donna extended her hand and introduced herself. "Hi Linda, I'm Donna Hoverdale."

Confused and taken aback, Linda shook Donna's hand and introduced herself. Jack was entering the back seat of the car, and Linda spun around toward Jack and said, "What's going on?"

Donna began, "Linda, I'm so sorry to do this to you, and ordinarily I would prefer to leave myself out of family matters, but there is a budding crisis with your family and you need to be brought up to speed."

Startled, Linda asked, "Are my parents okay?"

"Oh, I'm sure they're fine. This isn't about them. Do you mind if we drive while we talk? I don't want to have a discussion in the parking lot of your building," Donna said.

Linda looked at Jack, who nodded to provide comfort.

As the car exited the parking lot, Donna began the story that Jack had kept from his mother for what seemed like an eternity. In fact, it was well over a year since Jack began his search for his father. How could he possibly justify to his mother that he hadn't told her about it? For this, could he ever be forgiven?

"This is very difficult," Donna began. "But we have no choice. You initiated a police bulletin regarding Jack's father—"

"What!" Linda shouted. "How did you know? Who are you?" Linda spun around to look at Jack. "Jack, what do you know about this?"

Jack jumped in. "I know pretty much everything, Mom." Jack turned to Donna, knowing he had no choice about what to do next. "Hey, Donna, is it okay if *I* tell my mom the story up until the police report?"

"Sure, go ahead," Donna said.

Linda's head was abuzz, but there was one aspect of the situation that was glaringly clear... and equally bizarre: here was her son asking permission of a strange woman to tell her a story about his father.

"Mom, I've wanted to tell you about this for a long time, but I was scared. I accidentally found out that I had a real father, I mean a father who was not anonymous. I saw it on my birth certificate—"

Linda cut in. "I knew it. I saw that the envelope had been opened. That's why I thought you might have found out. When did this happen?"

"Mom, you'll have to believe me when I tell you that I wanted to tell you about this for the longest time." Jack knew he was about to ramble, so he just blurted it out. "Over a year ago."

"What? Over a year ago?" Linda asked, filled at once with shock, anger, hurt and confusion. "You've known for over a year, and didn't tell me?"

Donna interceded. "I'm sorry, I need to cut in. I don't mean to interrupt, and I know you two have much to discuss together, but I need to bring you up to date. This is a time-sensitive issue, and I've got to get back to my office as soon as possible. I work for an agency of the federal government. Stewart Jacobson works for the same agency. A few years ago, he was recruited to work on a special mission for us. A secret mission. When he agreed to do this, we had to give him a new identity. Naturally, we get very concerned when we think there is a security breach. It came to our attention that Jack was looking for his father. We intervened and arranged for the two of them to meet."

Linda turned abruptly to Jack again. "You met Stewart?" she blurted out, her voice uncontrollably high.

Jack nodded. Linda put her hand to her mouth, and she began to cry. Ever prepared, Donna handed Linda a tissue. Linda's cry quickly became soft, shifting instantaneously, it seemed, from anger or confusion to sadness. All of Jack's decisions and rationales over the long period of his search now dissolved into sheer regret. He should have told her, he realized. This is pain she should not have to bear. Jack reached toward her and placed his hand on her shoulder, moved by a desire to comfort her and trying to find some way to connect. For a moment it felt to Jack that everything that mattered to him — an innocent, unconditional bond with his mother — was lost. He too began to weep.

Linda turned to Jack. "Why didn't you tell me?" she pleaded.

He was stuck. Each time he had considered revealing his search to his mother — in his view, the right thing to do — he had given in to a calculation that compelled him to keep it a secret: he feared a loss of control over the process. But how could he say this, especially now, without intensifying her hurt?

"I don't know," Jack began. "When I found the birth certificate, I started to think about why you hadn't told me about him. I thought maybe he did something bad to you. Or maybe you guys broke up and you didn't want to ever see him again. I thought it would be good for me to find out a little about him before I told you about it."

"But over a year! Jack, over a year! You kept this from me for so long!" Linda exclaimed, her tears giving way to astonishment.

"It was all so strange," Jack said. "I thought it would be easy to find him. People find other people all the time. So, I started checking different sites. Pretty quickly things started to seem weird. Stewart didn't exist, his social security number—"

Linda cut in, "You got his social security number?"

"It's a long story, but yeah. But then when I went to check it out, I found that the number never existed. So, it wasn't as much a search for my father as it was solving this mystery," Jack said.

"But why didn't you tell me?" Linda persisted.

"Because if there was a problem between you and Stewart, then maybe you'd stop me from looking for him." Jack paused, then said, "And I guess I didn't want to be stopped." Another pause, then Jack uttered the words that stung Linda at the core of her relationship with her son. "Plus, Mom, let's face it, you clearly didn't want me to know about him."

A beat of silence ensued, then Donna got back to the business at hand. "Linda, the police report goes on a national police network. It gets monitored internationally. Bottom line: it created some suspicion about Stewart Jacobson."

"Is Doug Roberts aware of what's going on?" Linda asked.

Jack was amazed. In a heartbeat, Linda was able to switch gears, to move from the deeply emotional to the rational. It was extraordinary to Jack. His mother and Donna were not that dissimilar. But he also sensed for the first time that this outward shift from sensitive to task-oriented was not really a shift at all. There wasn't a subjugation of passion, but an emergence of what the moment called for. Both modes could operate simultaneously.

Things began to fall into place for Jack. He once saw his mother walk out of a patient care room with a bruise on her hand and eyes puffy from crying. The bruise looked fresh, and Jack asked where she got it. His mother told him about the patient she had just left. He was a twelve-year-old boy. He had a bright face and an infectious smile. He lost his left arm in a car accident about a year earlier. He was put on a therapy program to strengthen his right arm. Linda wanted to feel the upper limit of his hand strength, and she told the boy to squeeze her hand as hard as possible. That's how she got the bruise. It hurt, but it felt good to Linda because he was making progress. The boy came to Linda's facility twice a week for rehabilitation therapy. His mother told Linda that he didn't cry on those days. But Linda did, secretly, as she walked out of his room. Jack saw that his mother had to rise to the occasion, and as soon as she walked out of the room any number of situations and people would claw at her for attention. She might have to admonish a physician who ordered incorrect therapy, meet with a sales rep about a new product, counsel an employee on how to communicate more effectively with patients, or talk to an accountant about what seemed like the driest of matters. She could shift gears quickly; and a leader, Jack learned, could call upon wisdom to determine which gear was right for the moment. He had a new appreciation for his mother, and a better and more acute understanding of Donna.

"Yes. We've been in touch with Doug. He's issuing a follow-up report that Stewart Jacobson has been located," Donna replied.

"Will that take care of it?" Linda probed.

"We're not sure," Donna responded. "It's all a matter of timing. The quicker the report gets out there, the better. You put Stewart's college and where he worked in the report. That could be a problem because someone could look up his picture in a yearbook. God forbid this goes on, and people start circulating pictures."

"Donna, I'm so sorry. If I had any idea, I never would have done this."

"I know. No one is blaming you for anything. But the key now is to do absolutely nothing else. Is there anyone else you've discussed this with?" Donna asked.

"No. Wait. Amanda Roberts who works for me. Doug's sister."

"Just keep reminding her not to talk about this with anyone. Doug will avoid discussing it with her, and he'll just tell her that there's no news," Donna said.

Linda's posture eased. "What can you tell me about Stewart?"

"Obviously, I can tell you very little," Donna said. "He's one of the nicest people I've ever worked with. He became quite an expert in oil exploration. It's safe to tell you that because you already know his background. He's very well respected. Most of us get into my field and work our way up through the ranks. Stewart gave up a lot for his country. In a way, he gave up his career so that he could help his country."

"I guess I'm not surprised," Linda said. After a moment thick with silence, Linda asked, "Does he have a family?"

"Now he does," Donna said, smiling, pointing to Jack. "I know that's not what you meant. But he was quite taken with your son." Jack felt his face flush. He was surprised by how much pride that gave him. "No, he has no family. Stewart was engaged some years ago. From what I understand he had little luck with relationships before that. I know he came to believe his career would get in the way. And his job took him all over the globe. Literally. He'd spend six months on an oil rig in the Pacific, then five months with scientists testing alloys in Iceland. He met his fiancé in England at a conference on energy resources. She worked for a company developing applications of wind energy. Seems like an odd couple. But deep down, Stewart is a true environmentalist, and it showed in how he approached his work. Anyway, a couple of months into their engagement, Stewart got a call from a police captain to go to a hospital to identify her body. She was killed by a drunk driver in a hit-and-run. Needless to say, he was devastated. I didn't know him before, but it appears he's built some insulation around himself. You can't go through that kind of hurt twice."

Linda intuited that Donna was speaking from a personal place, but she didn't pursue it.

"What a story," Linda said. "What a life. I hope he's able to find happiness someday."

"I didn't know that about her. He didn't tell me. He said he would someday," Jack said.

Linda turned to Jack. "How often have you seen him?" she asked.

"Just once," Jack replied.

"Where? When?" Linda asked.

"A couple of months ago," Jack said. "It's a long story. I didn't get to see him for very long. Then he had to leave. He came here — back to the U.S. — just to meet me."

"I have to get back to Washington soon," Donna said. "Linda, Stewart's security, maybe yours and Jack's, depends on total secrecy. Your father's friend has made some inquiries to Meredith. He'll be told they have no records of Stewart."

Whoa, Linda thought. Who is this Donna? And who does she work for? It's amazing how much she knows. Jack couldn't help harboring a private smile — he'd been through this shock before.

"What about my parents? They'll ask if I know anything about Stewart. What can I tell them?" Linda asked.

"We discussed this at our meeting. We can't afford to widen the circle of people who are in on this. On the other hand, we know you and your parents are close, and they've been involved in helping you. Are they trustworthy people?" Donna asked.

"My parents?" Linda couldn't hide her shock at the question.

"Yes. Do you believe you can trust them?"

"How does someone answer that? Yes. Of course. About anything, but especially this. They're good people. And after all of these years, they've never shared anything about my pregnancy... or how it happened."

"I understand. But this is not a simple family matter. This involves national security," Donna said.

"They never even told my brother," Linda said.

"Why wouldn't you have told your brother?" Donna asked.

"I love my brother. But he's married, and I wouldn't want him to be tempted to tell his wife. That would put them in an awful, untenable position. Not that I don't trust them all. I just didn't want it to get back to Jack," Linda said.

"Fine. Then I am giving you permission to share this with your parents, but please make sure they know this does not go any further," Donna said.

"I promise," Linda said reassuringly.

They were nearing Linda's practice. "What next?" Linda asked. "Will Stewart see Jack again?"

"Yes. He very much wants to," Donna replied. "Much depends on how and when his work is completed overseas. We're not fully certain when and under what circumstances he can come back. I know you didn't wake up today thinking your life would change. Whether and how you and Stewart meet will be up to the both of you, depending on how his mission finishes."

"How will we be kept up to date?" Linda asked.

"I don't know. We'll be in touch when opportunity presents itself. I can't be any more specific than that," Donna said.

"I understand... I guess," Linda said, not sure whether she should even ask any more questions.

As they pulled into the parking lot of the practice, Donna asked Linda about her practice.

"I understand from Jack that you may be selling the practice," Donna said.

"I'm thinking about it. I'm weighing a few different options, none of which feel comfortable. The nutshell version is I either expand so I can distribute my costs over a greater volume of patients, or I have to get out. I'd love to expand, but I haven't been able to work out a way to buy this other practice I'm interested in. But I'm working on it," Linda said.

"Well, you have a wonderful reputation," Donna said. Then, smiling, she added, "We looked into it."

Donna parked, and Linda opened the door to exit the car. She turned to Jack, apprehensive about making eye contact. "We'll talk later, I suppose." She had a sad look, almost of resignation.

"Yeah, we will," he said. "I need to get back to the college to get my car." He too felt empty, drained.

Linda took a step away from the car, then turned and motioned to Donna to wait. Linda walked around to the driver's side. She bent down and leaned her head close to the open window. "Donna, I hope it's okay to ask you one more thing. Is Stewart angry with me?" Her voice was subdued, and she seemed, to Jack, defeated.

"Because you didn't tell him about your pregnancy?" Donna asked.

Linda sighed. "I never told him. I never told Jack. I completely understand if he's angry with me."

"I can't say for certain," Donna began, her tone pensive. "Since I've known Stewart, there have been many things he could have been angry about. Really angry. Things that would have made me furious. But I have never seen him get angry even once. I don't know where he puts it, or maybe he's just good at hiding it. Or maybe he just doesn't process things that way. I've never known anyone else like that."

TWENTY-THREE

Jack was driving out of the college parking lot when his phone rang. He saw it was his mother. He was anxious about talking to her but was also feeling relieved in retrospect that Donna was involved in how she finally learned the story of his search for his father. Jack stared at the phone, reluctant to answer, but did so on the fourth ring, just as it was about to go to voicemail.

"Hi," he said, his voice quiet and stern.

"Hi, Jack. Are you okay?" Linda asked, her tone soft and cautious.

"I guess. I don't know. I guess I don't know how I am. What about you?"

"In a fog. When will you be home?" Linda asked.

"I'm on my way home now. I need to make a few calls."

"About your father?" Linda asked.

The term "father" felt awkward to both Linda and Jack. Linda was going to say "Stewart," but it would have had a distant ring to it. But as Jack heard "father," it felt to him like Linda was sterilizing Stewart's relationship with both of them, as though Stewart's connection to Jack was predicated on a technicality.

"No, not really. Well, in a way, maybe. I'll explain later," Jack said.

"Only if you want to. I don't want you to feel any more pressure about this than you already have. I'll leave early today. It's slow around here anyway. We really should talk," Linda said.

"Yeah. Okay. I mean, good," Jack muttered, caught between apprehension and compassion. "I'll see you a little later."

Jack arrived home and immediately called Cathy. "Is everything okay? I thought something must've happened since you canceled," she said.

"I had an interesting meeting today," Jack said, deadpan.

"Who with, someone at the school?" Cathy asked.

"No, not exactly. And I really can't speak, but my mother and I had

203

a conversation today."

"Oh my god, Jack," Cathy answered, knowing full well she couldn't speak about it on the phone.

"And we weren't alone," Jack said.

"Oh, really," Cathy said, feigning nonchalance, a well-rehearsed practice on phone calls with Jack. "Maybe you can call me later, or we can set up some time to get together."

"Yeah, that would be great. I'll call you tomorrow before I go to work. Can I call you at eight?" Jack asked.

"Definitely. You know the number," Cathy said.

Jack hung up the phone and stared at it. He didn't know what to do. Shortly he and his mother would have a conversation that had been lurking in the wings for over a year, or maybe for twenty years. Well, at least he didn't have to break the ice, a daunting task he had assumed was surely in the cards. It was the natural outgrowth of the events, he reasoned. It had been at the core of his discussions with Cathy for months. *When will you tell your mother? How will you break the news to your mother?* There was never the thought that his mother would find out first, in some other way. It never even crossed his mind.

Now Jack's thoughts slalomed along an uncertain and inconclusive path. He could not understand why his mother hadn't told him about his father. Suppose she had told him when he was ten? What harm would there have been then? Even if he had wanted to meet his father, it would have been completely under Linda's control. Surely, she would have understood this. This deceit just didn't fit the kind of person she seemed to be to Jack. And he couldn't decide if he was angry. On the other hand, he was guilty of the same thing. Would she be angry with him, he wondered? To Jack, all the reasons for not telling her were like pieces in a puzzle, all adding up to a rationale that made perfect sense, and that was entirely justifiable. And it wasn't like he was never going to tell her. The right time simply had not found its way out of the morass. But his mother had kept her secret for his entire life. How could she explain that? he asked himself over and over. For now, he couldn't get a fix on how their questionable judgment calls were the same and how they were different.

Linda sat in her office, finishing off a letter to an insurance company

204

that had asked for details about a series of treatments that were not part of an original treatment plan. This would not be the most wrenching justification she would have to provide today, she thought.

Linda got into her car and started the ignition. She sat there, motionless, staring at the leaves fluttering in a soft breeze. Then she gripped the steering wheel with a ferocity not common to her temperament. As her grasp softened, her head dipped toward the steering wheel and she wept. How did this happen? How could her son not trust her? At least not enough to share his discovery? Could she blame him? After a lifetime of devotion, could one colossally dreadful decision wring the unconditional love and trust from the entirety of her relationship with her son? Would he hate her? The questions were painful and were speeding through her fast and furiously. Would he forgive her? He hadn't told her about the birth certificate. And he hadn't told her about the search. This was tormenting Linda. It was hard to believe that things would ever be the same.

Her crying became uncontrollable, more than at any time in her life. Linda had seen her share of despair — so many patients with lives turned upside down as a result of accidents. It's a despair that hits like a ton of bricks when the initial moment of clarity after a life-shattering event rings in the bulletin that nothing will ever be the same. And it hurts in a way no one else can imagine. And now Linda was hurting in a way she could never have imagined. She buried her face, hot and wet, into her hands, conscious only of her effort to contain her sobbing.

After a moment or two, her crying subsided, her wailing easing into spent sighs. She groped in the pocket of her blazer and found the tattered remnants of a tissue, hardly a match for the task at hand. Linda dried her eyes and caught a glimpse of herself in the rearview mirror. Her eyes were red, her face flushed. The lines on her face looked deeper. She felt ugly and insignificant. It was time to head home. At that moment she had no sense of how to initiate the discussion with Jack. Linda dabbed at the remaining wetness under her eyes and pulled out of the parking lot.

Jack was in his room when he heard the front door open.

"I'm home," Linda shouted, attempting to foster some semblance of normalcy.

"Be right down," Jack shouted back, his intention the same.

Linda was brewing a cup of tea when Jack entered the kitchen. "Want a cup?" she offered.

"No, thanks," Jack said, waiting for his mother to broach the topic that hung in the air like wet laundry. He sat at the kitchen table, gently tapping a pencil against it.

There was a pause filled with anticipation and anxiety. Linda sat down at the table, angled catty-corner to Jack.

"Jack, I'm a little lost with all this, and I don't know exactly where to begin," Linda began, her voice timid, a timbre that sounded unusual to Jack. "Are you angry with me?" Of all the bases for blame in the situation, the most severe belonged to her, and she began to understand it.

"I guess so," Jack said, looking away, the sting of his reaction mitigated by Linda's quivering tone. "Why didn't you ever tell me you knew my father?"

The question was right there, way at the beginning of the conversation. There was no building up to it for Linda. She had never before had the need to execute a confession. Her life had been a model of giving, of devotion. She viewed her sins as having been judgment errors, working too many hours when Jack might have needed her, firing an employee who might have benefited from a second chance. But there was nothing like this. Nothing in her experience had ever prepared her for this moment.

"Jack, for the first few years after you were born, this whole thing didn't matter. At least I thought it didn't. I adored your father. He was very special. But I knew early on that he was headed for a career that left no room for anything else. Especially me. After he left, I debated a thousand times about telling him that I was pregnant. I was worried that if I told him about the pregnancy and he wanted to be involved with you that it wouldn't be because of me. Look, I hoped that he would call or write. But he didn't. And I guess I just couldn't bear the thought of this man having a relationship with me only because of an obligation to a child," Linda said.

"But how would you know that would be his only reason? Maybe if he had a child, he would have wanted to settle down more. How could you possibly know?"

"I couldn't know. But it was clear to me — at or at least it seemed clear to me at the time — that he was absolutely destined to follow his career. Maybe it was faulty intuition on my part. Who knows? But I couldn't have it in my heart that I wasn't enough for him. Can you understand that?" Linda asked, her eyes swelling with tears.

"I don't know, Mom. It's just, how do you not let someone know they have a child? Isn't that the bigger issue?" Jack asked.

"Yes. And I see that now. And I've known it for years, I guess. But I didn't think of it that way then. About fifteen years ago I went to a counselor to talk about this. The counselor asked if I could find Stewart so that we could go to counseling together. I said that from the time I was pregnant I planned to raise you on my own. I explained the circumstances about Stewart's work and said I really didn't want to involve him. She was nice and sympathetic. She said that many women at the time were choosing to raise children as single parents. If I told Stewart, there would be the lifelong complication of custody — I mean if he wanted it — and who knows what else. On the other hand, I was even more afraid that he wouldn't want a child. Then you'd have a lifetime of disappointment. That became my greatest fear. Since he never contacted me, I thought I would probably never see him again. So, nobody gets hurt. You weren't going to have a life with him, and neither was I."

"But I wasn't going to have a life with him because *you* decided I wouldn't." Jack felt himself getting angry as the words were coming out. "That's a choice he should have had and maybe even I should have had."

Linda looked at Jack. His questions struck her as simple, not naïve simple, but dead on, right to the point. His line of reasoning was uncluttered, not buried under layers of emotional complexity that had confused and tormented her for a lifetime.

"Jack, I'm so sorry. I should have handled all this differently," Linda said, her voice almost pleading with him to understand.

There was a momentary silence. Here in the kitchen, the center of their home, the place unparalleled as a haven for Linda and Jack, here was a moment of chilling unease. Jack stood and walked to the refrigerator and realized as he got there that he could consume nothing. He turned toward his mother and leaned against the refrigerator.

"I read this article a few months ago about this guy who wanted to see his daughter whose mother had custody," he began. "They were divorced and really hated each other. The mother's lawyer somehow got the father to give up his visitation rights. The girl was eleven at the time. The father lived in New Mexico, and the mother took the daughter to Arizona. In the meantime, he remarried. After about a year, the daughter wrote to her father asking to see him. He then wrote to the ex-wife asking if he could come visit his daughter. The wife refused. The girl secretly wrote to him that she wanted to see him because she missed him and wanted him to be in her life. In her letters, she explained where he could pick her up at school. It would be their secret. She said she would never tell her mother or anyone about it. He never did that because he was afraid it would jeopardize his chances of ever having legal rights to see her. But, you know, I read tons of stuff about people who do just that, get together in secret. Anyway, it took over a year for the court to grant him a visitation permit. Over a year!" Jack walked back to his chair and sat down. "That's totally insane!" he continued. "One of the problems was that since the mother moved out of state all the records had to be transferred and one state had to decide how it would recognize the laws of the other state. It takes forever."

"Sounds like you learned a lot in the past year. I'm sure something like that can be devastating to a family," Linda said.

"Yeah. I can go on and on with loads of stories just like that," Jack said. "But the point is that here's a mother who kept a child from her father, and in this case the child and the father wanted to have a relationship. In my case, Stewart and I never even had that chance."

Linda put her hands to her face and began to cry. It wasn't an intense cry — her energy drained from the whole day. Jack sat and watched her. He couldn't bring himself to console her. He was angry and confused, paralyzed by the unwieldy synergy of the two emotions.

Linda looked up at him. "Jack, why didn't you tell me that you found the birth certificate?"

"I thought I would tell you about it every day. But, like I said in the car, I knew I would lose control of the whole situation. I was afraid I would lose the possibility of seeing him. I couldn't imagine why you wouldn't have told me the truth except that you didn't want Stewart in your life. If that was the case, I figured you'd put up roadblocks and I'd never find him. I realized that if he wanted to see me it would be easy. We didn't exactly disappear from Whistling Point. Rather than getting you involved I tried to find him on my own. I had every intention of telling you, but I needed to find the right time," Jack said.

"But you didn't even tell me once you did find him," Linda said.

"I know, but that wasn't my fault. I had to promise that I wouldn't tell you. Donna and the others couldn't let it get out. That could get Stewart into real trouble. They were very clear about that, and they told me on the day I met him."

"I guess. Yeah, I understand that," Linda acknowledged. "Are you still angry with me?" she asked.

"Yeah, I am," Jack said, more forcefully than intended.

"There's one thing you need to know. There was never a moment I regretted having you. That was always very separate from anything to do with Stewart being interested in me or a family," Linda said.

"I know. I know that's true, Mom. But still, I can't help thinking that I should have known I had a father. And Stewart should have known too," Jack said heatedly.

"I had always planned to tell you, Jack," Linda said. "Like you, I was waiting for the right moment. I didn't want to tell you when you were very young because I thought it really didn't matter back then. When you were very little, an infant, I always thought I would tell you before you turned ten. Then, when you were ten, I saw such an innocence in you. I didn't want to take that from you, or have you question yourself. How could a kid handle something like that? Then I thought I would tell you when you became a teenager. And on and on. Time just passed. It just never came up, and I thought, why rock the boat? Stupid? Yeah. Without a doubt. But as I said, I couldn't even dream that Stewart would become a part of your life, so why do something that would change things forever? But recently, I was planning to tell you. I had actually been talking to Grandma and Grandpa about it."

Jack cut her off. "They know about this?" Jack bellowed. Then just as quick, "What am I saying? It didn't register when we were talking in the car. Everything was moving too fast. But, of course, they know about this. Grandpa signed the forms on the medical record."

"What medical record?" Linda asked.

"Remember when I did the internship at the hospital? I was able to find the medical record from when I was born. That's how I found out that Stewart went to the New England Institute of Technology."

"How did you get the medical record?" Linda was astonished.

"Part of the internship was in the medical records department. Remember?" Jack asked, a hint of pride in his voice.

"Then you got in touch with the college? I would have thought that would be a dead end," Linda said.

"Yeah, but that's where all the mystery started. They had no record of a Stewart Jacobson ever going to that school. Then a few months later his name popped up on some housing record, and I was able to get his social security number. One thing led to another, and because he does sensitive government work, the government started spying on me."

"But I thought they took you to see him?" Linda asked.

Linda's question broke the tension and Jack laughed. "Well, *took* isn't exactly the word. It was more like I was kidnapped and—"

Linda cut him off. "Kidnapped! What do you mean?"

Jack described the entire episode, including all the details of the car chase. Linda sat listening, mesmerized, and as Jack saw Linda's worried look, he reassured her that he never felt he was in real danger. Linda, feeling relieved, asked what it was like to meet his father.

"It was the scariest moment of my life. In walks this guy who introduces himself to me as my dad." Jack was getting excited, and for the moment he forgot he was angry at his mother.

"Tell me about it," Linda prodded.

"I had no idea what to expect. It never crossed my mind that he didn't know about me. Never. I thought he just didn't want to have anything to do with me. Or with you. Either of us, I guess. Maybe both. I figured he was some asshole. Otherwise, why would you want to have nothing to do with him? That's what I thought, that you didn't want him in your life. I mean, with a year of looking and no success, I really built up some stories about him in my mind. Some made him out to be all right, but most were that he was such a terrible guy that you felt forced into making up the anonymous donor story. But right when we meet, he tells me that he just learned about me three days earlier, and he came here from some foreign country just to meet me. At this point nothing made sense. So instead of meeting some creep, I meet this smart, professional guy who's doing important work for the government. Not what I ever expected."

Linda cut in, "Doesn't surprise me."

"What doesn't surprise you?" Jack asked.

"That Stewart is smart and is doing important work, especially work that he believes is principled."

"And he remembered you," Jack said.

"What did he say?" Linda asked, trying to mute her eagerness.

"He liked you a lot. He remembered how you met at the hospital, and he even told me he was a jerk to you on that first day."

Linda laughed. "He remembered that? Yeah, he wasn't very nice. He practically kicked me out of his room."

"But he told me he really admired you. He said you were smart and cared about people. He said you had guts. He wasn't surprised that you were running your own business," Jack said.

Linda was taking it all in. "You know, you look a lot like him, Jack."

"Yeah. I thought that too, kind of," Jack said. "But neither of us said anything about it."

"How does he look? I can only think of him looking like, well, I guess, looking like he's closer to your age than someone in his forties."

"He's thin. Tall, I guess. He's in good shape," Jack said. He paused and smiled. "He still has his hair, and it's not gray."

"So, you have no idea what he does?" Linda asked.

"Not a clue. I've gotten to know Donna pretty well." Jack stopped and straightened up. "Wait. What am I saying? I actually don't know a thing about her, other than she works for the government. I mean I've now seen her a few times, and she hasn't let on at all about what Stewart does. It's a very one-sided relationship."

"I hope he's going to be all right," Linda said.

"Why didn't you tell me about Stewart once you thought I might have seen the birth certificate?" Jack asked.

"It was my plan to talk to you about it right away. But then I thought you might want to find him, and what if he didn't want you in his life? You could've been terribly hurt, and I didn't want that to happen," Linda said.

"But if I already saw the birth certificate, how would not telling me have helped?" Jack asked.

"That's a fair question. Well, for one, I wasn't positive that you saw the birth certificate. Either way, I was planning to talk to you. If you did see it… well, I don't really know. I just thought it would be good for me to find out what was going on with him before I told you. But I swear I was going to tell you," Linda said.

"You know what I can't understand?" Jack began, his voice growing stern again. "I can't figure out if you just didn't want me to have a relationship with my father. Before, you said that you wanted to see if Stewart was interested in you, and if he was then he could find out about me. But if he wasn't interested in you, then he wouldn't find out about me. It's like you put your own interest first," Jack said.

That stung Linda. "Wow. I never thought about it like that."

"But what other way is there to think about it?" Jack challenged, wanting desperately for his mother to produce an answer he could sincerely believe in.

"I only thought that once Stewart put his career ahead of a relationship, he would be involved with a child only reluctantly, and I wouldn't want that for you. I thought that would only cause more hurt. I saw that many times. I don't know if you remember Gypsy Rennata. I can't believe her real name was Gypsy. It sounds so strange to say it now. Anyway, she lived about two blocks from Grandma and Grandpa, but she moved away when you were about five. She babysat for you a few times. Maybe you remember her daughter, Raven? She was about four years older than you."

Jack shrugged his shoulders. "Nope. No memory of her."

"Gypsy wasn't married to Raven's father. The two of them met at some concert and lived together for a few years. I can't remember his name, but he would show up out of the blue maybe twice a year. His work involved a lot of travel. I think he used to install security systems in warehouses. So, when he was working on a project in the area, he would come by and ask if he could take Raven for the day. Gypsy would let her go, thinking, what choice did she have? After all, he was her father. When Raven was about seven, her father showed up and took Raven to a circus. Then he dropped her off at home. When Raven asked when he would come to see her again, he said he had no idea. Raven was devastated. She felt abandoned by her father, and she felt unloved."

"How do you know all this?" Jack asked.

"Gypsy told me. By the way, I never told her about Stewart — I told her the anonymous donor story. Anyway, she couldn't decide what to do, whether to try to get the father more involved or less involved. She went to therapy for it. The therapist thought that more involvement would be better. After all, that made sense. Gypsy tried to contact the father to work out a more regular visitation schedule with Raven, but he never even responded to her calls. In the meantime, Raven would ask about her daddy, and Gypsy never knew what to say. After a while she decided that the situation was too painful for Raven. So, she moved — she wanted to make it impossible for the father to simply come one day, once or twice a year, and expect to be a father for the day. It was way too heartbreaking for Raven."

"Is that why you never told me?" Jack asked.

"No. Well, maybe in a small way. I don't know. I could never get their situation out of my mind. It's not like I thought the same thing would happen. Stewart was way too responsible and way too decent to act like that. But I was afraid that maybe he wouldn't want to have a child. And even if he handled it better it still would have made life unbearable. Not for me, for you."

"I can't believe you're saying this to me. With Gypsy, that guy proved he was a scumbag. With us, it's like you're convicting Stewart before he commits the crime. Before he even knows there's a crime to be committed!" Jack exclaimed.

"It was the wrong thing for me to do, Jack. I know that. But it was very hard, heartbreaking, to watch that situation and not think maybe the same thing would happen to us," Linda said.

"But you just said you knew Stewart well enough to know he wouldn't do the same thing. It's like the story keeps changing."

"Jack, I wish I handled it differently. You have to believe me."

"I do. But I still feel like I missed out on something. And I'll never be able to get that back." Jack pounded his fist on the table. "I'll never get that back."

Linda felt crushed, devastated. This was not how it was supposed to be. The emotional turmoil was like a tornado inside her soul. She looked at her son and felt completely spent from guilt and sorrow. "I really am so sorry, Jack."

TWENTY-FOUR

Jacobson, Stewart. Deceased. Complainant Notified.

"Thanks for taking care of this so quickly, Doug." Donna hung up the phone. Now she had to see to it that this police report update would be properly circulated. A copy of the police report was transmitted to Olaf and Rafiq.

"Thank God," Rafiq sighed to himself. He sent the report as an email attachment to several colleagues along with the following note.

Yesterday, I was informed that a former classmate from the New England Institute of Technology may have been a party to a paternity suit in the United States. Some concerns were justifiably raised because of his early employment affiliation with Meredith Oil. Though I knew Mr. Jacobson only briefly and quite casually, I was saddened to learn today that he has died. A shame — he would have been in his early forties. In any event, I wanted to inform you that this police matter in the U.S. is now closed.

A few thousand miles away in the office of A.W. Kassing, Tom Gaines and Elaine Corrigan were reviewing the status of their operation.

"Look, Tom, you have to decide how much longer we need to keep this going."

"Elaine, I can't complete the final report until we can substantiate whether the Russians' new alloy will work."

"But you know it will work at thousand-foot depths."

"But I don't know the threshold effectiveness level at greater depths... if it'll work up to three thousand feet. We need to know that."

"Tom, everyone agrees the timing is such a minor point. If we don't know it now, we'll know it in a year. Maybe even before that. If the Russians think the alloy will work, you know damn well they're going to start manufacturing it, probably no more than eight to ten months from now."

"Yes, of course. Elaine, we've been at this for four years. Their technology will be upgraded by an entire generation if this works. If the U.S. is going to remain competitive on deep-water drilling, the sooner we know, the better. And you know it."

"Absolutely. But I'm worried about the potential fallout from Jack and now Linda. Now that there's a report making the rounds that Stewart Jacobson died, the heat should be off. Hopefully. But Jack and Linda, who knows how they will handle all this? They're not used to this stuff, Tom, and you can never be completely sure that they will be discreet. It's not that they don't intend to be careful. I have no doubt they want to be, but look at how Jack talked to the NEIT girl—"

Tom cut her off. "Her name is Cathy."

Elaine was growing adamant. "Sure. Cathy. Very sweet. C'mon, Tom. The point is, how can we be sure that Jack won't speak to anyone else? Or that Linda won't? Or Linda's parents? Or Cathy?"

"You're right. I know you're right. But I still think I can trust them."

"Trust them?" Elaine questioned, incredulously. "Linda didn't tell you she had your child. Now we should trust them?"

Tom wasn't used to seeing Elaine pontificate with sarcasm. Elaine was a genuine risk taker, but despite the magnitude of the risk, she was always meticulous about maintaining the proper safeguards. Trusting five innocent bystanders with matters of national security and the team's welfare fell outside her safe zone. And Tom was conflicted because her unease was completely understandable.

"Yeah, I don't know what to make of that. There's nothing about her that would lead me believe she would have been deceptive. I'm not excusing her, believe me, I'm not. But let's face it, the situation between Linda and me was a two-way street. Maybe I did something to scare her off, to make her believe I wouldn't be around for a child. Or that I wouldn't be around for her, for that matter. I made it quite clear that I was going headstrong into a career that took me out of circulation. I never even called her."

"I'm sure there's merit to what you're saying. And I appreciate that you're owning up to your share of the responsibility for what happened back then. But right now, today, we're facing a dangerous situation.

There are at least five people back in the States who believe that Stewart Jacobson has become a spy. They are not used to the sort of things we do. They are nice people, Tom, regular people. And they're completely wrapped up in you emotionally now. I'm sure they're unconditionally committed to maintaining confidentiality. No one doubts their intentions. But how can you be totally sure that a situation won't arise that would make one of them talk?"

"Jack is my son. I'm going to trust him. And I know Linda well enough to believe she can be trusted. And with patient records and malpractice issues, she deals with confidentiality as much as we do."

"Maybe it's more than trust, Tom. Don't you think it's unfair to them that we are putting them in this position?"

"Of course it's a burden for them. But it's not forever. This will all be over in a few months. In the meantime, I can sort out how to handle things with them."

"Ah, so that's it. Are you afraid that if our mission ends, you'll be forced to figure out what to do about them?"

"I've thought about that, Elaine. I ran it through my mind over and over. There's no way that I would compromise our mission. Period. I wouldn't extend it for any purpose other than for what we came here to accomplish. But truth be told, I really don't know what to do about them."

"Are you interested in seeing Linda?"

"Interested? Yes. Scared? You bet." Tom laughed, bewildered by the craziness of his predicament.

"Yeah, well. I don't blame you."

The past week had been one of unprecedented self-reflection for Tom. It left him feeling discouraged and heartened, lonely and connected, spent and energized. He realized — well, confirmed — that he had a powerful faculty for remaining focused on the task of the moment despite the presence of an enormous distraction beckoning for his attention. Probably a blessing and a curse, he thought. The benefit was obvious. But on the downside, it could account for why there had been little room in his life for other things, especially relationships. Tom concluded that this trait might make him a second-rate parent. It dawned on him that he employed a powerful rationale, cultivated over a lifetime, in which he was guided by his unconscious to remain alone so that he could spare a family from his absence. But there was something about meeting his child that shattered this explanation. His feeling about his son wasn't compatible with the system of logic he relied on to assess practically all areas in his life, especially work. But most of what he did — virtually all of what he did — was work. Then, along came Jack, and what had forever seemed to Tom like a sound basis for not having a family now looked like a pile of empty excuses.

"I'm not sure how to think about Linda," Tom confessed.

"But you will see her. It's unavoidable, isn't it?" Elaine asked in an effort to steer Tom to the practical reality of his situation.

"Yeah. I guess. But I just can't zero in on how to approach all of this with her. I need to hear from her directly why she never told me about Jack. You know, Jack has no clue. I asked him about it. He was under the impression that maybe Linda never wanted to see me again, like maybe I was just some horrible person."

"You know you don't bear any blame for this. It's not like you told Linda that if she ever got pregnant, you'd have nothing to do with the child. She took it upon herself to keep this from you."

"I agree. But as I said, she must have been pretty convinced that I wouldn't be around. And, Elaine, my life is like one huge ton of evidence. Exhibit A. I had exactly one relationship with a woman. Well, one serious relationship. And look what happened. The one time it just feels right, and I make a commitment, she's taken from me."

TWENTY-FIVE

Rafiq Farid was in his office in Riyadh preparing for a meeting on international shipping lane regulations. Security regarding the transportation of oil was an ever-present concern, occasionally rising to the level of significant worry. Rafiq was considered a strong player in this area. He was extremely knowledgeable about the intricacies of international treaties governing commercial use of waterways. But equally important, maybe more so, were his mediation and facilitation skills. His colleagues and his adversaries respected Rafiq for his fair-mindedness and willingness to hear all sides. Perhaps his greatest asset was that he could be trusted.

As he was reviewing a request from the Egyptian government for the transport of drilling equipment through Saudi waters, he was notified that his wife was on the phone. Jamila rarely called his office, so Rafiq thought there must be a problem.

"Jamila. Is everything okay?"

"Rafiq, I am so worried. Abdel did not come home last night."

"Did you call his friends?"

"Yes, of course. No one has seen him or heard from him."

"But wasn't he going with Abdallah to a study group?"

"Abdallah has not heard from him. He is worried too. He told me Abdel is changing, that he is growing angrier."

Rafiq sighed, but tried to be reassuring. "Remember, he did this last month. Twice he didn't come home or call. Then he came home. I'm sure he will be fine."

"Maybe you could ask your security staff to look for him," Jamila asked.

"If he does not call us or come home by the end of the day, I will."

"I'm so worried, Rafiq."

"I pray that this phase will pass. That he will come back to us."

"I pray as well. Sometimes I worry that God does not hear."

"God hears, Jamila. I hear you, too. Please let me know if Abdel calls you or you find out anything."

Rafiq walked to the window of his fourth-floor office in a modernized section of Riyadh. The vista was a sea of white limestone buildings. It all looked so sanitized and safe. But Rafiq knew this scene was a facade. Beyond this landscape was a world of poverty, simmering with underlying despair and rage. Maybe Jamila was right. Maybe God did not always hear. Or maybe he did, and perhaps God was relying on us, Rafiq thought, to demonstrate that as a race — as a species — we could make the proper choices, choices that would benefit and uplift the masses of people who had come to know deprivation and hunger too well. Then we could surely earn his proper devotion. Rafiq knew his exposure to other parts of the world made his faith complicated. What seemed simple to so many was convoluted for him. The balance between his faith and the acceptance of diversity was not easily resolved. His devotion to religion was fraught with questions and tests.

Jamila was nineteen years old when she and Rafiq met. He was five years her senior. She was the daughter of his grandmother's neighbor. He fell in love with her at once. She was radiant and filled with energy. Jamila loved to talk about politics and was generally the only woman sitting in the room with men as they weighed in with their opinions on world affairs. Whenever one of the men bullied his way into the conversation by virtue of his loud and shameless conceit, Jamila could easily tip his balance with a simple question about the purity of his views. Rafiq recalled the time he took Jamila to meet his uncle, Fahd. Fahd could be boisterous and arrogant, filled with himself and his pompous belief that he always knew more than anyone else in the room. After dinner, the men eased off to the living room to talk and smoke while the women cleaned the dishes and prepared dessert.

As Jamila was helping to clear the dishes, she overheard Fahd say, "I am so furious — I was taken advantage of. One of my workers was stealing from me." Fahd owned a trucking service. He had seven trucks, which were used to transport produce and bread to a central market.

"Who was stealing from you, Uncle?" Rafiq asked.

"A young girl, maybe sixteen years old. She's been with me for two years. She loads bread onto the early truck. Some loaves don't make it onto the truck."

"How do you know she was stealing?" Rafiq asked.

"Do I look stupid to you? No, of course not. Why? Because you are an intelligent man. But I must look stupid to her. She thinks maybe I don't know how to count. Three hundred loaves are loaded onto the truck and only two hundred and ninety-five make it to market. Does she not use her head to think? What — my customers are not going to tell me I'm short on my delivery?"

"But did you catch her? Do you have evidence it was her?" Rafiq asked. Jamila was listening as she worked.

"Yes. The next day I checked her bags. She always brings bags to work. Usually filled with clothes. She washes clothes for the neighbors to make extra money. I checked under the clothes. There were two loaves of bread there."

Jamila walked over. "Uncle Fahd, I don't mean to interfere, but how well do you know this girl?"

"I have many workers, Jamila. This girl is a peasant. I don't know her other than that she works for me."

"She is so young. Have you ever met her family?"

"No. She comes from a family of peasants. She should be grateful I had the kindness to give her a job."

"If they are peasants, they must be hungry," Jamila said.

"Maybe. Probably. What's the point?" Fahd demanded.

"Have you ever been hungry?" Jamila asked.

"Many times. But I did not steal."

"Maybe you did not know her kind of hunger."

"It doesn't justify stealing. She is like a street rat."

"I'm not condoning the stealing. I'm simply saying maybe we should understand her desperation before we condemn her. You would want the same courtesy."

"If her family is so poor, why not come to me and ask for something, for some help?"

"A better choice, surely. But sometimes pride or fear prevents us from making the right choice."

Rafiq was listening. Both people made sense. But Jamila's heart was deeper, filled with sensitivity; at the same time, she was not blind to the need for justice. For Fahd, justice was synonymous with punishment. And if punishment was applied to acts based on hunger, how would the world improve? he wondered.

Rafiq asked, "Uncle, what are you planning to do about it?"

"I am going to fire her and make it difficult for her to get another job," Fahd responded, haughty and stubborn, his chest swelling.

"Uncle Fahd, can I ask you a favor?" Jamila interjected.

"If it's about this matter, my mind is made up. This girl is a thief and I have an obligation to stop her thievery."

"Yes, it is not up to me to tell you what to do in your business. And yes, her deed should not go unpunished. But before you take any action, go to her home and speak to her parents. See how they live. See if you can find it in your heart to be forgiving if they are poor and hungry. This girl is only a child. If she can't find honest work, she will become a prostitute. You know that. You have a chance to turn her life around. Maybe her punishment can involve repaying you and adding a penalty, maybe working extra hours for free. I don't know. But please, go to her house, talk with her parents."

Fahd was taking in Jamila's words, much to the surprise of Rafiq. "Jamila, you are a persuasive young woman. I will do as you say. No promises, though."

"I cannot ask you for any. But thank you so much."

Fahd turned to Rafiq. "You are in for quite an adventure with this woman."

Since Fayza died, Rafiq had not seen this spirit in Jamila. She was cloaked now, guarded. She turned to more traditional dress — a black jallabia — less for the traditionalism than for the boundary it created between her and the world. Her spontaneity, her energy, her curiosity, had been siphoned from her. As he gazed out his window, he sensed Jamila's spirit had become like the poverty he knew existed; it was out there somewhere, but beyond his view.

A knock on Rafiq's door yanked him from his woe and feeling of helplessness. "Come in," he muttered.

The door opened. "Rafiq, I need your written opinion on this matter with the Egyptian government." Sami Al-Jamal, a colleague, was standing in the door with an impatient look. Sami was a senior attorney in the Ministry, which handled contracts with security personnel and was a liaison with the civil police.

"Rafiq, what's wrong? You look like you have the weight of the world on your shoulders," Sami said.

"No. I'm all right. Just lost in thought, that's all. The opinion is on my desk. I'll get it for you."

"Lost in thought, huh? The last time you were lost in thought we had to shut down one of our cargo ships."

Rafiq dragged his mind, but not his mood, back to business. "It was not up to code. It was unsafe. Those engines could overheat and start a fire. Would you want one of your relatives on that ship?"

"You did the right thing, of course. But it cost us a lot of money. Hey, Rafiq, I saw that memo you wrote about that guy in the States with the paternity suit, Jacobson. I hate these situations. Remember a few years ago there was a German who worked for Hecht Oil. They told us he died. Then he shows up as a consulting engineer at one of our drilling sites. I'm going to double check on Jacobson, just to make sure those police reports are not a scam."

"Oh, sure. Good idea. Sami, it might be easier for me to look into this. I'm still in touch with some of our classmates. I'm sure at least one has kept up with Jacobson."

Sami nodded. "Good. Saves me the trouble. Probably best if you do it right away — if it is espionage, we wouldn't want to give them too much time to cover their tracks."

"I'll take care of it immediately, Sami."

Sami turned toward Rafiq's door. "And Rafiq, get a photo of Jacobson. We'll circulate it — let's not take any chances."

TWENTY-SIX

The more people entered the intimate circle of Jack's life, the lonelier he felt. His mind was littered with confusion about his closest relationships — with his mother, his newfound father, and Cathy. Cathy, he wondered, how did she manage to get into the center of his life so quickly? He felt unsure of her motive and less sure of her staying power. And now he was on his way to meet her. They selected a different rendezvous spot, an Italian restaurant just outside Poughkeepsie, New York. It wasn't terribly far from Albany, and Cathy's family used to go to the restaurant on their way to visit Cathy's uncle and his family in New York City. They planned to meet at one p.m. for lunch.

Jack began to feel pangs of insecurity. Why in the world would she have any interest in him? He saw himself as small and aimless. His infatuation with her made supreme sense to him. But what he offered to her seemed, by comparison, insignificant and ordinary. Jack felt gawky around her, and he feared his awkwardness obscured whatever intelligence, humor, perceptiveness and logic he possessed — traits he had not yet bundled and exploited toward a career goal, or even a coherent set of interests.

Jack's apprehensions were getting the better of him. He envisioned Cathy spending her days around fiercely smart, powerfully goal-oriented people. The students at NEIT had promising careers ahead of them. He had visions of them clutching diplomas, arrayed in a long line, smiling and poised, marching toward — no, creating — the future. They were bright, ambitious and destined to leave a more respectable mark on the world than anything he could do, Jack rationalized, his intimidation growing with each self-pitying fantasy. He thought about his father as an iconic member of this group. Jack fixed on the notion that Cathy had more in common with his father than with him. Both were engineers (well, Cathy was on her way toward becoming one), and both were devoted to using their education and skill to improve the corner of the world they touched. Jack's thoughts nibbled at his confidence as he felt increasingly emasculated by the two new people in his life. Everything he did, his entire life, now seemed mediocre. His grades in school were good. But so what? he thought. Who cares? It's not getting me anywhere, he mentally mumbled to himself. He felt so average in contrast to his highly achieving and morally driven father and the equally impressive Cathy.

At once, his mother entered the mental picture: she also knew what she wanted to do with her life, well before she was Jack's age. An extraordinary role model, he acknowledged, but Jack felt devoid of an ability to mold his life in so inspirational a way. Sure, he had interests. Interests. What interests? he demanded of himself. It occurred to him that any interests he had didn't translate into anything that resembled a life plan. Jack hadn't felt rushed to find a career until now. He always knew something would come along that drew him in. But now, surrounded by a venerated father and a budding success story in Cathy, and fueled by a renewed respect for his mother's professional drive, Jack experienced a rush of pressure, a self-imposed coercion to be more vocationally inclined. Or, if not a career, then inclined toward *something*. Something that he could project into the world as distinctly his — a hobby, a belief, a talent, a taste for something. Anything. In the absence of that, Jack became certain that Cathy's fondness for him — rooted only in sympathy and fascination with the story of which she was a part — would surely wane.

The lower edge of the Catskill Mountains was a glorious sight. The mountains had soft, rolling peaks. Perfect topography for a gentle roller coaster, Jack thought. The mountains fed into one another, oozing into a flowing landscape like a breezy cascade. Set against the clean blue sky, the mountains' dense and richly leafed fir trees shone like a sea of green glitter against the sun. Many of the smaller hills were homes to farms, and groups of cows and horses grazed with unadulterated contentment. Red barns, old tractors and aluminum silos sprinkled through the scene, which appeared to Jack to have been frozen in a time far less complicated.

Jack arrived at twelve forty-five and pulled into the parking lot behind the restaurant. As he walked around the building, he saw Cathy sitting on a bench at the base of a small pond on the side of the restaurant. A family of ducks ambled alongside.

"Anyone sitting here?" he asked mischievously, pointing to the other end of the bench.

"Oh, Jack, you scared me," Cathy exclaimed as she jumped from the bench and embraced him. "I missed you."

Jack's self-doubts did not evaporate, but for this one fleeting second his world could not be more right.

Jack and Cathy sat at a table in a small outdoor area, overlooking the pond. Cathy reached across the table and took his hand. "Hey, it's really good to see you."

Mesmerized by her affection, Jack could offer only, "Yeah, me too," although his desire was to bellow his ecstasy. He wasn't sure what he would reveal, however. Maybe it would be a stronger expression of his fondness for her, or maybe a disclosure about the personal misgivings produced by all the recent events in his life.

"I can't wait to hear what happened with your mom," Cathy asked with a giddy eagerness. "Come on, fill me in."

Jack wasn't ready to discuss The Situation. He knew Cathy's affection for him was genuine. But a part of him believed it was grounded in her fascination with all the excitement and mystery in his life. And Cathy was not simply an observer; she was a participant, actively involved. Had it not been for Cathy, Jack might never have found his father. He sensed that it would be quite normal to convert such enthusiasm into affection for a colleague in a shared experience.

"Yeah... my mom," Jack responded quietly, his thoughts still locked into his personal perplexity. "Hey, Cathy." Jack looked up with a particular firmness of eye contact. "Can I ask you a question first? Do you ever think about where you'll be in ten years?"

"Is that a proposal, Jack? We really don't know each other that well." Cathy smiled.

Dishes of pasta and warm bread were delivered to the table. Jack's pensive mood would not be rattled. "I'm being serious, Cathy. Do you ever think about that?"

"Sometimes. I guess. Maybe. I don't know. Why are you asking me?"

"I don't know." Jack's tone was contemplative. "It's a feeling I have about my life, I guess. It's probably stupid, but I'm not sure how much to think about what's down the road for me. But I really want to know about you. Even if you don't think about it much, what goes through your mind when you do?"

"Well, for one thing, I—"

Jack cut her off. "Wait. Back up. When did you decide you wanted to be an engineer?"

"Never. I don't know what I want to do, actually. I know that sounds crazy, especially when you think about how much it costs to go to NEIT."

"But you told me you like sciences and want to get involved in alternative energy sources," Jack said, his confusion building and easing at the same time, building because he was convinced Cathy had a more defined career ambition and easing because he was not alone in having uncertainties about his future.

"I do want to. But I really don't know exactly what I want to do with it. I figure once I have an education about the technology side of it, I can think about what kind of work I want to do."

"How'd you get this interest? Where did it come from?" Jack asked.

"I really have no idea. I always did well in math and science. And I really liked those subjects. I probably never told you, but I won the ninth-grade science fair. I took a motor and created a working vacuum cleaner with an internal fan and a cylinder for the bag. It was very exciting." Cathy was smiling proudly as Jack was sliding into an impenetrable state of being smitten.

Jack marveled at Cathy's scientific prowess. "Wow. I'm not even sure I know how to use a vacuum," he joked. But in his heart, he needed to get some insight into what led her to a specialized school, one that attracted very bright students whom Jack assumed exercised great clear-headedness in developing plans for their futures. He couldn't consider himself to be compatible with her until he understood that and reconciled his own self-proclaimed aimlessness. "But really, what about your interest in alternative sources of energy? How did you get into that?"

"I don't know for sure. It's not like there was one big thing that happened in my life. I'm not carrying on some great family tradition or anything like that."

"But your interest didn't come out of thin air. You can't think of anything?"

"It's just something I always talked about with my parents. They used to talk to me all the time about how irresponsible we are with energy use in this country. A few years ago, we went to Europe. The cars were tiny compared to what we drive here. They seemed so cool, almost like toys. I wanted to get one to drive around in our backyard. My parents told me they have no choice but to have small cars in Europe. For one thing, it's not like people have garages and lots of property. So, space for cars is limited. But also, gas was so much more expensive in Europe that they can only afford small cars there. After our trip I looked up comparisons in energy use between the United States and other countries. It was amazing — we use something like a fourth of the world's total energy. And most energy consumption has a polluting effect."

"When was that?"

"About seven years ago."

"So, you've been interested in this field for that long?" Jack asked.

"Probably longer. That's just when it all came together for me. But way before our trip, my parents used to talk about it all the time. I remember when I was little, my father told me there's a fixed amount of oil in the ground and someday it will run out," Cathy said, recalling her astonishment. "I got scared and asked him if it would run out the next day. He said we have a long way to go. Not long after that, an oil tanker had a spill. It wasn't a bad one, but on the news, they showed seals and birds lying along the beach, dying from being completely soaked in oil. It was a horrible sight. On the news they talked about whether it was better to try to save some of them or to put them out of their misery. What a choice! I figured there has to be something better than all this."

"I've seen pictures of animals washed up on shore like that. I hate seeing that," Jack said.

"Oh, the suffering is incredible. It's like a form of suffocation for them. Their skin can't absorb oxygen, they can't breathe, and their mobility is completely restricted so they can't do anything to rid themselves of the oil."

"Horrible! But what do you propose, that we give up oil entirely?"

"Of course not. The world would come to a standstill. But we need to do a lot more with alternative sources of energy. Like solar and wind energy, hydrogen fuel cells, and nuclear fission."

"Aren't the hybrid cars helping?" Jack asked.

"Sure, anything we can do to make our energy use more efficient helps. But that's far from a permanent solution. And I worry that as more and more hybrids come on the market it may make us complacent."

"What do you mean?"

"It means we fool ourselves into thinking that because we've done *something* we've done enough."

"Ha, the same could be said for a lot of things we do. It's so nice hearing you speak about things this way. How are you not more sure of what you want to do with your future? You're so knowledgeable and passionate. I don't understand."

"I don't know! Sometimes my head spins with it all. I've taken a few courses on energy economics. In some countries there are some groups, like monarchies or oligarchies, that have massive control over the oil wealth. Unfortunately, the wealth doesn't get spread around, and the rest of the country is impoverished. I might want to get involved in an area related to economics and international relations. I applied to do an internship next summer in D.C. at the Energy Department. Wouldn't that be an awesome place to learn about all of this?"

"But that's not exactly dealing with engineering or science or technology, is it?" Jack asked.

"You know, the further I get into my program, the more I realize that all these things are linked together. It's hard to advocate for alternative energy sources if you don't understand the technology behind it. And how the technology is developing."

"I guess. It makes sense when you say it." Jack felt intimidated by Cathy's commitment. And even if she wasn't sure how her life would proceed, at least she had passion for something.

"So anyway, back to your question about where I'll be in ten years… I have no idea. Why were you asking? Do you think I should be further along in my planning?"

"Further along?" Jack was startled by even a hint of doubt from Cathy. "Are you kidding? You're already light years ahead of me. I don't even know what my interests are, let alone what kind of a career I should have."

"So, who's mandating a timetable for you?" Cathy asked.

"What do you mean?"

"I mean where does it say that you have to have your life plan by a certain date?"

"No one. Everyone. I don't know. My mom knew she wanted to get into health care when she was twelve. You were about the same age when you became interested in alternative energy sources. My father went to NEIT, obviously you know that, but I feel like he must have had a clue about what he wanted to be doing, or at the very least, what field he wanted to work in."

"So what?" Cathy said, realizing much of what brought this on was Jack's self-confidence going AWOL. "What difference does it make why something sparks someone's interest? What if my family didn't go to Europe? What if your mom didn't injure her ankle when she was twelve? What if I got interested in this field when I was thirty? What difference does it make? You get interested in something when you get interested in it. The only bad thing is to wait around for something to hit you and not be open and curious. Without that you might never get interested in anything at all."

"I can't argue with that. But I can't help but feel like I should have a better grasp on where I want my life to head."

"Did any of this matter to you before you met Stewart?" Cathy asked, thinking she was getting to the heart of the matter.

"Maybe, but I guess not as much as it does to me now." Jack paused and glanced down. "It's not just my father, Cathy. It's you, too. Sometimes I think about you at NEIT. There you are, Mensa candidates all around, ready to take over the world and do important stuff. And then you and I meet, and here I am at some local commuter school and—"

Cathy cut him off. "Are you crazy? You're just as bright as anyone I know at my school. Well, to be honest, there are a few people there with brains the size of watermelons, but most of them have zero social skills. There's one kid, Warren Zalickis… he can take a plumbing kit and jerry-rig it into a jet engine. But say hello to him, and he has no idea how to answer you. But other than people like Warren Zalickis, no one there is any smarter than you. That's not even the point. I don't even know exactly what 'smart' is. Or care. When you first called and told me about the party for your mother, I liked you right away. There was something very sincere in your voice. Pretty ironic, huh? But even though what you told me was some made-up story, your feelings about everything were sincere. And that's what came through."

"Well. Thanks."

Then something else occurred to Cathy. "If you ever start feeling stressed, or down about yourself, just remember who your parents are. They're both fighters, and strong, independent people. You couldn't have come from that and be the opposite."

That did give Jack comfort. Quickly and powerfully, he felt a bolt of positive psychic energy. More than Cathy even knew. He had been looking at his parents as standards against which he fell short. It occurred to him now that his thinking was purely arbitrary; he could adopt any position on his future prospects that he chose. Why not simply gaze into the future and see hopefulness? It would have been easy to embrace this position even before he met his father. Now that he knew his father was honorable and ethical and intelligent, there was that much more reason to feel optimistic. Jack knew his feelings might recede back to self-doubt, but for now Cathy's words worked a little magic.

"Hey, Jack," Cathy continued. "What's the one thing in the world that makes you the most angry?"

"Angry? Why angry?" Jack asked.

"Because I don't want to dwell so much on your self-proclaimed inadequacy," Cathy said, not realizing half the problem had been solved. "I think you're much further along in having interests than you think. I'm not talking about a career — that falls into place later on. So, what's the one thing in the world that really drives you crazy?"

"Honestly, in the past year — wow, way over a year, actually — since I've been looking for my father, I've been reading a ton of stories that are really horrifying to me. Stories I never would have thought about before. Like there's this ten-year-old girl, I think she lives in Utah. Her mother was fifteen when she got pregnant by her nineteen-year-old boyfriend. He actually threatened to kill her if she didn't have an abortion, but she was Catholic and didn't want to. Anyway, when she was in her eighth month of pregnancy, the boyfriend beat her up... I mean really beat her. Broken ribs, a broken collarbone, collapsed lung. I saw photos. You can't believe how horrible. The baby had to be delivered by an emergency C-section. It's a miracle the baby even survived. She was given up for adoption right away — the mother and her parents signed all the papers. Last year, when she was nine, she was told she was adopted. Meanwhile, the birth mother started to look for her daughter. The adoptive family didn't find out until after they told her she was adopted. They became so afraid that the girl would want to live with her birth mother if she met her that they made it impossible for that to happen. They moved a couple of times. And they even have an injunction against the birth mother, preventing her from contacting the child."

"How could they do that?" Cathy asked.

"Different states have different rules about everything related to looking for lost family members — who can have access to what information, how court cases are decided. Everything. In this case they were able to say that since the birth was related to an episode of violence, the child's interests would be better served if she was kept at an 'arm's length distance' from the birth mother. That's what they call it, an 'arm's length distance'. So, I guess that made me pretty angry. People having to go through that. Families feeling that pain and the courts dictating who can or can't see their kids. Or their parents. I mean, the adoptive family did a great thing by giving this little girl a family. But it seems like every side feels like they have to win, rather than come together or find some common ground. And the courts reinforce that. And in the middle of it is a ten-year-old kid who just wants to meet the woman who gave birth to her."

"Where did you hear that story?" Cathy asked.

"When I was searching for my father, I came across hundreds of stories like that."

"Where? On websites?"

"Websites, newspaper articles, journals. I even spent time in a couple of law libraries. I wanted to find out what or how much I can access from old records. And you know what? It's almost impossible. Especially without an expensive lawyer, which obviously I couldn't get. Can you imagine not having the money to find your child?"

Cathy was taking it all in. She had never heard stories like this.

Jack continued. "And you know what else? Lots of people never tell anyone about it. Like people are ashamed or afraid. Lots of times they join groups of people searching for others, but they don't even tell their best friends. Kids have it the worst. If an adopted kid who's like twelve or fourteen wants to find a birth parent, what do they do? Sometimes they're afraid to tell their adoptive parents. It's not like they would want to leave the adoptive family, but they're afraid the adoptive parents wouldn't understand. And, guess what? They don't tell them."

"You came across all this while you were searching for your father?"

"Yeah. It's amazing. I had no idea about any of this until I started looking for him. There's a whole world of people out there in similar situations."

"Well it seems like you're quite the expert, now. And you said you didn't feel passionate about anything," Cathy exclaimed.

"I guess so," Jack responded dismissively, but with a hint of pride because of how impressed Cathy seemed. "I guess I've learned a lot about which things work and which don't. Like where to find different kinds of records and how to present your case so that you can get through some of the bureaucracy. And about the websites that specialize in finding people. You have to be very careful."

"It's amazing." Cathy glanced down at Jack's plate. "Hey, you hardly touched your food."

"I was rambling. Sorry," Jack said. "You want to go for a walk?"

The pond was very inviting. They circled it. On the far side was a hilly embankment that led to an open grassy field.

"What now for you and your mom?" Cathy asked tentatively, uncertain as to whether Jack was ready for this topic.

"I have no idea."

"Do you think she wants to see your dad?"

"I don't know. I could tell she really cared about him." Jack's tone became stern. "But she's probably a little afraid because she kept his child a secret from him."

"I'm hearing angry."

"Angry? I'm completely pissed." Jack stopped in his tracks and turned to Cathy. "How would you feel in my situation? Here's my mother, who never told me about this man. Can you think of anything

233

worse? Yeah. Like maybe that she never told him."

"You spoke to her about it. What did she say?"

"Nothing. Well, not exactly nothing. But close to nothing. She told me some story about a neighbor who had a little girl and the father barely came to see her. The girl was very upset, but the father still didn't show up that often. I think my mom was afraid that would happen to us."

"But that would have been later on, wouldn't it? Like after you were born. Why didn't she tell him when she was pregnant?"

"She said she was convinced he would be completely involved in work. She said he—"

Cathy cut him off. "Did he agree? Did he tell you the same thing?"

"I don't know. I saw him for a total of ten minutes. Fifteen, max."

"But he must have said something about being surprised to learn about you. Something about why your mother didn't tell him."

"I guess. It's not like he came out directly and said, 'There's no way I would have hung around if I knew she was pregnant.' But he did say he had a demanding job that took him all over the world."

"Okay, then. So, your mother didn't lie about his job and what was involved in it?"

"No. But that doesn't excuse it, does it?" Jack demanded, his anger building.

"Nothing excuses it, Jack. But right now, you're just trying to understand it. Maybe you'll forgive her at some point."

"I don't feel like I can ever forgive what she did. I grew up without a father when maybe I could have had one."

"But she thought it was best this way. She didn't want to take a risk."

"Whose side are you on?"

"I didn't know there were sides. I'm not on anyone's side, Jack."

Jack was adamant. "Sometimes there are sides." They continued walking. "I grew up thinking my father didn't exist. That he wasn't real in any way. We'd never meet because my mom didn't know who he was. I lived with that my whole life. And it was fine. I never cared about that. I had one parent, and it was all I knew, and it was okay."

"As I see it, it was more than okay. Your mom sounds like a great mother, and she worked really hard to raise you."

"I can't believe you're defending her. It's as though keeping me in the dark my whole life doesn't matter. And what about keeping a secret from Stewart? This man could have spent his entire life not knowing he had a child."

"But she said she planned on telling you."

At this, Jack became livid. "When?" he barked. "When was she going to tell me? When I was ten? That came and went. When I was fifteen? Twenty? Thirty? When she read his obituary? When was I going to get told? I'm amazed you can defend that."

"I'm not defending it. Just trying to understand things through her eyes. And I'm not saying it was the right thing to do. We all make mistakes in—"

Jack shot her an angry glance. "Mistakes. Is that what you call it? A mistake? No, a mistake is when you tell the child when he turns five. A mistake is when you wait till the child is two or three to tell the other parent that you've had a baby together. That's a mistake. This is completely different. You don't see that?"

"I can." Cathy's devil's advocacy wasn't working, and she backed down. "So, what are you going to do?"

"I don't know. I feel like I have to get away for a while. I can't be with her right now."

"What's that going to solve?"

"Probably nothing. But I can't deal with her every day as though nothing's happened."

"What would it take to forgive her?"

"I can't even see that right now. I've lived my entire life, and I just found out I have a father."

"Jack, I don't see this as a side issue, but I'm on your side, if there is one. I'm just being sensitive to her, because here you are. Smart, sweet… she did a good job of raising you. I get that she made a mistake. A big one. And I'm not defending her at all. She made a decision based on what she understood and felt at the time. Maybe she would make it differently today. But I think she did a pretty mature and responsible thing by thinking the whole thing through. And it made her a better person. After all, it didn't stop her from finishing college, from getting her physical therapy degree, and from running her own business for all these years. And she never once made you feel like you came second."

Jack knew that Cathy was right. He had been so angry at having been deprived of knowing about his father that he had elevated his mother's wrongness into a capital crime. It was hard to think of her as a decision-maker at his age, making life decisions in the psychological context of uncertainties and vulnerabilities. But that's when she got pregnant. And Cathy understood that she did not shrink from the experience, but rather grew from it.

"Well, professor, what do you suggest I do?" Jack asked, his comfort level rising.

"Oh, 'professor' is not necessary. A simple 'Your Highness' will do. What do you mean what should you do? I don't think you need to do anything. The situation will play itself out. There's nothing you can do about your father. He seems to want to have a connection to you. See how it goes over time."

"What about with my mother?"

"You still think you need to get away?"

"Maybe not right now."

"Just continue talking to her. I know you're upset. But so is she. You guys need each other."

"Yeah. Maybe you're right."

TWENTY-SEVEN

"It's the most ludicrous thing I ever heard." Lurching across the room, his arms flailing, Tom was an outraged kinetic mess.

"Calm down, Tom, this isn't helping." Elaine tried to contain him.

"But an arms dealer? Of all things, an arms dealer!" he blared.

"Keep your voice down. They'll hear you in Stockholm."

Tom had made one too many trips to Saudi Arabia. Not that trips to Saudi Arabia triggered automatic alarm bells, but the German federal border police, ever cautious about foreign nationals who travel to Mideastern countries, had done a routine cursory review of Tom's background. The Defense Ministry was aware of Tom's mission, but not any branch of the state police nor the national customs agency. So, when travel manifests were reviewed, a standard check of Tom had been done by the federal border police. Unfortunately for Tom, a preliminary glance at the results suggested he fit the profile of an international arms dealer: multi-national ties, culturally fluent, and an association with an organization with all the appearances of a cover.

"Good, let them hear me in Stockholm. And why will it take two days for the Defense Ministry to notify the border agency?" Tom said, disgusted.

"I can only repeat what they told me. Since you are in this country as an invited guest under special circumstances, authorization to release information about you requires approval from the ambassador."

"I know. But the ambassador is not even aware we exist."

"That's why the delay. She has to be briefed, but she won't be returning from the United Nations until tomorrow. It's not going to be a problem."

Elaine was conflicted because this was just the latest wrinkle in an increasingly complex web of unanticipated problems. Too many people had become aware of Tom and his work. There was the small contingent of American family members dropped all at once into Tom's life, not the least of whom was a grown son Tom never knew he had. Elaine surmised the Jacobson paternity suit question appeared to have blown over, thanks to some quick action on the part of her colleagues in the United States. That clearly had the makings of a fiasco. But one can never be sure, she thought. The foray into Saudi Arabia to deliver a presentation was a good idea. It produced information about some quiet but potentially important efforts on the part of oil officials to advance peaceful long-term relationships with neighbors, and equally important, the identity of some key players. But was it worth the risk? In retrospect, Elaine thought not. The German federal border police would need to be notified by the Defense Ministry about Tom. It just widened the circle way too much, she concluded. It's tough enough in the United States when the FBI and Defense must collaborate; these massive organizations have different agendas, different roles, histories and cultures. What's important to one organization may be decidedly insignificant to the other. Now they were stationed in Germany, and Elaine's best guess about the consequences of a national border agency knowing about Tom ranged from 'can't hurt' to 'not good'. The ambassador's office should resolve the matter, but it would take a couple of days, and delays of this sort made Elaine antsy.

In the context of international terrorism, governments and police forces didn't take risks lightly. Ordinarily, since Tom didn't present as a national threat, the German border agency would wait to hear from the ambassador's office regarding his status and background. But a zealous member of the agency thought it wouldn't hurt to check unofficially with a counterpart in the Saudi government. Although it was outside international protocol — checking with the foreign national's host government first was general standard procedure — the agency representative fired off an electronic memo to the Saudi oil ministry to verify the legitimacy of Tom Gaines.

"Hey, isn't this the guy who gave the presentation last month?" Sami was standing in the doorway of Rafiq's office. The memo from the German border agency was passed from an oil official who managed agreements with contractors to Sami, the attorney responsible for security contract oversight.

"What's his name again?" Rafiq asked, careful to convey a blend of concern and detachment.

"Tom Gaines. You know anything about him?"

"I met him a couple of times. Why the interest in him?"

"I think it's just routine. He flew here a couple of times. They just want to make sure he is who he says he is."

"I have no reason to believe otherwise. He gave an interesting presentation to our ministry group."

"Strangest thing, though," Sami said, puzzled. "My office did a quick check on him. There's very little information on him before five or six years ago."

Rafiq's mind was racing. He could tell Sami the truth. Although the risk was minimal because Sami was a trusted colleague, it would place Sami in the untenable position of knowing about a national security affair regarding a United States citizen. Not a fair position in which to place a colleague. "What do you mean?" Rafiq asked.

"Before he worked for A.W. Kassing, he worked as a senior engineer for Lowen McGrady. You know them, don't you?"

"Yes. The rig consulting group."

"Aref al-Walla worked there. You remember Aref, he did some design work for us and teaches engineering at the university."

"Yes. I remember him."

"I called him to ask about Gaines. Said he never heard of him."

Ever quick on his feet, Rafiq responded, "That doesn't surprise me. Lowen McGrady is international. They have, what, twenty or thirty offices around the world? They must have over five thousand engineers working for them."

"Yes. That's what I figured. It's just that, well, it's just that someone of Gaines's stature, a senior engineer... I would have thought Aref would have known him. Or at least heard the name. It's just a little strange, that's all."

"It does seem a little odd," Rafiq agreed. "But you know how those multinationals work. A senior engineer gets assigned to a project and stays with it for years. He may not get to know the other members of the firm very well."

"You're probably right. But I'm going to look into it further anyway."

"Sure. Keep me posted."

"I will. All right, so that's the situation with Gaines. By the way, any luck with that other American, Jacobson? Any information on him yet?"

"I'm working on it."

As Sami turned to exit Rafiq's office, he looked back at him and said, "And don't forget the photo."

Rafiq watched the door to his office close. He took a deep breath, stood and walked over to a closet in which his suit jacket hung. He put his jacket on and exited his office. As he passed his secretary, stationed at her desk just outside his office, he mentioned he had to attend to a personal errand. He hustled past the elevators and took the steps down to the ground level. Filled with nervous energy, Rafiq walked briskly to an office building two blocks away. Nondescript, this law library housed archives on international criminal cases in which the Saudi government had some involvement. As a well-recognized member of the country's legal elite, Rafiq had complete access to the building and was able to brush by the security staff at the entrance with a simple, "Nice to see you." The basement had a communications system that was impervious to penetration and eavesdropping. It was here that Rafiq would often go to speak to counterparts in other countries or to have conversations he could be confident would not be overheard by other parties.

"Tom, we have a problem."

"What else is new?"

"My colleague is looking into the backgrounds of two Americans."

"Do I know them?"

"You are them."

***

Linda Davies stared at a glass of red wine held delicately in her left hand. She sat, relaxed, in her backyard. Her eyes were ringed with the telltale circles of tears coupled with little sleep. The yard was fenced off with posts and rails, creating boundaries while permitting visual access to everything outside it. It was an apt metaphor for how Linda's mind worked. Her life decisions were her own, for the most part... privately made, generally final, but having been reached after searching beyond the borders of her own thoughts. She swirled the wine gently in the glass.

She gazed at its circular motion, wishfully considering ways to gain some control over the predicament or praying for it to disappear. She sat in a wicker chair, an old pillow accepting her shape flawlessly as it had for years; her feet rested on the matching ottoman.

Until now, everything had been in order for Linda. For the most part, she felt fulfilled, though she also felt some void lurking in the background of her life. There was little beyond Jack and work. But Jack and work were big. For most people, it seemed, work and family occupied the vast amount of energy and time. Yet, for Linda, there was a peculiar emptiness. Not because she was a single parent. Not because her business needed to be seriously modified in order to make it viable. But she began to second-guess her decision about keeping Stewart a secret more earnestly than ever. This sort of second-guessing — a tough, sober, no-holds-barred self-reflection — occurred every few years. But now, with everything out in the open, the opportunity to retreat to a rationale for keeping it secret was no longer available.

Even if Stewart didn't want to have an active presence in their lives, she thought… even if that was the case, she knew he wasn't the kind of person who would completely turn away from them. He would have had some participation, some involvement. And what might it have been like? At the very least he would have appeared a few times a year to take Jack to some place or other. Or he might have shown up more regularly, maybe even desiring some version of joint custody. What would it have been like, Linda thought, to have had a partner to consult about raising Jack? Even if Stewart's relationship with them was predominantly tangential, surely the big issues and events would have been discussed with him. What school should Jack attend? Why isn't Jack paying more attention in school? Why doesn't Jack have many friends? Where should Jack go on his vacation? What's the most exciting birthday present Jack could get? Even if Stewart elected to have little to do with Jack, as long as this was understood from the beginning, maybe Linda would have done some good by telling Stewart when she was pregnant. As long as his peripheral involvement was established at the outset and known by all the parties, there would be few expectations. No expectations for a romantic life with Linda, no expectation to spend holidays together, no expectation for attention to be lavished on Jack. And with no expectations, there would be no disappointments. But Linda would have had the benefit of sharing the parenting, or at least the decision-making about the parenting. And maybe that would have made her feel less lonely. But more importantly, she thought, it would have given her greater confidence in her decisions.

Linda was getting wrapped up in this fantasy. How great, she thought, or minimally, how nice it would have been to be able to discuss momentous parenting issues with the only other person on the planet who had the same biological relationship to her son. When Jack turned eleven, he was due to switch from the elementary to the middle school. Jack enjoyed the elementary school — the teachers were pleasant and energetic and the class sizes small. But Linda was concerned about the public middle school. It was large and overcrowded — four elementary schools fed into it. Jack was not eager to go the middle school. His social universe had always been small and quaint; it generally consisted of one or two close friends, and he hated being a captive member of a large crowd, especially when the pressure for social engagement was so powerful. The middle school, although he could have handled it (after all, he wasn't socially inept, she thought), might not have been the best choice for him. Linda eventually enrolled Jack in a private school for sixth, seventh and eighth grades. She based her decision not on the curriculum (he'll learn wherever he goes, she thought), but on the fact that the private school offered so much more individualized attention to students. The disappointment was that Jack would be leaving his friends. Linda and Jack talked about this choice for several weeks. And while Linda talked to her parents, friends and teachers about sending Jack to the private school, she remembered thinking how she would have loved to discuss this matter with Stewart. She wasn't exactly sure what he might have offered, but she just knew that no one else shared her role as Jack's parent.

Ah, but all this was indeed fantasy, and Linda understood this completely. Real life doesn't work so neatly that each member of a relationship understands and respects the other's desires, goals and vulnerabilities. Suppose Jack had visited Stewart from time to time, she pondered. At some point, Jack might have wanted to stay for an extra week with his father. Then what? Or what if Stewart was married and wanted Jack to spend half a year with him, his wife and their five adorable and well-adjusted kids? What if Linda had decided to ask Stewart to pay for part of Jack's private school? What if he said no? What if Linda's romantic interest in Stewart was rekindled and wasn't reciprocated? Or, less likely, she was sure, the reverse. Expectations always form, no matter what, she resolved. It's inevitable; it's human nature. That's why it was better this way, Linda had reasoned.

But look what happened. The only way to have suppressed expectations forever was to have never told Jack about his father. But what a horrible ethical choice, Linda thought. The practical implications seemed clear and grounded in a sensible rationale. But now Linda felt haunted by her moral failing. How could she have deprived these two human beings of a right to know about one another? She made her decision based on her belief about what was best for her son and herself, in that order. For certain. Well, probably. Hmmm, maybe. And she made that decision because she could. There is no worse basis for making a decision, she thought now. How damning of her to assume ownership of a decision, she acknowledged, over the fate of others' lives, when it should not have belonged to her. She realized that she had never expanded her decision-making calculus to include what would be best for Stewart. Their sexual tryst was loving and respectful. But of the greatest significance at this moment for Linda was that it was mutual. There was pure symmetry and poetry in their transition from dinner to making love; they were swept along by a passion that transcended and unified their individual desires.

Linda had been surprised that a pregnancy resulted — she was sure she was not ovulating (and Stewart hadn't raised the subject of using protection). Nonetheless, their act produced an outcome that was not expected. And though their union was fueled by an evenness of purpose and passion, Linda had an ability to thwart that equivalence, and later she did. How incredibly selfish, she thought. She alone could take control over the consequences of an act that another person had shared equally. Moreover, being responsible for a baby was not any more difficult or convenient for her than it would have been for Stewart. From the moment she knew she was pregnant and would have a child, the course of her life would be changed forever. She would adjust, make it work. Why shouldn't Stewart have that same burden? And that same blessing? Why should she decide — her guts were churning now — that Stewart should not have that opportunity to adjust his life as well? Or not adjust. Either way. It was for him to decide.

Religion didn't play much of a role in Linda's life. But she came to feel at this moment that the conception of a child was not her decision, or any person's really, but that of some larger purpose. And here in her backyard, her haven, she arrived at the conclusion that she had sinned.

TWENTY-EIGHT

"What do you want me to do?" Tom asked after Rafiq gave him the details of Sami's investigations.

"I want you to come here one more time. You will be coming on business because you represent a client who is interested in ascertaining operating expenses down the road. You are reaching out to me because you want to help your client calculate the impact of tariffs on future labor costs. While you are here, I will walk you around the building, casually, so people will see you. A few brief introductions. You can be on your way. Then you should execute whatever exit strategy you have at once." Rafiq's tone was more resolute than Tom had ever known.

"You think this is actually necessary? What's the risk if I don't come?" Tom asked.

"Tom, let me tell you my greatest fear. We have all sorts of people in our government, and some are very suspicious of outsiders. Outsiders like you. Once they become suspicious, they get nervous that there is a threat. You have the potential of being perceived that way. Even if the evidence doesn't support it. More than the potential, perhaps even the certainty if we can't get you off the radar. But I think I need to get you back on the radar screen before I can get you off."

"Are we blowing this issue out of proportion?"

"I don't believe I am. If Sami starts talking — even though he means well... Listen, forget about Sami. Right now, you have Jacobson and Gaines on chains of emails questioning who they are."

"But Jacobson is dead. Gaines is not a gun runner. Tomorrow our ambassador will contact the German border agencies and state police to let them know Tom Gaines is who he says he is," Tom asserted.

"The logic of the situation will not prevail. The illogic will."

"I get it. And I'm not crazy. I understand that when people start asking questions, doubts don't go away. But all this will be resolved tomorrow."

"I'm afraid things just work differently in our part of the world. You haven't lived in a state of paranoia for decades, much less grown up in one. Problems don't get resolved the same way. I lived in both worlds. I saw what it was like there. There is a linear sequence, B follows A, C follows B. We took that class in argumentation together, remember? You are taught to strip away everything that is not a fact so that what is left can be explained by a scientific model. It's far more muddled here. Yes, facts prevail. But there is the additional prism of faith and religion through which the world is known to us. Too often those who have not understood this faith have harmed us. We may strike a bargain with others to sell oil, but we cannot let our guard down."

"Rafiq, what is the risk, in your opinion?"

"I can't say for sure. I don't know who else has the same access to the memos that Sami has. And I would hate to discover they are in the hands of skeptics. That could mean big trouble."

"Like what?"

"For one, if a spy were discovered to be mingling with senior members of the oil industry, that could be an embarrassment for both countries. But I'm mostly worried about you. Sami discovered what he believes are questionable patches in your work history. You allegedly worked at Lowen McGrady. He already checked with a professor here who worked there at the same time. It was odd to Sami that the guy didn't know you."

"Thousands of people work at Lowen McGrady. It wouldn't be unusual for an engineer assigned to a project to not know many people at the firm."

"Yes, I know. I told him so. And he bought that for now. But it's not the Samis I'm concerned about. It's the others who are not as reasonable. Or who are dangerous. I don't want to see anything happen to you."

"When do I come?"

"First thing tomorrow morning. I'll make the travel arrangements and have the documents dispatched to you. In the meantime, I have another chore to take care of."

"What's that?"

"I have to distribute a photo of Jacobson."

"A photo!" Tom blurted, shocked. "Why?"

"Because some people are not convinced that Jacobson died. They think it's a cover story."

"Why?" Tom asked, his voice filled with anxious incredulity. "Why wouldn't they believe a police report?"

Rafiq laughed. "A police report. That's the least believable information. Do you know how many police reports turn out to be plants?"

"Fair enough." Tom verbally shrugged. "Then, what about the photo?"

"I'm taking care of it," Rafiq responded.

Rafiq left the law library and headed back to his office. The day was clean and bright, barely a trace, a wisp, of a cloud in the sky. Rafiq squinted as the sun reflected vibrantly off the white asphalt.

***

Donna Hoverdale was in her office just outside Arlington, Virginia. She called Jack on the special cell phone she had provided him.

"Jack, I just wanted to reassure you we took care of the problem with the police report. I think it's pretty well solved."

"That's great, Donna. Where is he now? Or shouldn't I ask?"

Donna laughed. "You're learning."

An assistant came in and handed Donna a printed page from a website, which she read as Jack was speaking.

Donna's eyes widened as she interrupted Jack. "Jack, I'm sorry, I've got to run. I'll call again soon." She looked up at her assistant. "Goddamn it!" she exclaimed. "Does Tom know about this?"

"No."

"Elaine?"

"No."

Donna was stunned. She stared at a reference from an unofficial Saudi website that reported on shadowy activity in the Mideast. The website was developed by two former mid-level defense ministry officials and read more like a gossip blog than a bona fide information source. Royal insiders leaked information anonymously, and the juicier it sounded, the more likely it was to get printed. Among dozens of brief updates was a two-sentence reference to Tom Gaines.

Tom Gaines, an American energy expert with A.W. Kassing and stationed in Germany, has visited the Kingdom of Saudi Arabia on three occasions in the past two months. There is speculation he may be an arms merchant with contact to rebel groups.

Donna summoned an emergency meeting with Defense Intelligence Agency officials Julius Gold and Emmett Cosgrove, Attorney Deirdre Rothstein and Donna's supervisor, Carl Hodges. A conference call with Tom was arranged thirty minutes into the meeting. The group met in a small classroom used for training new recruits. Flip chart easels were arranged around the perimeter of the room and a blackboard took up the entire wall in the front of the room. Carl entered, carrying three large folders. Taken together, the stack was about eighteen inches high.

"I brought all the major reports Tom generated from Germany," Carl began. "We may want to go over some of this material with him. Donna will bring everyone up to speed."

The group was seated around a small wooden conference table. "This was on a Saudi website this morning," Donna said as she distributed copies of the statement about Tom Gaines. "The website is not really respected, and occasionally includes wild accusations that have no basis in fact. Some of it is laughable. But on rare occasions, the site reports something that appears nowhere else, and it turns out to be true. Last year, it reported on the defection of a troop of seven officers who fled the country with about two million dollars. Turned out to be true. But for the most part, it's generally a source of amusement for the military and intelligence communities."

Carl jumped in. "If we pull the plug on Tom's mission too quickly, it very well could generate more suspicion. I don't want people over there thinking Tom disappeared. It'll just confirm a story like this."

"But if we wait too long, Tom could be at risk. I'm not comfortable exposing him to it," Emmett declared.

"What's the risk, Julius?" Carl asked.

Julius was responsible for surveillance of groups who monitored DIA projects and personnel. "Ordinarily, a security detail of the state police will investigate. The good news is that they will ask our ambassador for details first. I've already alerted our embassy to confirm details about Tom's background and purpose for being in Germany. The bad news is that they may not believe the ambassador's communiqués. If they don't, they'll do a thorough investigation of his background and Kassing. They'll leave no stone unturned. The good news is Tom's background was pretty well constructed. Well, at least we think it is. The bad news is that they will assume certain people in their government should know Tom because of his lifelong association with the energy business. It may seem strange to them that no one ever met him before. Bottom line... it's a crapshoot."

"What's your recommendation about when to get him out of there?" Carl asked.

"I agree with Emmett on this," Julius said. "We could pull Tom out tomorrow, but that will surely trigger a more vigorous investigation."

"Donna, go over the exit plans with us on this, just so we're all up to date," Carl asked.

"Plan A... Tom closes down Kassing because he has an offer with Rangel Petroleum as Consulting Engineer. He works there for two years, retires, and takes another non-industry job. Plan B... Tom meets an unfortunate fate. We have a new identity for him and a job in the finance industry. I have all the documents for these plans in my office. We're ready to go on a moment's notice — letters to clients, press reports, bank account closures, legal documents, new IDs. Stop by to read the details after our meeting."

"Let's get Tom on the phone now," Carl said.

Tom was sitting in his office, expecting the call. On his desk sat an envelope with round-trip tickets to Riyadh for the following morning. Rafiq understood that Tom would have to discuss the plan with, and obtain approval from, the group. Ultimate approval rested with Carl.

"Hey, Tom, you're making headlines there. Soon you'll be chased by paparazzi," Carl teased, a prelude to a sober discussion.

"I told you a long time ago, I'm probably not cut out for this stuff," Tom responded.

"Bullshit, Tom. You're good at this and you know it. I'm sitting here with a stack of reports I can barely carry. This is probably the best documentation we have about Russian drilling capacities."

"And I'm a hair away from getting very important information about a new drilling alloy. The experimentation phase is almost concluded."

"Well, I'm afraid you may not get to it. We may have to shut things down sooner than we expected. Listen, I've got Donna, Emmett, Julius and Deirdre here. You know about the website report, right?"

"Yeah. Crazy, huh?"

"I've seen crazier. We all have. What do you make of things from where you are?" Carl asked.

The group stared at the speaker in the middle of table as Tom began, "I spoke to Rafiq. He thinks I need to put on a little show. He wants me to go to his office tomorrow. I'd be there under the pretext of getting advice from him for a client who's calculating the effect of proposed tariffs on labor costs. It makes sense that I would seek Rafiq's recommendations on that. He can then parade me around to some key people. Do some quick handshakes, 'Hi, how are you,' and I'm out of there. He thinks it's important to show I'm legitimate, and if I'm with him that will help a lot. Then he can talk me up to them once I'm gone. It should counteract the ridiculous gun merchant story."

Carl was the first to respond. "It's an interesting idea, Tom." He looked at the group. "Tell me what you think."

Emmett quickly jumped in. "Too risky. If it's not executed well, it'll look contrived. You think you have problems now? Just wait."

"I agree," Julius said. "Plus, this puts Rafiq in jeopardy. If the suspicion surrounding you continues after you leave, he'll be under a microscope too. Think of where that can lead. Questions about how he knew you, where he met you. He's not used to being in the hot seat. At least not that kind of hot seat. He'll look inept, naïve or like he betrayed his own government by failing to disclose his association with an American agent. But listen, he's got to know all this. Why would he be willing to put himself in a potentially dangerous situation like this? Doesn't make sense. I say you forego this."

"Deirdre, your thoughts?"

"My job is to protect the agency from legal problems. If we go ahead with this, if Tom goes along with Rafiq's plan and something goes wrong, there are all kinds of embarrassing situations we can face. And I mean embarrassing legal situations. Think of it this way. Rafiq becomes complicit in our activities by aiding and abetting an undercover operation. Just think of the risk… Rafiq's an official of another government. We could be in a lot of trouble because we either co-opted him into our service or enticed him. And if you think we could be in trouble over this, think about what could happen to him."

"Your bottom line, Deirdre?"

Deirdre was emphatic: "No way we do this."

"It looks like we're heading to a consensus," Carl summarized. "Donna, how about you?"

Donna glanced at the others. They were a picture of resolve. Then she leaned forward and quietly but firmly declared, "I say we do it."

Donna's recommendation was met with looks of shock.

"Even with these risks?" Carl asked, skeptically.

Donna edged closer in toward the group. "Yes. Even with these risks. Look, we can try to slide away from this problem, whether we do it all at once where Tom just falls off the face of the earth, or whether we do it slowly. We know the risk of the first option. That would be nuts. We'd have people buzzing all over the place trying to figure out who Tom was and what he was doing. But what does going slowly mean? Do we wait a week, a month, a year? And what happens in the meantime? We can't just sit still hoping ambassadors can persuade people who have no faith in what our officials say. Certainly not when it comes to spies. I like Rafiq's plan. It makes Tom a human being. It shows he has legitimate business dealings and respected business associates. I say we do it."

"Tom, what do you think?" Carl asked.

At once, the group turned toward the speaker set in the center of the table as though it were a human being. "I'm torn, because I don't want to put my friend in what could be an immensely dangerous situation. This guy doesn't deserve that—"

Donna cut him off. "Tom, I don't want you to think that I'm not concerned about Rafiq's welfare. I understand the consequences if this is blown. They will be worse for him than for you. Much worse. But Tom, he's no fool. He certainly knows what he might be getting into by suggesting this plan. And I think it could work. He is very well respected, and I think his credibility is strong enough to dispel any suspicions about you. It'll be like vaccinating his colleagues against any more crap they might read about you."

"Then I also say let's do it," Tom asserted.

Carl sat back, collected his thoughts and looked at the group assembled around the speaker phone. "Okay, it's a go. Tom, watch your ass there. Call us tomorrow when you arrive back in your office. I want a full report... who you spoke to... what was said... how they seemed... what questions they asked. Based on what happens, we'll all decide on an exit strategy. We'll talk tomorrow afternoon."

TWENTY-NINE

Rafiq worked in a twelve-story office building on the outskirts of Riyadh's business district. The building was fourteen years old and was intended to provide additional office space for the oil ministry, an organization of colossal proportions and complexity with an ever-mushrooming bureaucracy. This building was to house computer systems and documents regarding the transportation of oil from Saudi Arabia to other parts of the world. It continued to serve as a repository for documents, but over time the first few floors were increasingly used for the oil ministry's attorneys. Rafiq was the senior attorney, and the vast number of lawyers who occupied the first five floors reported to him. The security staff of the building had a dual reporting relationship. For all security matters relating directly to the building and its contents, they reported to a director of security, who, in turn, reported to Rafiq. For matters involving national security, the security staff reported up to a state-run internal police agency. This was a good arrangement for Rafiq, if for no other reason than that it gave him access to national security activity.

Since the building housed vaults of sensitive legal documents, and because senior oil ministry officials routinely visited the building, it was well protected by the security force. Three security officers were stationed in the lobby, and each of the four basement entrances behind the building had a security guard posted at it at all times. The building was equipped with a modern network of security cameras.

Tom arrived at Rafiq's building at eleven twenty-five a.m. He showed his passport to the pleasant, albeit businesslike, security guard, who was expecting his arrival. Tom was asked to wear a badge with his name and photo printed on it for the duration of his day in the building. He was asked to sit in the lobby and wait for Rafiq's administrative aide to escort him to Rafiq's office.

Like many buildings constructed in the previous decade, this one's architecture was dominated by chrome and glass. The lobby entrance had two revolving doors and one large center double door, which was controlled by a motion-detection system. As Tom waited, he watched some of the occupants of the building leave, presumably for an early lunch.

About ten minutes later, an impeccably dressed young man approached Tom, who was seated on a corner couch. "Hello, Mr. Gaines," the young man said. "My name is Ali Barouk. I'm Mr. Farid's assistant. Welcome to Riyadh."

"Thank you, Ali. It's a pleasure to meet you."

"Likewise. Please follow me. Mr. Farid is expecting you."

Tom followed Ali to an elevator bank behind the security desk. The elevator doors had a polished sheen. Tom and Ali exited on the fourth floor and strode down a long hallway toward Rafiq's office. Tom noticed that most of the door signs had both Arabic and English writing on them, and most included the word 'Attorney'. 'Rafiq Farid' was written in large block letters, in a font larger than that on any of the other nameplates. Ali opened the door and he and Tom entered a reception area with seating for about ten people. A rich burgundy carpet blanketed the floor. Seascapes adorned the walls. Off to the right, just behind the reception area, was a conference room. The door to the conference room was ajar, and Tom could see that it could accommodate at least twenty people around an exquisite oak table. Rafiq's office was off to the left behind the reception area.

"I'll let him know you are here," Ali said in a rehearsed, officially affable voice.

A moment later, out bounded Rafiq with some atypical unrestrained enthusiasm. "Tom, so good to see you. Please, come in."

As they sat in Rafiq's office behind closed doors, Tom announced his readiness for the day's activity. "I'm ready to go, I think. Though this will be the most anxiety-producing acting job I've attempted."

Rafiq laughed. "I am feeling the same, my friend. And I believe this will be my acting debut. Let me fill you in on whom you will be meeting." Rafiq described five or six people to whom he wanted to introduce Tom. He noted these were key opinion leaders in the oil ministry. Their views carried much weight. If they liked Tom and perceived him to be legitimate, well, then later if Tom's name was bandied about as anything other than a bona fide American businessman, they would decry it as 'rubbish'. And, according to Rafiq, if they dismissed accounts of Tom as a weapons merchant or spy as ridiculous, so would the multitudes of others who read scandalous website reports and gossip columns.

"Let's be on our way," Rafiq said with resolve, along with a hint of resignation.

Rafiq escorted Tom to the third floor. The layout was similar to the fourth floor, though there were fewer individual offices. The pair waited in the outer office of Aref al-Sharif, special assistant for economic affairs to the ambassador to the Organization for Petroleum Exporting Countries. A moment later, out walked a lanky, bespectacled, rosy-cheeked man. He was wearing traditional Saudi robes and appeared severely preoccupied.

"Aref, I know you are busy, but I wanted to introduce you to an American colleague, Tom Gaines."

Tom and Aref shook hands and exchanged pleasantries.

"Tom is a consulting engineer with A.W. Kassing, based in Germany," Rafiq began. "We have been chatting about the effects of tariffs on labor costs."

"A sensitive subject," Aref cut in. "I wish these were more predictable. It would help to make costs more predictable." It didn't take much to make Aref feel at home with this subject. "Are you an economist, Tom?"

"No. I'm an engineer by training. Our firm has clients that manufacture drilling materials, and we also advise them on the deployment of equipment and evaluate studies of oil and gas volumes."

"No doubt your job has been getting more challenging over these past years. The tariff issue will complicate cost calculations. I'm sure you're aware."

"I know. Two of my clients are unsure how much money to place in reserves for labor costs. Rafiq has been helpful," Tom said.

"Whatever he told you, double it!" Aref said, deadpan.

Sensing Aref was humorless, Tom's reaction was slow. Then Aref and Rafiq laughed, and Tom joined in.

255

"Well, I've got to move Tom along and I know you are busy, Aref. I just wanted to introduce you. Tom is a very progressive thinker."

"I hope we will have more time to talk the next time you visit. A pleasure to meet you, Tom."

"Very good to meet you as well."

A minute later, as Tom and Rafiq stood at the elevator bank, Tom asked, "So, how did that go?"

"Perfect. Aref is one of the most serious men I know. He rarely makes a joke. It's just not his nature. And he would do so only when he feels comfortable with someone."

"Good. Who's next?" Tom asked, relieved that the ice was broken in a positive way.

For the next twenty minutes, Tom was introduced in a similar manner to three other officials. The introductions went smoothly, much like the interaction with Aref. None to whom Rafiq introduced Tom believed him to be anyone other than who he claimed. Tom's easy manner and facility for speaking with great clarity and intelligence about engineering gave him instant credibility. All told, Tom and Rafiq were pleased that an effective foundation was being established among key gatekeepers in the ministry.

"I saved Sadad for last. We should try to do this quickly. I don't want to give him an opportunity to ask questions," Rafiq cautioned. Sadad al-Naimi was a former prosecutor, and for the past five years he had been the chief liaison between the oil ministry and the state security apparatus. Rafiq had some doubts about going forward with this little charade with Sadad, but if it went as well as with the others, Tom's reputation would surely be solidified.

"Sadad, good to see you," Rafiq said, extending his hand, as the three men stood in the reception area of Sadad's office on the second floor.

"Good to see you as well, Rafiq," Sadad replied, motioning the two men toward his office.

"And this is Tom Gaines, a consulting engineer I have known for a while. I wanted him to say hello to you before he left for the day."

"Nice to meet you, Tom. Please, come into my office for a moment."

Sadad's office was sprawling. And completely chaotic. On the far end of the office was Sadad's desk, and sitting atop were massive piles of paper strewn about. A large table in the center of the room, large enough to seat about ten people, was also densely populated with stacks of papers, folders, binders and assorted documents.

"Ah, Tom, I know what you must be thinking. How disorganized this office appears! But somehow, I manage to know exactly where everything is. My only talent, perhaps."

Tom laughed. "You must be quite at home here."

"And where is home for you?" Sadad asked. Sadad had olive skin much like Rafiq's, square shoulders and a foreboding appearance with a heavy mustache linking his rounded jowls.

"Home for the past few years is Germany. We established a German branch of our engineering firm there."

"What about in the U.S.? I spent about five years there studying law at Georgetown. Beautiful area. Where are you from?"

"Not far from Georgetown, actually. I'm from Baltimore."

"Baltimore. Oh, yes. I was there a few times. Wonderful city."

This seems jovial and light, Tom thought. Rafiq knew better.

"Tom, tell me, what brings you to our fair city?"

Rafiq cut in. "Tom and I met some months back at a conference. He is doing some work on calculating labor costs for drilling and wanted some information on tariffs."

"There is much variability in tariff estimates," Tom threw in. "A couple of clients are trying to determine how large a reserve to create."

"Was my good friend Rafiq helpful?" Sadad asked good-naturedly.

"We'll know that answer if my clients avoid bankruptcy," Tom replied with a smile.

Sadad also smiled. "If their businesses fail, I think it only fair that Rafiq represent them in bankruptcy court, since they are there as a result of his bad advice. But I think bankruptcy will start looking like a good alternative compared to paying his fees."

They shared a laugh. Then Rafiq rose from his chair and tapped Tom on the shoulder. "We should leave now, Tom. I don't want you to miss your flight, and we have taken much time from Sadad as it is."

Sadad interrupted as Tom began to lift himself from his chair. "Please remain for just a moment. I have a question for you, Tom."

Tom and Rafiq sat down and Sadad began, "Tom, I get a list of all of the visitors scheduled to come into this building. Rafiq is aware; he gets the same list. With foreigners, I have a member of my staff do a quick background search. You can never be too careful, especially these days. Anyway, I wanted to check, are you aware that a website has been reporting that you are a weapons dealer?"

"Yes," Tom replied, without hesitation.

"Any idea why there would be such a rumor about you?" Sadad asked.

"I haven't a clue, actually," Tom replied. "A colleague speculated that it was because I made a couple of trips to Saudi Arabia and have an international consulting practice. Seems crazy."

"Hmmm." Sadad was pensive. "That website goes out on a limb. Most of the stuff they print is laughable. But it is wise for us to remain wary, nonetheless. Therefore, I would like you to help me feel better about you."

"Sadad, Tom is a guest in our country, a guest of mine," Rafiq scolded. "Are you implying our guest should be treated with suspicion?"

"No, and please forgive me, Tom. I am not insinuating anything about you or your background. But when a report comes out stating that you are an international weapons dealer... well, it would be imprudent of me, in my position, to not follow up. I'm sure you understand, Tom."

"Sadad, with all due respect, I think the scrutiny should be directed to the authors of the website," Tom asserted, calculating how far to go with a show of defiance, bordering on indignity.

"Perhaps you are right. That website proffers sensationalism. We probably should not pay attention to it. But still, it is there. In black and white. Tom, tell me, you worked for Lowen McGrady, didn't you?"

Rafiq cut in. "Sadad, is this an inquisition of our guest?"

"Not at all. But at the risk of minor embarrassment, I just want to feel comfortable about who is entering our country. If there was no website report, we would not be having this conversation."

Tom intervened. "Rafiq, I completely agree with Sadad. If he didn't exercise some suspicion based on that site, he would not be fulfilling his responsibility. So, Sadad, please ask any question you like."

"Thank you, Tom. And again, I would be more than pleased to have no doubts about you. Please, Lowen McGrady — I understand you worked there."

"I did."

"Which office did you work out of?"

"I was affiliated with two offices. One in Copenhagen and the other in Colorado Springs."

"The managing partner of Colorado Springs... wasn't that Martin Ruffington?"

"Yes. Do you know him?" Tom calmly asked Sadad.

"I met him twice. Very smart guy. I believe he left Lowen about three years ago. Where is he today?"

Martin Ruffington had been recruited by the CIA as an energy analyst. He was part of a team that was responsible for developing safeguards for the strategic petroleum reserve. His cover story was that he retired to do freelance consulting work. Martin was solicited to assist in developing the alias for Stewart Jacobson when the DIA was fashioning his new identity.

"I haven't kept up with Marty," Tom said. "As far as I know, he retired."

"You know, Tom, we have some people in our ministry who worked with Lowen McGrady engineers. I called a couple of them this morning — seems our meeting is fortuitous — and I can't find one who knows you."

"I spent very little of my time in the office. You know one of the disadvantages of not having a family is that you get labeled as the one willing to travel. I spent a good deal of time working on projects overseas."

"It is possible to be so isolated?" Sadad asked, his voice tinged with skepticism.

"That's a tough one to answer. I would be happy to give you the names and contact information of some colleagues. And, of course, you are more than welcome to contact Marty."

Rafiq jumped in. "Sadad, I appreciate Tom's willingness to be questioned. He does this out of courtesy. I think it only fair that we extend a similar courtesy."

"Tom would be surprised if we didn't follow up on a security matter.

259

I think it is a courtesy that we are not doing it behind his back."

"I agree," Tom asserted, looking at Rafiq.

"I first met Tom at one of our energy conferences about two years ago. Then a couple of months ago he was invited to speak at a conference here in Riyadh to a group from the oil ministry. His talk was on the future of oil exploration from an engineer's perspective."

"I see. So, you met him twice?"

"Yes, twice," replied Rafiq. "And I would add that he came to us highly recommended by Olaf Neelson."

"Olaf has been an honest partner to us," Sadad said, looking pointedly at Tom. "What was your relationship with Olaf?"

"I've known Olaf for years. We first met at a conference about twenty years ago. Both of us have little interest in politics, and we struck up a friendship. Our firm has done much work for his government."

"Have you ever worked directly for your government?" Sadad asked pointedly.

"No, not directly."

"Indirectly?"

"Many of the clients I've had over the years have government contracts," Tom responded, matter-of-factly.

"In the course of your relationship with clients, have you ever had contact with government officials?"

"It depends on your definition of 'official'," Tom said.

"My definition is not hair-splitting. I'm wondering if government officials ever asked you to do business on their behalf."

"I wouldn't say if they did. You know that. However, I can say that I never worked on behalf of my government."

"What if I said I have proof you did?" Sadad asked, his look growing sterner.

"I'd say I'd like to take a look at it."

"Tom, would you excuse Rafiq and me for a minute? I'd like to discuss something about this in private."

"Sure, I'll wait in the reception area." As he stood to leave, Tom and Rafiq both resisted the urge to make even the most subtle of eye contact, lest they reveal concern.

"Sadad, what is going on?" Rafiq began.

"Rafiq, I don't trust him. He's a spy."

"What?" Rafiq was astounded. "Is this something you know or are you guessing?"

"I'm not usually wrong."

"Do you have proof of your accusations?"

"His answers were too rehearsed. If he wasn't a spy, he wouldn't have said he would like to see the proof. He would have said something like 'that's ludicrous, that's insane', or gotten angry or nervous... something other than his acknowledgement that proof may exist."

"You are jumping to a conclusion."

"Why are you so eager to protect him?"

"Sadad, listen to me. I spent quite a lot of time with him today, and at the conference at which we met. You think I would meet with just anybody? Why would he waste his time coming to see me to talk about mundane matters of tariffs? And I'll tell you why your suspicion is upsetting me. This man came here as my guest. He should not be subjected to an investigation. This is not the hospitality we extend to a guest. It is shameful."

"He seemed too eager for me to ask questions. It was as though he wanted to discuss his story. I felt he was too compliant. And Rafiq, you should be more concerned with the security of our affairs than with a stranger."

"We do our affairs no justice when we engage in humiliation sport toward our visitors."

"Well, I don't trust his story. And I plan to look into it further," Sadad declared.

"I'm no fool, Sadad. I had him checked out before I met him the first time. He is who he says he is and he does what he says he does."

"Rafiq, I'm responsible for security for the ministry. If my gut tells me to look further, you would lose all respect for me if I didn't follow up."

"Have it your way. But no more of this embarrassing inquiry."

Rafiq departed Sadad's office. Then Tom and Rafiq went back to Rafiq's office. They sat at his desk, sipping espressos.

"You know Sadad will be looking into your background," Rafiq said.

"Should I be concerned?" Tom asked.

"I don't know. Listen, Tom, we never discussed this matter much. It's none of my business, but your mission, whatever it is, I want to be comfortable that we are not the focus of it."

Rafiq pre-empted Tom before he could answer. "No, don't respond. I know you well enough that you would not exploit our friendship."

"Thank you, Rafiq. You're such a good friend to me. After all these years, I still feel more comfortable with you than I do with most people. It's refreshing, after where my job has taken me. I don't want this to spill over to have them questioning you."

"Tom, I've been loyal and faithful to the ministry. Everyone knows that. No, I'm not worried for me. But tell me, when they start checking into your background... it will look legitimate and thorough?"

"It should. The people back home who work on these identity matters – they're exceptionally good. Enormously thorough. I have college degrees, a strong resume, and people who will vouch for me. I think I can weather a storm."

"Let's hope, because Sadad is quite adept at creating a storm. So perhaps we can head him off at the pass." Rafiq allowed himself a wry smile. "I heard that expression in an American movie and always liked it."

Tom was preparing to leave, but as he was about to walk out of the office, Rafiq said, "Wait, there's one more thing I want to show you." It was a page from an old college yearbook. "Do you know this man?" Rafiq asked, pointing to a picture above the name "Stewart Jacobson."

It took a second for the photo and the yearbook page to register. Then Tom laughed. "Don't tell me that's Chris Latkins?"

"What a memory! Unfortunately, Chris died three years ago. Heart attack. Lived in Wyoming. Seems like a good stand-in."

"I didn't know you were so devious, Rafiq," Tom teased.

"I don't hold a candle to you, my dear friend."

Tom and Rafiq grasped hands warmly, then Tom exited the office.

Tom was to meet a driver in the lobby of the building, but when Ali brought him there, he was informed by a security officer that the driver was running approximately twenty minutes late. Tom asked if there was a lounge or cafeteria where he could get a cup of coffee. The officer directed him to the building's newly renovated cafeter[...] level of the building.

About five minutes after Tom left the lobby, a young ma[...] the building. A thick crop of hair and a wispy beard garnished[...] features. A khaki backpack was slung over his shoulder. Dre[...] casually in jeans and sneakers, he had on a loose-fitting flannel shirt an[...] a bulky desert-tan jacket, zipped midway. He approached the security desk and was greeted with a smile by the officer on duty.

"How's school?" the officer asked.

"I haven't been going that often," the young man replied, an almost glazed look on his face.

"Got your mind on other things?"

"Sort of. Hey, is my father here?"

"He's in his office. Should I tell him you're here?"

"No, not yet. I want to have lunch first."

"Sure. Sorry, you know I need to check all bags coming into the building. Could you please open the backpack for me?"

Inside were books and some CDs. "Okay, go ahead. See you later," the officer said.

Tom was impressed with the cafeteria. It was a sterling site, bright, clean and large. It had been reconstructed in the past year, largely as a convenience for employees. An assortment of hot and cold foods was offered; there were traditional Saudi offerings as well as European cuisine. Tom ordered coffee and a serving of flatbread, then walked to a table close to the entrance. He wanted to make sure his visitor's badge would be visible to the driver who was instructed to meet him there.

As Tom settled into his chair near the entryway, the young man entered, passing directly in front of Tom. Tom took quick notice of the young man because he was scanning each person who entered, as it might have been his driver. The young man did not go the food court area, but instead walked to the rear of the cafeteria. This section had a row of windows from floor to ceiling, which looked out on a promenade of walkways in the rear of the building. This was a beautiful spot, replete with a garden and a small fountain. Cafeteria guests typically chose seats along this back wall so they could enjoy the garden view.

It was about two o'clock, the final half hour or so of the lunch period

... man sat at a small round table. About a
... se proximity, and a few other scattered
... here the young man sat and the cafeteria
... d. No one took notice as the young man
... a prayer book and placed the backpack
... ge toward the middle of the book and
... . He remained fixed on that page,
... hatter from the nearby guests in the
... the book, he quietly mouthed the words. He
... and forth ever so subtly as he read. His motion was soft and
lyrical, but became progressively, though only slightly, energized during
the course of a three-minute period.

This young man was now in a bubble, completely alone. He had
become severed from anything other than this one momentary and
momentous commitment, isolated from anything other than the
fierceness of his personal hell. Years of private torment collided now
with a morbid sense of purpose. It all came together in a burst of despair
and mission, a mix of virulent combustibility. This young man sat by
himself, moved only by churnings so deep within they were completely
indiscernible and inaccessible to all, even those closest to him. His world
had become quintessentially concealed; he became reclusive not in a
social sense (for he did have acquaintances and intermingled in the
world), but rather he adopted a particular spiritual isolation. Devastation
had set in as he became certain that peacefulness would forever elude
him. He projected his distraught soul onto a purpose which could give
his life meaning, even if he had to package his grand sense of purpose
into a flicker. The world had become too fuzzy, so much so that any sense
of coherence lay in extremes, far away from the muddled and agonizing
center where different views could live side by side.

Most dismal, the connection to both his parents had vanished. His
mother and his father, who had suffered a tragic loss, failed to glean from
it how horrifyingly unjust the world seemed to him. The death of his
sister, a young girl, such innocence snuffed, and the world continued to
go on, accepting all the fundamental premises — we buy things, we see
movies, we dine, we talk about the mundane — that hold it together. This
is wrong. This cannot be, he fathomed. And there was something about

this building — this ministry — that represented the greatest poison of all. For it was here that people came each day to defend those premises. Each and every person who worked here, every one of them was responsible for holding relationships with outsiders so that business could continue to be conducted. As he plunged deeper into his tormented abyss, it became impossible for him to see people from other places and with other perspectives as anything but monsters. These people in this building were complicit in tearing down the purity of his culture. How could they sit and eat while his world crumbled? How could they not know better? How could they not see the pain their actions, their murderous ignorance, inflicted?

And with that he reached down and placed his hand under his jacket. Around his waist was a thick burlap belt. Arrayed about the belt in holster-style receptacles were three hand grenades, each neatly and tightly packed in a deadly wrapper filled with ball bearings. A small black detonating switch was anchored to the front, covering his belly button. He never looked at the faces of the people near him. Had he, he would have noticed Haitham, a fifty-five-year-old maintenance worker who, two days earlier, had celebrated the birth of his first grandchild. So joyful from her birth it was impossible to wipe the smile from his weathered face. Haitham was on a fifteen-minute coffee break. He would also have noticed, just to his right, two secretaries finishing a late lunch. Farooha, twenty-four, had been married for eight months. She was effervescent. Her lunch partner, Roba, worked in the security department. Roba was only nineteen, and she was worried that she was not catching on to the information system quickly enough. Her father was a soldier in the Saudi army. At that very moment, Farooha was providing encouragement to her, and Roba was beginning to feel more confident about her job. He would have noticed two lawyers, Mohammed and Khalid, seated at the next table. Between them, they had six children ranging in age from six months to twenty-five years. They had been colleagues for almost ten years. Khalid's brother had died of cancer four years earlier, and he and his wife did volunteer work at a cancer clinic, which was very important to them. At that very moment Mohammed and Khalid were talking about a case involving theft at an oil facility. Two cafeteria employees, a teenaged boy, Givon, and girl, Atifah, were cleaning another nearby table. Also gone unnoticed by the young man, they had arrived only half an hour earlier to work the afternoon shift. Last week she had discovered he loved soccer and he had learned she loved to dance. Atifah's mother had pneumonia when Atifah was two years old, and she had not been able to have additional children. Givon's older brother, whom Givon idolized, was a pilot in the Saudi Air Force. At another nearby table sat three people, two of whom were dressed in traditional Saudi robes and the third dressed in a well-tailored western suit. The two Saudis, Emir and Hamal, were mid-level oil ministry officials and the third man, Robert Harrington, was a dean visiting from a British university. He was eager to establish an internship for engineering students in Saudi Arabia and had waited four months for the meeting that day. At that very moment they were discussing eligibility criteria for the interns. All three men were married. Emir and Hamal had nine children between them. Hamal had two grandchildren. Emir's oldest daughter was getting married in six months. A son had just moved to France to study culinary arts. Robert and his wife had been trying unsuccessfully to have a child for six years. Recently, they had decided they would adopt an orphaned child from Africa. Their trip to Kenya was three weeks away and they had arrangements to meet with an adoption agency there. The agency had presented the Harringtons with a photo and story of a two-year-old boy who captured the couple's heart. None of these people had caught the young man's notice.

And not one of these people had a chance when Abdel Farid pressed the detonator button and blew himself and every one of them to shreds.

At that instant an incomprehensible departure from reason occurred. The blast produced a deafening roar that lasted only a second, thunderous, but at once done. Abdel and the people nearest to him were ripped into pieces, the unforgiving shrapnel piercing limbs and torsos with startling effortlessness. The explosion did not distinguish between people and things, so furniture and Roba and Farooha and Haitham and Atifah and all the rest were heaved into a mighty and random collision, their lives ended by a singular act of unimaginable butchery. The cafeteria became a cathedral to blood, smoke, death and chaos. Body parts were strewn about in a catastrophic human mauling. All of them, Hamal and Emir, Robert and Khalid, Givon and Mohammad, Atifah and

Haitham, Roba and Farooha, all of them, as well as Abdel Farid, lay mingled and mangled together, their lives ending in that one second. And the lives of every person who knew and loved them would never be the same.

The first on the scene was one of the two security officers from the lobby. The other remained at his post in the lobby and invoked the emergency protocol for the building. This involved seizing control of the elevators, securing emergency exits, and contacting police and other authorities. The officer entering the cafeteria had been trained in the army. Despite experience seeing corpses and other disfigurements resulting from violence, he balked, as this grisly scene was singularly revolting. The first person the officer encountered was Tom Gaines, the American he had directed to the cafeteria not twenty minutes earlier. Tom was on the floor, the table at which he sat now on top of him. Blood trickled from his forehead. He was alive. And conscious. The officer pulled the table off Tom and asked if he was all right.

"My leg," he voiced weakly, "I think it's broken."

The officer looked around. Just then Rafiq appeared, having been granted permission to use the stairs from a member of the security detail. He was puffing from racing to get to the blast site. He saw Tom and fell to his knees beside him.

"Tom," he shouted, his voice hoarse, his hands trembling. "Are you hurt? What happened? Can you speak?"

"A young man, over there," Tom said in a feeble, strained voice. He pointed to the human mass of blood and remains on the far side of the cafeteria. "A kid over there, he blew himself up."

The scene defied comprehension. Water was pouring down from the ceiling, emanating from a severed pipe and coursing through a pond of blood, bloating it and causing it to seep and swell. A gruesome stench, acrid from smoke and death, settled in with devastating rapidity. The smoke thickened, plunging the scene into a smoggy darkness.

The officer heard Tom and bolted around. "The young man, was he wearing a khaki jacket?"

"Yeah."

The officer staggered, and a look of horror came over his face. He turned to Rafiq. "Mr. Farid. I'm so sorry. I'm so sorry. That was Abdel.

267

Your son, Mr. Farid. He came down here about ten minutes ago."

Rafiq looked at the officer as though he alone possessed the power to issue a miraculous denial. "Are you certain Abdel came down here?" he pleaded.

The delivery of such catastrophic news was almost too much for the officer. "Mr. Farid, I am so sorry."

Rafiq sat back on his knees, placed his hands over his eyes and erupted in a shriek, "No, no, no, no, not Abdel, not Abdel."

Tom tried to lift himself up. His knee was burning with pain. Tom put his arms around Rafiq, and he too began to cry. Neither man said anything. This was just too much.

After a few seconds, Rafiq looked Tom directly in the eyes and said firmly, "I must take care of this." Rafiq stood and looked at the officer. "I need to find my son."

With that, Rafiq waded into the carnage, the officer following him. Most of the bodies were so ripped apart that they were unrecognizable. Their clothing was a scorched mess, drenched from blood and the onslaught of water. The dense smoky haze filled the room, impairing visibility. Electrical wires lay bare on the floor. Rafiq knew he should not be entering this area, but he needed to see his son. Police and firefighters had begun to arrive. Rafiq heard Sami's voice at the entrance, shouting to police about how loud the explosion was, how it rocked the building several floors up. Rafiq felt something under his foot. He looked down. It was a woman's hand.

Ambulances and police converged on the scene. Emergency medical technicians and state police descended upon the cafeteria, which all at once was in the grip of organized chaos. The smoke was thick and the risk of conflagration high. Firefighters rushed in and secured emergency water sources. Everyone was screaming.

Rafiq waded further into the bleakness, stepping over body after body. Debris and limbs intermingled in ghostly concoction. The large windows were all blown out. The smoke hung and produced a dusk-like darkness. Rafiq staggered across a pile of chairs. A familiar object caught his eye. There, under a chair, was a tattered and singed backpack. It was his son's. He lifted it and gazed at it. It was charred and was barely held together, the outer flap ripped away. Rafiq knelt and looked around. Two feet away, partially submerged in a pool of blood, were what appeared to be a few pages of a prayer book. He leaned toward the burned clump of pages and lifted them, blood dripping off the bottom edge. The drops fell onto a small remaining piece of a canvas book cover lying below. Rafiq recognized the fabric as the cover of his son's prayer book. He placed his hand on the blood-soaked remnant. He knew it was Abdel's blood. It was all so incomprehensible.

"Rafiq. I am so sorry, but we must step away from this area. Maybe there is another bomb." The voice belonged to Sadad, though Rafiq could not see him through the smoke.

"Sadad, where are you?" Rafiq shouted.

At once, he appeared next to Rafiq.

"This was my son's prayer book," Rafiq said, holding the drenched book. "My son is somewhere in here." Rafiq gestured toward the massacre.

"I am so sorry. They told me Abdel may be responsible."

"That's what I heard as well," and Rafiq began to weep. "Oh, no. Jamila. I need to tell Jamila. I need to tell his mother."

"I can stay with you, Rafiq. I'm here. But let us move from the area. This site is too gruesome, especially for you. It is too much to take in. The only one who survived is your American guest. It will do you no good to agonize here."

"I need to see him," Rafiq whispered.

"We need to get out of here. The police need to scan this area for any more explosives. Please, come with me," Sadad said.

"Sadad. I must see Tom. And my son. My son. I need to see him and I won't leave until I do. He is here, Sadad. My son is here."

Rafiq walked through the dense smoldering cloud toward the entrance of the cafeteria. Police and emergency medical technicians were combing the area. A medical technician was attending to Tom. He was given oxygen and was gingerly lifted onto a stretcher.

"Wait!" Rafiq shouted. "I need to speak to this man."

"Sorry, sir." The medical technician declared, "Our orders are to get him medical attention and to the police for questioning."

There was no way Rafiq could allow Tom to be questioned by state police.

"You must listen to me. I am in charge of security for this building. Nothing happens without my authorization. I must speak to him. Privately."

"Sorry, but no way," the technician protested. "If anything happens to him, it will be my head."

"That will be the least of your problems if you don't get out of my way. This man may die soon, and I'm not about to lose an opportunity to find out what happened in my building. With my son." And with that, Rafiq pushed passed the technician and toward Tom, who was sprawled on a stretcher. Perhaps it was his shock, but he resumed his businesslike demeanor and at once was composed again.

Rafiq leaned in toward Tom. "Are you all right? Can you hear me?"

Tom looked up and nodded. He was weak, his breathing labored. "Yes. Rafiq, I am so sorry."

"We have no more than a few seconds, Tom. Listen carefully and do exactly as I say." Then Rafiq leaned in very close, practically touching Tom's ear, and whispered his plan. In another minute, Rafiq walked back to the technician, who waited a few feet away.

"Attention! Listen to me," Rafiq yelled. "We must follow international protocol. This man is seriously injured and may die. Our instructions are to bring him to the American Embassy. Doctors will be there waiting for him."

"Are you crazy?" the technician shouted. "Of course he might die, especially if we bring him to the embassy. There's no way they can take care of him there."

"Now, you listen to me," Rafiq countered, glaring at the technician. "This man is an American citizen. He made a specific request to go to his embassy. Are you prepared to take responsibility for creating an international incident?"

"He never said anything to me about going to the embassy."

"Well, he just told me exactly that. Go ask him," Rafiq demanded. Time was running out. At any second the police would turn their attention to Tom, the only witness to survive the blast.

"Come on. Go ask him," Rafiq ordered.

The technician turned to Tom. "Sir, do you wish to be brought to your embassy?"

Feebly, Tom nodded.

"Now, move! Quickly, move!" Rafiq shouted.

The technician scowled at Rafiq. "If this man dies, it will be your responsibility."

Rafiq glared back at the technician and inched toward him. "Everything down here is my responsibility. Now go."

Tom was ushered out on the stretcher and lifted into the waiting ambulance. About fifteen minutes later he was at the rear gate of the American Embassy. The officer at the gate was awaiting him and motioned the ambulance to pass through into the embassy grounds.

The driver and technician lifted the stretcher and slid it out of the ambulance. An American physician signed a form authorizing the transfer of custody of the patient from the Saudi emergency medical technicians to the United States. The physician dispatched two medical aides to bring Tom into the compound to the medical unit. As Tom was wheeled away, the Saudis had doubts about whether he would survive.

THIRTY

Rafiq was waiting outside the front of his office building as a sleek, black Mercedes pulled up. The door opened and a small figure, clothed and veiled in black, emerged from the back seat with frantic abandon.

"Rafiq, is it true? Where is he? Where is my son?" she cried as she ran to him and grabbed his arms. Her grasp was like a choke hold.

He embraced her as she melted into his chest. "Jamila, I'm so sorry. I'm so sorry."

Her sobbing was uncontrollable. She pulled back and again clutched his arms, her grip more powerfully intense than her small frame should allow. Screeching now, "It's not true. It cannot be true. Take me to him. Rafiq, I need to see him. I need to see him now."

Rafiq was caught between his own shock and his instinct to protect his wife from merciless pain. "Jamila, you cannot see him. It was so quick. He felt nothing. They all told me this. Everyone who knows about these things. The police. They said no one would have felt anything."

Jamila shot a hard look at Rafiq. Her eyes widened with a new sense of horror, a sobering realization. "Others were killed too?" Jamila demanded.

"Yes. They don't know how many. Maybe five. Maybe ten."

"Oh God. Mercy. God. Mercy. Where is he?" Jamila was wailing.

"They are taking care of him. No one is allowed in there now. It's too dangerous." Then, adding, "You would not want to see him like this."

A member of the investigative police force approached. "I am sorry to disturb you. But we have some questions which must be answered immediately."

Rafiq and Jamila looked at him. The stark reality hit home— their personal tragedy was also a crime.

"Of course," Rafiq replied. "Jamila, are you able?"

She nodded.

There was compassion in the police officer's eyes. "I am deeply sorry for your loss. For all of this. We will need to do a more thorough interview later. Right now, we need to know whether your son was acting alone or whether he has colleagues who might strike elsewhere."

Rafiq began to respond, "I believe Abdel—"

Jamila cut him off. "Abdel was alone. He was alone. His life became impossible. Now he is out of his misery." Rafiq was surprised that Jamila had stopped crying.

"How can you be certain?" the officer asked.

"He fell into despair. We should have seen it sooner. He had no friends," Jamila said.

The officer turned to Rafiq. "There was an American. Why was he taken to his embassy?"

"He insisted," answered Rafiq.

"Do we have information about him? Why was he here?"

"His name was Tom Gaines. He was here to visit me about oil tariff issues. He was leaving when this happened."

"We will need to speak to him. He's the only witness."

Rafiq cut in. "We all know what happened. The American will add nothing to this tragedy. My son committed a terrible act. Others have died. The American Embassy will contact me after he receives medical attention. He was in very bad shape when he was taken from here."

"Is he expected to survive?" the officer asked.

"I pray his will not be one more life taken by my son," Rafiq said. "I will let you know as soon as I hear something from the embassy."

"Thank you. You know, you are not allowed back in the building at this time. Please go to the hotel across the street. I will escort you both. They have prepared a place for you to stay where you will be comfortable. We can talk later."

About twenty-eight hundred miles away, Elaine received a call from a military liaison in the United States Embassy in Riyadh. She was briefed on the event and on Tom's condition.

"Will he... will he recover?" she asked with atypical tentativeness.

"He's been in surgery for fifteen minutes so far. The blast took a toll on him internally. He took in a lot of smoke. Blood loss wasn't severe. His knee is broken. We'll know more in an hour or so. He was very insistent that I tell you to activate an immediate closure plan."

There were multiple plans for the cessation of A.W. Kassing's operations. Closure plans ranged from immediate to protracted, each determined by circumstances. The clear preference was to permit the organization to fade. The game plan was easy: Tom and Elaine decide to take new jobs. Wrap-up takes a few weeks to a couple of months. Communications are dispatched announcing an orderly and planned phasing out. In one of these scenarios, A.W. Kassing achieves its demise through incremental lessening. It becomes less noticed, less of a target. It simply disappears by shrinking into nothingness.

The greater concern always lay with the need for an abrupt shutdown. This would occur only in the face of some emergency like a breach of security or a heightened suspicion about the nature of the organization's work. The challenge with this option was not in the operation. Tom and Elaine required no more than a couple of hours, maybe even less, to organize a shutdown. Every A.W. Kassing document was scanned and encrypted; hard copies were maintained, when necessary, only in offices in the United States. The office was in a building owned and operated by a government affiliate. Phone lines were secure and managed by contractors of the Defense Department. The military was prepared to take Tom and Elaine to a military installation for transport out of the country if necessary. This could all be put in motion instantaneously. The bulk of the challenge involved the aftermath. New identities and reintegration plans would need to be put into effect for Tom and Elaine.

Elaine hastily arranged a conference call with Donna, Carl and Deirdre. By the time she reached them, about ten minutes following her call from the embassy, they had already been briefed.

"Any update on Tom's condition?" Elaine asked.

"Nothing more than what you were told," Donna replied.

Carl jumped in. "I arranged for a team to close down the office by eight p.m. your time, Elaine. Use the next couple of hours to make sure all files are secure. You'll be picked up in two hours and taken to the embassy."

"Okay. When will I return to the States?" Elaine asked.

"We'll evaluate that once we have an idea of Tom's condition," Carl responded.

"You may need new passports and visas," Deirdre suggested. "I'll arrange for them to be at the embassy for you. You'll have a packet with new identity information."

Donna added, "I'll notify your contacts in Europe to let them know we're shutting down."

"What about Rafiq?" Elaine asked. "What do we tell him?"

"The truth," insisted Carl. "Tom has a lot of faith in him, and he went way out on a limb for us."

"For Tom," Donna noted.

"Yeah, for Tom," Carl acknowledged.

"I'm going to get an update on his condition, then I'll call Rafiq. We're going to need him," Donna said.

Rafiq and Jamila were huddled in a quiet room of a small hotel across the street from Rafiq's building. A state security officer was with them. He was a young man, not quite thirty years old, and was very conscious of their need for private space. A heavy silence darkened the room.

Rafiq's cell phone pierced the stillness. "Yes, hello?" he answered with energetic anticipation, as though awaiting news that might undo this most tragic moment.

He listened for a couple of seconds, then cupped the microphone. "It's the U.S. Embassy," he whispered to Jamila and the officer. He went back to listening. His eyes widened, and his face grew grim. "Thank you for notifying me," he said, and then hung up.

Rafiq turned to Jamila and the officer. "It was about Tom, the American. He didn't survive the blast."

"He died?" confirmed the officer.

"Yes," Rafiq replied somberly. "He's gone."

THIRTY-ONE

Linda knew she needed to speak to Stewart. The realization came into focus in a flash. She had spent twenty years second-guessing the correctness of her decision not to tell him about Jack… and twenty years not telling Jack about him. A big part of her knew all along it was not the right decision, but the rationale she cultivated took on a certain persuasiveness and a life of its own. Linda understood that she had become a captive of her own decision. After a while, the story of the anonymous donor became almost real. And the more real it became, the more it needed to be protected. Now, it had become a myth that had shattered. Not only had the truth been discovered, but the moral underpinnings she had constructed for it had also crumbled.

She needed to speak to Stewart right away to explain how sorry she was. Access to him, however, was impossible. Perhaps Jack had a way of reaching him. She doubted it, but she also recognized that she was still not privy to everything in the situation. Linda started to call Jack, but quickly realized their phones were probably tapped, and any discussion about Stewart should be conducted in person. It occurred to her that until recently this lifelong story involving three people was completely under her control; now she was the one in the story with the least control.

Jack arrived home in the late afternoon. Linda felt a little anxious about seeing him. Everything had changed in the last few days. The tension over the obvious was draped with layers of confusing unease. She feared Jack was in an early stage of pulling away from her. Not only because he had discovered Stewart, but because, quite simply, he was getting older. Her life had been organized largely around her son, and he was entering the stage of life where this was no longer necessary. She knew the day would arrive when he would come of age and his independence would draw him from home, but she also felt dread that the discovery of his father could accelerate its inevitability. Moreover, she believed it could cause him to be resentful.

Linda had been treading softly around Jack for the past days. "Hi, where have you been?" she asked softly after he entered and offered a breezy wave to her.

"Just spending some time with Cathy." The tone of his voice was neutral.

"When do I get to meet her?" Linda asked.

"Soon. Well, I guess. I mean, I really don't know."

"Okay, whatever suits you," Linda replied, wanting to avoid any tension.

Cathy's words played themselves over and over in Jack's mind. She had tried to help Jack appreciate the predicament his mother had been in as a young, pregnant woman. "But it's not like we have a relationship or anything. She's really just a friend—"

Linda cut him off. "That's how the best relationships start off, as friends," Linda said.

Linda's observation made Jack feel better. Even as he tried to stay angry with her, he appreciated his mother's reassurance. His fondness for Cathy was growing. He knew it was reciprocal, but the physical distance between them and what he regarded as her head start into adulthood deflated his dream that the relationship could fully evolve in an intimate way.

"I don't know," Jack said as he slunk into a chair. "She has so much going for her. She's so smart, and she goes to this amazing school."

"You're so smart, and your school is very respectable," Linda said, craving the opportunity to be comforting.

Jack laughed. "Well, maybe."

"Does she know what she wants to do after school?" Linda asked.

"Definitely something related to alternative energy sources."

"Good for her. NEIT is a great school for that," Linda said.

"Did you hear of it before you met Stewart?" Jack asked.

The sound of his name coming from Jack was a little unsettling for Linda. She tried to react to the substance of his question rather than this feeling. "Of course. It's one of those schools that most people know of." And then, seizing the opportunity to discuss Stewart since it was Jack who introduced his name into the conversation, Linda asked, "Jack, I've been giving a lot of thought to this. I'd like to speak to Stewart. I've decided I really need to talk to him."

"Why do you want to talk him?"

"Well," Linda said with a small laugh, "for a lot of reasons, I suppose."

"Yeah, but like, something specific?"

"I'd like to share with him what I shared with you. That I'm so sorry I didn't tell the truth. I never meant for anyone to be hurt, and I never imagined it would come to that." She paused, and then asked, "Do you have any way to reach him?"

Jack shook his head. "I have no way of getting in touch with him. They felt any information I have about him could become a problem."

"What about Donna? Do you have a way of contacting her?" Linda asked.

Jack couldn't help laughing. "These are not ordinary people who say, 'Here's my phone number. Don't hesitate to reach out anytime.' Donna tells you just what's necessary and no more. The way it usually works is that I mess something up, then Donna hunts me down to scream at me."

"Scream at you?" Linda asked, her maternal instinct kicking in.

"Well, not exactly scream. But let me put it this way, she's not shy about letting me know I've pissed her off."

Linda was comforted that Jack was engaged positively in a discussion with her. "How often has this happened?" she asked.

"I guess about three or four times," Jack responded. "First, she appears out of nowhere. You see a car getting closer in the rearview mirror. Or you see her parked in a spot where you were heading. She actually gets there before you get there. She knows where you are going before you even thought about going there. She's always ten steps ahead of you. Then once you're in the same car, she'll ask a couple of questions, which I think is really just to let you know that she's aware of everything you've been up to. It feels like an interrogation, but she's not asking questions because she needs the information. She already knows what she needs to know. It's to let you know that she knows. Then she'll hit you with some big accusation. It's honestly really kind of amazing, and it scares the crap out of me."

"Wow. But she seems to really like you. That's the impression I had in the car."

"Maybe. I don't know. It doesn't really matter, anyway. I don't know if she *likes* people. I feel like she'd turn her own mother in if she got in the way of her mission."

"Her mother would be smart to leave the country."

Jack laughed. "Her mother would need to leave the planet before Donna couldn't find her. Then again, she'd organize a team to search Mars."

They shared a laugh, and it felt good to both — natural in a way that it hadn't in a while.

Then Linda asked, "But, Jack, what if there was some emergency? What if there was a need to find her? I don't mean like for me to reach Stewart. I suppose that can wait a while. But a real emergency?"

"Like what?"

"Suppose someone who knows what Stewart is doing for the government — someone who's an enemy — finds out he has a son. Maybe it would put you in some kind of danger. I don't want to be an alarmist, but what if that person comes looking for you?"

"Donna and her people are on top of that. They are very aware of the possibility of danger. That's the main reason they don't want me to have any information, because the more I know the more trouble I could get into."

"But how would they know if someone came looking for you?" Linda asked.

"They would know. I'm sure of it. She's aware of everything I do. And I'm sure they're aware of who might find out about me and what the risks are."

"I hope you're right. And I'm sure it helps that your father is one of the people looking out for you."

That pleased Jack enormously. It was a connection between his parents.

"Mom, I've been thinking about all this a lot lately. And Cathy has actually been helpful. I want you to know I've been trying to understand why you made the decision not to tell us. I don't know that I get it all. Maybe I never will. But I'm not angry anymore. I want you to know I forgive you."

Linda's eyes welled up. She stood and walked over to him. She leaned down as he sat on the chair and put her arms around him, cradling his head. "I love you so much."

***

Elaine was driven directly to the medical facility at the United States Embassy. Although Elaine had been to the embassy at least a half-dozen times, she had never been to the medical facility. It seemed like a cross between a small infirmary and an emergency room. She was ushered down a hallway by the physician, Dr. Kherrington, who had attended to Tom, but was jolted when her eye caught something resting on a table in a small room — more a glorified closet than a room — on the left side of a hallway. It was a casket. They headed to the far end of the hallway toward what appeared to be a patient's room. Tom was lying in a bed, his head propped up. He was groggy, but cognizant. Elaine walked briskly to him and hugged him.

"How are you feeling?" she asked, relieved to see him.

"Alive. Broken knee. But better than everyone else in that cafeteria. How many were killed?" he asked, his voice weak and his tone grim.

Elaine turned her attention to the physician. "May I speak with Tom alone?"

"Certainly," replied Dr. Kherrington, and he exited the room.

She turned back to Tom. "We think eleven, including the boy who did it."

"Oh, my god. How horrible. Was it definitely Rafiq's son? It was all so quick, and I was out of it. Apparently, I also have a concussion."

"Consider yourself lucky. Yes, it was his son. His name was Abdel. Tom, listen, we need to get you out of here as quickly as possible. Rafiq set up this plan. The embassy just told him you didn't survive. He's conveying that information to the police and the authorities at the site."

"Why are we involving him in this? His son just killed himself and ten other people. Give the man space. Some respect!" Tom was shouting, his voice strained.

"He orchestrated this, Tom. He needs to pull something out of this situation for you or it will be even more unbearable for him."

280

"My god, that poor man, that poor family. What does he want us to do?" Tom asked.

"Are you able to travel?"

"The doctor said at least not for a couple of days. But I'm okay. I can go now if you want."

"The plan is to leave as soon as possible. I'll accompany the casket. We're going to make a bit of a show of my leaving with it. Quiet, but still we want it reported that Tom Gaines' body was leaving. He was the American killed in the blast. You'll be leaving with an alias a few hours later."

Dr. Kherrington entered the room and, turning to Elaine, said, "I have an urgent call for you."

Elaine took the phone. "Hello?"

"Elaine, it's Rafiq. You must listen to me. When Tom was being escorted through our building, there was one person who was suspicious. His name is Sadad al-Naimi and he is an important person in our ministry. He was a prosecutor and has had a number of experiences that made him mistrustful of foreigners. There was something Tom said that aroused some suspicion. He insists on coming over there and talking to someone about how Tom actually died. He saw Tom after the explosion and saw that he was alive and had some mobility. It's not that he doesn't trust me. He doesn't trust that I was told the truth."

"Rafiq, can't we arrange for him to speak to someone by phone?"

"I offered that, and he was quite insistent. I didn't want to resist too much because it would arouse his suspicion about me."

"If we can't stop this, I'll arrange for Dr. Kherrington to speak to him when he gets here. He can explain how they tried to do everything to save Tom, but it was in vain."

"I'm going to come with him. Perhaps it will ease the encounter and make it go more quickly."

"Rafiq, you and your family have suffered so much. Please don't feel an obligation to be involved any further. You are so appreciated, but if you need this time for yourself no one will question you for it."

"I'm going to come."

"And your wife. How is she?"

"She is with her two sisters. She's in shock. Her sisters are wonderful though, and I know are providing her comfort. I can't think beyond the moment. I must come."

Rafiq and Sadad arrived at the embassy about an hour later. They were escorted into an office in a small building adjacent to the medical facility. They sat at a small round conference table in the corner of the room. Within a couple of minutes, Elaine and Dr. Kherrington entered and, following introductions, sat at the table.

Rafiq began, "Thank you for agreeing to see us. We are so very sorry for your loss."

Elaine jumped in. "And for your loss, Rafiq. Words cannot express the sorrow we feel for you and your family."

"I want to express my sorrow as well," said Sadad. "This is a very tragic and sad day for all of us. I do not want to take up much of your time. And I know that Rafiq must return to his wife shortly. I will get right to the point. Although we are in the early moments of an overwhelming tragedy, I cannot permit my responsibilities for the security of our country and our ministry to be compromised. Therefore, please indulge me. I need some additional information about the death of Mr. Gaines. It's a little puzzling to me to have seen Mr. Gaines up and about following the blast only to learn that he did not survive. I want to put my mind at ease, so please, if you will, explain to me how it came to pass that he has died."

"I can appreciate your concern, and I will be happy to explain," said Dr. Kherrington. "Mr. Gaines sustained several injuries from the blast. The most serious was trauma to the brain, which resulted in bleeding. This is called intercranial bleeding, which produced a hemorrhage. The supply of blood to the brain became constrained, and tragically, death is not uncommon. Since the bleeding was relatively slow, Mr. Gaines had some physical mobility immediately following the explosion, but, sadly, his death was all but certain. He had internal bleeding in other organs as well. The smoke compromised his lungs, which put additional strain on his heart."

"If he was treated immediately, could he have survived?" asked Sadad.

"It would have been virtually impossible to treat an injury like this at the site. It requires invasive brain surgery."

"Thank you so much for your explanation, Dr. Kherrington," said Rafiq. "Sadad and I will let you return to your work."

As Rafiq and the others began to stand, Sadad said, "I have just one more request, doctor. Would you mind terribly if we saw Mr. Gaines' body?"

Elaine tried to mute her alarm. "Mr. al-Naimi, this would be highly irregular. And we are interested in protecting the dignity of Mr. Gaines' body. He will be transported back the United States to be with his family."

"I certainly understand. Did he have children?" Sadad asked.

"No. He will be reunited with his parents," Elaine said.

"Please convey our deepest sympathies to them," Rafiq said. "At some point, when I can determine how to say it properly, I will want to write to them. I owe them my personal message of sorrow and regret."

"Absolutely," replied Elaine. "And thank you for coming. I hope we have allayed your concerns."

"You have," responded Sadad. "But I must confess, only ninety-nine percent. That last percentage point may linger. So, as we leave, I would be most grateful if I might see the body. And it will give me the opportunity to pay respects suitably to a guest of our country whose last breath was taken on our soil."

"I'm afraid Mr. Gaines' body is being prepared for transport in a casket."

"A quick look is all I ask."

"Sadad, I feel like we are intruding on something sacred," said Rafiq.

Elaine recognized that Sadad's request was not going to disappear. She needed to buy time. "Permit Dr. Kherrington and me to review the status of the work on Mr. Gaines, and we will return shortly." They left the room while Rafiq and Sadad sat at the table and waited.

Elaine and Dr. Kherrington returned after about fifteen minutes. Dr. Kherrington explained that Mr. Gaines' body was being readied for burial. They would be notified when it would be acceptable to see his body.

Several minutes passed, and the office phone rang. Dr. Kherrington answered the call, turned to the group and announced, "Let's go." Elaine and Rafiq felt an excruciating tension as they walked from this building into the medical area.

The four ambled somberly down the corridor and approached the small room that held the casket. Elaine saw the room was dimly lit, the only light emanating from a flickering fluorescent ceiling fixture. The four stood motionless at the base of the deep reddish-brown casket. Brass handles on each side were supported by two thick lug bolts. The top of the casket was curved, and the lid protruded slightly over the sides.

Dr. Kherrington moved to the top of casket and placed his hand under the lid. He lifted it, careful to keep it at a forty-five-degree angle. The light creaking sound of the hinge punctured the silence. There lay Tom, motionless under a white blanketed shroud, the top tucked around his neck, only his head exposed. His skin had an almost porcelain, crystalline sheen, not quite waxy, not quite chalky. His hair glistened with a fresh, slicked wetness. His eyes were closed, the lids pale. He was completely still, limp. All eyes were frozen on Tom. Elaine glanced at Sadad but could not surmise how he was processing the sight. After about five or six seconds, but what seemed like an eternity to Rafiq and Elaine, Dr. Kherrington gently lowered the lid of the casket.

Sadad remained fixed on the casket for a second. Then he sighed and turned to Elaine and Dr. Kherrington. "Thank you very much. Your cooperation in this very trying time is most appreciated. I apologize for doubting you."

"You are looking out for your country," Elaine said.

"Do you anticipate this incident will receive much attention in the United States?" Sadad asked, looking at Elaine.

"I can assure you there is little interest in this becoming a highly publicized incident," Elaine replied, privately acknowledging that Sadad had no idea of the basis of their common interest on this matter.

As they said their goodbyes, Elaine and Rafiq exchanged a knowing glance. The events of day began to crash on an otherwise numb Rafiq. As he turned to leave, he quietly wept.

THIRTY-TWO

Doug Roberts typically spent about twenty minutes each morning reviewing briefs from the State and Defense Departments with the potential of involving police activity in his San Francisco district. A four-sentence report, buried below what seemed like less newsworthy events, caught his eye. He called his sister, Amanda, who was at work at Davies Physical Therapy. When she didn't answer her cell phone, he called the office and asked for her.

Doug began, "I tried to reach you, but it went to voicemail."

"I was with a patient, so I turned it off."

"Okay, got it. Have you seen Linda today?"

"Yeah, why?"

"How does she seem? How's her mood?"

"Linda seems more relaxed today than I've seen her in weeks," Amanda replied.

"Amanda, let's hang up. Find a private place to sit down. Then call me from your phone."

They reconnected a minute later.

"Are you sitting?"

Amanda felt flushed and her pulse quickening. "Yeah, I'm alone in a conference room. Is it about Linda? What is it?"

"I get a briefing of news bulletins from the State Department every morning. Listen to this one: '*Riyadh, Saudi Arabia: A suicide bomber detonated a homemade explosive in the basement of a building housing a legal affairs division of the oil ministry. A Saudi investigation confirmed the bomber was a deranged youth and was not motivated by political interests or religious fanaticism. Up to ten Saudis and one American were killed. The American was identified as Thomas Gaines, an oil industry consultant.*'"

"And…?" Amanda asked.

In a deliberate and slow tone, Doug said, "Thomas Gaines is Stewart

285

Jacobson."

"What?" Amanda blurted. "How do you know?"

"I made a few calls after the whole thing broke with Linda. I have some contacts at Defense who filled me in. I just didn't want to get blindsided because I was the one who put out a bulletin looking for Jacobson."

"I'm sure Linda doesn't know."

"I'm going to reach out to the woman who's been handling this thing. In the meantime, don't say anything to Linda."

Amanda walked out of the conference room. Mid-morning was a busy time at the practice. A full complement of staff was on duty and the patient waiting room was full. Amanda felt shaky. She was grateful for the high level of activity at the facility, hoping it would prevent anyone from noticing that she had become a wreck. She took a drink from the water cooler and resolved to bury herself in her work.

About an hour later, Amanda was in a patient room with a man who had recently had a hip replacement. Linda poked her head in and, recognizing the patient as one of her long-term clients, called to him, "Hey, Mr. Davenport, you look like you're doing great." Her mood was lively. Then, turning to Amanda, who was doing her best to avoid eye contact with her, Linda said, "Amanda, please stop in to see me for a minute when you and Mr. Davenport are finished."

Linda was doing some paperwork when Amanda stopped by a short while later. "Hi, Amanda. Close the door. I need to ask you something confidentially."

Amanda felt her throat closing. "Sure, what is it?"

"A ton of stuff has happened since we spoke to Doug. I'm really not allowed to talk about it, but you already know the basics and I need to ask a favor." Linda was beaming, and her giddiness about Jack's forgiveness was fueling her need to share more of the story than she intended. "I found out that Jack really was searching for his father, and I still have to pinch myself over all this, but he found him," Linda began. "Amanda, they met. It turns out that Stewart Jacobson — Amanda, you have to swear this is all going to remain between us — had to have his identity changed because of his government work. They couldn't tell me a thing about it. Anyway, I explained to Jack why I never shared the truth with him. He was angry in the beginning. I don't blame him. I know I did the wrong thing. I don't know how it happened, but he said he has forgiven me. Amanda, for twenty years I've been walking around with this panicky feeling that Jack would reject me if he found out the truth. And now he says he forgives me."

Amanda was listening to Linda's story and felt stunned. Her mind was racing, and her hands began to tremble. If there was any uncertainty about whether Linda knew about Stewart's fate, it was now crystal clear to Amanda that Linda did not.

Linda continued, "I think Jack's new girlfriend might have had something to do with this. This is why I wanted to talk to you... Amanda, I need to speak to Stewart." Linda noticed that Amanda looked ashen. "Are you okay?"

"Sure, yeah."

Linda was so immersed in her thoughts that she failed to notice Amanda's labored breathing. "Anyway, I decided that I must speak to Stewart. I need to explain to him why I kept my pregnancy and Jack from him. I don't know how it will go, but I really, really need to speak to him."

Amanda was feeling desperate to leave. "Wow, Linda, I'm so glad Jack is okay with all this. But, hey, I have a patient waiting and I—"

Linda cut her off. "I'm sorry, I didn't mean to ramble on, but I just wanted to get Doug's phone number from you. I have no way of reaching the people who can connect me to Stewart. But I'm sure he can." Linda noticed that Amanda was physically trembling. "Amanda, what's wrong?"

Amanda was caving in to emotional overload. She always envied her brother's ability to remain cool and collected, even under the most stressful circumstances. Amanda did her best to steer clear of stress-inducing triggers. She was a wonderful therapist. Her clinical competencies, though still developing, were sound. But her major strength was sensitivity to patients' social needs. More than any other therapist in Linda's practice, Amanda could zap the anxiety from the most apprehensive patient with her warmth and caring nature. Linda didn't need to be beaten over the head to recognize that Amanda's reaction to her story and request for Doug's phone number was bizarrely uncharacteristic. "Nothing's wrong, Linda. I don't have Doug's number with me. I have to go." She turned pale and was clearly shaken.

Linda got up and walked to other side of the desk, where Amanda was seated. She reached down and took Amanda's hands. "Amanda, talk to me. What's wrong?"

Amanda took her hands from Linda's and covered her face. She didn't know what to do. She didn't want Linda to be hurt, but she felt trapped by the devastating emotionalism and an inability to navigate through this situation with even the slightest degree of cool-headedness. She was compelled to charge ahead, feeling a complete absence of control over how to approach this. Her eyes filled as she looked up and made eye contact with Linda for the first time all day. "My brother called me about an hour ago, Linda. He told me he had a report that Stewart was killed."

Linda froze. She could say nothing. Her head began to buzz with a tingling sensation that felt like soft electrical jolts. Amanda stood and put her arms around her. "I'm so sorry, Linda, I'm so sorry. I wasn't supposed to tell you. This all just happened. Doug doesn't even have the whole story."

Linda felt dazed, and the room was beginning to blur. Amanda thought Linda would faint, and she held her and lowered her into the seat she had just vacated. Linda looked at Amanda, and in a soft, barely audible voice, asked, "How?"

"There was an explosion. A suicide bomb in a building. It was in Saudi Arabia."

"Jack. What am I going to tell Jack?" Linda murmured, her eyes glazed.

Amanda crouched beside the chair, her arms around Linda. They were both crying. They stayed like this, speechless, for about two minutes.

Linda abruptly looked up. "I'm not ready to believe this. How does Doug know?"

"He got a report. I think he said it was from the State Department."

"I want to speak to him."

"Linda, he didn't want me to tell you. He's calling some woman from the government who would know more about this."

"Amanda, I need to speak to him. Please call him for me. Please call

288

him now."

"He would only talk to me on my cell phone."

"He knows that my office phones here may be tapped."

"This is all too much, Linda."

"Let me use your cell phone," Linda insisted, a sharp sternness to her voice.

"Linda, I'll call him. I need to tell him that I told you."

Amanda called Doug from her cell phone. "Doug, I'm with Linda. I'm so sorry, but I felt like I had no choice but to tell her about Stewart."

"Why would you do that?" he demanded, angrily.

"I wasn't planning to, but she asked me for your number. She was going to ask you to get in touch with that government woman so she could contact Stewart. I felt like I had no choice. She wants to talk to you." Amanda handed the phone to Linda.

"Doug, is it true?" Linda asked very matter-of-factly.

"I have no reason to doubt the story, Linda. I'm so sorry."

"Can you read it to me?"

"The story includes Stewart Jacobson's new name."

"Is there any reason I can't know it?"

"There are plenty of reasons you can't know it."

"Is the story you received classified?"

"No. It's from a State Department bulletin."

"Who else would have access to it?" Linda asked.

"Anyone. But no one would know the name is an alias."

"So, the only people who shouldn't see the report are those who can make the connection?" Linda's questions had prosecutorial-like precision. Amanda was confused by this sudden shift in Linda's demeanor. Then she understood — Linda was in denial.

"Linda, you're putting me in a bad position."

"Doug, it's not your fault that I know about this."

"I understand, but I don't want to do anything that will compromise anyone."

"Is the story available online?"

"I'm sure it is."

"Then I'll look it up."

Doug resolved that he couldn't — and even shouldn't — make this more difficult for Linda. "Listen, I'll save you the trouble. I'll read it to you."

Doug picked up the news bulletin and read it to Linda. There was a pause when he finished. Then Linda said, "How horrible. How horrible." She was crying again. "Thomas Gaines. Thomas Gaines, that was his name?" she said, her voice barely above a whisper.

"Yes," Doug replied.

"How did you find out?" Linda asked.

"I'm sorry. I don't mean to focus so much on the business of this all, but you know I can't tell you that," Doug replied.

"Are you sure that Stewart was Thomas Gaines? Completely sure?"

"I'm very sure. And I'm so very sorry."

Several thousand miles away a funeral service was being held. The remains of Abdel Farid, shrouded in a plain, brown cloak, were lowered into a grave. Koranic prayers for the dead were chanted. Relatives of the family and business associates openly wept, all strained from answerless pondering about how this could happen.

Rafiq and Jamila were overcome with loss. Both children had now been taken from them, both lives ending horrifically, in violence. Rafiq's and Jamila's pain was so extraordinary that it seemed, at this very moment, to be entirely incompatible with what God intended for the human spirit.

THIRTY-THREE

Amanda insisted on driving Linda to her parents' house. Linda spent an hour there but wanted to be certain to be home by the time Jack arrived. The hour with her parents was good for Linda. She was in a daze when she first got there. The news of Stewart's death was reverberating through her like an ambiguous painful force. She wasn't sure how to present the news to Jack, and her parents encouraged her to just explain it straight, but with sensitivity.

Linda heard Jack's car pull into the driveway about a half hour after she arrived at home. She couldn't bear the thought of telling him that his father — this man for whom he had searched so diligently for well over a year — was gone. Jack bounced into the house, bubbly because much of the world had become good for him. He saw his mother standing in the kitchen. Her face said it all. It was drawn and red and pale at the same time. Her eyes were puffy, and her hair an uncharacteristic mess. His heart began to race.

"Jack," she began, her voice quivering. "Come into the living room and sit with me."

He tossed his jacket on the kitchen table. He said nothing as she took his hand and escorted him to the couch in the next room. They each sat on the edge of the couch, facing one another.

"I received the most horrible news today, Jack. I don't know how I can say these words to you." Linda felt her throat tightening. "It seems as though Stewart... your father, was killed."

Jack plunged into a stunned silence. His heart began to pound, and he could feel pulsations cascading down his arms. His mother stared at him and gripped his hands tightly in hers. "What? How? How?" he asked.

"In Saudi Arabia. A bomb exploded in a building he was in."

"How do you know?" Jack asked.

"I heard from Amanda's brother, that detective in San Francisco. He got a government report with the news."

291

Jack sat, bewildered, astounded. He looked intently at his mother and declared, "It's not true. I don't believe it." With that, he bolted from the chair and ran over to the phone, which was hanging on the wall in the kitchen.

Before he could dial, Linda shouted to him, "Who are you calling?"

"The police. They'll get me to Donna."

"No, Jack, wait." Linda raced and grabbed the phone from him. "Jack, you can't do that. We can get into big trouble, and maybe make things worse for Donna. Maybe others will be killed. You can't call the police."

Jack hung up the phone. His mind scrambled for an idea. "My phone is tapped. I know it's tapped. I'll call the State Department asking for Donna. They'll ask me some things. They'll see I know about Stewart Jacobson. They'll know I really need her. Next thing I know she'll be calling me, or she'll just show up." He was ranting. "This is completely false, completely. We need to get to Donna. No way he died. There's no way."

"We don't know that she works for the State Department. No one is going to tell you anything."

Jack was shouting. "I'm not going to believe this. You can. But I don't. I won't."

"Jack, calm down. I want to explain how—"

Jack cut her off. "Calm down? Are you crazy? Calm down? I finally find my father and now he's dead and I should calm down?" he screamed.

Then Jack picked up a wooden stool. He gripped it tightly and lifted it to shoulder level. His muscles tightened, and he felt himself losing control over impulses to restrain his behavior. With great force, Jack smashed the stool down on the floor. The legs flew in different directions and the wooden seat splintered into three chunks. Shards spun about, taking a full five seconds to come to rest.

Linda moved to him and grabbed him by the shoulders. "Jack, listen to me. Listen. We are trying to find Donna. Doug Roberts, you know, Amanda's brother, the detective, he can get ahold of her. He's going to call me as soon as he hears from her." She looked at him firmly and warmly. He could always get strength from her. But not now, not this time. He melted in her arms and began to cry with dizzying passion.

Linda escorted Jack back to the couch. Jack stopped sobbing and looked at his mother. "I want you to tell me this is not true."

"I can't," Linda replied. "I wish I could, but I can't."

"Why?" he demanded.

"Because Doug said the report comes from a reliable source."

"A reliable source doesn't mean the report is true."

"There was a suicide bomb in Saudi Arabia just like Doug said. I was able to find news about it online. I looked it up when I was at Grandma and Grandpa's."

Jack didn't respond. Denial ran its course and was beginning to exhaust itself, and he knew it. Although he was in shock, it was beginning to settle in that Stewart's death might be real.

"Why was he in Saudi Arabia?" Jack asked, his face flushed and wet.

"I don't know, honey," Linda replied, wiping Jack's forehead with a tissue.

"Were they out to kill him? Was it him they were going for?" Jack asked.

"The report said it was a deranged young person. Others were killed as well. I don't remember how many. Four or five, maybe. Maybe more."

Jack's mind was racing in different directions. This had to be deliberate, he thought. He stood and began to pace in front of his mother. He began to hook onto the only explanation that could fit the tiny number of facts about his father's life to which he was privy.

"This wasn't an accident, then. There wasn't some crazy person. It was on purpose. I'll bet it was because of the paternity report that went around on the police bulletin. I'll bet that's what put him in danger. Then people went after him to kill him. They found out who he really was."

"Oh, Jack. No, no," Linda pleaded. "That wouldn't be it. That's so far-fetched. Plus, the government wouldn't have allowed him to stay there if it was too risky a situation."

"He's been doing this for so long," Jack responded. He was beginning to believe this scenario he was constructing was accurate. "Now, all of a sudden, he's in danger. A bunch of years, no problem. Now there's a report with his old name and everything, and the next thing you know he's killed. There's no other way to look at this." Jack's shock was like an accelerant, pushing this fantasy along. He was getting angrier as he was homing in on his target.

Linda tried to dampen his embrace of his story. "We have no idea what his job was, what he was doing, where he was doing it and who he was doing it with. We're not in any position to say when he might have been placed in danger and why."

Linda's efforts were working against her as Jack was investing more and more credulity into his concoction. "Of course, you don't want to believe it. You're the one who got that whole paternity story started," he spat at her.

Jack was glaring at Linda now. His distress was gnawing at him, stifling his capability to think sensibly. He was overwhelmed with shock.

Linda couldn't muster a response. She began to cry and plead with Jack. "Jack, don't say that. You know that's not true."

Jack just stared at her. Then he shouted, "I don't know what's true. Only that I have to leave. I have to get out of here. Now."

Jack turned and briskly walked through the door, slammed it shut on the way out, practically leapt into his car and drove off. Linda stood in the kitchen, stunned and crying, a jumble of wooden shards strewn about the floor. She saw that Jack had left his jacket on the kitchen table. In it was his cell phone.

Jack backed his car out of the driveway and sped toward the New Jersey Turnpike. Realizing he had forgotten his phone, and not willing to return home, he stopped at a gas station to call Cathy. "I'm on my way to see you," he shouted into the phone, sounding exasperated and electrified at the same time.

"Why? What's wrong?" she asked.

"It's my father. He was killed."

"What?" she blurted. "Jack, where are you?"

"I can't talk now. I'll see you in a few hours. And don't call me — I forgot my phone." He hung up the phone and tore off on the highway toward Massachusetts.

Jack was in a state of frantic rage the entire five-hour trip to Cathy's apartment. He had never been there, but he had mapped it out one evening when he thought it would help him feel closer to her. The miles slid by and he could think of nothing other than his father. It all felt unreal now, the entire episode of the search, just as it did months ago when he felt overwhelmed by confusion and uncertainty. The catalog of events he experienced in his search felt like they were dissolving into twisted mental clutter. He felt incapable of placing any of the actions he undertook to find his father in a framework of coherence. Did he really even meet him? It morphed into a dreamlike experience. A horrific sense of unease for the blame he directed at his mother for the fate of his father began to swell in his mind. Maybe it was deserved, he thought. After all, she deprived him of a father in his childhood. Now her actions would deprive him of a father in his adulthood. Maybe it was not her intent to hurt him, but hurt him she had. How could he forgive her this time? It was all getting to be too much for him.

He arrived at Cathy's apartment in a Boston suburb at about midnight. She lived on a quaint street, crowded with small brownstones, on the third of three floors of a small building. The brownstone had been converted over forty years ago from a single-family house into a six-unit apartment, occupied mostly by NEIT students. He rang the buzzer at the entrance, and immediately heard a buzzer back releasing the lock from the entrance door. He walked up the two flights and saw Cathy in her doorway, waiting for him. As he approached her, Jack saw she was animated.

"He's alive," she shouted, her face sparkling.

Ill-prepared for another shock to his mental system, Jack could mutter only, "What?"

They were standing in front of each other now. "Your father. He's alive. They faked his death to get him out of the country."

"Are you sure?" Jack demanded, his eyes widening into circles.

Cathy was smiling. Jack knew it was the truth.

Jack didn't know whether to shout or cry. Cathy grabbed him and pulled him into her apartment and shut the door. He fell into her arms, trembling.

After a moment they moved to her couch. "Tell me," Jack said, clutching Cathy's hands.

"About an hour ago I got a call from Donna. She asked me to go to a neighbor's house and call her on a number she gave me. My friend Janice lives on the second floor, so I went there. Anyway, I called her back, and she told me that the story about Stewart wasn't true. Well, some of it was true. He was in a place where a bomb went off. And several people were killed. He got hurt pretty badly. But he survived. They needed to find a good way to get him out of the country before anyone could ask him questions. That's the reason. That's why they created a report that said he was killed. Donna had no idea that Doug, the police guy your mother knows, found out. She had no idea that any of you knew about the report. Doug was trying to reach her all day, but she didn't get the messages. Anyway, I guess she just got in touch with him a little while ago. He called your mother, and Donna called me."

"Holy shit. But Cathy, I swear I knew it, I knew it wasn't real." Jack was smiling.

"So, you stormed out on your mom, huh?"

"How do you know?"

"Your mom said she found your phone in your jacket and then called me. She was really worried about you and thought you might be coming here, so I told her you were."

"Wow, I guess there really is no such thing as privacy anymore," challenged Jack.

"Not about this, it seems. But, hey, can you blame her? I asked her if she was all right. She said she was, but I could tell that she really wasn't. She was really worried about you."

Jack was taking it all in. "That's fair. So, what do I do now?"

"Call her."

"Okay. You're right." A smile came to his face. "And by the way, you being right all the time is getting to be a big problem between us."

Jack called his mother. They expressed relief and regrets, careful to refrain from discussing specifics about Stewart since they understood their call might be monitored. She asked when he would be coming home. It occurred to him that he hadn't thought about that, the realization of which introduced a hint of trepidation. Probably tomorrow, he suggested. Linda also had some news for Jack — she would be seeing Stewart the next day.

After the call, Jack sank into Cathy's couch. Freed from his anguish, he was beginning to take in her environment. Her apartment was small and quaint, consisting of two rooms and a kitchen adjoining the living room. It was neat, neater than Jack expected any student's living quarters to be. One entire wall, about eight feet long, was entirely covered with shelves that were filled with books. They were organized by theme: engineering, art and novels were the biggest categories. There was an uneven assortment of drawings and photos adorning the walls, stuff going up, it seemed, wherever space permitted. One was a photo of Cathy, her parents and her older sister. Jack stared at the picture, getting a glimpse of where Cathy came from.

"My mother is going to see Stewart tomorrow," Jack said.

"How do you think it will go?"

"No idea. I know she's planning to say she's sorry... you know, for not telling him about me. I'm guessing he'll understand. But I really don't know."

"When do you think you'll see him?"

"I don't know. Until ten minutes ago, I thought it would be never again," Jack replied. "I'll have to ask Donna. So, where is she, under the couch, in the refrigerator, on the roof? Maybe she's hiding in the toilet. I can just see it, a little snorkel bobbing out of the water with a listening device and camera on the tip."

Cathy was laughing. "Yeah, I'll bet she implanted one of those locator chips they use for dogs in your mother without her even knowing it."

"I'll bet I have one in me," Jack said. Then, "Speaking of my mom, why is it you're always defending her?"

"I never thought of it that way, like I was defending her. I guess I just rely on someone's intentions, you know? I mean, she didn't mean to hurt you, so why hold her accountable?"

"Don't you think you can hurt someone even if you didn't intend to?" Jack asked.

"Of course. But when you were talking about your mother, you were implying that she had a disregard for what was best for you. And maybe even for Stewart. But that wasn't the case. She didn't disregard anything. She just thought it all through in a way that made the most sense to her at the time. She'd probably do it differently today."

"Fair enough, I guess."

Cathy leaned into Jack and put her head against his shoulder and

297

clasped his hand. They relaxed in this position for a few minutes. Then Jack feebly disclosed, "When I left my house and drove up here, I didn't think beyond seeing you so you could help me deal with, you know, my father…" His voice trailed off.

"I know. So…?" Cathy said, delighting in knowing Jack was about to squirm.

"So…? So, now I don't really know what to do," Jack responded.

"About what?" Cathy said with feigned innocence.

"About what to do next."

"Well, then, it's good I do," Cathy said as she stood up, took his hand, and began to escort him into the next room.

The worst day of Jack's life became one of his best.

THIRTY-FOUR

The day had been about as emotionally jarring as any in her life. The news that Stewart was alive, coupled with a peaceful resolution with Jack, was a sedative for Linda. As a result, her sleep was more restful than anticipated given the momentous nature of the upcoming day. Linda was to meet Donna for lunch at a restaurant in a northern suburb of Washington, D.C. Donna wanted to brief Linda on the events surrounding Stewart over the last few days and update Linda on his new identify. It would be important for Linda to know what to call him and how far to go with questions. All this was significant because the staff at the hospital were aware only of the specific government agency with which Stewart was affiliated, and certainly nothing of his role or identity changes.

Linda's visit with Stewart was set for three o'clock. He had arrived from Saudi Arabia the previous day and was convalescing in a Veterans Administration hospital. As she showered and dressed, she realized how fortuitous it was for her visit to be hastily arranged. She knew if she'd had weeks or even days to prepare for the visit, she would have driven herself crazy obsessing over it. This worked out fine, she thought. It was impossible for Linda to avoid thinking about what Stewart's life had been like. She knew some of the basics: engineer, government assignment, never married, lost a fiancée to a car accident. How utterly heartbreaking, Linda thought. Her curiosity around all these matters was bubbling over, but she had no feel, no sense of boundaries or permission for how much she could pursue them.

Linda drove from New Jersey to the Washington D.C. area, her mind racing with questions about Stewart. She arrived at the cozy Italian restaurant just a few minutes before Donna. Overcome with emotion, Linda embraced Donna, who uncharacteristically gave in to the display of affection. They settled into a booth in the corner of the restaurant and were comforted by the sense of privacy it offered.

The conversation began with Donna apologizing for not being able to move more quickly on the message from Doug Roberts. She felt terrible that Linda and Jack received her message so late into the evening after spending a torturous day believing Stewart had been killed.

"In a strange way, it crystallized just how important he is to me," Linda said. "I don't mean in the same way as twenty years ago, of course. But he's Jack's father, and my son finally got to meet his father — to learn that one exists — and just like that, he's taken from him. It absolutely devastated Jack."

The conversation shifted to Linda recounting the bewilderment she felt when they first met, when she observed her son deferring to an unknown woman who was issuing an explanation about his father. Donna confided that the revelation of Jack's existence was as much a bombshell to her, to Stewart and to their colleagues. As a matter of fact, Donna said, there was some discussion of the relationship between Stewart and Linda when he was going through due diligence early in his recruitment with their agency. They had decided it was sufficiently brief, in the past and unlikely to resurface; as a result, they never bothered to perform an even rudimentary investigation into Linda's life.

Donna, grinning, added, "In a million years we wouldn't have guessed it would have resurfaced this way."

Linda smiled. The conversation with Donna proved effortless, casual and comfortable. It was a far cry from the first encounter, which was couched in urgency and in which Donna exuded a powerful authoritativeness. Donna violated every facet of the imagery Linda held for a woman in the center of a world of espionage. She was warm and caring, had an easy smile and a sense of humor.

Linda also knew Donna could transform into the hard-charging, no-nonsense version at the drop of a hat. This edition had a commanding presence and no tolerance for rule-breaking, emotion or violation of the chain of command. It conformed more to Linda's conception of a commanding officer in the military: mission first, all else second. Ironically, Linda recognized this was precisely how some thought of her. While no one would accuse her of disregarding feelings, Linda understood she was admired because she could easily mobilize people to a common cause.

Conversation topics drifted to family and upbringing, and how they each found their way into their careers. "Jack is so proud of you," Donna noted at one point.

Linda beamed, and Donna continued, "You should know he really looks up to you, not only because of your success, but because he knew it took a great deal of hard work and because you've always been so respectful of others. He's talked about that with us."

"Wow, isn't that nice to hear," responded Linda, experiencing an exuberant rush. "I'm so proud of him, too. He really is a great kid."

Conversation shifted to Linda's practice. "Are you still thinking about selling it?" Donna asked.

"I don't want to. But you know how the financial picture in health care has changed. It's real hard to have just one facility and make it work. I'm facing the reality of that every day."

"That's another reason why I wanted to meet. My cousin is an economist who consults for Medicare. I was telling him about your situation — I hope you don't mind — and he suggested that you give him a call. He said there may be some ways for restructuring payments that could help. He also said based on who your patients are, you might qualify for loan financing if you wanted to buy that other practice. Here's his card. No promises, but if anyone knows about these things, he does."

Exceedingly grateful, Linda took the card, and assured Donna she would call him.

"Now, let's talk about Stewart," Donna said. "First things first. Stewart has a new name. David Landau."

"David Landau," Linda repeated. "Sounds so simple, like an actor. How do you come up with these names anyway?"

"It's called the New Name Division," Donna joked. She leaned back in her chair. "You know, the funny thing is that when I first started working for the government, I thought there were all sorts of clandestine operations with groups of agents making all this stuff up. The truth is that we try to come up with something that sounds kind of ordinary, benign. We do research to make sure we cover the right bases, like making sure there's not an existing lawsuit or other problem with someone who's got a similar name. Not terribly exciting."

"Do I call him David Landau?" Linda asked.

"Absolutely. Please make no reference to Stewart or Tom or that he has a new name. The rule of thumb is that anyone in earshot could become curious if they think David is not who he says he is."

"Got it. Is there anything we can't talk about?" Linda asked.

"Just follow David's lead. He'll know how far to go. Well, maybe I'm jumping the gun a little here. David is not, and never was, a professional at this. He's an engineer, not an operative. But I'll give him credit — if he errs, it's generally on the side of caution."

"Can we talk about Jack? Can we talk about how Stewart—" she caught herself, "I mean, David spent the last twenty years? What about his family? Where he lived?"

"He'll know how far he can go. If any of the hospital staff get too close, he'll probably change the subject. Other than that, ask him anything. He definitely won't talk about the past few years, you know, since he's been working on this project with us."

Linda's anxiety level escalated during the twenty-minute drive to the hospital. She knew the message she wanted to convey — that she was sincerely sorry — but her confidence in predicting how he would respond was ebbing.

Linda entered the hospital and approached the visitor's desk in the lobby. She signed in, was given a visitor's badge and was directed to room three forty-seven to visit David Landau.

As she walked through the corridors, she saw a sign that read, 'Rehabilitation Services'. Linda couldn't help but peek in. It occurred to her that about half the equipment appeared to belong to a generation of equipment long considered obsolete.

She took a few deep breaths in the elevator. When the door opened, Linda exited, turned left and walked down a rather long hallway. Her pace was slow and deliberate. The telltale hospital odor, a blend of antiseptic potency and lingering staleness, though familiar to her, felt new, as her senses were on heightened alert. She passed several patient rooms, glancing in and noticing men of different ages, shapes, colors and sizes. Toward the end of the corridor, farthest from the centrally located nursing station, was room three forty-seven. Linda approached the room and stood in the doorway for a second. A few feet away, in a bed, lay a man she last saw half her life ago. He was wearing blue pajamas, and the

302

bed sheet covered the lower half of his body. He appeared a little groggy, and his leg was in a cast.

Linda leaned against the door jamb. "So," she said, getting his attention, "Every time I meet you for the first time it seems you have a broken knee."

"Oh my, Linda!" Stewart said, lifting himself up with some difficulty; then, just as quickly, he collapsed onto his back.

Linda moved to him quickly. "Here, let me help." She maneuvered a pillow under his head, her care-giving instincts propelling her into action.

It was at once natural and overwhelming. In fact, they both felt overwhelmed. For Linda, this moment had been the subject of two decades of anticipation, though in all her fantasies she never expected it would come about as a result of events spinning so weirdly out of her control. All the maddening internal debates about whether to tell Jack about Stewart or whether to seek Stewart out conspired to produce a jumbled mass of self-doubt. For Stewart, there was a profound sense that his life would never be the same. He'd had episodes of misgiving and regret about having never married and never having children. But that had all changed in a flash. At this moment of their coming together, Linda's past and Stewart's future were meshing, becoming integrally interwoven and fundamentally redefined.

"Thanks. Let me look at you," he said. Linda stepped back, stifling tears.

"You look wonderful," Stewart said. Indeed, Linda did look wonderful. Her hair was shorter than he remembered, but it still had an auburn sheen. Her eyes were filled with life and her energy was just as he remembered. "You've hardly changed."

She couldn't help but say, "You've hardly changed as well. Busted knee, mussed up hair. Taking up space in a hospital."

Stewart managed a laugh, but it was subdued because he was achy and was on pain medication that made him drowsy.

Linda was taken by how much she remembered him. Other than a hint of gray in his hair, Stewart did impress her as having changed very little. He was trim and in good physical condition. She remembered staring at his eyes while he talked, feeling secure and embraced.

"How are you feeling?" Linda asked as she stood at his bedside.

"I've been better. The good news is they tell me I'll make a full recovery. How about you? How are you? There's so much I want to hear," Stewart said, with an eagerness in his voice that seemed to defy his condition.

"Oh, yes, we have a lot of catching up. But I don't want you to do too much if you need to rest—"

He cut her off. "All I do is rest. Resting has become my new profession."

Linda smiled. "What happened? Can you tell me?" She moved a chair over to the side of the bed and sat on the edge, leaning forward.

"You may know some of it." His voice was soft and there was a melancholy look on his face. "I was in a building when a bomb went off. I was with a bunch of other people in a basement cafeteria. I was the only lucky one. It was only because I was waiting for someone to pick me up, so I was waiting right near the entrance. The bomb went off in the back. Just horrible. In so many ways. I think ten or eleven people were killed." He looked away from Linda, and appeared to her a drained figure, disheartened in spirit and body.

Linda was at a loss. More instinctively than intentionally, she reached down and placed her hand gently on his shoulder. She tenderly rubbed his arm. For Stewart, it was the first physically comforting gesture he had felt in a long time. They sat in silence for a moment, a silence that felt good and eased away some of the apprehension and awkwardness they felt.

"I'm so sorry," Linda said softly.

"Thank you," he replied.

"I'm sorry for a lot of things—" Linda began, but cut herself off as a nurse entered the room.

"Time for your meds, David," the nurse said.

It felt odd to Linda to hear this man being called 'David'. Sure, she was prepared for it, but hearing his new name spoken out loud, reintroduced a strangeness about him, a sense that his life was shrouded in mystery and that she would probably never have any real grasp of it. She quickly removed her hand from his arm, an abrupt reflection of the distance between them once again.

Stewart leaned up and took a small cup of water and two pills from the nurse. He thanked her, and she left the room.

"How's Jack?" Stewart asked as soon as he saw the nurse was gone.

"He's fine now. Yesterday was devastating for him. He thought you were killed."

"I heard. Donna told me you all saw the report. I'm so sorry about that."

Stewart had no frame of reference for calculating how much he meant to Jack, and he would invariably underestimate Jack's feelings for him. Linda's reference to Jack's reaction to his death caught him by surprise and added to his incomprehension about being a father. "He was devastated?" he asked, his tone vulnerable and hopeful, curious and confused.

"I've never seen him that way," Linda said.

"I have to confess this is all so new to me. I mean having a son. Being a parent. When I saw him, I was stunned; I thought—"

Linda cut him off. This was the moment. She could not bear Stewart opening up about Jack without him hearing how sorry she was. "There's something that's very important for me to say to you. Something I have wanted — needed — to say to you for a very, very long time." She took a breath and slowed down, and in a very deliberate tone, said, "I want you to know how sorry I am that I kept Jack from you." It was a declaration that was at once so simple, yet so rehearsed. Linda stared at him and inched forward in the chair. She looked for some reaction. Getting none, she continued, "It was never my intention to keep my pregnancy a secret. I was so scared about having a baby and I was so scared that you wouldn't want to be involved, that you wouldn't be around. That's how I thought of it then. Obviously, I know now how unfair that was. I should never have made that decision for you. Never. I'm not asking you to forgive me, because I don't deserve it. I just really needed to tell you how sorry I am. And how sorry I am for Jack. He deserved to know he had a father." She put her hand to her mouth, almost to contain the flow of words. Then Linda stopped speaking.

Stewart was looking at her and saw her eyes welling up. It took him a minute to react. "You know, I think about our time together a lot. It meant a lot to me then. It still does. We were both such bundles of energy

305

back then. Couldn't wait to get out there and conquer our worlds. I didn't give you much confidence, maybe any confidence, that I'd be around for anything, did I? I can't put myself in your shoes, but I know that whatever decisions you made weren't easy. I have to ask myself, if it was me, would I have been able to depend on myself knowing how much scampering around I was in for? I don't know. When I discovered I had a child, I was in absolute shock. I couldn't believe it. And it was only a couple of days later that I met him. I didn't even know what to talk to him about, what to say. We had only a few minutes. It seemed like we were together for a second, and poof! He was gone. As the days passed, I started to feel bad about missing so much of his life... his whole childhood. Maybe bad is the wrong word. Empty. Vacant. I'd be lying if I didn't say I felt, from time to time, like I was betrayed. So were the important people in my life, like my parents who never knew they had a grandchild. And I became convinced it wasn't my fault. After all, it wasn't my decision that Jack wouldn't be in my life. And it wasn't his either. So, I couldn't seem to get past the idea that we — Jack and I — were deprived of each other because of the decision you made."

Linda was beginning to quiver. She hadn't anticipated that Stewart would not accept her apology, that it was going to be rebuffed so sternly, so emphatically. She felt her heart racing. If Stewart would not forgive her, surely Jack wouldn't either.

Stewart continued. "It's not that I was angry all the time, at least not seething angry. More like confused angry. I went back and forth, amazed at the whole thing, that we had a child. And I also became incredibly happy about it. Honestly? I didn't know what to feel. It was all so unexpected. But after I met him, and he became a real person to me, I was thrilled. And even though I had no role in his life, I felt a surge of pride. Crazy, for sure. I know it was undeserved, but I felt it anyway. But another feeling would come over me from time to time. The feeling I had been cheated — robbed — of what could have been the most important thing in my life."

Linda was now softly sobbing. She felt an urgency to reiterate her apology, praying it would mitigate Stewart's feelings of being betrayed. She started to speak, but Stewart, weak and achy, held up his hand as if to stop her.

"Linda, please, I need to finish," he continued. "But everything changed in the last few days. Since the bomb went off. I need to share this with you. The bomb was brought in and detonated by the son of a friend, someone I knew in college. We hadn't seen one another in twenty years. This man was Lebanese and was working as an official in the Saudi government. I'm pretty sure I told you about him, Rafiq Farid?"

Linda dabbed her eyes as she thought for a couple of seconds, then nodded. "Oh, yes, Rafiq. I remember the name. Wasn't he the one whose grandmother died, and he was afraid to miss the class?"

"Nice! Good memory! That's the one. We met again by coincidence several months ago. He's become a good friend again. More than a good friend, actually. He's had a tough life, though. He and his wife lost their daughter a few years ago when she stepped on a land mine. Of all the ironies in life, this happened while she was on a peace mission. Apparently, their son couldn't handle it and his life took a horrible turn. None of us may understand his pain or confusion. He's the one who detonated the bomb in Rafiq's building, killing himself in the process. I can't imagine Rafiq and Jamila, his wife, ever recovering from this. Losing two kids? Devastating is an understatement." Stewart's voice trailed off, weakened from his wounds and his deflated spirit. He gazed at the ceiling and regained his thoughts. "And then there were all those people killed in the building. And all the families of those people were destroyed. It made me see things differently about Jack. And about you. Jack is a very special kid. Well, young man, I should say. He means well in whatever he does. I was able to see that right away. Whatever you taught him, you taught him well. You should be very proud. Life is so fragile, Linda. If I was a few feet farther into the cafeteria I would have been killed. Something or someone felt it was important for me to still be here. It made me understand something. When I was angry, I was angry because of what I missed out on. What I felt was that you had deprived me of something. But you didn't set out to deprive me of anything. You set out to do what you thought was right. What was right for Jack. And who am I? I didn't give a scared, young, pregnant woman the feeling that I could be counted on to be there for her. I understand that better today. If I continued to blame you, I'd be denying that I played any role in it. That's not fair. The people who were killed would forgive anyone for a second chance. Not because forgiving is easy. It's because you get to know just how precious life is. Linda, I'm not angry anymore. I admire you for doing an incredible job of raising Jack." He looked at her and offered a reassuring smile. "Maybe we can move on now?"

Linda was weeping. "Thank you so much, Stewart."

"David," he said, grinning.

"David," she repeated, smiling back, wiping the last trace of tears from her cheeks with the back of her hand.

They bathed in the relief of getting that out of the way, each silently acknowledging the significance of the moment.

"Tell me about Jack," Stewart asked as he settled into the bed.

A burden lifted, Linda leaned back in the chair beside Stewart's bed. "He is truly a gift. I'm sure you'll get to see that. Let's see what I can tell you about him. He's just as happy to be by himself as he is to be with others. When he was little, maybe about three years old, I took him to a play group. There were about ten kids involved. I'd watch as the other kids formed their little groups, and there would be Jack playing alone in the corner fascinated by some toy. As other kids would wander by, Jack would play with them, and he'd be happy about it, but his instincts were to be by himself. And that's how he's always been over the years. He's always done really well in school, especially when it came to the social sciences or current events. And especially when he felt there was some social injustice."

"Nice! What sparked that interest?" Stewart asked.

Linda mulled over the question for a couple of seconds. "I used to think it was because he just cared about the underdog. I didn't think too much about why. Maybe because he saw lots of patients in my practice who were having a hard time. But I think a lot had to do with you. I never put it all together. When he was little, I know he felt like he was different because he didn't have a father. In preschool once, on Father's Day, he asked me about his dad because all the other kids were making cards and he was making a card for his grandfather. No matter how much I tried to make him feel comfortable, I know he felt different. Now that I know how much time and effort he put into finding you, I realize how important being different has been. I wish I had a better understanding of that all along. So much for motherly intuition."

"It seems to me you did an incredible job."

Linda smiled. "You know, maybe if I understood he was going to feel so different, I would have looked for you right away."

Stewart laughed. "Well, as you know, finding me wouldn't have been easy. Do you have any advice about how I should handle things with him?"

"Jack very much wants you to be involved in his life. He needs to know that you want that too. The worst thing for him would be to feel that you don't. That is, if you agree."

"I do want that. I want that very much. But I have no experience being a parent. Or even know how to think like a parent."

Now Linda laughed. "Experience is no guarantee that it will go well. I think the best thing is to let him know that you want to be in his life, that it's important to you — assuming it is — and the rest will fall into place."

Stewart pondered the advice. The first commitment he had made in his life, his engagement, ended in devastation and tragedy. The most recent restoration of a relationship — with Rafiq — was a precursor to tragedy. Of course, he understood this was different. And while he knew it was irrational to think that tragedy inevitably struck the people he cared about, he couldn't let go of the thought that he might bring bad luck to Jack. But that wasn't the type of tragedy he was concerned about. He was concerned about disappointing Jack. He didn't understand that Jack didn't set a high bar for him.

"You look worried," Linda observed.

"I don't want to disappoint him."

"You won't," Linda reassured him. "He's not thinking about you that way. Once you come to terms with whether and how much you want to be his father, the rest will flow naturally."

It occurred to Stewart that Linda was the only person in the world who could offer this advice as well as feel unbounded love toward Jack. Linda was not a friend or confidante encouraging him to have a relationship with his son but was someone who was unconditionally invested in protecting her son; she recognized that Stewart's relationship with their son would not interfere with or replace Jack's relationship with her, but instead would add to Jack's life in important ways. Stewart was not only beginning to understand the view from a parent's perch but was beginning to feel it.

"Thanks. I guess we'll see how this goes," he said, intuiting it would take some time to sink in. "Now, Linda, tell me about you. I know how great your practice became, and I'm not surprised. What about your personal life? You never got married?"

"I guess I just never met the right person. I had some relationships, but nothing terribly special. Truth is, I never gave myself many opportunities to meet someone. Between Jack and my business... I don't know... it seems like the time just flew by. I can't say I regret it, because Jack turned out great, and until recently the business has been great as well."

"You never felt lonely?" Stewart asked.

"What a question!" Linda replied. "I never felt alone. Jack has been the center of my life. My parents live nearby, and I see them a lot. I've got some great friends. And I've had people who have worked for me for over ten years. I feel we're more of a family than a business lots of the time." She paused. "But lonely. I guess. Not often, but I'd be lying if I said 'never'. How about you?"

Stewart shrugged, almost in resignation. Until recently, he hadn't really stepped back to take stock of his life. "The past twenty years seems like a roller coaster. I was never able to stay in one place very long. I may have been lonely but was too busy to notice."

"Donna told me you were engaged. She told me about what happened, too. I'm so sorry."

"Thanks. Yeah, she told me she shared that with you."

"Can I ask her name?"

"Madeline. She was British. She was a very special person."

"Did you know her for a long time?"

"About a year." Stewart paused and leaned up in the bed. "Listen, Linda, I haven't really talked about this much. I've tried to just remember the nice things about Madeline, and try not to think about—"

Linda cut him off. "I understand. No need to talk about it. I'm sorry."

"No, it's okay that you asked. The one part about her accident I take comfort in is that she died instantly. There was no pain."

Linda nodded and leaned toward Stewart and placed her hand on his arm, testing out the gesture again, with a bit more confidence. "What was she like?" she asked.

"She was full of energy. Always busy with something. Passionate about her beliefs. Curious. Smart. And she was lots of fun. She could always make me laugh. Brightened up the room as soon as she walked in. She could always put me in my place, too." Stewart hesitated and smiled. "She reminded me a lot of you."

Linda offered a faint smile. "I'm sorry that you lost her." After a brief pause, Linda asked, "And you? What you have been doing all these years?"

"You know I can't really tell you that. What I can mention is that I was recruited to do some work for our country. I hope it will be helpful. I don't want you to have the wrong impression — I wasn't doing anything terribly exciting or exotic. Mostly engineering work."

Their conversation rambled across a range of topics — their families, Linda's practice and Donna's offer of help, what it's like to spend six months on an oil rig. They reminisced about a story from their time in the hospital together, when Linda had gone to a little-used supply closet to get a prosthetic device. She had heard a faint sound coming from behind a freestanding shelf area and discovered a radiology technician and a nurse's aide having sex.

"Can you believe, they politely asked if I could come back in five minutes?" Linda said, laughing.

"I hope they were on their break, so my insurance company wasn't paying for that," Stewart said.

"You never know, maybe your health plan covers that sort of stuff."

"You have a point. I think it does cover physical therapy."

A nurse entered the room with a tray of fruit and placed it on a bedside stand. The sun pierced the window with its late afternoon intensity, slicing the room into rigid halves of glare and shadow. Two figures stood silhouetted in the doorway, their eyes fixed on an exhausted Stewart and Linda as she sliced an apple for him.

"Is it okay to come in?"

"Oh, Jack," exclaimed Linda, jumping from her chair and running to embrace her son. "And you must be Cathy," she blurted before Jack had an opportunity to introduce her. "I can't tell you how excited I am to meet you."

The moment was filled with poignancy for Stewart. He watched in awe as Linda threw her arms around Jack, and then Cathy, in a spontaneous gesture of affection. Seeing Jack and Linda together, Stewart suddenly felt like a stranger to both, and observing such heartening expressions of warmth intensified this feeling. As much as he could understand that Jack would return the hug with effusiveness, he marveled at how instantaneously Linda was able to convert Cathy from a stranger to an intimate. It was one of the first traits he had seen in Linda, and it was one of her most endearing.

"Come in, come in! Cathy, meet Jack's father," Linda said, grabbing them each by the hand and ushering them toward the bed.

Linda had always appreciated that Jack's appearance was inherited more from Stewart than from her. But at that very moment, seeing them together for the first time in her life, she was awestruck by the physical similarity. She was also startled by the realization of how much Jack looked just like Stewart had when she and Stewart first met. Linda also understood that each man was anxious about seeing the other, each wanting to reveal so much, yet not knowing how to begin or quite what to reveal. Or how to do so in a relationship so old and so young, so defined and so uncharted. This relationship lacked a vocabulary that could be shaped only by experience and history. Jack doesn't even know what to call him, she thought. Linda understood that it would take time, and until then, knowing both of them, they would be polite and err on the side of not forcing closeness and later wishing they had. Linda realized she was coming to understand Stewart by what she already knew about her son.

"It's great to see you again," Stewart began. "I thought about it every day."

"Yeah, me too," Jack said.

Turning to Cathy, Stewart said, "I'm so happy to meet you. I don't know that we'd all be here if it wasn't for your persistence. I'm in your debt."

Cathy was grinning. "Thanks. But Jack was the persistent one. How are you feeling?"

"Right now, I'd say pretty good," Stewart said, smiling and looking right at them, his eyes more alert than they should be, taking it all in. "Everybody, sit, please. There's so much I want to hear about."

The next hour flew by. Stewart flooded the conversation with questions about school, events in Jack's childhood, his friends growing up, favorite books... he couldn't get enough, it seemed. He reminisced with Cathy about NEIT. She was amazed at how current his knowledge base was about how engineering practices evolved, and he was duly impressed with her mastery of engineering concepts from twenty years ago. They shared a laugh about Professor Hobst still teaching at the university and still traumatizing students.

"Were you scared to go to his class?" Cathy asked.

"Scared? I was scared of normal things like Armageddon and nuclear annihilation. But those things were nothing compared to Hobst. My stomach churned every time I walked into his lecture hall."

"Same with me," Cathy said as they both laughed. "His latest thing is to do a conference call with the dean and your parents if you miss a homework assignment. Parents are scared of him too."

Stewart shook his head. "Sounds like things are getting worse with him. I do have to say, the guy is a genius with alloys and conductivity. He's still one of the best researchers out there."

Jack was genuinely enjoying Stewart's banter with Cathy. He was getting to know his father, observing him smile and chat, seeing him as a human being. Stewart saw that Jack was pleased that he was engaging Cathy. He understood how easy it could be for Cathy to feel left out of this very strange family reunion and he recognized that Jack was happy for Cathy to be included.

After some more light conversation, Stewart turned to Jack. "Any idea about what you'll be majoring in?" For the first time, his tone sounded paternal to Jack. It was new and reassuring.

"Well, actually, I do. I'm pretty set on political science so that I can go to law school," Jack said. Then, turning to Linda, he continued, "I've been thinking about it a lot lately and wanted to talk to you about it over the weekend."

"That's wonderful, Jack," Linda said, smiling.

"Great," echoed Stewart. "How'd you decide that?"

"It wasn't just one thing. I've been thinking about all these people who were doing what I was doing, you know, looking for relatives. It was such a tough thing to do, and not just because of your work. So, if I become a lawyer, I think I can help."

Cathy jumped in. "Jack knows so much about this. I think he knows way more than people who've been studying it for years."

"That's an exaggeration," Jack quickly asserted, simultaneously uncomfortable with and pleased by the attention and praise.

"I think Cathy's right," Linda said, unable to conceal her motherly pride.

"So do I," Stewart said. "I've become very familiar with the steps you took to find me. Believe me, we did our absolute best to make sure no one, and I mean no one, could find me. Every step you took presented roadblocks and dead ends and, in some cases, serious threats. And yet, you figured out how to get around each one… dodge it, confront it or outmaneuver it. The people I've been working with are professionals at that, and they're amazed at what you did."

Cathy jumped in, "Jack, tell them that story you just told me, about that family in Wisconsin."

"Maybe another time. I think everyone is getting kind of tired."

"No, no, Jack, please," Stewart requested.

"Absolutely," echoed Linda.

Jack began grudgingly, "Just a couple of nights ago I was reading about this case in Wisconsin. A husband and wife were watching the local news on TV. A story came on that involved this young woman, I think in her early thirties, who was looking for her birth parents. Turns out she was the founder and president of a small local organization that helps adopted people find their birth parents. The woman, get this, is the adopted daughter of the husband and wife who were watching the news. They never even told her she was adopted. She never told them she knew, let alone that she runs an organization that helps people in her situation."

"So, what happened?" asked Linda.

Jack was becoming more animated and energized as he described the story. "There was a big blow-up in the family. The adoptive parents confronted her the next day. She told them she loves them and was grateful to them for raising her. She said she had a feeling she was adopted, mostly because she looked so different from them. She explained that she did some research and confirmed her suspicion. Then she was able to get the name of the adoption agency and was petitioning the courts to allow the records to be unsealed."

"What's happening with it?" asked Linda.

"The adoptive parents hired a lawyer to make sure the court doesn't permit it."

"Do you have any idea how it'll get resolved?" asked Stewart.

"In this case, the court will probably appoint a mediator," Jack explained. "Court rulings almost always rule in favor of what they regard as the best interests of the child. That makes sense. But here you have a thirty-year-old woman who doesn't require legal protection. So, it comes down to this frustrating clash of what everyone thinks is the right thing to do. Everyone kind of sees each other as being at war, which seems so selfish. And then the legal process can make this worse because the lawyers want their clients to see the other side as the enemy. The kids are usually left in the middle, which obviously sucks."

"Jack has told me how tough custody battles are," Cathy said.

"That's for sure!" Jack jumped in. "Custody battles can be insane. For everyone. The kid's life ends up all over the place. Two days here, one birthday there. And it varies state by state. Some places usually rule in favor of the mother, which isn't always the best option. Lots of times things work out fine. But when the custody fights go on and on, it's the kids who wind up suffering."

Jack was invigorated and couldn't stop himself from telling his parents all that he had learned throughout the past year. Stories that had touched him, taught him and made him feel alive.

Linda and Stewart were mesmerized by Jack's display of maturity and authoritativeness. Despite being physically groggy, Stewart was entranced and was learning about his son with wide-eyed eagerness. Seeing Jack with Cathy and listening to him speak about these issues with such well-developed coherence made Linda feel that Jack was leaving his childhood behind and transitioning into adulthood, right there, right before their eyes. For Stewart, this was the only side of Jack he knew. He was struggling to get his mind around the child who grew into the man sitting in front of him. Here they were, Linda and Stewart, celebrating their parentage, sharing the recognition that their son's sense of purpose was taking shape, joyful in their tacit acknowledgement that Jack's intellect was serving the mission of his heart.

"You'll make a wonderful lawyer, Jack," Linda said.

"I hope," Jack said. He could see his parents had a look of pride in their faces. So did Cathy. His focus was brought back to Stewart, who seemed so happy, yet was clearly struggling as he battled his increasing bleariness.

Jack offered a concluding thought, "In the meantime, I set up a meeting with the dean next week. I'm going to volunteer to do support work for students searching for lost relatives or birth parents."

"That's great, really great," said Stewart.

"And don't worry, I won't mention a thing about how I got interested in this."

"I never worried for a minute," Stewart said, smiling.

Cathy looked at Jack and asked, "Have you come across any cases where the birth parent didn't want to be reunited with a child?"

"It happens a lot," Jack said, uncertain why Cathy was introducing a point of departure for a new conversation. "Why?"

Then Cathy turned to Stewart. As an engineer, Cathy was accustomed to thinking in terms of calculations. She was about to take a calculated risk, but because she was getting to see that Stewart was a good person, she surmised it had favorable odds for a successful outcome. "I know I may be completely out of line, but do you think you would have wanted to have a relationship with Jack if you knew about him?"

Jack jumped in. "Cathy! That's a weird thing to ask."

"Oh, it's fine," Stewart said, cutting him off. "And appropriate."

Stewart looked at Jack, Cathy and Linda, all of whom were staring at him. He began to speak. "It's an important question. And I'll answer it. But I want to settle another question first," Stewart said, focusing on Jack. "And it's this. Did your mother do the right thing by not telling us about one another? It's important we resolve that first. When your mother was pregnant, she had some choices to make. One choice was to share the pregnancy with me. Looking at it today, we might all think it would have been better to tell me. No one is more sure of that, than she is. But that's the benefit of hindsight. I want you to know that back then, I gave your mother no confidence that I would be there for her. Or for you. I was all gung-ho with a career that was taking me all over the globe, hopping from one continent to the next. Oh, sure, she could take a chance and tell me, not knowing whether I'd be there, whether I'd drop in from time to time, or whether I would completely abandon her and you. Would it have been smarter of her to introduce that kind of uncertainty into a child's life? Or into hers? That's a pretty scary proposition. Or, should she raise her child on her own, knowing full well she could depend on a stable support system with your grandparents? You could make an argument either way. But she made a perfectly understandable decision that was based on wanting the best thing for you. The most important thing to understand is that her decision was based on her love for you. Not only do I forgive her, but I commend her. Jack, I have no right to demand anything of you, but if I could ask one thing, it would be to forgive her, as well."

Jack nodded. Linda understood this matter was settled.

"Now, as for the question Cathy asked. Look at you, Jack. You're an amazing, remarkable person. Would I have been there? There's nothing on earth that would have kept me away."

Jack heard the words he had needed to hear since the moment he discovered the birth certificate.

"And one other thing," Stewart said. "You know I was involved in an explosion last week. Eleven people lost their lives. I was lucky. I have a second chance. We have our whole lives ahead of us. The way I see it, I just think we're getting a bit of a late start."

Jack reached over and placed his arm on Stewart's shoulder. "Thanks," he said.

A nurse poked her head in the room. "David, I'm afraid your visitors will have to leave. Visiting hours are over."

"What happens to you next?" asked Linda.

"I have to leave for about six weeks starting tomorrow. I wish I could tell you where I was going, but they won't let me — for all the right reasons." Then, in a mock whisper, he said, "They have to make sure I get this David thing right."

Linda laughed. "I'm learning not to ask too many questions about this stuff."

"It took me a while to learn that as well," Stewart said, smiling. He turned his attention to Jack. "Hey, Jack, I was thinking about something. I need to make a trip overseas once the cast is removed. I'll be gone for just a day and a half. I'd love if you could come with me. That is, if it's all right with your mother."

Jack looked at Linda. She nodded weakly, more of an affirmative shrug, as if to communicate that not only was it okay, but her permission was not required.

"Sure. Where to?" asked Jack.

"To visit a friend."

THIRTY-FIVE

Stewart spent the next six weeks in a military training facility in Colorado. His cast was removed, and he was making good progress, his limp becoming increasingly slight. This facility was selected because of its excellent physical rehabilitation program, and it was where he could become acquainted with his new identity. David Landau's resume looked remarkably like Stewart Jacobson's, and once rehabilitated, he would be on permanent assignment directing research and working on policy development for the Energy Department.

Stewart had one request of his managers. He needed to pay his respects to the family of the friend who risked so much so that he could get safely out of Saudi Arabia. His officers at the Department of Defense were reluctant, but Stewart helped assuage their apprehension by assuring them that he would be in the country for less than five hours, and he agreed to fly in a military transport to avoid going through customs. Oh, and one other thing, he said — he would like to bring his son.

A week later, Stewart and Jack were airborne. This was the first time they had been together for an extended period, and their free-flowing conversation left little time for sleep on the ten-hour flight. It was exactly what Stewart had hoped for when he asked Jack to accompany him on the trip. He also explained his history with Rafiq and how important it was for him to see him. And Stewart very much wanted his old friend to meet his son.

The plane landed in an air force base about two hours south of Riyadh. A military car was waiting to drive them north to the capital vicinity. Stewart and Jack sat in the back and took in the scenery. Jack was fascinated by the bustle and look of Riyadh. The car wound its way to the outskirts of the city. A mosque was situated at the end of a long road. Standing in front of the white building was a familiar figure.

Jack watched as Stewart exited the car and embraced Rafiq. Neither

319

man said anything. These men are like brothers, Jack thought.

"Rafiq, I want you to meet my son. This is Jack Davies." Then, turning to Jack, "Jack, meet Rafiq Farid." After a couple of minutes of introductory talk, Stewart asked, "How is Jamila?"

"We'll talk after. I know you have only twenty minutes. Please come with me," Rafiq replied.

Rafiq led Stewart and Jack around the side of the mosque. It was a beautiful building, about two stories high, surrounded by pillars of white stucco and magnificent painted glass windows. Around the back was a courtyard, and behind that was a cemetery. Small marble stones with Arabic writing dotted the landscape.

"Over here," Rafiq said, pointing to a nearby stone. "This is our daughter, Fayza."

The three men stood in silence at the graveside of Rafiq's daughter. Jack had never been at the grave of a child before. He had no experience with anything like this. He had spent well over a year learning about the pain that young people experience when they yearn to find a loved one and face an endless series of frustrating obstacles. But with life at least there was hope. Not blind hope. But hope that enables you to envision a dream and try to bring it to fruition. This scene, this young girl's fate… this was not something he could understand. Stewart had recounted Fayza's story for him on the plane. Jack had come to admire her for her faith that people with different interests, different histories and different cultures could somehow find common ground. In the world he discovered — people searching for loved ones — common ground often seemed elusive; competing interests pulled people apart, their positions hardening with each increment of polarization. At that moment, standing there in Fayza's presence, Jack understood that it took much more courage to find common ground than to resist it. He glanced over at Rafiq, overcoming his anxiety to look at him while he stood in silence at his daughter's grave. Jack could see that this man's pride in his daughter, glowing still and lasting forever, kept him from breaking from grief.

After a few minutes, Rafiq motioned to Stewart and Jack. They walked about fifty yards to a newer area of the cemetery. "This is where my son Abdel is buried," Rafiq said, pointing to an area of dirt marked off by a white stone.

Stewart felt a powerful connection to Abdel. He was the last person to look into Abdel's eyes. Stewart felt he should have had no reason to fear someone who, at his core, was so fundamentally innocent. Stewart could not understand the despair to which Abdel had surrendered and which had led to the moment that brought them together. But he understood that Abdel had lost his place and had traveled a lonely road toward utter hopelessness. His parents couldn't know that road, though Stewart knew they would never free themselves from the belief that they could have, and even should have. That, thought Stewart, would be their ultimate unfair burden. Standing next to him was his own son, a son he discovered just as his friend's son perished. What's in Jack's mind? Stewart wondered. He really didn't know. He knew only that he had but a glimpse into this young man's dreams and could only guess at the historical arc that gave shape to those dreams. Stewart's thoughts about how he could help Jack on his path were layered with insecurity and uncertainty. But he understood now, with more resolve than ever, how blessed he was to be there to help him on his journey.

The three men walked in silence back to the courtyard and alongside the mosque, back to the street. The car was waiting about twenty yards away.

Stewart broke the silence. "How is Jamila?"

"She was lost in a very dark place for many weeks. One morning she said to me, 'Rafiq, we must visit the families.' So, we reached out to all the families who lost someone in the explosion. We wanted to learn about the people who perished. And we needed to let them know how sorry we were. We also wanted to let them know Abdel was not a horrible person, that he was a sad boy who was sinking in torment. Not everyone was willing to see us. We had to beg a few, and in one case we found some distant relatives who served as intermediaries. We met with the last of the families last week, the parents and husband of a young woman who worked in our ministry. Her name was Farooha. The family did not want to see us at first. They were adamant. They were so dreadfully angry. We persisted and finally they agreed. They were wary when we got to their home. They sat stiff. Their eyes were vacant, as though they had cried so much, they had nothing left. Jamila took the mother's hands and said we wanted to know about her daughter. After a few minutes she began to talk. We sat with them. We prayed together. We listened while they told us about their daughter, how happy she was. Farooha was a song of life. She was only twenty-four, just starting out. After a while, they asked about Abdel. Why would he do such a thing? They could see we suffered a terrible loss too. There is so much healing that has to take place. Maybe this was a start. I hope. When it was time to leave, they hugged us and we cried together. We all needed that. I spoke to her parents again yesterday. We — her parents and Jamila and I — are creating a scholarship in her name at the ministry."

"That's beautiful, Rafiq. And incredibly noble and brave," Stewart observed.

"Noble? No, not noble at all. As for brave… I'll admit I was nervous about meeting the relatives. I was afraid they would see our son as a stain among people, that he would be cursed forever. I was also afraid that Jamila and I would see suffering that was unbearable. And you know, sadly, I was right. But Jamila and I also learned something else. We learned that each person who died was loved and graced the world in a special way. We learned that the family could move on a little once they knew we cared. By the time we left, they didn't hate us. And I don't think they will ever hate Abdel again. What I discovered is that the human spirit has a tremendous capacity for forgiveness."

"I only wish it wasn't born out of the pain you experienced," Stewart said. He looked at his friend with awe. Destiny had intervened in their lives with a stark and powerful reversal of fortune. Just as fate deposited a son into his life with suddenness and surprise, so too had it plucked a son with devastating finality from his friend's.

Stewart knew Rafiq misunderstood what he meant by 'brave'. Stewart didn't intend the term for finding the courage to face the families of those who lost a loved one. Rather, Stewart's meaning was more profound; he meant it to capture Rafiq's courage to face himself, to transcend his personal tragedy and devote himself to the needs of others who suffered. His wife, Jamila, whom he had yet to meet, must be a remarkable person, Stewart thought. These two people could have drowned in a state of immeasurable grief and unyielding guilt. And such pain would no doubt be within inches of their lives forever. But rather than succumbing to it, Rafiq and Jamila used their sorrow to open their eyes to the suffering of others. This was not the time to correct his friend's misinterpretation; Rafiq was too humble and too gentle to accept adulation of character. This was the time for Stewart to silently marvel at the wealth of goodness in this man.

A faint smile lightened Rafiq's face. "I want to show you something," he said as he reached into the inner breast pocket of his suit jacket and pulled out an envelope. He opened it and pulled out a photo and showed it to Stewart and Jack. It was a picture of a young boy who appeared to be about two years old. The boy had a wide, bright smile, and his eyes shone like white crystals against his deep ebony skin.

"Who is this?" Stewart asked.

"One of the people who perished was a man named Robert Harrington. He was British. He and his wife, Margaret, were going to adopt this little boy from Africa. Margaret isn't in a position to adopt him now. But we are. Jamila is in Kenya now, meeting him. He will be our son. His name is Ronald."

"Rafiq, that is so wonderful," said Stewart, beaming.

"And we have made another decision," Rafiq said. "I have made arrangements with the ministry to be transferred to the United States. Jamila and I need a fresh start. And Ronald will not look different to people in the United States."

The two men embraced. "You're an extraordinary person, Rafiq," said Stewart. "When will you be coming?"

"There is much bureaucracy with the adoption. It will take several months to work everything out."

Stewart smiled. "I know someone who can help you."

"Great. Who?"

Stewart pointed to Jack. "Jack has become something of an expert on situations like this."

"If that's true," Rafiq said, turning to Jack, "I would welcome your help. The process appears daunting."

"I know a lot about the law firms who deal with this back home. I could probably make some recommendations. And I can probably help you get through some of the red tape, you know, some of the paperwork and regulations."

"Thank you so much, Jack. I will never forget that you came all this way. You are an honor to your parents." Turning to Stewart, Rafiq said, "You have done God's work by coming here."

"I had to come here. To see you. With Jack," Stewart said.

Stewart and Jack turned to walk toward the car. Stewart put his arm around Jack's shoulder. It felt good. And right, to both. As though they had been walking that way that forever.

CPSIA information can be obtained
at www.ICGtesting.com
Printed in the USA
BVHW030748120721
611729BV00005B/69